PETER

FISHER OF MEN

Noni Beth Gibbs

Pacific Press® Publishing Association
Nampa, Idaho
Oshawa, Ontario, Canada
www.pacificpress.com

D0092345

Cover design by Lars Justinen
Cover art by Lars Justinen
Inside design by Steve Lanto

Additional copies of this book may be obtained
by calling toll-free 1-800-765-6955
or online at http://www.adventistbookcenter.com.

ISBN 13: 978-0-8163-2189-6
ISBN 10: 0-8163-2189-2

07 08 09 10 11 · 5 4 3 2 1

Dedication

To Jack,
my dear husband,
my best friend.
Thank you.

Acknowledgments

My mother, Susan Kahrs, has gone above and beyond the call of motherly duty and appreciation in her hours of encouragement and tireless editing, preparing this book for submission. In addition to reading it through several times, she has also read it aloud (in a slightly edited version) to all my children, which means I am also grateful for that many hours of peace!

My sister, Tina, helped so much with housecleaning and homeschool during the most intense segments of writing. She is an inspiration, full of encouragement (nagging, but in a nice way), and guidance (bossy, but also in a nice way). She keeps everything running, and I don't know what any of us would do without her. She is the perfect blend of the superorganized Martha and the devoted Mary.

I have never been a "finishing" sort of person; I possess many more half-finished doilies, dolls, and dresses than I would ever want to admit publicly. That I have completed a *second* full-length book is a testament to the quality of assistance I have received from my family, as well as the desire God has given me to share His stories with others.

My early education was greatly shaped by my teachers. In second grade, Mrs. Segoria helped develop my lifelong love of books. In third and fourth grades, Mrs. Savage—a friend of my mother's, even though she didn't look that old—held spelling bees that delighted my little heart. In fifth and sixth grades, poor Mr. O'Neill put up with all my "clever" stunts and unchecked wit with far more patience than I deserved. (I was suspended only once.) Luckily for Mr. Duckett, I had settled down a bit by seventh and eighth grades and was eager to learn everything I could, so he made an extra effort to challenge me. I have always appreciated the time and attention each of my teachers spent with me, no matter which phase of life I was in.

Thank you to the editors and proofreaders at Pacific Press for all your hard work. I look forward to getting to know you during the process of preparing this manuscript for publication.

And my darling husband: It was no accident that led you to meet the men from the publishing house that day and talk to them about me and this book. Thank you for being proud of me and so supportive of my writing. Many times as I was writing this book, I thought of you. After ten years of marriage, I still love you with all my heart.

Characters

Angels	Demons
Aitan	Ares
Arion	Bozkath
Bahir	Eidolon
Chanok	Elazar
Deron	Gillulim
Elazar	Goiim
Gurion	Hamath
Jabir	Oreb
Matthan	Igal
Menachem	Set
Meraioth	Shihab
Misbah	Sirion
Nadiv	Zeeb
Nissim	Zuar
Taberah	
Tarik	
Zohar	

Abelia, Andrew's four-year-old daughter
Adalia, Andrew's three-year-old daughter
Atalia, Andrew's baby daughter

Aretas, king of Nabataea

Bakbukiah, a doctor
Baram, a farmer
Batia, Peter's mother-in-law
Betzalel, man healed by the pool

Elhanan, a fish seller

Hazelelponi, woman at the wedding
Hezron, a leper

Jered, Peter's son

Kenan, a priest in Capernaum
Keren, Andrew's wife

Najiyah, a princess of Nabataea; Herod's first wife
Nahshon, a madman

Ornah, mother of the boy of Nain

Ranon, a boy of Nain
Rimona, Simon's wife
Riphath, man lowered for healing through roof

Seth, Peter's son
Shillem, Philip's former employer

Talib, a male believer

Yasirah, a female believer

Contents

Chapter 1

With a thud and a groan, the little fishing vessel ran aground just at daybreak. Simon and Andrew leaped over the side and began pulling in rhythm with the waves to drag the boat onto the shore. Only half filled with fish, it responded better than they would have liked.

Simon stretched and yawned, waving a greeting to his friends, James and John, who were helping to bring in the boats for their family. He looked wistfully at the sleek, modern craft their father, Zebedee, owned and operated. Each piece of equipment was of good quality and contained the latest innovations.

Looking back at his own small boat, Simon sighed. He had made it himself with Andrew's help. They had fashioned it from oak, so it was sturdy enough. But the only modern thing about it was the way the ends of the boat curled up and around to form two lantern hooks. Andrew had modified them so they could swing out over the water, a real boon for night fishing.

"Hey, sleepyhead, are you going to help me sort these or not?" Andrew's voice interrupted Simon's envious thoughts.

"I sorted more of them yesterday," Simon grumbled good-naturedly. "It's your turn today." The banter flowed freely as their practiced hands rapidly processed the night's catch. They were almost done when James and John walked over.

"Catch anything?" Andrew greeted them.

"We did all right," John replied. "Have you heard the latest about the Baptist?"

Andrew sat up straight. "What about him?" he asked eagerly.

"He's preaching at Bethabara," James interrupted, "and John is going to hear him."

John laughed. "Officially, I'm going to *sell fish*—for Elhanan. You know how Father feels about the Baptist."

James rolled his eyes. "He thinks he's a fanatic or a lunatic. Maybe both. He would never waste time listening to him."

"Anyway," John continued, "do you two want to come with me? Maybe Elhanan would let you bring something to, uh, sell too."

"Of course he will!" Simon exclaimed. "As long as we promise to tell him all about it when we get back. When do we leave?"

Andrew's face fell. "Keren is so close to her time that I really shouldn't leave her. But maybe I can go next time."

"Maybe the Voice will speak again." Simon was as excited as a child.

"I saw the Dove coming down out of heaven," James reminded them. "Do you think it might be there this time too?"

"Could that man really be the Messiah?" John asked.

"I'm not sure," admitted James. "I thought so at the time, but in the last month or so we haven't heard anything more about him. It's like he just disappeared."

"It doesn't matter," said Simon. "I'd be glad just to hear John preach again."

"When can you meet me?" asked John.

"Give me an hour," Simon said quickly. "I can be back here by then. I just have to help Andrew get last night's catch carried over to Elhanan, gather a bit of food, and pack my share of the fish, and I'll be ready."

"And break the news to Rimona," Andrew reminded him. "You're not going to leave that for me to do."

"All right, all right." Simon threw up his hands. "I'll tell Rimona before I go."

Andrew shook his finger at his brother. "You'd better."

James and John stood to go. "We'll see you in an hour, then, Simon," James said.

"You can use one of our donkeys to haul your fish," John offered.

"Andrew, I hope God blesses you with a son this time."

"Amen," was Andrew's heartfelt response.

Just over an hour later, John was surprised to see both Simon and Andrew trudging toward him, each with a large sack of dried fish and bread slung over his shoulder. Simon seemed excited, an enthusiastic grin on his face; Andrew just looked glum. They approached and stood looking at him, until John had to ask, "I give up. What happened?"

Simon grinned even wider. "Well, I told Rimona. And let's just say she wasn't happy."

"At least you're here," said John. "What else?"

"Not much," Simon replied a bit too innocently. "I said Goodbye to my lovely wife, my mother-in-law, my sons, and my nieces. *All* my nieces."

John looked questioningly at Andrew, who dropped his gaze and nodded. "Another girl? I'm sorry, Andrew." John tried to sound sincere in spite of the chuckle that escaped his lips.

Simon let out a whoop. "You should hear what this one is named!"

"Let's see," John tapped his chin as he thought. "You already have Abelia and Adalia. I give up. What is it?"

Andrew rolled his eyes. "Atalia. You know how Keren is when she gets an idea into her head. The worst part is, she is planning to name the next one Abitalia."

John's eyes twinkled. "You'd better hope it's a girl, then."

"Please, no," Andrew groaned. He glanced over his shoulder. "We'd better go before it gets any later."

They followed the road south, remaining silent for a time, but soon the beauty of the late-spring morning lifted their spirits. All thoughts of unhappy wives and living conditions that would now be even more crowded faded from their minds. The prospect of hearing the Baptist again was thrilling, and hope of the Messiah, intoxicating. For that day and the next, it was all they could talk about.

Tarik, Nadiv, and Arion stood patiently in the road, waiting for the men to finish loading the donkeys. The Guardians didn't bother to look at the

three nearby demons, Oreb, Zeeb, and Shihab. Oh, they had no doubt the three would make trouble enough if they could, but the Father would tolerate no interference with this journey, and they all knew it—Guardians and demons alike.

"They're almost ready," Tarik said. "I can't wait to see if Simon decides to be baptized when he hears John's appeal."

Arion nodded. "Maybe John will too. I've noticed lately he's grown closer to the Father than ever before."

"You know," said Nadiv, "the humans may not realize this at all, but this trip is definitely part of the Plan. They think they are just selling some fish and listening to a few sermons, but the Father has much more in mind. Maybe all three will answer the call."

Tarik had just opened his mouth to reply when he heard the unmistakable sound of the dimensional barrier being breached. In a flash, six more Guardians stood beside them. The tallest, Aitan, greeted them. "Tarik, Jabir and I have been assigned to help you. Bahir and Misbah will be with Nadiv, and Chanok and Menachem will assist Arion."

"It will be good to work with all of you again," Tarik rejoiced, embracing each in turn. "Praise the Father for sending you," he said, as Arion and Nadiv also welcomed their companions.

A few paces away, Oreb, Zeeb, and Shihab exchanged a look of horror. After a hasty whispered conference, Shihab disappeared to deliver an emergency report and bring back reinforcements. As the little party of fishermen and donkeys walked along the road, Oreb and Zeeb followed as closely as they dared. Finally Oreb said, "Go on ahead, Zeeb. There's not much we can do until the others get back, anyway. Maybe you can find some bandits or something."

Zeeb was gone only a few minutes. He returned wearing an evil grin. "Succoth," was all he said, and winked at Oreb.

Tarik's mind churned with questions as he followed Simon. What could this mean? Why would three obscure fishermen need so much protection? Was he being called into action once more? He knew nothing, but he was sure that time would bring him the answers.

Tarik's previous assignment had been such a difficult one that he was given a full ten earth-years of light messenger duty, plus a few short-term assignments as an assistant Guardian, before receiving his next *full-time duty. After Herod, the poverty-stricken baby boy of Bethsaida had been such a pleasant change that Tarik had welcomed the respite. At times, some of the other angels must have wondered why his unique talent was being poured out in the backwaters of Galilee, but if Tarik himself ever thought of this, he never said so. He just felt thankful to be near his beloved Master, even if he served only on the fringes of the great struggle.*

But the unexpected presence of Aitan and Jabir could only mean that Simon had some part in the war, a part none of them had suspected until now. Beings from many worlds had watched Simon often, since he belonged to Tarik, without ever seeing in him any hint of remarkable promise. Only God knew the depths of his heart—and just what his place in the Plan might be.

They traveled hard, following the road east of the Jordan, stopping for just a few minutes in each small town to sell fish. At noon of the second day, they entered Succoth, the last village before their destination.

"Fish for sale," called John softly as he walked briskly along the street.

"Aren't we even going to stop?" Andrew asked.

"Not this time," John said, then even more quietly, *"Fish for sale!* We want to make it before dark. *Fish for sale!* The roads are too dangerous, even if there are three of us. *Fish for sale!"* He saw a woman peek out her doorway. She looked as if she might actually buy something, so he sped past her.

"You know, John, I really admire the way you sell fish," Simon said, running to be first through the narrow gate in the village wall.

"Thank you," John grinned. "Now, let's hurry!"

"Pray for protection," Tarik, Nadiv, and Arion whispered to the three men. Simon and John continued talking as if nothing had happened. Off in some bushes beside the road, Oreb and Zeeb smirked.

The new Guardians drew near. "Pray for protection," all nine said aloud. Oreb and Zeeb stopped smirking.

Simon, Andrew, and John stopped in the middle of the road, their voices trailing off into silence. "I think we should pray," John finally said.

"It's not even the Sabbath," Simon began to protest, "and there's no synagogue here . . . but I think you're right."

"So do I," Andrew said, shaking his head as if to dispel a strange feeling.

Awkwardly, they bowed their heads as John haltingly asked for whatever protection God saw fit to provide. Feeling oddly relieved once their prayer was over, if a bit sheepish, the three men led their donkeys along the dusty road to Bethabara.

The angels shouted for joy, seeming to glow even brighter as they encircled the fishermen in a ring of white flame. Nothing evil, whether human or demonic, could pass through the energy flowing from them. Even with the reinforcements that had returned with Shihab, the demons could do nothing but veil their eyes against the blinding radiance of the prayer shield.

A massive tangle of trees and brush grew all along the winding course of the Jordan. In it, wild animals found shelter, as did the roving bandits that plagued the area. Ahead, where the path of the river was nearer the road, a gang of vicious robbers concealed themselves in the undergrowth on each side of the road. Any hapless traveler they attacked was beaten to death without mercy, his body left discarded by the wayside.

Upon seeing the Galileans approach with their heavily laden animals, the leader chuckled to himself. "Looks like we're having fish tonight," he whispered.

When their prey reached the place of the ambush, the chieftain opened his mouth to shout the signal, but no sound came from his lips! He tried again. Nothing. Frantic, he tried to rush at the three men, hoping his gang would follow, but he couldn't move! Some force held him back. He strained desperately, but all his efforts were useless. As his quarry passed along the road and out of sight, the leader blinked once. His eyelids seemed to be all that worked.

Tarik, Nadiv, and Arion waved happily to their friends in the underbrush. The other angels waved back with one hand, each holding down a robber with the other. The demons that usually clustered around the ambush sites to feed on the sights of death and bloodshed were nowhere to be seen.

After the intended victims had passed by safely, the Guardians holding back the would-be murderers stepped away reluctantly, giving them back into the keeping of their demons.

Oreb and Zeeb turned on Shihab in fury. "Is this the best you could do?" Zeeb screamed. "I set up a better ambush the very first time I took the class!"

"But the angels . . ." Shihab began before he was cut off by a hard shove. Outraged, he zoomed back toward the site of the thwarted ambush, hoping to vent his anger and spite on the inept tempters.

He skidded to a sudden halt when faced with twenty-four irate devils, all larger than himself, and reconsidered his approach. Sanity ultimately prevailed, and Shihab contented himself with fiercely glaring at them before stomping over to where the leader of the robbers was bent over, trying to regain his balance. For several minutes Shihab stormed around, cursing the bandit as if it had all somehow been his fault. Then he flew off, feeling better until he heard the laughter of angels behind him.

The leader of the robber band felt a pain in his side and winced. Why was it so hard to breathe? Slowly he raised himself, glad he could move once more, and turned to face his men. They stared in shock, eyes wild. The men tried hard not to look at each other, not wanting to see a mirror of the fear each of them felt.

"We didn't do it this time, either, Barabbas," a man of gigantic proportion finally stammered. "None of us was even close to you." A red-headed youth nodded in confirmation.

"We couldn't move, either," said another. He gulped. "Something was holding us."

Just then they heard it—laughter all around them—but they could see no one.

Barabbas looked at each of his men. The terror in their eyes spoke the truth for them. "That's the second time today," he said, trying to keep his hands from shaking visibly, "and the fifth time this week. You know I'm not a superstitious man, but this is getting tiresome. All in favor of going back to the Jericho road say 'aye.'"

"What was that?" Simon asked.

"It sounded like a shout," said John, frowning.

"I didn't hear anything," Andrew said. "I was too busy talking. It was probably just an animal or something."

Simon shrugged. "Oh, well. Now, let's draw straws to see who has to stay behind and sell fish tomorrow."

As the time for the evening meal neared, Simon again bemoaned his short straw and waved his arm to shoo the flies out of his face. It was hot, and his robe felt stiff and uncomfortable. He missed the fresh breezes of Galilee. Even a dip in the muddy waters of the Jordan sounded delightful, but no, he had to stay with the fish. The stupid, stinking, dried fish!

Simon cursed the fish. He cursed the heat. He cursed John and Andrew for taking so long, and when he ran out of things to curse, he started over again. Just then he heard the sound of running footsteps and looked over his shoulder.

"Simon! Simon!" He could hear Andrew before he saw him. "We found Him! We've found the Messiah!"

Impulsively, Simon leaped to his feet, racing to meet Andrew. As an afterthought, he scooped up the clanking bag containing the proceeds from their fish sales. "Where is He? What is He doing? Is He calling together an army? I'll go enlist right now!" Simon didn't even look back at the score or so of fish he left lying on a mat.

Andrew tried to explain as best he could. "He's not gathering an army—not yet, anyway. Just wait till you meet Him, and you'll understand. One thing, though; He doesn't look exactly like you'd expect."

"Why would I care what He looks like?" Simon gestured grandly with the money bag. "All I care about is getting rid of the Romans and having our own king on the throne. I'll be a free man!"

"You'd better put that away," Andrew cautioned, glancing quickly around. "You never know when a robber might be nearby."

Chastened, Simon slipped the bag inside his robe. "What is His name? Where is He staying? Did you actually get to talk to Him?"

"One question at a time, my brother." Andrew couldn't help but laugh. "Yes, I got to talk to Him. I, Andrew, son of Jonas, have personally spoken to the Messiah. His name is Jesus."

"Jesus," Simon repeated thoughtfully. "That means 'Jehovah is salvation.' Well, He's going to save us, all right, and it's about time. Where did you say He was staying? I didn't see any nice inns around."

"Funny you should mention that," Andrew replied mysteriously, "because I asked Him the very same thing." He lapsed into silence, watching his brother out of the corner of one eye.

"All right, all right, what did He say?" Simon scowled at his brother and shook him by the shoulders. "Don't make me guess."

"He said . . ." Andrew inhaled and exhaled with excruciating slowness, savoring the moment. Simon tightened his grip. Andrew held up his hand in mock terror. "He said we could come and see."

In his surprise, Simon nearly knocked Andrew to the ground. "Why didn't you say so in the first place? Where is He?" Andrew pointed to a grove of trees. Simon shook his head in disbelief. "I don't know what the most important Man in Israel wants with a poor Galilean fisherman, but I'm going to find out right now!" He sprinted in the direction his brother had indicated.

Andrew straightened his rumpled robe. "He wants us," he said wonderingly, "because He's just like us."

Tarik knelt beside the place where Simon stood. Even though his Master's human eyes filtered out the unseen world around Him, Tarik knew He was aware of his presence. He closed his eyes in blissful worship and relaxed, for no demon could ever approach this close to Jesus without permission. Strengthened, revived, he stood once more and spoke words of encouragement to Simon's mind. "This is the Messiah. Listen to Him, for He speaks only the truth."

Jesus looked on the proud, impulsive fisherman with glad welcome. He knew every cell in Simon's body, for He had formed them. Every day of Simon's life, from birth to death, He saw as if unrolling a scroll. As His eyes traveled from the untamed brown hair to the rough, dirty feet, such love flowed from Him that Simon felt as if he had suddenly come home.

"You are Simon, the son of Jonas," Jesus told him, without waiting to be introduced, "but after this, you will be called Peter, for you are My little stone."

Simon gulped, trying to grasp what his eyes told him. How could this thin, poorly dressed man be the Deliverer of Israel? Although He appeared kind, He was emaciated and hollow-eyed, as if He had been ill for a long time. His clothes, though neat, were roughly spun and had been mended many times, their original color impossible to guess. His hands were calloused by a life spent in hard manual labor, and His feet obviously had done a lot of walking.

But at the very instant when doubt rose up, something else inside Peter's heart assured him, *"He is the One."* An amazing feeling flowed over him, a feeling that all creation bowed to this Man. Seating himself on the ground beside John, Peter felt a new, unfamiliar peace flood his heart. He didn't even notice his brother had not yet joined him until some time later, when Andrew walked up, carrying the fish Simon had left behind and leading three neglected donkeys.

"We might as well try to cook some of these fish," Andrew suggested, turning the donkeys loose to graze. "I was able to trade some fish for fresh bread, so we can have quite a feast. Simon, can you help me with this?"

"Peter," said his brother.

"What?" Andrew asked, puzzled.

"My name is Peter," Simon explained. "Jesus said so."

"All right," said Andrew slowly, "but maybe I should call you Simon Peter until I get used to it." He set down the fish. "Now, are you going to help me, or not?"

By the time night fell, Peter was not too surprised to see Jesus wrap up in His cloak, lie down on the ground, and pillow His head on one arm.

Peter smiled wryly. After all, he had wondered what kind of fancy room the Messiah would sleep in. Peter yawned and stretched out on his back. Looking up at the night sky with its stars bending near, Peter thought, *It can't be long until He sets up His kingdom. This is just some kind of test before He brings out all of His riches and calls for His army. Only a test.*

At last he slept, dreaming of a triumphant parade with Jesus riding into Jerusalem on the back of a fine donkey. Multitudes chanted His name and sang His praises; the wealthy laid palm branches in His path, and children threw flowers at His feet. Through it all, Peter was at His side, waving to the crowd and sharing the glory of the new kingdom.

Chapter 2

"Hosanna, hosanna, King!" mumbled Peter. "Thank you. Thank you very much, all of you. Are those for me? Ow!"

John nudged him hard in the ribs. "Wake up, it's time to go."

Peter propped himself up on one elbow, blinking sleepily. "Throw flowers, not rocks."

"Simon, uh . . . , Peter, we're leaving now." Andrew shook his brother by the shoulder.

"But it's still dark," Peter protested. Andrew grabbed his brother's arm and tugged. John yanked away Peter's cloak. "Hey, what are you doing?" Peter punctuated his protest with an oath.

Andrew winced at Peter's language. "Shhh, we're going with Jesus, remember?"

Peter gulped. "Oh. Right. Let's get going, then."

To their surprise, Jesus did not at once turn north toward the province of Galilee. Instead, He led them to Bethabara, stopping just outside the city. For no reason that they could see, He sat down comfortably, smiling at them.

"I could have slept in," Peter mumbled to himself. He rested his head in his hands and tried to relax.

"Philip!" Jesus called out. Peter raised his head to see a short, stocky man walking toward them, grinning.

"I hoped I would find you, Teacher," Philip exclaimed. "I wanted to hear more of your stories. Oh, there you are, Simon. Andrew and John said you were here, but I hadn't seen you."

"This is a surprise," said Peter. "I hardly ever saw you once I moved away from Bethsaida, and now here you are, miles away. Does this seem as odd to you as it does to me?"

"It's probably not that strange," Philip chuckled. "We both seem to be here for the same reason—to see Jesus."

Jesus reached for Philip's hand and clasped it. "Follow Me," was all He said.

Philip's eyes got round. "You're leaving? Right now? But Nathanael is . . . I'll be right back!" He turned and ran without dignity, puffing from the exertion.

Jesus' eyes crinkled in a smile as He squinted at the rising sun. "Right on time." A few minutes later, Philip was back, his lanky friend in tow. Hazel eyes swept the group with a bright, honest gaze.

Jesus spoke before either of the men. "Look, here is at least one Israelite who is sincere."

Philip's friend frowned. "How do you know me, Lord? I'm sure I've never met You."

"It's simple," said Jesus. "Before Philip called you, I saw you praying underneath that fig tree."

The man's mouth dropped open. "Teacher, how did You know that? You *must* be the Son of God!"

Jesus looked intently into his eyes. "Do you believe in Me just because I said I saw you under the fig tree? I will show you much greater things than that." He turned to the others. "The truth is, after this you will see the heavens open wide, and angels ascend and descend on the Son of Man."

Peter looked questioningly at Andrew. Andrew shrugged and whispered, "I don't really understand, either."

Nathanael fell to his knees. "Master, I will follow You anywhere."

"Good," Jesus said. A satisfied look came over His face as He stood to His feet. "Then, let's go."

The wedding was in full swing when they arrived at the little town of Cana in Galilee. Jesus slipped into His cousin's home through a side door and led His followers to the kitchen. Though the evening was cool, the kitchen blazed with heat and light. Inside, a veritable army of bakers and servants hastened to carry out the bidding of a small, lovely woman in a light-blue robe. Her waist-length black hair, just starting to gray, was pulled back in a loose braid. She caught sight of Jesus as He stood in the doorway and ran eagerly to greet Him.

"There You are; I've been so worried," she scolded gently. She reached up to cup His tanned face in her hands. "Haven't You been eating anything? You're so thin!" Her keen eyes searched His face, finding new dignity and awareness there, written in lines of struggle. "You look very different."

Jesus took her hands in His and kissed them lovingly. "It's good to see you too, Mother. Come meet My friends." Mary peered around His shoulder to find five young men, shaggy and travel soiled. Their eyes watched her Son's every move with something that could only be called reverence. Her heart swelled with pride.

"Let me show you where you can refresh yourselves," she said to them, "and then you can tell me all about what my Son has been doing. I'm sure Hazelelponi can get along without me for a little while." She called across the room, "Hazel, I'll be back in an hour or so, all right?" Without waiting for an answer, she set off briskly, leading Jesus by the arm and chattering all the way.

"This is more like it," Peter said to Andrew and John, his voice muffled by the clean linen as he dried his face. Well-trained servants unobtrusively whisked off his sandals, bathing his feet with cool water.

"Just think," Andrew added, "pretty soon we'll get to live like this all the time. I could sure get used to it, you know."

John grinned, but said nothing. His house wasn't as ornate as this one, but his father had had servants for as long as he could remember, and he was used to being waited on.

Mary's timing was perfect; more servants carried in the first servings of stew just as the men finished washing and the last of the muddy cloths were carried out. The ravenous men fell on the food, answering Mary's rapid questions the best they could with their mouths full. They told her what they had seen and heard at Jesus' baptism and how He had suddenly reappeared only a few days before.

"Your Son is the One the prophets and Moses all told us about," Peter said enthusiastically.

Mary beamed at him. Since Joseph's death the year before, there had been no one who would listen and share her memories of the angel or the prophecies in the temple. Certainly her stepsons didn't believe Jesus was anything special. Now, the appearance of these young men seemed to indicate that the time was almost here for her Son to become king. And that would make her . . . "Did you ever hear about all that happened when my Son was born?" She turned firmly from the prideful hopes threatening to flood her.

"A little," John answered her.

"Tell us," Peter urged.

So for the first time in many years, Mary spoke of the visit from the angel who announced to her that she would bear the Messiah, of Joseph's hurt when he thought she had betrayed him with another man, and of the dream that had convinced him to marry her. Peter listened intently as she told them of the shame heaped on husband and wife at their wedding, when even the flowing lines of her gown could not hide the bulge in her middle.

The men almost forgot to chew when she came to the part about the decree from Caesar Augustus. They had heard the story from their parents about how every man had to return to the city of his ancestry to register for the tax roll. How could they have known, while they listened to their fathers tell of the Counting, that it had forced Mary to make a dangerous journey over steep, rocky roads, all the while heavy with child?

Tarik seated himself next to Peter, curving an arm and a wing about his charge. He loved stories, and the birth of his Commander was one of his favorites. He often wondered what it was like to be human, each day filled with uncertainty and strife. The stories he heard them tell offered glimpses into their hearts, and he treasured each one.

Unable to come too close, Satan ground his teeth as he was once again forced to listen to the tale of this extraordinarily painful defeat. It had been such a good plan. First, he had wanted to stir up the townspeople enough to stone Mary. It wasn't legal, but so far north it could have been kept quiet. Joseph had spoiled that part by marrying her, even when the whole city believed her to be a whore.

Then there was the decree. Augustus was malleable enough; it appealed to his pride to count those under his dominion and collect more taxes for his overflowing coffers. The road to Bethlehem was hazardous, and a special contingent of demons went ahead, digging potholes, forming rockslides that would trigger at the barest whisper, and washing out the road in places and then making it appear as if the footing were still solid. It should have been so easy to arrange a simple stumble down a slippery slope. One little misstep. A single freakish fatality.

A peculiar sound caught his attention. In the sudden silence he became aware that his underlings were looking at him strangely. He surreptitiously unclenched his teeth, and everyone wisely pretended not to notice that the grinding promptly stopped.

Against his wishes, Satan's thoughts returned to the journey by Mary and Joseph from Nazareth to Bethlehem. Gabriel had led a squadron of his mightiest warriors to surround the couple, shielding them from each unseen danger and even physically supporting them in several especially difficult places. They never knew that more than once they had walked across open air, supported by nothing but the power of their Guardians.

"Uh, Mr. Lucifer, sir," Oreb stammered. He hadn't been this close to his leader since before the Rebellion. "I was just thinking, . . . well, you know that Mary is in charge of the food for the feast."

Satan fastened Oreb with a steely glare. "Yes." His strong voices were melodious yet frightening as they intertwined, "I do."

Oreb gulped, shifting his eyes to where Simon sat, still engrossed in Mary's story. "I was just remembering what you said in your talk—about how we don't have to make Him do something really bad, like kill someone; all we have to do is to get Him to step outside His Father's will the very tiniest fraction. Then He'll be ours, right?"

Satan crossed his arms, drumming the fingers of one hand impatiently. "Go on."

"Well, the way you explained it to us with the prophecies and everything, His kingdom isn't an earthly one which is why . . ."

Satan lunged forward suddenly, gripping Oreb by his bony shoulders. The *little demon's eyes bugged wide, and no sound came from his open mouth. "The feast," hissed Satan menacingly. "What about the feast?"*

Oreb tried to collect his scattered thoughts, one eye rapidly developing a new tic. "The feast," he echoed. "Yes, the feast." He swallowed hard. "With Mary in charge of the food, if they ran out of something, it would be her fault. Jes— I mean, He—would have a choice to make, wouldn't He? He could perform some kind of miracle to help her, one that an ordinary human couldn't do. Or He could do nothing and see more shame heaped on His mother and His family. Any way it turned out could be to our advantage."

The look of cunning that spread over the rebel leader's face chilled Oreb to his protoplasmic marrow. "You could be right." Satan leered. "Let's see, . . . what would be best? I know. You and Zeeb each dispose of three jars of wine. The timing is critical, so be ready when they run out."

Walls were no barrier as Tarik looked across the compound to see Oreb and Zeeb stalking along, each carrying a large stone urn filled with wine. It was useless to protest the menial assignment when it came straight from their commander, but their gloomy faces told the tale all too clearly. Behind a sheltering bush, they poured out the wine onto the earth, covering the jars with branches so the humans wouldn't find them until it was too late.

"What are they doing?" Tarik whispered to Gabriel, who hovered beside Jesus as always.

"Don't worry," Gabriel whispered back, his eyes full of mischief. "It's part of our Plan."

"It was nearly a week before I heard what happened less than two hours after we left," Mary said, wiping her eyes. "The soldiers swept through Bethlehem and all the surrounding villages, killing every baby boy two years old and under. If it weren't for the angel who woke us, Jesus would have been . . . " She paused to wipe away a tear. "I've always wanted to thank him."

Gabriel patted her hand. "You're welcome."

Catching a glimpse of the darkening sky through the room's one high window, Mary jumped to her feet. "I'd better get back to the kitchen. It's become late, and Hazelelponi will be wondering where I am. Make yourselves at home at the feast!"

Over the next several days, Peter relaxed and enjoyed the festivities. Jesus seemed to be the center of attention wherever He went, and Peter was seldom far from His side. Every day Mary took time away from her duties to sit and talk awhile with Peter, James, and John. She was so beautiful and vibrant that Peter had no trouble picturing her in royal robes, surrounded by maids-in-waiting, as befitted the mother of a king.

Everything had gone so smoothly that he was surprised on the last night of the feast when Mary practically ran to them, eyes wild. "Jesus, you've got to help me," she cried, panting. "The most awful thing has happened, and I don't know what to do."

"Of course, Mother." Jesus motioned for the five to follow Him.

Outside the kitchen door she motioned to a row of waist-high jars lined up against the wall. "Those six are all empty, and six more are missing. There is no more wine for the feast! You have to help me," she pleaded. In her mind, she finished the sentence: *and then everyone here will see You were meant to be king.*

Jesus pulled her into His arms, smoothing her hair as He answered her unspoken wish. "Dear Lady, it's not time for that yet. You don't understand what you're asking."

Every time He spoke to her like that, Mary remembered His first Passover trip, when she found Him in the temple with the rabbis. "Don't you know," He had said, "that I must begin My Father's work?" He was only twelve, but His gentle rebuke cut to her heart, just as it did now.

"I'm sorry. I didn't think . . ."

"It's all right, Mother." He kissed her forehead. "I know, and I will still help you."

Hope shone from her eyes, and the tears threatened to spill over. "Thank You." Leaning into the brightness of the kitchen, she called two of the men to come. "Do whatever He tells you." She motioned toward Jesus.

Peter stood tall, in case Jesus needed anything from him. No, his Master just told the men to fill the jars with water. Peter's brows lifted in a question. To serve water at a feast like this was unthinkable, and insulting to the guests, but the servants did as they were told. Peter looked back over his shoulder several times to make sure they were following their instructions exactly.

"I might have known He would go for the old water trick." Satan turned to Oreb. "This was your idea, so you can stay and make sure no one tries to add any kind of coloring. We want our good host to catch the full impact of water at his feast. The rest of you, be ready. I want everyone here to know just who is responsible for this insult."

Jesus seemed particularly happy as He led them back to supper. "Master," Peter ventured. "Why did You do something, when You said it wasn't time yet? And what did You do, anyway?"

Jesus smiled and put one hand on Peter's shoulder. "It is always the right time to build faith in your heart, as well as in the others who are following Me. As far as what I did, you'll find out soon enough." He laughed at the thought of the anticipated surprise.

As they sat, John managed to keep the coveted position at Jesus' right hand. Peter hardly had to push Andrew at all to stay at His left. Vastly curious, he kept a close eye on the proceedings, instantly recognizing one of the men from the kitchen when he came in carrying a pitcher of water. The man walked slowly, his face strained; the host saw him and motioned him to come.

"More wine? It's about time!" the host snapped irritably, waving his empty cup. "Quickly, serve this table first!"

Oreb watched carefully as the molecules in the water separated, rearranged themselves, and came back together in a dark, fresh juice. "Uh-oh, I wasn't quite expecting that. Uh, Mr. Lucifer, sir . . ." His voice came out as a squeak.

"Is everyone ready?" Satan bellowed. "The timing is critical. When the water hits the host's cup, that is our signal."

"Wait! Wait!" Oreb flew through the walls in his haste. "The water has been turned into . . ."

"Wine!" the servant exclaimed as a rich, sweet juice splashed down into the cup. The host looked at him strangely. "Um, I mean, of course, it's wine!" the servant laughed nervously. "What else would it be?" Trying to hide a grin, he moved down the length of the bridal table and filled each cup in turn, even though he could hardly pour for looking in amazement at Jesus.

Satan froze, his arms poised to give the signal. It took the barest moment for the full implications to run through his mind. "Quickly! Right now!" he screamed. "We can still salvage this!"

"Crown Him!" The demons shouted unhesitatingly, each trying to influence his sinner to offer Jesus the throne of Israel. "Crown Him as your King!"

Satan massaged his aching temples. "And try to keep them from drinking that awful stuff!"

Peter blinked slowly to clear his eyes. The fluid pouring from the pitcher was dark, shimmering in the torchlight. His mouth watered in anticipation. Even from across the room he could catch a hint of the fragrance.

The host took a careful sip. Surprise covered his face. "This is excellent," he shouted to the servant. "I thought we would have used the best wine first, but this is the finest I've ever tasted!" He drained the cup and shouted across the room, "Where did this delicious nectar come from?"

Peter could stay still no longer. He jumped to his feet, gesturing grandly to his right. "I know who did it! He's right here!" All eyes turned first toward him, then in puzzlement to the empty bench at which he pointed. Peter looked around in confusion, his ears red with embarrassment. "He was just here. Where did He go?"

"Come over here and sit down, young man," boomed the host. "I want to hear more."

Those guests closest to Andrew and John pounced on them as well, demanding the full story. "After all," one woman said, "you were there. You saw what happened."

Within moments the story had traveled around the room. "We should crown Him as our King," the host exclaimed decisively.

The guests took up the cry. "Crown Jesus! Crown Jesus!" But although they searched for Him, they couldn't find Him. With His quiet disappearance, the first of many coronation attempts ended as quickly as it had begun.

The Guardians stepped in quickly, whispering to their charges the truth of the New Kingdom and encouraging them to drink deeply of the wine provided directly by the Creator. Untainted by any foul, earthly fermentation, its refreshing flavor awoke in those present a longing to know the One who made it. Even the ordinary juice of the grape carries wondrous healing potential within it, but the wine at that feast was so potent that each one who drank it was not only untouched by illness of any kind for many months, but carried extraordinary vigor to the end of his or her days.

The demons, forced into yet another retreat, spent the night in even more rancorous bickering than usual. "Well," Zeeb gloated to Shihab, "at least now I don't have to worry anymore about getting into trouble over the bandits."

"Shut up," whispered Oreb, squeezing between two larger demons in an attempt to avoid the direct gaze of his pacing leader. "Nothing ventured, nothing gained. Besides, this wasn't any worse than that."

Tarik sat by Peter, speaking to his mind, helping shape his words as he told the host everything he knew about Jesus. The angel glowed brighter and brighter, resonating with praise. This was what Tarik had waited for, had longed for, and he exulted in the Father's victory. All through the night the universe watched as a beacon of light passed through the dark reaches of space, illuminating the city of Cana with its warmth, and the Father's heart yearned after His people.

It seemed to Peter he had been in bed only a minute or two when a lantern flared to life. He squinted, his blurred eyes finally discerning the cheerful face of Jesus. "Is it time to get up already?"

If Jesus had spent another night without sleep, it didn't show. "Yes, Peter, it's time. We'll be leaving now, and My mother and brothers will follow in a few hours."

The others sat up and rubbed their eyes. "Where are we going?" John asked.

Jesus' smile was not without sympathy. "We need to spend some time in Capernaum."

Peter's face froze. "How nice that we'll be able to see our families again," he managed at last.

Andrew looked stricken. "Yes, how lovely."

John tried to encourage them. "At least we can tell them our trip was a success. We sold our fish, most of them, anyway. And just think of all the things we have to tell them. We saw a miracle with our very own eyes, and we have met the Messiah."

Peter groaned, looking pleadingly at Jesus. "Master, You're going to have to help me. I don't think I can face my family after being gone this long, unless You're with me."

"I always have been with you, Peter, and I'm not going to leave you now. Don't worry."

"Yes, but You don't know Batia."

Chapter 3

What do you mean, 'I had to go to a wedding'? You went off and left me for days—weeks!—to go to a wedding?" Rimona stomped her foot.

Peter opened his mouth. "Don't answer that," she interrupted before he could speak. "I can't believe you just left us!" she wailed.

"You men think only about yourselves," Batia agreed.

Peter's famous temper emerged, and without stopping to consider what Jesus would have thought of his outburst, he hurled several choice bits of sarcasm at both his wife and his mother-in-law before stalking out of the house.

Batia began to weep, holding up a pleading hand toward her daughter. Rimona raced to her mother's side, and the older woman clung pitifully to her. "Do you see?" she sobbed. "Do you see what I have to put up with? Oh, that man will be the death of me yet!"

"I know, Mother," Rimona patted Batia soothingly, blinking back the tears in her own eyes. "We'll be fine, though. We always have each other."

Nissim folded his wings, looking sadly at Tarik. "Rimona hasn't listened to me even once since you left. She has been treasuring each grievance, storing them up, just waiting for Peter to get back. Meraioth did his best with Batia, too, but you can imagine how that went."

"They do seem to feed off each other," Meraioth agreed. "Igal hardly even needs to suggest hateful words anymore; they come up with them just fine on their own."

Peter looked across the small room to where Andrew sat by his sleeping mat, hands out in supplication. He couldn't hear what his brother was saying, but judging by the stony expression on Keren's face, things weren't going too well for him, either.

"You always take your mother's side," he complained to his wife. "Why can't we just try to get along?"

"I'm not the one with the problem here," Rimona insisted. "You both just do whatever you want, whenever you want, without a care for your families."

Peter lowered his voice. "What we were doing was very important, you know. We found the Messiah."

Rimona sighed. "So how much is it going to cost us this time?"

Peter ran his fingers through his hair in frustration. "You know we can't afford a new house right now. Besides, what's so bad about this house? It has four walls and a roof."

As the argument continued, Oreb, Zeeb, Igal, and the others sprawled comfortably on the dirt floor to enjoy themselves. As Meraioth had said, they didn't even have to take an active part; they just shouted an occasional suggestion to make sure no opportunity was missed. As the evening wore on, more of the evil forces congregated to feast on the discord that was spreading in such plentiful supply. From a distance, the Guardians wept.

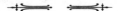

Peter slumped down next to Jesus by the shore of the lake, completely discouraged. He picked up stone after stone from the ground at his feet, throwing them into the water. "That didn't go so well," he finally admitted, "but I'm at my wits' end. I don't have any idea how to get my wife to change. Or her mother, either, for that matter." He shook his head and sighed. "I've tried everything."

"Do you love your wife?"

The question startled Peter. "Well, of course. That is, . . . I suppose I do. I'm not sure!"

Jesus couldn't help but chuckle at Peter's wry expression. Then He grew sober. "Why don't you see what happens when you love your wife? I mean truly love her and think of her before you think of yourself—love her as if she were your own flesh and you were each a part of the other. For in God's eyes, that is the way you are."

Peter rested his chin on one knee. "That won't change Rimona."

"The love of Adonai will change *you*. That is where the change needs to begin, in your own heart. Let me tell you about a man who had a plank in his eye."

Tarik, Aitan, and Jabir stood close to Peter as he pondered Jesus' words. Oreb paced afar off, unable to add even one wicked idea to Peter's thoughts. The little demon had to work hard to keep away from his commander, for wherever Jesus was, Satan was sure to be as near as he was allowed.

Soon Andrew joined Peter and Jesus, surrounded by Nadiv, Bahir, and Misbah, all speaking words of peace to his troubled mind. When both men stood, braced to return to their cramped home, all six guardians drew their swords, prepared to battle Igal when he contested their authority.

Peter fought the urge to grasp Andrew's shoulder for support as they paused outside the open doorway of the one-room dwelling. "It's no use waiting. We might as well get it done."

"I'll watch out behind you," Andrew offered bravely. Both men instinctively flexed their enormous muscles as they ducked into the house.

"How nice that you could stop by," Rimona's voice could surely have shattered iron. "Do you think the fish will just swim up to shore and jump in the boat for your convenience, so you won't have to bother going out tonight?"

The veins at Peter's temples bulged alarmingly, and only a nudge from his brother saved him from losing his temper. He took a long, slow breath and let it out. "I'm sorry."

"That's right, make your excuses like always. I don't know how much longer I can . . . what did you say?"

Clearing his throat, Peter repeated a little louder, "I'm sorry."

Andrew turned to Keren, who sat nursing the baby. "I'm sorry too." The shy woman didn't look at him, but her face softened just a fraction.

Impulsively, Peter kissed Rimona on the cheek. "I'll take the boat out in just a minute or two." Leaving his speechless wife, he crossed to Batia, who watched him with narrowed eyes.

"You're sorry, eh? I'll say you're sorry. It was a sorry day my husband ever met you." Her prominent nose bobbed up and down as she nodded for emphasis.

Peter acted as if she hadn't spoken. "I am sorry, um, Mother. I was . . ." His voice faltered and sputtered to a gurgling halt. He shook his head, coughed, and tried again. "I was wrong."

"Simon Peter, it's time to go. The fish are waiting." Andrew's interruption came at just the right moment, while Batia was still trying to think of something cutting to say. Peter didn't have to be asked twice. He flew out of the house faster than King Saul's javelin.

The instant Igal saw the angels coming and that they were armed, he drew his warped gray sword and faced them at the step. "Hamath, Bozkath, you'd better get out here," he called over his shoulder.

"Step aside and let us pass. We have the right of way," Tarik warned him.

"Absolutely not." Hamath pushed in next to Igal, with Bozkath right behind him. "This is our exclusive territory. By what right do you presume to intrude?"

"The right of prayer. The Master Himself is praying for them right now. All of them." The angelic weapons flashed with power, sending the demons stumbling backward.

"Run, Igal, they're too strong for us!" Hamath covered his eyes, blindly stumbling away from the light. Igal never even heard the warning. He was already safely out of range.

For the first time the brightness of heaven shone into every dark corner of the house, cleansing and purifying it. As if freed of some awful taint, the very air

seemed fresher. In her shock at the unexpected apology, Rimona didn't notice it at first, and even when she did, she wasn't quite sure what was different.

Her mother, completely free of Hamath's influence for the first time in years, couldn't think of a single thing to say the rest of the day. She lay down on her mat that night, propped up her swollen ankles, and tried to compile a list of insults to hurl at her son-in-law the next morning. Hours later, when nothing useful had come to mind, she finally gave up and went to sleep.

Rid of Bozkath, Keren fetched the water for both families for supper, earning her an incredulous stare from Rimona. In her quiet way, she helped to settle Jered and Seth for the night, in addition to her own daughters. Her Guardian, Zohar, eased her way as much as he could. The evening was smoother and more peaceful than any of the women could remember, and the angels were thankful beyond words. Rimona, still busy cleaning up supper, was puzzled, but merely shrugged.

An uneasy truce prevailed over the next several days. Simon Peter and Andrew launched their boat each evening before sunset, fished all night, and returned exhausted. Each morning, Jesus met them on the shore, where He had prepared a bed of coals laid with fish and bread. James and John joined them, too, but their father had no time for what he termed "ridiculousity."

Zebedee did allow Jesus to stay as a guest under his roof, but he ordered that Philip and Nathanael share the same room. Jesus seemed to find no discourtesy in his host's brusque behavior and unfailingly invited him to join the simple repast.

On the Sabbath day, even Zebedee laid aside his nets to attend the synagogue. Every son or daughter of Israel in the small town was there to hear the visiting Rabbi speak. According to the custom, Jesus rose when asked, seating Himself in the front between the slender marble pillars to read the Scriptures. His clear, mellow voice brought the ancient poetry to life in a way none of them had ever heard before. Peter sat by Andrew on the men's side, striving to catch every word.

The desert and the parched land will be glad;
the wilderness will rejoice and blossom.

Like the crocus, it will burst into bloom;
*   it will rejoice greatly and shout for joy.*
The glory of Lebanon will be given to it,
*   the splendor of Carmel and Sharon;*
they will see the glory of the LORD,
*   the splendor of our God.*

Strengthen the feeble hands,
*   steady the knees that give way;*
say to those with fearful hearts,
*   "Be strong, do not fear;*
your God will come,
*   he will come with vengeance;*
with divine retribution
*   he will come to save you."*

Then will the eyes of the blind be opened
*   and the ears of the deaf unstopped.*
Then will the lame leap like a deer,
*   and the mute tongue shout for joy.*
Water will gush forth in the wilderness
*   and streams in the desert.*
The burning sand will become a pool,
*   the thirsty ground bubbling springs.*
In the haunts where jackals once lay,
*   grass and reeds and papyrus will grow.*

And a highway will be there;
*   it will be called the Way of Holiness.*

After the service, Jesus spoke quietly with Peter and Andrew, Philip and Nathanael, and the sons of Zebedee. "Our stay here at Capernaum is over for now. Be ready to leave for the Passover in the morning." The men quickly agreed, not willing to be separated from Jesus for any length of time.

Early the next day, Peter and Andrew met the others on the main road. "How did it go?" James asked Peter.

Chapter 3

"Better than I thought it would. Rimona wasn't happy about it, but she wasn't angry, either."

"Look," Andrew added, "our wives even packed us some food for the trip."

"No, don't tell me." James scrunched up his face. "Dried fish." At Andrew's rueful nod, he burst out laughing. "Don't worry, we brought some too."

Peter was the only one who noticed when they veered to the left, away from the main road to Jerusalem. Quickly he asked, "Master, what are we doing? This is the way to Jericho."

Jesus gave a wide grin. "I know. Isn't it beautiful?"

"But I thought . . . well, that is . . ." He trailed off, not quite sure how to question Jesus.

"We have an appointment to keep before the feast. Someone is waiting to meet us in Jericho." And with that, Peter had to be content.

As the travel-stained men approached the north gate of the city, the sun was not yet high, but a steady stream of people passed them. Most were on their way to the Passover, but a few were working their way back to the north. Peter saw one such man approaching and instantly recognized by his clothing that he was a Samaritan. "Hey, Andrew, look," he said quietly.

As the man drew near, leading a donkey, Peter moved hurriedly to the far side of the road, and the others followed suit. In fact, all the Jews gave the Samaritan a wide berth, inadvertently making his passage that much easier. The man was almost past when Jesus stopped abruptly. "Wait," He said, "I need to talk to you."

The Samaritan looked behind him to see if Jesus was speaking to someone else, but there was no one. "Me? You want to talk to me?"

Peter could hardly believe it when Jesus crossed over and began talking with the man. At first he tried to listen to what they were saying, but instead, he kept hearing the comments of his fellow Jews as they passed by. "Is that one of *our* people talking to a Samaritan?" "Maybe he's crazy." "I know I'd never be seen with an idiot like that!" Peter grew indignant, but just as he was about to leap to Jesus' defense—maybe even knock down one of His detractors—he realized that if he did, they would know he was with the "idiot." He remained silent.

43

Much later, far too much later as far as Peter was concerned, Jesus resumed His journey, calling back, "Goodbye, Samuel." He led His followers into Jericho, mingling with the happy crowd. Peter gawked like a country yokel; it was his first time in the famous city of trade. Almost all the streets were narrow and winding, hard to navigate, but full of fascinating sights. "Look at that tax collector." Andrew, his voice rigid with disapproval, nudged Peter sharply in the ribs. "You'd think he was king of the city or something."

Peter looked with a mixture of awe and disgust where Andrew pointed. The tax collector sat in his booth, a line of traders extended as far as Peter could see, each with a bag of coins for payment. Even from where he stood, Peter could see that most of the money never made it into the government's tax chest. He felt a stirring of envy until Jesus led him into the best inn the city had. *Ah,* he thought, *at last. Looks like tonight we'll finally be staying somewhere fit for a king.*

But instead of requesting a room, Jesus simply asked the innkeeper for a man named Tobias. "He arrived here only last night, and he was gravely injured."

"Oh, yes, I know the man you mean. Let me take you to him." The innkeeper led them down the corridor, stopping at one of the finer suites.

Tobias lay on a soft, low bed. He was covered with bandages everywhere that could be seen. The thought crossed Peter's mind that it was a sad waste of such luxurious surroundings on a man who clearly was in no condition to appreciate them. But before he had time to give this much thought, Jesus crossed the room and sat beside the man's bed, taking one shaking hand in His own. "My name is Jesus. I came from Galilee to meet you."

The man's cracked lips barely moved. "But I just arrived here."

"I know." Jesus smiled. "I sent Samuel to bring you here."

They stayed only a few minutes, as Tobias was still very weak. Peter thought he looked far better as they left, though, as if he had somehow received strength from Jesus' touch. As they walked back onto the street, Peter gave one last, wistful glance at the banners over the door of the Comfort Table Inn. It didn't look as if they were going to have these superior accommodations for the night after all, but he was willing to tolerate something a little less fancy—at least for now.

Chapter 3

To Peter's surprise, Jesus didn't seem to be interested in any kind of accommodations at all. He merely led the men back out of town and into the countryside. When the road began to climb up toward Jerusalem, winding through a treacherous valley, the fishermen surrounded Jesus, hands on their swords. Fully alert, they scanned the brush and rocks in all directions for signs of an ambush. At one place, where a rock blocked part of the road, Jesus said, "This is where it happened. Over there is where Tobias lay after he was left for dead." They could still see rust-colored stains on the rocks where Tobias had waited to die.

Nervously they all looked around, but the robbers that had attacked Tobias the day before must have been long gone by now, for everything was quiet. Still, Peter felt much better with a sword in his hand. Its weight reassured him. No one tried to take his place when he took the lead, searching for any hint of danger.

Tarik, Nadiv, and the other angels waved at their friends, who were sitting behind rocks and shrubs. Happily, they waved back, watching lovingly as their Supreme Commander paused in the roadway to speak to His disciples. Tarik was very grateful that this time around he had not been assigned to a robber.

Twenty-four demons, fit to be tied, watched history repeat itself as the angels again held the bandits immobile. The forces of Satan were powerless against the Guardians. Then one demon recognized Shihab. "Hey, there's the genius that made this happen the first time."

"Get him," yelled another, and with nothing better to do, they took off after the smaller demon, chasing him in spirals and loops until enough of their anger was worked off to return to their work. In full flight, Shihab swooped past Oreb and Zeeb, calling, "I'll meet you in Jerusalem."

"Where are we going?" John asked curiously as they turned aside from the main road only a short distance from Jerusalem.

"Right there." Jesus nodded to a large farm surrounded by fields of sheep, goats, donkeys, and a few exquisite horses. "We will buy our sacrifices before we go into the city."

A middle-aged man, wiry and fit, came out to greet them, holding out both hands to Jesus. "How good to see You again and to meet Your friends. Your family is well?"

"As well as always. How is yours, Baram?"

"My wife is in good health, and my niece is splendid. Her husband has been promoted to be Caiaphas's chief servant, so she has done very well for herself." He sighed. "Still, no children, though, and after all this time I don't expect any, may the will of Adonai be done."

"Amen," Jesus said. "Have My brothers been here already?"

"Yes, James was here the day before yesterday; he purchased a fine lamb for Your family."

"Perhaps you can help my friends with their sacrifices. Do you have any extra lambs?" Of course he did, as Jesus well knew, but this was just the polite beginning of an amiable discussion of price, much too gentle to be called haggling. At the end, the head of each family held a lamb bought for an amount that would have purchased only two doves inside the temple.

"Stay here tonight," Baram urged. "You are welcome to whatever I possess."

To Peter's relief, Jesus gratefully accepted the generous offer. "Thank you, Baram. We will stay the night, and then tomorrow we will go into Jerusalem to carry out the atonement." He reached over and caressed the lamb in Peter's arms. To Peter's surprise, Jesus' eyes filled with tears as the doomed creature leaned soundlessly into the curve of His hand.

Chapter 4

A cacophony of animal noises and the clinking of coins by the temple moneychangers assailed Peter's ears even before he entered the temple court. At first he thought there might be a riot going on, but then he remembered. It was the sale of the animals used for the sacrifices. He had seen it once before, when he was twelve, and as far as he could tell, nothing had changed.

First came the moneychangers, row upon row of them. In order to buy an animal at the temple, visitors had to use Tyrian shekels, the only currency accepted at the temple. The exchange rate heavily favored the temple—naturally—and the animals themselves sold for exorbitant prices. The moneychangers brought in a huge profit; the priests, and especially the high priest, grew rich; the merchants got rich; everyone benefited. Everyone, that is, except the worshipers.

Leading his lamb by a cord, Peter stepped ahead of Jesus to clear a path for Him through the sheep gate. As he finally broke through the milling barricade of humans and animals, and into the courtyard, the whole amazing scene spread out before him.

For a moment, Peter paused grandly between two mighty pillars. He could just picture himself, another two or three years in the future, standing in the same spot, shouting, "Make way for the King! All hail the King of Israel!" He smiled at the thought. How everyone would stop and stare! In fact, everyone was staring now.

Silence washed across the temple court, starting with the money-changers and spreading through the merchants. The priests ceased their labors mid step, and each worshiper froze in place. All eyes turned to Peter. *This is more like it,* he thought. "Hello," he called to them, lifting his free hand in an uncertain wave.

No one waved back. In fact, no one seemed to notice that he had moved. Puzzled, Peter turned to ask Jesus what was wrong. As Peter's eyes sought and found Jesus' face, the lamb's lead slipped through nerveless fingers and fell to the stone floor. Whatever he had been about to say sank into the blackness of his panic-stricken mind. Jesus stood still, scanning the crowd. Righteous fury lashed out of His eyes, slicing into the souls of each one there, laying bare the pride, lust, and greed.

A surge of power came from Him, a tangible wave of some celestial force, and the very foundations of the temple shuddered in response. The multitude waited in fearful thrall for God Himself to pass judgment on them, wishing the walls would fall and hide them from His face. Jesus stepped forward, and the trumpetlike tones of His voice echoed through the temple. *"Get these things out of here!"*

Striding down the stairs, He came upon the first table of money. The moneychanger still sat there, one hand unthinkingly outstretched to receive coins that had already dropped to the ground. The look on Jesus' face goaded him into action. Scrabbling and undignified, he abandoned his table and ran, clawing the air as he tried to add speed to his flight. Jesus took hold of his abandoned table and tipped it over with a crash; Roman and temple coins mingled in a stream and spilled across the stones. For just a moment, the silence again descended.

Jesus snatched up a braided whip and held it aloft. "This is My Father's house, and you have made it a den of thieves!" Hundreds broke and ran at that, instantly becoming a seething mass of humanity that poured across the temple grounds. Pandemonium reigned supreme. With unstoppable force, Jesus moved through the courtyard, upending each table with a crash, the abandoned coins rolling musically over the floor. Working quickly, He freed the animals that had been held for sale, and they trotted purposefully out of the courtyard. Though He still held the whip, He did not strike anyone. There was no need to do so. By the time He reached the other side of the temple, nearly everyone was gone. A few white feathers floated to earth in the hush that followed.

Peter leaned his head against the marble pillar behind which he had found shelter, ashamed to note that his whole body still trembled. At first he didn't notice the elderly priest who shared his hiding place, but the old man clutched his arm. "Did you see it?"

Peter managed a shaky nod. "Yes, I saw it, all right."

The aged son of Levi let his faded eyes drift, unfocused, into the distance. Tears fell as he quoted from one of the sacred scrolls.

The Lord, whom you seek, shall suddenly come to his temple. . . .
Who may abide the day of his coming? and who shall stand when he
appeareth? for he is like a refiner's fire, and like fullers' soap:
And he shall sit as a refiner and purifier of silver: and he shall purify
the sons of Levi, and purge them as gold and silver,
that they may offer unto the LORD an offering in righteousness.

"He came suddenly, all right," Peter muttered, "and now I can hardly stand."

Proving his point, he rose with cautious unsteadiness to his feet, leaning against the column to keep his balance. Behind him, the old man, still filled with rapture, repeated softly, "An offering in righteousness."

Tarik followed Gabriel as he led the ranks of angels approaching Israel's capital city. The temple that human eyes found so delightful looked revolting to him just now. So many demons filled it that the white marble appeared black to his eyes, absorbing all light. They walked on every inch of the courts, crawled over the walls, and sat on the furniture. Even the gleaming dome was encrusted with them. He shuddered. It had been sad to watch his former friends change in the years since the Great Rebellion, growing ever uglier and more devoted to evil.

The change was most noticeable in Satan. Being shut off from the presence of the Father for thousands of years, deaf to the voice of the Spirit, had left his mind shrunken and misshapen. Though still extraordinarily tall and regal in appearance, he bore in his forehead the mark of unremitting sin. To meet the challenge of battling with God in human form, he had moved his primary headquarters from ancient Babylon to a temporary location in Jerusalem. Now, hands on his hips, he stood defiantly at the tip of the temple dome, waiting for them.

The shining host drew their swords, prepared for battle. They surrounded their beloved Commander and His little company of men with a blanket of light. The demons at the edge of the city had to fall back into the precincts of the temple itself. Angrily, Satan assembled them into orderly rows, ready for a frontal assault if need be.

Jesus stepped forward where all could see Him. Deliberately He allowed the veil of human flesh to slip, and none who saw Him at that moment had any doubt that they stood in the very presence of God. The courtyard commerce halted instantly, every eye fixed on Him with dread. "Kill Him!" Satan shouted. Fiercely he led the charge, and his troops had dutifully begun to follow him, even if without real enthusiasm, when they were abruptly stopped in midair, unable to get any closer.

"Get these things out of here!" Jesus cried. Before the evil angels could regroup, a cosmic pulse radiated from Jesus. So strong that even the humans could feel it, it was devastating to the rebel army. Every single demon within a furlong was blasted clear of the holy place. As the effect rippled around the world, each evil angel felt it as well and paused momentarily in his dark work.

Jesus went from one heavy wooden table to the next, upending each one with ease. Panicked people raced everywhere, until the courtyard was virtually empty. Tarik could have twirled with joy. For the first time in centuries, the holy temple was clean and pure again. Little children crept out from behind pillars, overturned tables, and hesitant adults. A tiny girl began to sing, and one by one the rest joined her. The angels added their voices, and true praise rang once more through the house of God.

Peter waited for the unsteadiness in his knees to pass. His shock was deep at seeing the sudden transformation of his quiet, gentle Friend into the Majesty of the universe. Just when he was starting to feel really comfortable with the future King, Jesus had changed all the rules. Shaken, Peter looked around to see where He was.

Chapter 4

Heedless of the fortune heaped all around Him, Jesus held out His arms to the children. The little ones laughed and chattered, clustering around Him. Even those who had just seen Him drive out the money-changers and merchants were not afraid. Their hearts were loving, with no blot or blemish that might cause them fear in His presence.

Peter had begun an absentminded search for his lamb by the time Andrew arrived, bringing it with him. The brothers stood for a long time without speaking. Then Peter remembered a verse the rabbi had read in the synagogue one Sabbath. For some reason it came to his mind now. *"Zeal for your house consumes me."*

Andrew nodded. "It truly seems like God's house now. I didn't realize how noisy and irreverent everything was until they all left. The air seems cleaner, somehow. Even the walls are brighter."

"The priests aren't going to like it, though," said Peter thoughtfully. "I'm afraid He made some powerful enemies today."

It took a while to find a priest capable of performing the sacrifice. Peter confessed the sins of his family, laying his hands on the lamb's head. The priest ritualistically slaughtered the quiet little animal by slitting its throat, draining the blood into a special vessel. More than ever before, Peter found himself wondering exactly what it all meant. Why did the lamb have to die once he placed his sins on it? What did that have to do with forgiveness, with atonement? He was just a fisherman from the north country and had never given this part of his heritage much thought.

The priest carried away the blood to dab on the horns of the altar, pouring the remainder at the base. Strangely saddened, Peter gathered up the limp body of his lamb to roast later that day as part of the Passover Feast. With his brother, he went in search of Jesus.

They heard the shouts before they could see Him. "Let's go," Peter called to Andrew. "They must have attacked Him while we were gone." Both men raced toward the sound, stopping short when they saw Jesus sitting on the bottom of the temple steps, a huge smile on His face. A crippled man had just thrown aside his makeshift crutches and was leaping for joy. The crowd shouted again, even louder.

A bent old woman, blind eyes turned unblinkingly into the sun, came near to Jesus. He took her hand, passing His fingers lightly across her face. The woman straightened, turned her head slowly around in amazement, and shouted, "I can see! I can see! Oh, praise God, I can see!" The lamb slipped from Peter's grasp for the second time that day.

One after another they came, the hurting, the maimed, and the outcasts. Each found healing and comfort in the touch of their Messiah. No one was turned away, and Jesus had a kind word for all. When the last suffering one was made whole, Jesus stood, motioning for Peter and Andrew to follow Him. "The others are waiting for us, and it's nearly time for the Passover supper."

His voice sounded cheerful and calm, as if He had not just taken on the entire priesthood of Israel, threatening their control over the people, breaking up their livelihood, and then performing wondrous miracles the like of which had not been seen since the days of the prophets. Most of the priests had returned by this time, huddling in little hate-filled groups around the perimeter of the courtyard. Peter figured they were still too afraid to approach, but he couldn't help wondering if Jesus—and the rest of them, too—would be safe once darkness fell.

Jesus seemed to have that thought, too, for as soon as supper was over He led His companions into the night. Using only the unlit back streets and avoiding the temple with its blaze of light, they made their way to the eastern wall and left the city.

"Are we going to Bethany?" Peter asked, eager to see more of this part of the country.

"We might go through it later, but that's not where we're headed now."

Peter gave up asking questions, just following Jesus through the Kidron Valley and up the slope of Olivet. Well before they reached the crest of the hill, Jesus turned to the left, climbing a narrow stone stairway into an olive orchard. The wind softly rustled the leaves, and the light fragrance of flowers hung in the air. In this peaceful atmosphere, the tensions and worries that had built up in Peter during the day slipped away. Surely no danger could find them in this secluded place.

Andrew, Philip, and Nathanael decided to sleep just inside the entrance, in case someone did happen by. Peter, James, and John followed Jesus deeper into the olive grove. The full moon lit the meandering paths, though it was darker underneath the shelter of the trees. Jesus stopped on the far side of an open circle of cushioning grass, motioning to the men to enter a small cave in the hillside. Peter ducked in, immediately lay down, and began snoring, wrapped in his cloak against the cool air. But Jesus knelt as always to hold a lengthy conversation with His Father.

It must have been only about an hour later that the murmur of voices roused Peter from his slumber, and he rolled over. At first he thought it was James or John still talking with Jesus, but then he heard the cultured tones, so different from his own rough Galilean accent. He crept to the mouth of the cave and peered out. The strange man wore dark clothing, so Peter could see very little, but from what he could tell, the robes appeared to be of the highest quality.

"If you want to be a part of My kingdom, you have to be born again," Jesus was saying earnestly.

The man bridled in indignation, deliberately misunderstanding Him. "Are You saying that I should re-enter my mother's womb at my age? That's preposterous! Surely You don't mean to imply that there is anything wrong with me." He drew himself up with pride. "My family is one of the best in Israel. I have been educated by the greatest of our teachers. Now, many consider me to be among the greatest of our teachers. I have led a good life since I was born—the first time. I don't need to repent; that is for the heathen!"

"The birth I am talking about comes by baptism and being filled with the Holy Spirit. That is how you are born into My kingdom." Jesus met the man's sarcasm with His own special wisdom, yearning to show him greater truth.

Peter wondered sleepily how the man had found them, but dismissed it as unimportant. The rich stranger seemed to mean Jesus no harm, and Peter was very tired. All too soon he was snoring lightly.

Tarik sat by Peter's side with one hand resting on the fisherman's shoulder, keeping Oreb at bay. Though saddened that Peter had chosen to sleep while the most beautiful words on earth were being spoken, the angel sat spellbound as he listened to his Commander.

"For God so loved the world," Jesus said, "that He gave His only Son, so that whoever believes on Him shall not perish, but have everlasting life." He

paused to let the words sink into Nicodemus's heart. "For God did not send His Son into the world to condemn the world, but that the world, through Him, might be saved."

Tarik wiped his eyes. He loved this charge of his—this stubborn, temperamental fisherman—and he prayed anew for more chances to help him realize that he walked day by day with the Source of salvation for the whole sin-stricken planet. He broke bread with the Bread of Life. He lay in the night with the Light of the World shining on his face. And still, he did not understand.

"Psst, Andrew, come look at this," Peter hissed early the next morning.

Andrew frowned, but followed his brother quietly, trying not to awaken the others. "What is it?"

"At first I thought it was just a dream, but then I found this footprint. See? It was made by an expensive shoe, not any of our old sandals. I wonder who he was."

"I didn't hear anything. Who was it?"

"I just told you. I'm not sure, except that he was pretty important. Don't you ever listen to anything I say?" Peter scowled at his brother. "At one point I heard Jesus call him a 'teacher of Israel,' whatever that is supposed to mean." He shrugged.

Andrew's eyes widened. "Do you think it was one of the Sanhedrin? They're the only ones I've heard being called by that name."

"It couldn't have been. After what happened yesterday, none of our nation's judges will speak to Him for a good, long time. Or if they do, they won't be speaking nicely."

Andrew grinned. "You're right. In fact, I'll bet they're talking about Him right now."

"Oh well. I doubt we'll ever figure out who it was. It's probably not important anyway. What's for breakfast?"

After the little group passed through a small town on the way back to Jericho, Jesus stopped. "I have a special job for all of you," he told the men. Many people will follow Me, and some will want to be baptized. I want you to baptize them."

As usual, Peter rushed in ahead of everyone else. "What about Your cousin, the Baptist? I thought he was the one who was supposed to do all that."

"We're not rabbis," added John. "We don't even know what to do."

Jesus chuckled. "I'll teach you everything you need to know. You will baptize them in the name of the Father, Son, and Holy Spirit, and as they go down into the water, it will show that their sins are washed away. As they come out, new and clean, it will be as if they have been born a second time, into My kingdom."

"That's it," Peter said in a low voice to Andrew. "Now I remember. That's what He was talking about to that man, but the man was arguing with Him. I wish I'd paid more attention; that's all I can think of." Andrew elbowed him to be quiet, in true brotherly fashion.

They were all nervous the first time. A crowd soon gathered where Jesus was preaching, and several hundred accepted His invitation to join in the new kingdom. Jesus nodded encouragingly, and His five followers stepped out into the murky waters of the Jordan. Peter's first convert was a bulky man who towered head and shoulders above him.

How am I going to get him back out of the water? was his first panicked thought. But he gamely held one hand toward heaven as he had seen John doing, and said the words Jesus had instructed them to say. "I now baptize you in the name of the Father, the Son, and the Holy Spirit." He plunged the man under the water with both arms and drew him out again. Really, it wasn't nearly as hard as he had expected.

Tarik wiped his brow. "That was close. He would've dropped that one if I hadn't caught him."

Nadiv helped Andrew with his candidate. "I agree they certainly do need some practice, but Jesus will see that they get it. In the meantime, we'll just make sure that none of our brand-new 'lambs' is discouraged by a nose full of muddy water." As they worked, they also kept a careful watch on their enemies lest any of them come close enough to cause a problem. The demons hated baptisms and avoided them whenever possible, but occasionally desperation drove them to attend. This time, though, they were unable to disrupt anything. All they could do was heckle.

"They'll never stick to it," Shihab shouted. "We'll make sure their good feeling doesn't last more than a week."

"That hypocrite over there won't make it until nightfall," jeered Oreb. Zeeb cackled along with him, but their laughter rang hollow. The crowd grew ever larger, as did the line of people waiting along the riverbank. With each new decision for truth, the angels sang louder and louder until they entirely drowned out the dissenting cries. In the end, the frustrated tempters could do nothing except sit and sulk.

One after another Peter baptized them. Most were smaller than the first, but still his arms ached when he came to the end. "Looks like that's all for today," he called to his friends as he splashed over to the riverbank. "I feel like I've been hauling in nets for two days straight."

"You have," Jesus laughed. "Except that My nets are filled with people, not fish." He embraced them each in turn. "You'll see; this is just the beginning."

The word quickly spread that Jesus was baptizing in the Jordan. The angels shouted for joy each time a sinner repented and chose to be baptized. Legions of angels were dispatched throughout the nation to assist in the work of drawing every soul to Jesus. In the face of such power, there was little Satan could do in the way of a direct attack, but of course, his crafty mind soon thought of a plan to take advantage of the little groups of the Baptist's followers who came looking for Jesus.

"Bring Sirion to me," he ordered. A moment later, Sirion appeared and bowed before him. "Your sinner is perfectly set up to accomplish my plan. You are to have him sow jealousy and anger in the hearts of the disciples of the Baptist. Emphasize the danger John faces if he loses support to this upstart, and that will align perfectly with what we have in store for him."

"Ah, I see," Sirion nodded admiringly. "If we can destroy their unity, it leaves an opening for us to destroy them, as well. Excellent choice, Majesty."

Satan preened at the flattery. "The best part is, we win no matter which way things go. Yes, discord will give us great opportunities, but even if nearly everyone follows our great enemy, all that will happen is that the Baptist will be left exposed and unprotected." He laughed his terrible laugh, making all within hearing shudder in fear and loathing.

True to his command, Sirion easily influenced his sinner, the high priest's servant, to turn many away from Jesus and create strife between the two groups of the Father's people. At last a delegation approached the Baptist, indignant at the many who had left their beloved teacher to go after Jesus.

Matthan stood behind the Baptist as they came, his hands on the shoulders of the man all heaven esteemed as great. The men in the crowd all tried to talk at once, airing their grievances against Jesus while Zuar added his voice to the chaos. "It's not fair! You did all the work, and now look—they're all following Him instead! What will become of you? Doesn't He care that you are in danger?"

John ignored Zuar as always. He held up his hands to silence the men. "You," he indicated an older man out in front of the crowd, "please explain what this is about."

The man nervously laid out his grievance against Jesus and his fears for his master's safety. Zuar tried one last time to awaken even one tiny fear in John, but it was useless. "Well, now He's having baptisms too," the man was saying, "and everyone is going to hear Him preach. We were so worried for your safety that we came straight here to warn you that He is trying to steal your followers."

John sighed and said patiently, "I have told you many times that I am not the Christ. I was simply sent before Him, to prepare His way." With a clear idea of what his faithfulness would cost him, he smiled and stood tall. "You could not have brought me better news. It means I have accomplished what I was sent to do. He must increase, and I must decrease. That has always been the plan of Elohim."

Sheepishly the men drifted away. Matthan could not hold in his delight, shouting, "Glory to God in the highest!" His charge's earthly fate had just been sealed, but the name of John glowed brightly in the Book.

Chapter 5

"I still can't believe He would talk to them," Peter grumbled. For once he dragged his steps, lagging behind at the rear instead of pushing his way to the front.

"Especially that one woman." Andrew shook his head at the memory. "You could tell, just by looking at her, that she was especially wicked, even for a Samaritan."

"We never should have left Him alone when we all went to get food." Peter frowned fiercely. "He always gets into some kind of trouble."

Andrew shuddered. "Yeah, you'd think He didn't even know that we aren't supposed to talk to that kind of people."

"Especially *her* kind of that kind of people. Ugh!" Peter made a face. "He sure has a lot to learn, doesn't He?"

"Peter has so much to learn," Tarik sighed sadly. "How can he walk with Jesus day after day and not see it? Gentile, Jew, Roman, slave, free—those artificial human distinctions don't matter to Him at all. He's trying so hard to teach them to love each other, but Peter just isn't paying attention."

Nadiv's shoulders drooped. "Andrew certainly isn't paying attention, either. There it was—the first time Jesus came right out and said plainly that He is the Messiah—and they were so busy whispering back and forth that they missed the whole thing."

"Yasirah was listening, though, and it did the Master so much good to be needed with such intensity and to be accepted so fully. Even though it hurt her when He had to show her the sin in her life, she obeyed."

"You know, if Talib hadn't believed in Jesus, too, and hadn't asked her to marry him, she was ready to sever their relationship in order to be true to her new faith. What a wonderful moment! I wish they could have shared it with us."

Tarik glanced over his shoulder. "Of course you know the first of many spies is not far behind us. It won't be long until he finds out where Jesus has gone."

"That one's going to be real trouble." Nadiv nodded knowingly. "Did you know Abr—I mean Sirion, was assigned to him? You know how good he is at subtly inserting thoughts of pride and the lust for power. Few of the rebels are better."

"Deron has his hands full, that's for sure. Maybe it will do his charge some good to sit for a while and listen to Jesus talk. And it can't hurt for us to help keep an eye on him."

"How can I keep an eye on him when I can't even see him?" Andrew craned his neck to scan the crowd.

"Get down! I said don't look now," Peter gritted through clenched teeth. "He's staring right at us!"

Andrew's eyes rolled wildly in his effort to spy inconspicuously. "Oh, you mean that one over there, sitting right next to the woman with the green headdress? How do you know he's bad? He looks like a beggar to me."

"That's why I'm going to be in charge of the security forces, and not you!" Puffed up in his new role as self-appointed head protector of the next king, Peter was fast becoming unbearable. "Just because you're my brother doesn't mean I need to share everything with you."

"Just because you're ten months older than I am doesn't mean you can look down your long nose at me all the time, either!" Andrew shot back.

"All I had to do is take one look, and I knew he was up to no good. And my nose is not that long!"

The man they were discussing broke off a piece of bread, holding it up in dirty fingers. His mouth opened to reveal gapped yellow teeth, spotted with brown stains and decay. "See?" John snickered. "If he were really a spy, he would've been able to afford better teeth."

"That's just what he wants us to think." Peter was smug. "It's nothing but a clever disguise meant to fool us into thinking he's some harmless wanderer who happened to sit down right there and listen to a story. With all the tricks they have today, that could be Caiaphas himself, and you'd never know it."

Andrew looked dubious. "He seems just like everybody else, at least to me."

"Well, he's not. I knew from the moment I saw him that he was up to no good. Go ahead and laugh if you want, but someday you'll see that I was right."

A crippled man threw away his crutches, leaping and shouting for joy, but neither man noticed. "Simon Peter, no matter how much you want to, you can't go around seizing every suspicious-looking character in the crowd. Besides," Andrew looked up mischievously, "the most suspicious person here is you. Of course, I'm second," he added modestly.

The sound of a grown man sobbing quieted the crowd. Something about him caught Peter's attention before he could deliver a scathing comeback. "Impossible! It can't be! That man looks just like—"

"Elhanan," finished Andrew. "I wonder what's wrong?" Elhanan, a nobleman of Capernaum and the supervisor of their fishing industry, knelt in the dust at Jesus' feet, not caring that his fine garment was being soiled. In all the time the brothers had known him, he had always been so careful of his appearance, and they were shocked to see the change that had come over him.

Elhanan was weeping almost too hard to speak. "My son, my only son is sick," he finally gasped. "He's not quite four, and he means everything to me. I'll do anything, even believe that you are the Messiah, if you'll only come and heal him."

"How wonderful," Peter thought. "All Jesus has to do is one simple little healing, and an important man has sworn to be His follower. Elhanan is someone who could really smooth His path to the throne."

Jesus didn't seem to share this happy idea, only saying sadly, "Unless you see miracles, you won't believe." The words hung heavily in the air, and no one moved as His eyes met and held those of the young father.

Elhanan swayed in horror. *Dear God, what have I done?* He thought. "Lord, I believe!" he assured Jesus. "No matter what, I believe!" He shuddered, nerving himself to ask again. "Please come and heal my son. If You don't, he will die."

Jesus reached out and embraced Elhanan as he broke down completely. There were tears in His eyes, but a smile on His lips as He said, "Don't worry. Your son is already doing just fine."

Peter thought the nobleman would leave then, but he didn't. As if he had all the time in the world, he sat there right next to Jesus, listening carefully to every word. Not until it was time for the evening meal did he stand and with thanksgiving take his leave. Peter leaned back and closed his eyes.

"He could have been home tonight if he'd wanted," Andrew commented. "Now he won't make it before tomorrow. He must really believe what Jesus said about his son being well."

"What's so special about that? I believe it."

"Quick, open your eyes!" Andrew shook Peter less than gently. "He's leaving."

"Who? What?"

"The man we were looking at earlier—the one you were convinced was a spy or something."

Peter jumped up. He could just see the beggar disappearing through the main gate of Cana. "He's acting suspicious all right. Let's follow him." The length of Peter's stride strained against the confines of his robe as he led Andrew toward the gate almost at a run. Without warning, he came to such an abrupt halt, hands flat on the stones of the city wall, that Andrew crashed into him from behind.

"Simon Peter, what on earth do you think you're doing?" Andrew let loose an oath as he nearly tripped and fell.

"What do you mean, what am *I* doing? Watch where you're going!" Peter returned, with an even worse oath, his face pressed into the smooth rocks. "He's almost out of sight, anyway."

The two brothers crouched in unison, peering at the road to Capernaum. Elhanan was only a small figure in the distance now, and the beggar followed behind, his manner a study in nonchalance. "He looks too natural," Andrew concluded. "I think you're right, after all; he is suspicious."

"Well, if he's spying on anyone, it must be Elhanan; that's good."

"Do you think we should warn him?"

"He's already too far away. Besides, he's been doing his job for a long time. He knows how to take care of himself. Just keep your eyes open, though. We're going to want to spot that fellow if he ever comes back."

"Tarik, you'll never guess what I just found out," Deron shouted to his friend. "I get to make another appearance to my charge in his dimension!"

"That's great news!" Jealousy was not a part of Tarik's nature, nor indeed of any part of the heavenly kingdom. "I'm so happy for you. What does this make now, thirteen times? Fourteen?"

"Fifteen, actually," Deron laughed. "My charge has led a busy life."

"So I've heard, Deron," Tarik called. "I'll see you later in Jerusalem." Deron waved with enthusiasm, floating low to the ground near his charge.

Sirion lurked nearby, but knew better than to interfere until Deron's personal appearance was over. Then he would be free to move in and try to bring fresh confusion into the mind of the high priest's servant, ensnaring him in cords of darkness. Deron would spill as much celestial light as he could, but ultimately he would be bound by the choice of the man he so lovingly guarded.

With a sense of guilt mingled with eagerness, Peter glanced to the east and home. In spite of the danger, he was glad to be on his way to Jerusalem once more. After all, Jesus would surely be crowned king in the capital city. "It's all right," a voice said beside him, "I miss my family too."

Peter started nervously. "John! I didn't even hear you come over here. I was busy thinking."

"So I noticed."

"I can't help wondering all kinds of things about the New Kingdom Jesus keeps talking about—when will it come, how long will we have to fight, who will be put in charge?"

"Obviously Jesus has important positions in mind for the five of us; that's why He chose us. Just think, we'll be noblemen, all of us, the princes of the New Kingdom," John warmed to the subject. "We'll have palaces for our families, hundreds of servants to wait on us, and we'll never have to fish again!"

"Hey, wait a minute," Peter protested, "I like to fish. In fact, I want to fish a lot. But just for fun, you know. Whenever I'm not too busy meeting diplomats and kings from faraway countries, leading processions through the capital city, or sitting in my own golden throne at the right hand of the king."

"But I'd already planned to put *my* throne there!"

Peter laughed heartily. Of course his best friend was just joking.

Tarik wiped away a tear. "Oh, Arion, how can they be so wrong? Can't they see that the New Kingdom comes in their hearts, not in the clash of swords or the struggle for thrones?"

Arion shook his head wordlessly, unable to speak. Oreb was not so afflicted. "Ah, Simon, you are great; you are wonderful; and no one should be more important than you." He spoke quietly to Peter, running gnarled fingers soothingly through the fisherman's wind-tangled hair. "You will sit on a throne. You will be rich, and everyone will bow to you. Especially Batia." Encouraged by Peter's dreamy smile, he went on. "You could have her thrown in prison if you want. All the power in the world will belong to you."

"Pray, Peter. Pray for deliverance from these wicked thoughts. Pray to have your sinful pride taken away. Pray that you will understand the truth of why Jesus came to your tiny planet." Tarik's voice trembled in its earnestness.

"He's not listening," Oreb gloated, quickly flicking a nervous glance at Jesus to make sure He wasn't paying attention. "He spends day and night with your Commander, and still he listens to me. You might as well give up hope for these miserable humans right now."

Tarik ignored him, focusing all his energy on Peter. The battle was increasing with each passing day, as the men spent more time fantasizing about what they imagined their lives would soon be like. How much longer could it be before a higher-ranking demon was assigned to oversee each of Jesus' followers, a mark of their newly acquired status? He was surprised it hadn't already happened. If Peter couldn't even see through the artifices of a low-level tempter like Oreb, what would be the result when he was beguiled by one of the most cunning, most alluring of the enemy army? Tarik squared his shoulders. He would work even harder—that's what would happen.

Peter yawned, sat up, and stretched. Their secret garden hideaway was exquisite in the early morning light. He left the cave and looked around the familiar little clearing. James and John had just been stirring, and Jesus' place was empty. Peter smoothed his hair and straightened his rumpled clothing. "I guess I'd better go look for Him. No telling what trouble He's gotten Himself into already this morning, without any of us to supervise."

"We'll meet you in the temple," James mumbled.

"Shabbat shalom," Peter said, his feet crunching in quick steps on the narrow stone path. "Have a peaceful Sabbath."

He entered the city at the northeast corner of the temple. Unsure where to look first, he stood by the sheep gate, scanning the crowd. Less than a minute passed before he heard Jesus call his name. Jesus' face glowed as He embraced Peter. "You came looking for Me! Thank you. Where is everyone else?"

Peter flushed slightly. "Just getting up. What have You been doing? I mean, not that it's any of my business or anything. I was just asking." His ears grew redder.

Jesus held His hands toward heaven, sublime happiness shining from His face. "The only thing I've been doing is My Father's business."

Peter felt emboldened to ask, "You haven't been making anyone angry, have You?"

"Satan is always angry when I carry out My Father's will." Jesus put His arm around Peter, leading him into the temple court. "I haven't made any people angry, if that's what you mean. Not quite yet." He looked over His left shoulder.

Peter looked back too. He saw a commotion in the middle of the street. A thin, ragged man carrying a bedroll stood arguing with two priests. The man gestured emphatically, turning his head this way and that as if searching for help. A well-dressed man joined the fray; his back was turned, and Peter could not see his face. He held up his hands to gesture for silence, but before Peter could see what happened next, Jesus drew him farther into the temple.

"Who was that man? Why was he carrying a burden on the Sabbath? He can get in huge trouble for that, You know." Comprehension dawned. "You? You did that? Why?" Peter groaned. "Oh, no. Now You've really made them mad. We've got to get out of here!"

"Impetuous Peter," Jesus' voice was filled with love. "Don't worry like this; I have everything under control. Let me tell you about Betzalel. Yes, he is the man carrying his bed. Until this morning, he had been paralyzed for thirty-eight years. . . ."

Peter, caught up in the gripping story of vice, greed, and betrayal, forgot his fears for the moment. Still, he stayed close by Jesus through the service, watching everyone closely, just as the head of kingdom security should.

During a break, Jesus slipped away from him while he was admiring the grand marble architecture of the house of worship. Peter felt a stirring of uneasiness when he saw Jesus talking to the same man he had seen earlier. He had put aside his bedroll, washed, and changed into a borrowed robe several sizes too big, but there could be no mistaking Betzalel.

Jesus was back in a moment, but Peter feared the damage had already been done. People were whispering and pointing, with many a frown directed at Jesus. Jesus took no notice; He sat down calmly in the courtyard and began to tell stories to those who gathered round. Peter scrutinized each face carefully, figuring there would be more spies in Jerusalem than anywhere else. One woman in blue caught his eye, her face as beautifully formed as one of the fine sculptures the Greeks loved to create. She focused so intently on Jesus, tears in her lovely eyes, that Peter immediately eliminated her as a suspect.

James and John found him then, but before Peter could bring them up to date on all they had missed, John blurted, "Herod has taken the Baptist prisoner. He's being held in Machaerus."

Peter's eyes widened in shock. He had heard much about the giant fortress east of the Dead Sea, all of it bad. "Why? When did it happen?"

"It's been almost five weeks." James spoke in a low, worried voice. "No one knows why, for certain, but everyone seems to suspect . . . *her*."

Peter swallowed hard. "I hope she doesn't come after any of us next. Jesus is John's cousin, after all." Even in the sacred precincts of the temple, he dared not speak aloud any criticism of Herod's illegitimate wife. The cruel tetrarch had been married to Najiyah, a princess of Nabataea, when he first caught sight of Herodias, his half brother's wife. The two began a passionate affair only a few doors from where her husband, Philip, slept. When Herod returned to Palestine, Herodias was with him.

In the biggest scandal for decades, Herod banished Najiyah to Machaerus; from there the scorned wife was able to escape into her father's loving arms. This error was to cost Herod dearly. King Aretas, outraged at the treatment of his daughter, made war on Herod, destroyed his armies, and overran his territory. The Baptist had waded into this political turmoil without hesitation, fearlessly denouncing the unholy liaison between Herod and his illicit bride. What Peter would not whisper in the temple, John spoke directly to the adulterous pair. Now, at the behest of Herodias, the prophet had been cast into the deepest dungeon Machaerus could boast.

"As far as I know, Jesus has never said those things." James looked around nervously. "You know what I mean."

None of them saw the temple police approach until several officers stood right behind Jesus, their white linen uniforms crisp and gleaming. "You'll have to come with us," one of them said uncomfortably.

"Of course," Jesus answered politely, "is there some way I can help you?"

"Ask the high priest when you see him," another interrupted. At his curt tone, Peter, James, and John each took a step forward, but Jesus motioned them back. Surrounded by scowling guards, He walked peaceably into the heart of the temple complex, a serene expression on His face.

Peter, James, and John stood indecisively, rocking nervously from one foot to the other. They did not look serene. It had all happened so fast, giving them no time to prepare, no time to react. After obeying Jesus' wordless command, they were in shock. They watched Him fade into the stone as if the building had somehow devoured Him.

Peter rubbed his eyes in disbelief, his voice a flat monotone. "They took Him away. They actually took Him away. What will happen to Him now? What will happen to us?"

Andrew was more practical. "Let's go. Now! We can figure it all out later. It won't do Him any good if we get caught too." He set the pace, running at top speed for the city gate. The others were not far behind. Not knowing what else to do, they hid as far back in Gethsemane as they could, waiting, hoping, praying.

Chapter 6

*B*y *dawn, most of the seventy members of the Sanhedrin had assembled,
ready to hear the strange case. Caiaphas, the high priest, had been there
for hours, meeting with his advisers. One by one, the torches went out, unre-
freshed, as the new light of morning crept in. Gleaming pillars of marble, rich
drapes, and the glitter of gold brought an atmosphere of imposing solemnity
to the stately room.*

*The air in the Hall of Hewn Stone seemed crowded and stifling to the
humans gathered there, although they had no clear thought of anything amiss.
Unknown to the august religious leaders of Israel, the answer to their vague
discomfort lay just outside the spectrum of their sight, where thousands of
demons jostled for the best positions, muttering curses at each other. The room
was so filled with their evil that not a single angel could enter. Even the Re-
cording Angels had to work from a distance.*

*In the center of the crowd, next to Caiaphas, stood Satan, personally
speaking into the priest's mind, stoking his hatred and pride. A few minutes
earlier, he had made a rare appearance in human guise to this most powerful
man in the nation of Israel. In his own strength, no mere human could resist
the thrall of that charming being, and Caiaphas was no longer fully his
own.*

*By the time of the morning sacrifice, the judges had seated themselves on
a half circle of cushions, awaiting the arrival of the prisoner. It seemed odd
to see Caiaphas as the leader of the seventy elders, a seat Moses had held*

long before the Sanhedrin had a name. Back then it was simply called "the Council."

Two temple guards brought Jesus in to face the charges. They could not see the angels that enveloped Him protectively as He stood there in the middle of the room. The accusations were presented in ringing tones—healing a man on the Sabbath and commanding a man to bear a burden on the Sabbath. Once, those charges would have carried a death sentence upon conviction, but now only the procurator of Rome held the power of life and death for the condemned. Of those in the room, none but Satan knew for a certainty that a religious conviction in this Jewish court could result in condemnation by a secular arbiter, if the right political pressures were brought to bear.

"Do you wish to answer these charges?" Caiaphas asked Jesus. "After all, many witnesses can testify as to what happened." The council members nodded sagely. Satan rubbed his hands together in glee, unable to restrain an inner chortle. This was going just as he had planned.

Jesus paused a moment. His reply was the last thing any of them expected. "My Father has been working without stopping, and so have I. Would you have My Father stop the sun in the sky on the Sabbath day? Or perhaps the flowers should pause in their growing, and the trees produce no fruit. Should My Father halt the waves at the shore of the sea one day each week?"

Some of the judges laughed aloud in spite of themselves. Whatever else might be said of them, the most brilliant scholars in the nation were not without a sense of humor. Satan abruptly snapped his head up. This was not part of the script. "Blasphemy," he ad-libbed to Caiaphas. "He is calling Himself God's equal!"

Caiaphas sputtered, his face turning red. "Do you call yourself equal with God? That is blasphemy." Ignoring the many times he had also referred to God in the same way, the high priest gestured widely, turning to the Sanhedrin. "You see what a danger this man is. He calls God his Father."

Jesus went on. "My Father will show you greater works than what you have already seen. My Father gives life to the dead, and in just the same way, His Son will give life to whomever He chooses."

Veins bulged alarmingly in Satan's neck. By the look on his face, he might have been thinking of Moses. Although there had been a handful of resurrections since then, none had offered him the utter humiliation he had suffered when the Son chose to give the aged leader of Israel his life back again. And Jesus' words held the clear promise of more resurrections to come.

Among the council members, a frenzied squabble erupted between proponents of the two main schools of religious thought: the Pharisees, who believed in the resurrection of the dead, and the Sadducees, who claimed that there was no life past the grave. How Jesus pitied the ignorance of the Sadducees and the blindness of them all.

Caiaphas almost shouted in his fury, "Your own testimony condemns you. You are a Sabbath-breaker and blasphemer. According to the Law of Moses, you should be stoned to death. Do you think to accuse us and escape blameless?"

Tarik was stunned. "How can they even think to accuse Him when they themselves are the ones who should be accused?" His heart was sorrowful beyond measure, but the Spirit whispered His peace, soothing the distress. "This, too, is part of My plan." And although Tarik and his friends didn't understand why they were not allowed to intervene, they trusted the Spirit implicitly.

A hint of a smile playing at the corners of His mouth, Jesus stood calmly before the court. His gaze flicked briefly upward. "I do not accuse you before God," He replied with dignity. "However, there is one who does." An expectant hush fell over the members of the council. "That man is Moses."

A shocked gasp went up, and the heavenly host smiled in delight. The story of Moses' resurrection just three days after his death was a long-held tradition of Israel, but never before had anyone dared speak of it with such assured authority. Many times the angels must have wondered just how much of the celestial realm Jesus was allowed to recall in His human form, but this answered the question beyond doubt. Tarik felt warmed and cheered by the revelation.

"What do you mean?" Caiaphas snapped, gesturing at the council. "We all have believed Moses from our birth."

"No you don't," Tarik replied, though they could not hear. "Moses, my dear friend Moses, wrote about the Messiah, and you haven't believed one thing he told you. If you had, you'd know Jesus was the One!"

"You say you trust the writings of Moses, but that is not true." Jesus looked keenly at His hearers as He spoke. "Moses wrote about Me, and you do not accept what he says. So will you then accept what I say?"

"We follow the Law of Moses," Caiaphas replied pompously, *"which you stand accused of breaking."*

"There they go again," Tarik shook his head. *"Moses had nothing to do with this! Jesus didn't break any law of Moses; He broke only those precious traditions of yours that you use to bind the people under a heavy load."*

"Show Me from the Scriptures just which law I have broken." A hush fell on the room at His challenge, and the accusers had the uncomfortable sensation that they were the ones facing judgment. *"I have broken nothing except the human traditions, which have been laid on the people of Israel like a heavy yoke. The Sabbath should be a delight, never a burden."*

Won by His inescapable logic, many of the council members nodded in agreement. Caiaphas glanced around the room, instantly realizing he had lost his support base. A superb statesman, he knew when to retreat. His face mottled red, he choked out the words, "Release him!" Temple guards jumped to carry out his bidding as Caiaphas turned on his heel and stomped from the room.

Satan was almost comical in his anger and dismay over the sudden and unexpected turn of events. When he could finally get his mouth to work again, he barked, "Meeting at the main headquarters in Babylon. Now!" With much flapping of wings, his subordinates hastened to comply.

The band of loyal Guardians were all that remained. Even the low-level tempters were gone. An atmosphere of peace pervaded the premises. No one moved to interfere as Jesus left unescorted, in search of His followers.

"We're going to have to eat sometime, you know," John observed as his stomach rumbled.

Peter put a hand to his middle. "I know, but do we have to go yet? I can wait a little longer."

"You aren't afraid, are you?" Andrew knew just what would goad his brother to act.

"Afraid? I'm not afraid! Let's go right now."

For all their brave words, it was a spectral group that approached the Garden gate, flitting soundlessly from bush to bush. They paused at the top of the stairs leading down to the Bethany road, looking and listening both ways.

"I hear someone," James said softly. "They're coming this way."

At the sound of male voices just around the bend, all four abandoned secrecy in favor of speed. Back to the farthest corner of Gethsemane they fled, shaking as they rushed down the path and dove among the trees. Their hope that the men were only passing by proved vain, and Peter vowed he would never again allow himself to be caught in a trap like that.

"John, come out. The rest of you, too. Jesus wants you."

The four men crawled out of the foliage with as much dignity as possible. "Philip? Nathanael? We thought they must have gotten you, too. What happened?"

Philip beamed, his round cheeks damp in the heat. "It was really the cleverest thing. When Jesus left the city, He had all these people following Him. He wanted to come get you Himself, but that would have given away our little hideaway, so He asked Nathanael and me to fall back gradually, and come into the Garden when everyone was out of sight. We did, and here you are."

"Not that," Peter said impatiently. "What happened at the temple?"

"They just let Him go."

"Just like that? That's all there was to it?"

Philip shrugged. "We couldn't go in, but it didn't take long."

John sidled over to Peter as they started off. "I'm so ashamed of myself. I've been with Jesus even longer than Philip and Nathanael, and I still ran like a frightened child."

"Well, we've been with Jesus only a few hours longer than Philip or Nathanael, but I know what you mean. I don't feel so great right now, either."

John hung his head. "We deserted Him just when He needed us most. Until now I've always thought I was so brave." He pounded his fist into his palm in frustration. "I can tell you this much, it will never happen again. No matter what the danger may be, I'm going to stay beside Him and face it."

Seized by a grandiose impulse, Peter raised his hand to heaven. "I swear in the sight of Adonai that I will forfeit my life before I ever desert Jesus again." Not quite satisfied, he added, "And if I ever break this oath, I vow to end my own life rather than face another day with such treachery on my head."

John was amazed. "Are you sure you're just a fisherman? That was almost poetic. How could I hope to match such boundless eloquence?"

"Elo—what?" They laughed together, suddenly feeling much better.

"Be bold! Be courageous! You can't let him outdo you," Oreb hissed in Peter's ear. "Swear you won't do it again." A wicked look came over his face. "Swear on your life!"

"Don't do it, Peter," Tarik warned. "Be humble. Pray that Adonai will keep you in the right path. You are so weak without Him." But the fateful words were already spoken.

Oreb danced in victory. "I did it! I got him!" He spat contemptuously at the ground near Tarik's feet. "And it's going to be so easy. All I have to do is get him to run away one more time, and he is mine!"

The crowd made its way north as slowly as a flock of sheep with springtime lambs. More than a hundred people followed Jesus everywhere He went, camping under the stars with Him each night along the way, finding shelter in the groves of trees. As usual, He was in no hurry, often carrying the smaller children by turn. Peter inhaled deeply as he ambled along beside Jesus, enjoying the now-familiar scenery along the road by the twisted course of the Jordan River. With so many people, the danger from bandits was minimal, and the self-appointed head of kingdom security could relax for a while.

On the afternoon of the preparation day, when they reached the crossroads between Capernaum and Nazareth, Peter was surprised and unhappy when Jesus stopped, embraced them, and told them to go ahead without Him. "A prophet is without honor in his own country, but I have a duty to carry out. I will come to Capernaum soon."

By mutual agreement the men camped beside the road to spend the hours of the Sabbath. If they had hurried, they could have made it all the way before sundown, but none were very eager to return home. They didn't want to be away from Jesus for even a moment. So it was all too soon, the day following the Sabbath, that Peter saw Capernaum looming larger with each step. At the path to Zebedee's house, he bid

James and John goodbye. Peter and Andrew walked slowly toward their home.

Peter's sons, Jered and Seth, played in the dust on the hillside, bathed in the rays of sunlight. Jered, the oldest at seven, waved absentmindedly. "Hello, Abba," he called, returning to his miniature village. Absorbed in his play, Seth didn't even look up.

One of the hinges of the rough door had come loose, and Peter had to lift the whole thing carefully to open it. He ducked as he stepped through, Andrew right behind him. In the gloom, all he could see at first was the cooking fire in the middle of the floor. As he peered uncertainly into the darkness, a dim shape detached itself from the shadows and moved toward him.

"Well, well, well. Look at what we have here. If it isn't the prophets," Rimona sneered. "They can go all over Israel—don't think I haven't heard all about it—but they don't have any time to take care of their own families."

"The door has been that way for two months," Batia shrilled from her mat. "I can hardly get in and out of the house. What if it caught on fire? Think of your sons, at least!"

Her loud voice woke Keren's baby, who began to cry. That woke four-year-old Abelia and three-year-old Adalia. The noise was deafening. Peter turned to Andrew and grinned sheepishly. "Welcome home."

Chapter 7

"What would Jesus do?" Tarik stood behind Peter, hands on his shoulders, willing him to stand firm against the enemy's attack. "Love is the key to the New Kingdom. Love them."

"What would Jesus do?" Nadiv repeated the words to Andrew. "He will give you the strength to deal with this if you just ask."

What would Jesus do? What would Jesus say? Peter asked himself, thinking hard. *Actually, when the guards took Him away, He didn't say much of anything. I guess it can't hurt to try it.* And he and Andrew stood like the temple columns, tall, straight . . . and silent.

"Do you hear the way she's talking?" Oreb slithered in close. "You've been with Jesus. How dare she talk to you like that?"

Nadiv and Tarik moved in protectively. "Don't listen to them. In the Father's strength you can do anything. All you have to do is ask, and He will help you."

Rimona wasn't through. "And as if it isn't bad enough that we can hardly get in and out of this hovel we all call home, we've had to put up with the Madman of Capernaum too! The last three nights he's been here, sneaking around the house and snooping through everything. I've hardly slept the whole time for fear he would murder us all in our beds, and you weren't even here to protect us!"

Stung by worry for his family, and angry at his wife for pointing out the dangers facing a family of undefended women, Peter snapped out an oath, turned around, and stomped to the door, only to find it jammed shut. With Andrew's help he was finally able to pry it open; both men ended up swearing at the door and their bruised fingers. Neither noticed Keren as she tried, unsuccessfully, to cover the ears of all three of the girls at once. "Come on, Andrew, let's go fishing," Peter barked.

He tried to slam the door behind him, but it budged barely a few inches before it stuck again. He yanked on it, getting several splinters in his palms. Frustrated beyond endurance, he kicked the offending door, forgetting he was wearing only thin sandals!

Andrew supported his brother as Peter hobbled down to the shore. Jered and Seth waved to their father as they slipped into the house. It was nearly dark, but there on the shore was their fishing boat just as they had left it before going off to find Jesus. Hastily Peter and Andrew checked their nets for holes; they found a few, but nothing that couldn't be repaired in the morning. "Let's get out of here," Peter said. "Somehow I don't think this was our day."

Taking pity on the injured Peter, Andrew pushed the boat out into the water, jumping in before the waves reached his waist. He was just about to unfurl the sail when a cold wetness spilled over his feet. At the same time he heard Peter begin to swear. Water poured in through a large crack, and the boat foundered!

"Back! Back! Help me get her back!" Forgetting his wounded toes, Peter leaped out of the boat. Most of what the brothers said during the next few moments was unrepeatable, but at last they dragged the boat back onto the shore. They bailed till their backs ached before the boat was light enough to move out of the reach of the hungry waves.

"I don't know about you," Andrew remarked, "but I don't really want to go back in there." He nodded toward home.

"Me either," Peter grimaced. "Let's draw straws to see who gets the wet end."

"Maybe you haven't noticed. It's *all* the wet end."

Peter swore again, wrapping his wet cloak around him. "I didn't want to go fishing tonight anyway."

It was one of the most uncomfortable nights either of them could remember. The boat tipped slightly to one side, making it difficult to stay on the low seats, and the bottom was curved just enough to keep them from stretching out completely in any direction. At sunrise, Peter stood slowly to his feet, his back and knees cracking as they adjusted to the new position.

Andrew sat up and tipped his head from side to side as he tried to work the knots out of his neck. "Let's fix what we can before it's time for breakfast. That way we can definitely be ready to go out tonight."

"That sounds like a plan."

They decided to repair the nets first, as that task would not take long. Their powerful hands worked quickly, yet deftly, as they braided new segments into their nets, filling the holes until each weak spot had been strengthened. Together, they held the net up at the corners, giving it one final inspection.

"Here is some bread for you, Abba, Uncle Andrew." Jered ran to them, carefully holding a fresh loaf of flat bread in each hand. He looked around, and tears filled his brown eyes. "Abba, where are the fish? Mama promised me I could have some of whatever you caught."

"She probably knew we couldn't get anything," Andrew muttered under his breath.

"What, Uncle Andrew?"

"Nothing. He didn't say anything worth listening to." Peter spoke gruffly, frowning at his brother. "I'll tell you what. We're going to go fishing tonight for sure, and if you are a good, brave boy, you may go with us."

Jered's eyes lit up. "Really? Go with you? Oh boy, wait till I tell Seth! He'll be so jealous!" The boy raced off, eager to see his brother's face when he told him the good news.

"Now you've done it," Andrew said sourly. "We'll get no peace until Seth has had his turn too."

Peter threw back his head and laughed heartily. "Let's just hope he doesn't give Abelia and Adalia any ideas."

At the look on Andrew's face, Peter laughed so hard he fell over against the boat. When he finally sat up, he looked around and said, "I wonder what Jesus is doing right now."

"You know, being here is so familiar and yet so strange all at the same time, and I'm not sure why."

"You mean it's boring."

"Not really boring exactly," Andrew thought for a moment, "but maybe kind of flat. I mean, it's great to be back fishing, or at least it will be when we go tonight. It's just that nothing has changed here. Look around. It's the same sky, the same water, the same boats, the same people, the same town. Everything is exactly the same."

Peter nodded slowly. "Except for us. *We've* changed."

"Not only that, but somewhere, right this minute, Jesus is telling stories, a crowd gathered around Him, each person listening and hoping to see a miracle too. I miss the excitement."

"So do I. I love fishing and sailing, especially when there's a storm." They both laughed, picturing many nights of gale-force winds, lashing sleet, and small fishing boats scudding along nearly out of control. The flashes of lightning would illuminate their faces lifted toward the sky, teeth gleaming in fearless grins. Galilee's sudden storms brought a fierce contest between man and nature, with Peter and Andrew emerging victorious each time.

Peter went on, "Still, though, I think it would be hard to come back here for good, knowing that this is what we'd be doing, day in and day out, for the rest of our lives. We've had a taste of the good life now, and it's hard coming back here after planning all the details of our very own palaces."

Andrew's eyes took on a dreamy, far-away look. This was his favorite subject too. "I wonder what I'll get to do when they crown Him king. You've already decided to be head of palace security, but what about me? Maybe I'll be the prime minister."

"How about 'Palace Security Assistant'?"

Andrew picked up a tiny piece of driftwood and hurled it at his brother. "Your assistant? Never! Maybe I'll be the treasurer, and then you can come beg me for your salary."

"My palace will be bigger than your palace."

"I'm sure it will be. After all, you'll have to make sure it's big enough to hold Rimona and Batia."

Peter rolled his eyes. "Anyway, we'd better finish mending this crack in our boat. As Rimona would say, 'It won't mend itself.' "

At last the crack was as secure as they could make it. Gathering their nets and lanterns, they loaded the boat and pushed it to the edge of the water. Peter removed his outer robe, tossing it with his cloak under one of the seats. Modestly, he checked to make sure his undergarment was securely fastened before wading out into the water.

This time the boat floated easily, rocking gently as the waves lifted it. Peter quickly plugged one small remaining leak with a piece of cloth cut from the hem of his robe. When further inspection revealed no more problems, Andrew climbed into the boat and unfurled the sail while Peter pushed him out into waist-deep water.

A stray breeze caught the sail and pulled the boat insistently away from the shore. "Andrew, of all the novice stunts to pull!" Peter swore at his brother as he clung to the side, his legs dangling far above the bottom of the lake. "We've been gone only a couple of months, and you can't even remember to help me in before you raise the sail?"

Andrew cursed good-naturedly. "If you're not nice to me, I won't help you in." He held out his sinewy brown arm to Peter and yanked. With another oath, Peter landed in a sodden heap on the pile of nets. "Look on the bright side," Andrew suggested. "We won't have to row."

As the sun went down, Peter checked the oil in the lamps, hanging them carefully on their hooks at each end of the boat. He and Andrew turned the lights so that they shone directly over the water, hoping to attract fish from the depths below the steep eastern shore. "Let's wait an hour or so until it gets really dark; then we can throw in our nets."

"Sounds fine to me," Andrew shrugged. "We've got all night."

Peter sat back, stretching out his legs and folding his hands behind his head. "Have you ever thought about the devil? I mean, *really* thought about him?"

"Sure. Who hasn't?" Andrew rolled his eyes. "Why?"

"I was just thinking about that story Jesus told us about the argument He had with Satan out in the desert. It got me to wondering whether Satan ever tries to do anything to us."

"I just assumed that was another one of His parables. Hardly anybody really believes in a real devil anymore."

"That's why I've been thinking about it. If that story happened, it would have to have been right before we met Him. Remember how thin and pale He looked there at Bethabara? I thought then that maybe He'd been sick for a long time, but lately I've been wondering if He actually had been involved in a huge struggle with a powerful, intelligent, evil being."

"Satan?"

Peter nodded. "It makes perfect sense. There's more too. What about all the demon-possessed people we've seen Him heal? This would explain it. It's like there's a war going on all around us, but we can't see it."

"That's a spooky idea." Andrew scratched his beard thoughtfully. "I never thought of it quite that way. I've heard doctors before, though, explaining about these supposed demon-possession cases. Old Doctor Bakbukiah says these people have a particular disease of the mind that makes them hear voices and do terrible things."

"Maybe some of them are that way." Peter shrugged and then continued. "But whenever any of those people come to Jesus to be healed, the first thing He does is tell them to be quiet. I always thought He was just talking to the person, but what if He's actually talking to demons? Forbidding them to speak?"

"Their eyes are all so creepy until Jesus heals them." Andrew shuddered. "Just like the Madman."

"Nahshon?"

"That's right. He's been crazy so long I'd forgotten who he was before."

"Maybe we should ask Jesus to help him."

"It couldn't hurt, I guess."

"Anyway, he's a perfect example of what I'm talking about. And if he's somehow infested by demons, it could mean they're stronger than we ever imagined."

"Not stronger than Jesus, though."

"Of course not. But if He's even stronger than they are, they must hate Him terribly for getting rid of them."

Andrew nodded. "I see what you're getting at. If they hate Jesus, then they would also hate anyone who's close to Jesus."

"Like us. Haven't you noticed that things are even worse than usual at home?"

Andrew snorted. "You're just hoping Batia turns out to be possessed."

"It would explain a lot," Peter insisted seriously. "I wouldn't go so far as to say that she's actually got a demon living in her, but it sure wouldn't surprise me if she had one sitting on her shoulder and whispering in her ear!"

"Maybe both shoulders," Andrew said with a rueful laugh. He knelt forward and gathered the nets to throw overboard. "Maybe even whispering to us, too, to be honest about it. But what on earth would Satan want with us? We're just fishermen."

"I don't need your help. He's only a fisherman," Oreb said, clenching and unclenching his fists. "Trust me; I can handle him all by myself! I may only be a Level III tempter now, but I'm going to qualify for Level II—just like that," he snapped his fingers. "At least, as soon as I pass the test."

"You little devils are so cute when you're angry," sneered the red-haired demon towering above Oreb. "Since you care so much, I am a Level I tempter, as well as a commander in the Second Echelon. I've opposed Tarik successfully for centuries and have been assigned here by Lucifer himself. So if you have any complaints, I suggest you take them up with him. In the meantime, step aside. I have work to do."

Oreb had no choice but to move, his wings folded stiffly in anger. Zeeb sidled over to him. "Can you believe this? We've had them all their lives, only to be replaced just like that." He spat into the water. "I feel sorrier for you. You have to work with Set. Don't worry, though. Not all the stories we've heard can possibly be true."

"Thanks." Oreb was bitter. "Well, let's watch the 'expert' at work."

Set drew his obsidian sword and glided toward the fishing boat, keeping about a cubit above the waves. "Tarik, my good friend! So this is where you've been keeping yourself." He scanned the stinking boat contemptuously. "Charming."

Tarik stood between the demon and his charge, holding his blazing sword aloft in steady hands. He made no response to the taunts of his one-time friend, barring his way in silence. Aitan and Jabir drew their swords as well, remaining close to Tarik's side. Behind him, Tarik was aware of another high-ranking demon approaching Nadiv.

"You won't find your battles so easy now that you have me to deal with and not that backwater crust, Oreb," Set gloated. "I've seen his file. It's only

a matter of time until your precious charge kills himself or someone else. Then he will be mine!"

Still Tarik made no answer, but began to sing softly, an earth-song whose haunting melody had been passed down from one generation to another for hundreds of years. The choir had sung it the day King David was laid to rest.

> *He who dwells in the secret place of the Most High*
> *Shall abide under the shadow of the Almighty.*
> *I will say of the LORD, "He is my refuge and my fortress;*
> *My God, in Him I will trust."*

> *Surely He shall deliver you from the snare of the fowler*
> *And from the perilous pestilence.*
> *He shall cover you with His feathers,*
> *And under His wings you shall take refuge;*
> *His truth shall be your shield and buckler.*

Set snarled as Aitan and Jabir added a flowing harmony, the song almost unbearably sweet. "You think you can win, but you can't. I will haunt this man in the night watches. I will feed on his fear in the noonday sun." He raised his fists, wings opening majestically above him. "I will plague him endlessly. I will cause him to fall. I will bring him down to destruction!" His sinister laughter echoed along the shores of the whole lake.

As Peter and Andrew pulled the fish to the surface and into the boat; the nets groaned under their load. A sudden chill passed over Peter, and he shivered. He looked around but saw nothing amiss; the night was as warm as before. "Let's talk about something else. All this stuff about demons and darkness is getting a bit scary."

"You're the one who brought it up," Andrew snapped, rubbing his arms to smooth down the hair.

"You felt it, too, didn't you?"

Andrew glared at his brother. "I don't know what you're talking about."

"Then why are you shivering?"

"I'm not! Well, so what if I am?" Andrew straightened up with determined nonchalance and busied himself with the net. "That still doesn't prove anything."

Peter gazed thoughtfully toward the distant shore. "Just think," he mused, "there could be a fight going on around us right now, and we don't even know it."

Andrew rolled his eyes. "Whatever you say. Just help me throw out this net again."

Tarik and his companions made no reply, but they sang even louder. Not even the rebel leader himself could have passed through their song unscathed. Before they reached the second verse, Set could not bear to hear it any longer and flew to the center of the lake. The beautiful words, flowing out into the night, wrapped the tiny vessel in celestial peace.

You shall not be afraid of the terror by night,
Nor of the arrow that flies by day,
Nor of the pestilence that walks in darkness,
Nor of the destruction that lays waste at noonday.

A thousand shall fall at your side,
And ten thousand at your right hand;
But it shall not come near you.
Only with your eyes shall you look,
And see the reward of the wicked.

Because you have made the LORD, who is my refuge,
Even the Most High, your habitation,
No evil shall befall you,
Nor shall any plague come near your dwelling;
For He shall give His angels charge over you,
To keep you in all your ways.
They shall bear you up in their hands,
Lest you dash your foot against a stone.

"Did you feel that?" Peter gestured excitedly. "I just felt something strange wash right over me—a new kind of peace or something. I don't quite know how to describe it. Listen."

They sat still, straining their ears, but there was no sound except the creaking of the boat and the weak flopping of the fish. "I don't hear anything," Andrew said after a moment, "but I guess I do feel sort of peaceful too. I'll admit things seem different from the way I was feeling just a minute ago."

Peter sat in silent contemplation for a few moments then shook his head. "Oh well. We'll probably never know for sure." He sighed deeply. "Here, I'll help you get the net."

They eased the net into the water, arcing it to catch the fish as they rose to the surface. The moon shone high overhead, rippling its silver beauty across the lake they had loved since childhood. Again and again they cast, until the first hint of brightness crept into the sky, and the fish lost their attraction to the lanterns and made their way into the shallows.

Peter rubbed his bleary eyes and splashed a handful of cool water on his face. All at once, he straightened up with a sharp oath. "I promised Jered he could come fishing with us tonight! And then I forgot all about it. He'll be heartbroken. Oh, well, there'll always be other nights." He shrugged. "Let's go home."

Several leagues away, Set and Ares circled the boat like hyenas, watching and waiting for a weak spot in its defense. But the Guardians tirelessly held to their posts. "Oreb, come here," Set ordered. Oreb obeyed with noticeably poor grace. "Go back to the house and get the other Level III tempters together." Set's voice dripped with scorn. "Let them know about the changes in our orders."

"Yes, sir," Oreb said sullenly and flew off to do Set's bidding, Zeeb at his side.

Unable to resist, Zeeb needled, "See? I told you they wouldn't forget about the wine incident. I tried to tell you, but you just wouldn't listen."

"Shut up, Zeeb," Oreb replied.

Chapter 8

How little Peter truly understood about the nature of the war raging unseen about him. True, it was great progress that he would even speculate on the existence of a spiritual conflict in a spiritual realm, yet he had only begun to scratch the surface. Jesus was patiently teaching him, but he still had so much to learn. Just a short time before Peter had met Jesus for the first time, an epic battle in that war had taken place. All heaven, indeed, all the universe, had watched as Satan poured out millennia of hoarded sophistry while the destiny of humankind hung in the balance. Oh yes, the war was very real.

As the voice of the Father rumbled from the heavens, saying, "This is My beloved Son," the Spirit's voice spoke to the heart of the Son, commanding, "Go into the desert." And so, not knowing why the order had been given, He humbly obeyed. Without stopping to gather any provisions for the journey, He walked through the crowd and into the wilderness.

What followed was almost more painful than the watchers could bear. Jesus, the Majesty of heaven, the Creator of the universe, the angels' dearest Friend, was hungry. No, not just hungry—starving. Wasting and shriveling in the heat, He lay panting on the very earth His hands had formed—famished, without a crust of bread.

During the day He crept down to the river, drinking from His cupped hands, pouring the cool water over His head. In the noonday sun He rested under the shade of a tree, sleeping very little in His growing discomfort. By night He wandered out into the desert, a long way at first, but shorter and shorter distances as His body grew weaker. Always He prayed ceaselessly to the Father, preparing His heart for the work He was to do. And only that constant connection with heaven kept Him sane, kept Him alive.

None who kept that vigil with Him found themselves able to eat or drink. It didn't seem right that they should enjoy the bounties of the universe while their Maker suffered such deprivation. But the worst was watching Satan and his hosts press ever closer, whispering their evil lies. Gabriel, forbidden to interfere, stood guard at a distance. The Almighty One would not suffer the demons to touch Jesus, but He did allow them to bear down on His mind with every artifice their diabolical minds could invent.

They tried to distract Him, to break His lifeline of prayer, but He resisted them. They filled the air with fear, imitating the sound of vicious beasts about to attack, but He remained at peace. They chanted again and again that God had forsaken Him and left Him to die, but His love and trust never wavered. As days went by and the rebels made not the slightest gain, they became increasingly cruel and desperate.

At evening on the fortieth day, the Spirit commanded Him again. With the last of His strength, he staggered on across the rocky desert, far beyond the reach of any human help. As the sun set, He collapsed, every system in His body shutting down. Jesus was dying. He groaned aloud in torment, "Your will, Father. Only Your will." His cracked lips barely moved. His eyes fluttered shut.

Then a meteoric light flashed across the sky and landed beside Him. At the brightness, He opened His eyes and looked straight into the face of Gabriel, who bent lovingly over Him, gently lifting Him. "You don't have to worry anymore," the angel said tenderly. "I'm here now. The Father sent me to help You." He hesitated a moment, his brows lowering slightly in puzzlement. "At least, I think You are He."

Gabriel—the real Gabriel—quivered in outrage. "He can't do that! How dare he pretend to be me? There must be something I can do!"

His frustration was felt by all, but the Spirit spoke patiently. "Wait and watch. This, too, is a test He must face."

Every evil angel from across the globe had assembled, circling the drama below them. They watched silently, poised to strike at Jesus and rend Him into subatomic particles the moment He failed.

The false Gabriel brushed the hair out of Jesus' face with his hand and looked keenly into His eyes. "Please understand that I must make sure You are the One I was sent to help. I don't know how much You remember from before, but there was a war in heaven. The wicked angels were cast down to this earth. We have been sternly warned by the Father to beware of this rebel's tricks, so I just need to make sure who You really are before I can complete my mission. It would be disastrous if the life-giving food I bring fell into his evil hands."

The angel caressed the fallen Man soothingly. "All I need is for You to show me that You're really God's Son. See all these rocks around us? Just turn one of them into bread, and then I'll know for sure." He picked up a round, smooth stone and slipped it into Jesus' trembling hands.

The scent of freshly baked bread wafted through the desert, more delicious than any aroma from a palace bakery. Jesus' mouth tried to water, His empty salivary glands pricking painfully. Then He smelled the newly pressed grape juice. He could almost hear the rush of liquid being poured from the pitcher into a cup. His throat contracted, and He couldn't speak.

"Oh, no." The angel began to look worried. "I am afraid I may have made a terrible mistake. Captain Elazar warned me something like this might happen. Why do I find You here, alone in the desert, forsaken by God and cast off by men? What if You are the one he told me about? What if You are that wicked angel?" His face was pained, his voice pleading. "Please, if You would just show me one little miracle, it would set my mind at ease. I just need to know for certain."

The heavenly beings held their breath, waiting to see what Jesus would do. The assault on His senses was nearly overpowering. Satan was using every possible human feeling against Him at once, tempting Him in the area of man's greatest weakness—appetite. It was this that had been the downfall of Adam and Eve and the cause of untold sin and suffering since.

Jesus could so easily have done it; the stone was right there in His hands. All He would have to do was speak a word, and it would become bread. It would take but a single thought for a banquet table to appear before Him. But before He ever came down to earth, He agreed that He would not use His own power for Himself; He would rely completely on the Father, just as any other human must do. For Him to break that agreement now would mean

God's power was not sufficient to keep human beings in the path of obedience. It would show that Satan had been right all along and would be the end of God's kingdom.

From the very start of the rebellion, Satan's primary complaint had been that God's rules were too hard to obey, that it wasn't fair to punish him for breaking them when they were impossible to keep anyway. A large part of what Jesus was to accomplish during His time as a man was to prove Satan's accusations false.

The rock slid through His fingers, landing with a thud on the hard soil. Jesus finally spoke, His voice raspy and almost inaudible. "It is written in God's Word, 'Man shall not live by bread alone, but by every word that comes from the mouth of God.' "

The angels let out a great shout of victory. Of course they recognized the words; they were from the scrolls of Moses, written by inspiration of Jehovah. As Gabriel remembered the rest of the passage, a shock ran through him. As Moses had led the people through the years of wandering in the wilderness, as the aging human charge of Tarik had written the words that Jesus now quoted in the desert, Gabriel had little realized that Moses was actually living out the foreshadowing of this very day. Forty years for forty days. He recalled the original words:

Remember how the LORD your God led you all the way in the desert these forty years, to humble you and to test you in order to know what was in your heart, whether or not you would keep his commands. He humbled you, causing you to hunger and then feeding you with manna, which neither you nor your fathers had known, to teach you that man does not live on bread alone but on every word that comes from the mouth of the LORD.

Gabriel raised his hands to the Father with joy. By His grace, Moses had helped to provide Jesus with the weapon He needed to defeat His enemy, many hundreds of years before the moment arrived when his words would be needed. The angel's heart was filled to overflowing with humble gratitude at the unsearchable mysteries of Adonai. Surely the victory had been won!

For a moment anger flashed in the guileless blue eyes of Gabriel's look-alike, but he stifled it so quickly it was barely noticeable. "You're right," he nodded. "I hadn't thought of it that way. Still, there must be some way You can confirm Your identity."

He scooped up Jesus' frail body in his arms and launched himself into the air. Indignant exclamations could be heard everywhere as Gabriel followed behind, wondering that the Father would permit such contempt to be heaped on the Son.

The unholy angel flew with tremendous speed to the highest peak of the dazzling temple. He landed and set Jesus carefully down, supporting Him with one strong arm. "It's so simple; I can't believe I didn't think of it earlier. All You have to do is jump. If You're God's Son, He will make sure You don't get hurt. The Scriptures say, 'He will command his angels concerning you, and they will lift you up in their hands, so that you will not strike your foot against a stone.' Take God at His word, and trust in His promises. That's what You'd do, if You were really the One."

Jesus swayed and tried to swallow. The torches were so far below and seemed to spin around in a wide, sweeping circle. The humanity in Him longed to make some grand display, a vast declaration of His sovereignty. He knew the power rested in His hands to leap off the pinnacle and drift gracefully down to the marble floor. The priests would be amazed and might even crown Him right there.

But that was not a part of His Father's plan, and He was determined to obey. He spoke with effort, "It is also written, 'Do not put the Lord your God to the test.' "

Again, cheers erupted from the heavenly watchers. Again they thrilled as Jesus used words from Moses' Book of the Second Law to defeat His wily foe. Yet their joy was mixed with sorrow at the remembrance of the day Moses had disobeyed before the entire assembly of Israel. Later, he had written the passage from which Jesus had just quoted.

Do not test the LORD your God as you did at Massah. Be sure to keep the commands of the LORD your God and the stipulations and decrees he has given you. Do what is right and good in the LORD's sight, so that it may go well with you and you may go in and take over the good land that the LORD promised on oath to your forefathers, thrusting out all your enemies before you, as the LORD said.

Jesus had fulfilled every bit of that counsel, keeping the commands of the Lord and doing only what was right and good. Surely this would bring His test to an end. He had been tempted far beyond the limits of any man or woman to walk the planet, and had emerged victorious. All eyes went to Gabriel—the real Gabriel—knowing he would be the first to receive the order to intervene.

But to everyone's surprise, no order was given. Even the demon horde expected to be sent away as usual and fidgeted impatiently as they waited to see what would happen. They were nervous and edgy, fully realizing that their own destiny, balanced against the fate of fallen man, stood on the blade of a knife. Yet in spite of this awareness, deep in their hearts they felt a spiteful smugness at the gross humiliation of their proud leader.

The angel straightened, an odd gleam in his eyes. "Two points for You. Very good," he murmured. His features blurred and shifted. He no longer resembled Gabriel; he was now transformed into Lucifer, bearer of light. He looked a great deal as the angels remembered him during his time in heaven, though darker and somehow degenerated. In this latest metamorphosis, some trick caused his receding forehead to appear as noble as it had once been, before sin first made its mysterious appearance in his thoughts. Oddly enough, he chose not to appear before Jesus in his truest form.

All pretence of holiness and sympathy had dropped away. "Look," he sneered, "look how Your so-called Father of Love has treated You. He has abandoned You, just like He's abandoned everyone else down here. Do You know what He has planned for You? Do You think I don't know the prophecies as well as You do? I've read them too." Leaning in close, he whispered, "There's another way. You don't really have to die. Come with me now. Let me show You a better way."

In a show of superior strength, he seized Jesus by the shoulders. Together they shot into the sky above the city of Jerusalem and descended with a rush. Emboldened by the lack of any imposed restraint, Satan raced along just above the ground, Jesus held firmly in his huge hands.

In the darkness, the ride was petrifying. Jesus' stomach heaved, but His mouth remained parched. In less than a minute they had reached their destination—the top of Mount Nebo. Satan dropped Jesus precipitously on the hard ground and stood to his full height, towering above the Man crumpled at his feet. "Here You once showed Moses the land of Your infernal promise. Here I show You the world."

He swept his hands grandly, and the sky lit up. Suddenly, he was standing *in an Egyptian palace, with Jesus prone on the floor before the Pharaoh. All around them were brightly painted reliefs created by the finest artists of the time.*

The picture began to move as if they were moving through a royal tour. They skimmed along the Nile and rested atop a pyramid. One after another, the sights, sounds, and smells of the world's greatest civilizations flowed by in gaudy array. Faster and faster they flashed into an overwhelming display.

At last they melded into a single image, frozen in time. A beam of light illuminated Satan as he spread his arms wide, lifting himself into the sky and slowly rotating. "I am the god of this world!" His shout echoed for miles. "All that You see is mine!"

He laughed fiendishly, dropping to Jesus' side. In suddenly hushed tones, he added, "And I will give it all to You. No more pain, no more hunger. You can escape the hideous death awaiting You at my hand and win back every-thing lost by Adam. The power and wealth of the earth can be Yours; all men will bow before You to call You Lord."

His voice was silky, hypnotic. "Yes, I will give it all to You if You will do just one little thing. Bow down and worship me. Just once will be enough, and then it will all be Yours." He put his face very close to Jesus, grasping His chin and lifting His head. His gaze bored deeply into Jesus' eyes, the blue of his own shifting smoothly to black. Satan focused his full mental energy, honed by thousands of years of practice, toward bending the will of Jesus to his own. "Worship me," he whispered again.

Each angel wondered what Jesus would do, how He could counter this cunning deception in His weakened state, and they prayed that He would not fail. Jesus raised His eyes toward heaven, refusing to look upon the devil or argue with him. "Get away from Me, Satan." The powerful being next to Him lurched and tumbled end over end, sprawling ungracefully on the ground some distance away. He could barely hear the hoarse whisper as Jesus said, "It is written, 'Worship your God, and serve him only.'" The Creator slumped over with the effort, His life measured in minutes.

In the human realm, that command would have seemed very weak. But the barest murmur of one of God's children can topple the most fearsome forces of unseen evil. Not only Satan, but all his angels were thrust far out of sight, well past the distant horizon. Sinking into unconsciousness, Jesus didn't even know they were gone.

In the blink of an eye, Gabriel was at His side, holding sweet, soft manna and life-giving water. He picked up Jesus and held Him on his lap like a child. Jesus opened His eyes. He mistrusted the information of His senses. He shook His head weakly, refusing to eat just yet. Then He closed His eyes and moved His lips in prayer. A few moments later He opened them, a smile of relief on His face, as He saw Gabriel still there. "We won." Gabriel nodded silently as Jesus reached up and shakily touched the angel's tear-stained cheek. "Thank you." This time He accepted the nourishment gratefully, feeling the life creep back into His body.

His stomach was greatly contracted from the ordeal, and He could eat only a handful of food and drink a few sips of water before falling into exhausted slumber. The sun was just rising as Elazar helped Gabriel move their Commander under the shade of a scraggly tree.

Throughout the day they sat beside Him, shading and fanning Him with their wings. When evening came, He awoke briefly and consumed another small meal before dozing once more. Three days passed thus before He was sufficiently recovered to travel. Jesus clung to Gabriel and Elazar a long while, stepping back reluctantly as they faded from sight. He touched His fingers to His lips and raised His hand in a gesture of farewell before turning once again toward the Jordan.

"Go to Bethabara," the Spirit said. "I have arranged a meeting for You there." So, having been fed and revived by the same heavenly food that had nourished the people of Israel for forty years, Jesus walked slowly but steadily out of the wilderness.

Peter and Andrew wearily beached their boat, all thought of supernatural goings-on forgotten. They sorted the fish quickly and efficiently, preparing them for the market. Peter rubbed his eyes. "Let's just leave these here for the women. I'm tired."

"Sounds good to me," Andrew replied. "We've been gone so long we're out of shape. I can't wait to lie down." Peter's only response was a groan.

The walk up the hill to their home strained every aching muscle. Peter forgot about the broken door and slammed his head into it. "We've got to fix this cursed thing right away," he muttered.

"Let's do it when we wake up," Andrew yawned.

Inside, Rimona eyed them coldly. "Where are the fish? I suppose you wasted all that time and didn't catch anything again."

"They're down at the boat." Peter couldn't meet her gaze.

"Down at the boat? Doesn't that just figure? He sits around all night long and then is too tired to carry a few fish up to the house."

"Sheer laziness, that's what it is." Batia pursed her lips in distaste. "He wants you to do the work of a slave—and a donkey too! You, who could have married a rich man, had servants of your own, and that nice, big house, big enough for all of us." She sniffed in disdain.

Peter did his best to keep his rising temper in check. "That does it! I want everybody out of here now! And don't come back till we wake up."

Rimona's face took on a set look, and she gathered up the kettle and loaves of bread—every shred of the breakfast she was preparing. Standing imperiously, she called, "Come, Mother. Come, boys. Simon does not want us in his house. You might as well come too." She turned to Keren. Keren glared at Rimona first, then at Peter, but she picked up Atalia and left without speaking to either of them.

Andrew staggered over to his sleeping mat and groaned in exhaustion as he lay down.

Peter tried to be cheerful. "Did you notice? They forgot to take the basket with yesterday's bread. It's right over . . ."

Rimona burst back into the room, picked up a closed basket just inside the door, then marched back out again.

". . . there," Peter finished lamely with a sigh.

"But I'm starving."

"Me, too, but I'm too tired to go after her."

"Just think of a small fish wrapped in bread and baking over the coals of a fire."

"Oh, stop it. You act like we haven't eaten in a week. We've missed only two meals."

Andrew clutched his belly. "I'm going to die if I don't get something to eat soon!"

"Go to bed. The sooner we fall asleep, the sooner it will be time to get up and eat."

Chapter 9

Oreb and Zeeb sulked together, refusing to take part in any of the merriment. "There's got to be some way to get rid of them," Oreb said. He flicked a glance at Set and Ares as they systematically and seriously carried out their task—a little flame of hate in their eyes, the only evidence that they were enjoying their work.

Zeeb swallowed a snarl. "Those two think they're so much better than we are, like they can just come trotting in at the last minute and ruin everything after we've worked so hard. Just because we're not part of Central Command doesn't mean they can treat us like we're dirt."

"It's true that we didn't exactly bargain for such close contact with our greatest enemy, but I think under the circumstances we've done really well."

Zeeb preened. "The situation has brought out our best qualities, and Lucifer would have to be a fool not to see it."

"He sent Set and Ares, didn't he?"

"You just wait. By the time we're through here, the names of Oreb and Zeeb will be on everyone's lips. Even our enemy will be forced to recognize our power." The two diminutive demons chortled together, momentarily lost in their swollen dreams of grandeur.

Tarik and Nadiv stood at attention outside the shabby house with Zohar, Nissim, and Meraioth. Aitan, along with some newly assigned forces, formed a second row. Although wrong choices by the humans who lived here had temporarily prevented them from intervening, the angels wanted to be near,

94

ready at the first opportunity. At the moment, however, the only busy angels were the Recorders, their pens flying over the pages, preserving each word and thought against the day of judgment.

"At least the Guardians of the little ones can be inside the house," Tarik tried to sound encouraging.

Nadiv nodded. "We'll be back in, too, as soon as they repent."

"Picking up the pieces just like always," Meraioth said sadly. "Hoping it's not just a waste of time."

"It's never a waste of time," Tarik said with conviction. "The Spirit has won harder cases than these. Do you remember when I was assigned to Jonah? Even though he was a prophet, he was an angry, contentious man, who allowed himself to be greatly influenced by Set for many years. He actually wept when our Lord had mercy on the repentant city of Nineveh, but by the time the Spirit finally finished with him, he had the heart of love God looks for in all of His people."

Tarik sadly kept his vigil. His charge did so much better away from the influences that assailed him in his own home; he didn't yet know that God's power was sufficient to keep him in the way of obedience, no matter what the circumstances. Tarik strongly suspected that until Peter learned that lesson, he would be brought back to this test over and over.

"Call on Jesus," Tarik urged one last time as Peter sank onto his bed. "He will help you. It's not too late. It's never too late." His voice trailed off. "You can't fight Set, you know," he whispered as Peter's eyes began to close. "You will never defeat him in your own strength. You must call on the power of God."

It was very quiet the rest of the week. Simon Peter and Andrew woke in the afternoon, slipped some bread and fish into a bag, and went down to their boat. After the brothers were safely out of the house, the women filed in silently and set to work preparing the evening meal. In the morning, they left the house before dawn, leaving more fish and more bread for the men when they returned. No one spoke to anyone, and an uneasy truce prevailed.

Peter avoided James and John, telling himself that he was too busy to socialize; after all, he never knew when Jesus would come by and call him to leave, and he had a family to support. The thought that he had not always cared how much or little he provided his family never crossed his mind.

The week seemed to stretch on forever, as if to emphasize to Peter just what his life would be like if he failed to secure a place in the New Kingdom. He reached his lowest point during the night before the preparation day.

"I've been thinking," Andrew ventured. When no polite expression of interest was forthcoming from his brother, he went on anyway. "It really doesn't look too good for us."

Peter worked in unison with Andrew to drag the waterlogged nets into the boat. "You're right. Maybe we're under some kind of curse or something. Half the night gone, and still nothing."

Andrew sighed heavily, throwing the nets back into the lake. "Lately it's just been bothering me, thinking of the Baptist in prison all these months. Part of me even feels guilty for being out here with no walls, as free as can be, while he's chained in a dungeon."

"You aren't the only one. But I think what bothers me most is that he's Jesus' cousin, a member of His own family. Why hasn't *He* done something by now?"

"Maybe He's just afraid of Herod and the priests. Our last visit to Jerusalem didn't go so well, if you remember."

"And if Jesus loses His influence, what will happen to us?" Peter pulled up on his side of the net. "We'll be lucky if we just get to spend the rest of our lives as fishermen, and not underground, propping up some stone wall instead."

Andrew surveyed the net glumly. "Still empty. We'd probably starve if we had to do this for a living again."

Peter rested his head on his hands in discouragement. "I was so sure He was the Messiah too. Now I just don't know. I want to believe in Him, but all these questions keep coming into my head. I can't seem to stop them."

"Is Jesus really the Messiah? He doesn't act like He even cares about setting up His kingdom." Set hovered beside Peter, his great hands encircling the *fisherman's head. He spoke softly, and Peter did not refuse his suggestions.*

Chapter 9

"And what of the poor Baptist, all alone? See how God has forgotten him, and all his friends and supporters have abandoned him? Even your precious Master doesn't care about him anymore. If He can do that to His own cousin, you know He'll surely leave you to your fate, too, at the first hint of trouble."

Ares picked up the struggle, weaving sinuously around Andrew. "Poor John. All he ever did was to try to prepare the way for Jesus to become king. You know he grew up in the wide-open spaces of nature, wild and free." He paused for emphasis. "Just like you . . ."

Set slid in smoothly. "Now he's rotting away, locked up in the dark. At least you still have a lantern . . . for now."

"Do you like prison?" Ares winked at Set. "I hope so, because that's where you'll wind up if you stay around Jesus much longer. Get away while you still can, before the priests learn you were His follower. If you don't, you'll surely die!"

"Pray," Tarik urged Peter. "Turn your thoughts to the Father and His love for you. In His strength, resist these thoughts of discouragement, and the devils will be forced to flee. Trust in Adonai, who seeks only your salvation. Yes, it is true that you might be sent to prison and suffer greatly for His sake, but He will always be with you—even there."

Tarik's voice scarcely registered with Peter, so wrapped in depression was the glum fisherman. All he could hear were the whispers of doubt, the words seeming to clash discordantly in his mind. The more he heard, the greater his disquiet grew, until he could hardly sit still. Andrew fared no better. On and on, Set and Ares spewed their hideous propaganda all through the long, lonely night.

"We might as well give up and go home. We're not going to catch anything tonight anyway."

Peter slumped over, weary and sore. "You mean we might as well give up, end of story. Nothing is going the way it's supposed to. I was so sure that by now I would be leading the coronation parade into Jerusalem and shopping for a summer palace. It's bad enough having to give up all that and realize that we're nothing but fishermen, after all, but the worst truth is that we can't even catch fish anymore. We've worked all night without even one lousy fish to show for it."

Andrew chafed his hands together, trying to warm them. "I had a lot of plans too." He swallowed hard. "But this is where we belong. Our father and grandfathers were fishermen, going back at least two hundred and seventy-four years, and that's all we'll ever be too. Right here is our future. We were fools to think anything different."

Out of force of habit, they aimed their boat unerringly for the strip of shore below their house, pulling the boat up on the land. The very picture of dejection, they pulled the heavy, wet nets from the boat and began spreading them out to dry.

"What's going on over there?" Andrew squinted into the rising sun. "That's odd. It looks like a whole crowd of people coming this way."

Peter, standing in water up to his knees, didn't even bother to look up. "Who cares? As long as they don't bother us, we won't bother them." The nets sloshed rhythmically in the tiny waves. A short distance away, James and John stood in the shallows, caring for their nets as well.

"Simon, I think they're coming this way. It looks like they've left the road, and are walking down to the shore."

"Good for them."

"If only we had some fish to sell them," Andrew said wistfully, "we'd probably get better prices here than we ever could in the marketplace."

Peter glared malevolently at his brother. "Yes, we could have made a lot of money today—if we had any fish. But do we? Do we have even one little finger-long fish to sell to the very smallest child of Capernaum? No, we do not! And I thought our luck could not possibly get any worse." He continued muttering, scowling darkly.

"Uh, . . . Simon, you might want to take a look." The ripple of many voices drowned out the sound of the sea. A cloud of dust from many feet drifted over the two men as they worked, stinging their eyes and choking them.

Peter finally straightened and turned. A mass of people filled the usually quiet countryside. A glad cry suddenly burst from Peter's lips, and he hurled himself joyously at the Leader of the procession. "Jesus! You came back!"

Jesus embraced the damp fisherman, smiling reassuringly. "Of course I came back. Didn't I say I would?" He walked past the boat, shouting, "James! John! Come over here!"

They looked up from their work with the nets to see Jesus beckoning to them. Without hesitation, they dropped their nets half in and half out of the boat and ran toward Him. Behind them, Zebedee looked up at the sound, only to see his sons' backs receding along the shoreline. He jumped up and down in his rage. "Get back here and finish, you young wastrels! There are fish to sort and pack, the nets to finish, and, ugh . . . !" he grunted in frustration, "I give up! Just don't come crawling back to me when you're hungry." James and John never looked back.

The crowd pressed so tightly around Jesus that He was forced to the very edge of the lake, nearly tumbling into the water. Peter gripped His elbow to keep Him from falling in. "Would You like to come to my house? It's just right over there." He made the invitation unwillingly, cringing at the thought of Jesus in his shabby, strife-ridden home.

To his relief, Jesus simply laughed and said, "If it's all right with you, for now, I'll just borrow your boat."

"Where do You want to go?"

"Nowhere." Seeing Peter's puzzled frown, He went on, "Just push the boat out a few feet from shore and let Me sit in it."

Within moments Peter and Andrew had the nets pulled onto land and the boat hauled into the water. Jesus gathered up His robe, waded out into the water, and stepped into the small craft. He seated Himself and raised His hands, calling for the attention of the crowd. "Brothers and sisters," He addressed them with a smile, "come as close as you can and sit down. There is plenty of room here for all of you."

The gradual rise of the hill stretching away from the shoreline provided a perfect vantage point for each person to be able to see and hear Jesus clearly. The beauty of nature spoke to each listener, turning thoughts to the One who had designed the splendor that surrounded them.

"The time has come!" Jesus' first words startled them into attention, quieting the undercurrent of whispers. Peter sat up straight, so excited at the implication of these words that he almost dropped the rope that held his boat near the shore. "The kingdom of God is near. Repent and believe the good news!"

Just then the door of Peter's house opened, and Rimona stepped outside to see what was taking her husband so long. Her irritation deepened to downright disgust when she spotted him anchoring the boat with his own body just so someone could sit in it. A step or two closer, and she knew the Man in the boat was Jesus. For a moment she was almost tempted to go and listen, but stopped herself. "That good-for-nothing husband of mine," she muttered. "Him and that insane radical. And I don't see any fish, either." Still grumbling, she stomped back inside. If it had been possible, she would doubtless have slammed the door behind her.

Jesus spoke so vibrantly and with so much enthusiasm it was impossible not to be stirred by His preaching. His stories, drawn from everyday life, taught the lessons of the Father in a simple yet profound way that no rabbi could hope to equal. Every word was spoken to lift and strengthen those who had been cast down by the enemy, and as Peter listened, the great weight of discouragement lifted from his heart, leaving him refreshed and at peace.

Chapter 10

*T*arik stood between Peter and Gabriel, glowing happily. He could almost see the Holy Spirit rushing down, flooding Simon Peter with power from on high. It was so good to be among all of his friends and to see the Spirit sweeping across the group. Out of a crowd of more than four hundred, only three still had demons at their sides. The rest of the evil army was in full retreat, and all heaven rejoiced.

"Stay here," Set ordered Oreb and Zeeb. "Watch for any weakness, and get back in if you can." With that he and Ares flew off to a high-level meeting with Lucifer, out over the lake.

" 'Stay here!' 'Do this!' 'Do that!' You're not advanced enough to take care of one fisherman by yourself or important enough to go to any meetings. Just do what I tell you, then I'll take all the credit for myself,' " Oreb griped, making faces behind Set's back.

"That's no joke," Zeeb agreed. "He thinks he can just dance in here and tell us what to do. You wait and see; we'll fix him good one of these days." With so little to occupy their time, revenge was nearly all the two demons thought about.

"Hey, look at that." Oreb jerked his head toward Peter's house and laughed. "At least that's one place He hasn't been able to mess around with."

The house was crawling with demons, it being the only place they could find a foothold so close to Jesus. Igal jockeyed for position in the shifting mass.

"I was here first, and this is my job! Move over and leave me a little room to work. Hey, Rimona. Better see what your husband is up to now. He should have been here already with the fish."

Obediently, Rimona stood and walked outside the house. Her eyes were quick to discern the form of her husband, sitting idly on the shore without a fish in sight. And the Man in the boat, why, that must be Jesus! Here He was, interfering with her life again. Simon would probably leave with Him when He moved on, leaving the family to starve for all he or Jesus cared. Rimona scowled, while Igal eagerly fanned the flames of anger.

Nissim reached for her hand. "Just go and listen for a while, Rimona. Aren't you even a little bit curious to know what He's saying to all those people? You don't know it—not yet—but that Man is your only hope. He is the ladder in Father Jacob's dream, stretching from earth to heaven, connecting humans to God. Please, just listen to Him."

"Like that will really work," Igal sneered. "She listens only to me. Just watch." He took Rimona's other hand. "Think of all the trouble that radical preacher has already caused you. And in your heart you know it's not going to stop, either. The trouble is just beginning. Go back inside and start thinking of what you want to say to Simon when he finally comes inside."

"No, Rimona, please just come and hear Jesus. Let the Spirit speak to your heart." Rimona hesitated, considering Nissim's thought.

Seeing the possibility of his defeat looming larger, Igal tugged at the woman subtly, using an argument he knew she would not be able to resist. "Sabbath begins tonight, and you have so much to do to get ready. It's not like Simon is going to be any help, either. Now get busy!"

Igal shot a triumphant glance over his shoulder as Rimona turned abruptly on her heel and walked briskly into the house, taking out her frustrations in frenzied cleaning. Undaunted, Nissim squared his shoulders and followed, ready to use any circumstance to try again to reach the resentful woman.

In the doorway, he met Zohar walking out by the side of Keren and her daughters. "Are you going down to the lake?"

Zohar nodded. "Keren is just following the leading of the Spirit, and as you can see, nothing will be able to stop her."

Nissim watched with amusement as Bozkath threw himself on the ground at Keren's feet. "No! You can't go! I won't let you," the demon wailed. He tried to hold on to her ankles, but she walked through him as if he didn't exist.

"I see what you mean," Nissim grinned. "I'm so happy for you, and for her, too."

"Your turn will come," Zohar promised. "No one can be this close to Jesus and stay unchanged. Soon I will rejoice with you." Feeling much cheered, Nissim returned to his labors with a renewed sense of purpose.

"Mother, get up. It's getting late, and Sabbath will be here before you know it." Rimona bent over Batia and shook her gently.

Batia opened her eyes, wincing against the light that filtered in from the high, narrow window. "Hurts," was all she said, her voice sounding queer and strained.

Rimona held the back of her hand against her mother's face. "Why, you're burning up with fever. How long have you felt like this?"

Batia just shook her head ever so slightly and closed her eyes. Rimona worked fast, stripping away the covers and removing Batia's outer robe. "Jered, take these three coins to the marketplace. Go to the herb seller and get as much fever remedy as you can. Seth, bring me some water and a cloth." She sighed. "It's no use asking the physician to come. We don't have the kind of money he charges."

Without his usual spate of questions, Jered tightened his hand around the coins his mother held out and scurried out the door. Seth picked up a small earthen water pot and carried it carefully to his mother, spilling only a little.

"A cloth too," Rimona reminded him, holding her mother's head in her two hands. For once she didn't scold him about the puddle he had made on the dirt floor.

Seth stood with his finger in his mouth, watching as Rimona wrung out the cloth and wiped Batia's face with its damp coolness. Finally he took his finger out long enough to say, "Mommy, I want to ask Jesus to come."

She stared at him a moment, her hands still moving of their own accord. Most of the time, Seth was content to let his precocious older brother speak for him. "Seth, we just can't do that."

"Why not?"

Though Rimona tried to control her anger, her voice had a sharp edge to it. "Because I don't want Him here, that's why."

"Why not?" The little boy's lips began to quiver. "Jesus can make Grandma well."

Rimona wiped the hair out of her face with one bent wrist. "I don't know where you heard that, but it's not true. Besides, Grandma is going to be fine. Mommy will make her well."

"But I want . . ."

"Not one more word, young man," Rimona said firmly. "Just go out and play."

Tears spilled down Seth's chubby cheeks as he turned to go outside. As soon as he was sure his mother couldn't hear him, he whispered, "Jesus, please make my grandma well."

"Yes, yes, yes. Oh, yes!" Hamath gloated, shaking gnarled fists at the sky and cackling gleefully. "All her life I've waited for this moment, and now it's finally arrived. I'll get a promotion this time for sure."

"All you did was to make her sick," Igal said, rolling his eyes.

"Yes, but he," Hamath nodded toward Meraioth, "has always been able to keep me from making her this sick before. Now, I've done my work so well he has no choice but to step back and let me carry out my will with her."

"He looks awfully happy," Igal replied doubtfully, glancing at the Guardian. Sure enough, Meraioth was smiling as if nothing at all were the matter. "You'd almost think he wanted this to happen."

Hamath ground his teeth. "He must have some plan we don't know about. It's so frustrating trying to guess what these humans will do next."

Igal rubbed his chin. "Let's see. What could the enemy gain by allowing us to do this?"

"Well, usually when He permits us to bring disaster, it's to try to draw these stupid humans away from us and closer to Him, but that won't work this time." Meraioth's smile grew wider, though he pretended not to be eavesdropping.

"What do you mean?" Igal looked nervously over his shoulder. "Jesus is right here. I'm not saying it can't work, but I still think we need to be really careful."

"Don't worry," Hamath boasted, "I've seen to it that nobody will ask Jesus to come, and you know He won't show up without an invitation. It doesn't make any sense to me, but that's just how He works—you can count on it."

"I sure hope you're right."

"Of course I am!" Hamath beamed. "Now will you just quit your worrying and enjoy the sights and smells of death?"

Nissim grinned slyly at Meraioth. "It's better that we don't say much at this point, isn't it?"

Meraioth smiled back. "That's right. We say nothing. We just stand back and let the Spirit work."

Peter stood and stretched as Jesus dismissed the crowd. "I'll be gone only a short while," Jesus told the people. "We can talk more later; right now, there's something I need to take care of."

"Are you going to be at the synagogue tomorrow?" someone called as the crowd began to break up and move away.

"Yes," Jesus called back. "I'll see you there." Then he turned to Peter and Andrew. "Come, take me out in your boat. James and John, go get your boat, too, and come with us." Peter started to wade directly into the water, but Jesus asked, "Aren't you forgetting your nets?"

"These?" Obviously Jesus didn't know much about fishing. "No, they're the wrong kind of nets, even if we sailed to Seven Springs or toward Bethsaida. Just give me a minute to go home and get our throwing nets, and we'll at least have a chance."

Jesus smiled, His joy bubbling up from a hidden fountain inside Himself. "Peter, your deep-sea nets will be fine. And we're not going to Seven Springs."

Peter shrugged and dragged the nets into the boat. "Fine," he muttered under his breath, "don't believe me. I guess You'll just have to see for Yourself."

Already the day was growing hot, and the breeze had stilled. Andrew leaped for the tiller, leaving Peter to struggle with the oars. He waved to John, who had managed to commandeer the tiller of his father's boat in a similar fashion. Andrew started to turn the tiller to the right, but stopped. "If I'm going to steer this thing, I really need to know where I'm going."

"Just out there somewhere." Jesus waved His hand noncommittally toward the center of the lake. "Any deep water will do."

Of course any deep water spot will work as well as another, Peter thought disdainfully to himself, *because they're all equally useless this time of day. Every last fish in the lake has moved to shallow water, as any real fisherman knows.* Without even meaning to, he shook his head in obvious disbelief.

"Peter, Peter, you have so little faith in Me." Jesus' tone was loving, but His face was sad. "There's so much I want to teach you, but you must first believe in Me. Stop here and let down the nets."

Peter secured the oars and peered curiously over the side of the boat. He could see far down into the clear water, and there were definitely no fish anywhere. Just to be sure, he checked the other side, but found it equally empty of fish. He sighed. Obviously, the only way to show Jesus how impossibly foolish His idea really was would be to go ahead and do as He said. "Here, Andrew. Give me a hand with these things, will you?"

The two men threw the nets into the water, each keeping hold of one end. James and John looked on, trying hard to contain their amusement. "Aren't you glad they're the ones doing that, and not us?" James said softly to his brother, his lips barely moving.

Peter and Andrew worked in unison to send the net down into the depths and drag it up again. Peter watched carefully, but as far as he could tell, their efforts were useless—just as he had known they would be. He pulled as hard as he could, eager to end this foolish endeavor.

When the nets were about six cubits from the surface, Peter let go with one hand to wipe the sweat from his forehead, still holding tight with the other. "Well, this doesn't seem to be working," he said, trying hard to keep any smugness out of his tone. "We have just fished all the way from the bottom to the top, and the nets are still . . . !" A loud splashing noise cut off his comment in mid sentence, and the flaccid net sprang suddenly to life, tugging sharply at the ropes. Without warning, Peter found himself draped over the boat's edge, his head and shoulders under the water as the vessel listed sharply to one side. He let out a gurgling roar, and cloud of bubbles rose to the surface. Only a few feet from his bulging eyeballs, Peter saw an enormous school of fish writhing within the confines of the net.

Chapter 10

Almost losing what little air he had left, he grabbed the net with both hands, holding on as best he could, trying to draw it closer to the surface. Someone's hands—they could only have belonged to Jesus—pulled steadily on him until at last the sweet air surrounded his dripping face. Peter let out a shaky laugh, hardly noticing the ache burning itself into every muscle in his arms. "I see it with my own eyes," he gasped, staring at the largest single catch in the history of Galilee, "but I can still hardly believe it."

Andrew strained to secure his end of the net, the silvery mass of flopping, wriggling fish threatening to break the cords that held them captive. The net had frayed in several places, and the brothers began to fear they would lose the whole catch. With great difficulty, they drew the huge load to the surface, but every time they tried to pull it aboard, the boat threatened to capsize.

"James and John, we're ready for you now," Jesus called. "Bring your boat as close as you can and help us."

A new thought struck Peter. "You knew, didn't You?" He stared, amazed, at Jesus. "You knew all along."

By the time the sons of Zebedee had maneuvered close enough to help, Peter and Andrew were nearly exhausted. Jesus slid between them and took hold of the net. "All right, let's pull together, and we can get this done."

It was a struggle, and all five men were soaked by the time the fish were safely in the boats. As long as he lived, Peter would never forget the sight of Jesus sitting there on the rough seat with fish piled up nearly to His knees, hands raised in thanksgiving to heaven and sheer delight wreathing His face.

Even through the veil of Jesus' human flesh, Peter sensed anew the goodness, purity, and holiness of this Man. John had called Him the Lamb of God, and although the rough fisherman didn't yet know just what that meant, he looked down at himself, feeling somehow horribly dirty and almost naked. Every spiteful word, each doubting thought rose up before him in condemnation. Throwing himself down in the bottom of the boat to kneel among the fish, he cried out, "Master, You have to leave—I mean it. Oh, Lord, just go away from me, because I am such a wicked man that I don't even deserve to be here with You!" But even as he begged Jesus to leave, Peter clung to Him with all his strength, unable to bear the thought that He might really go.

"I'll never leave you." Jesus laid a reassuring hand on Peter's bowed head. "Even when you can't see Me, I'll still always be with you."

Andrew cleared his throat. "We probably should be getting back. These boats are awfully low in the water, and besides, we still have to get these fish taken care of. It's past noon, and Sabbath will be here before we know it."

Jesus nodded. "James, John, are you ready to go too?"

"Yes, Master," was John's fervent reply.

"Anywhere, anytime," James added.

Peter wearily picked up the oars. "Here, Andrew, it's your turn."

"Sorry, brother. If I move, the boat might capsize. You're going to have to row us in."

Peter stifled a groan. "Let's go, then."

Jesus took pity on him. "Pull the oars in and secure them. You, too, James. Then unfurl the sails."

Without thinking, Peter began to disagree. "But Master, the prevailing winds are coming from the other direction, and if the sails are unfurled . . ." He caught himself. "Yes, Lord." He opened the sails, knowing all the time that it was the wrong thing to do. But as soon as the sails were fastened in place, the breeze died. A moment later, it began to blow behind them, swelling the sails and pushing the boats forward.

The little crafts were sluggish and heavy, but the strange wind continued until they had both reached the shore. With the short rest, Peter's vigor had returned, and he leaped out into the water, helping Andrew pull the boat up as far as they could, which wasn't very far as heavy as it was. Jesus went back and forth between the two ships, lending a hand until the wooden vessels were safely beached. Wordlessly, the fishermen set to work sorting the immense haul, still seized by a sense of awe but unable to stop grinning like boys.

As soon as the last fish had landed in one of the two big piles on the beach, they turned to wash out their nets for the second time that day. Peter and Andrew finished first, and as they were dragging in the long, cumbersome deep-sea nets, Jesus stepped into the water to meet them.

"Up until now you have caught fish," Jesus said solemnly to them. Their hearts beat faster at His keen, searching look. They sensed that this was somehow an important moment, one that would affect every day of the rest of their lives. Peter and Andrew almost stopped breathing as Jesus went on. "Follow Me, and I will make you fishers of men."

Though not having any idea what duties might be required of a "fisher of men," both brothers understood one thing—knowing everything about them, good and bad, Jesus still wanted them; He had chosen them to have a part in His kingdom. And suddenly, that was all that mattered.

Jesus embraced them, reading their response plainly on their honest faces. As He raised His radiant face to heaven, Peter was startled and puzzled to hear Jesus say, "Adonai, My Father, thank You for these first precious grains of wheat in Your harvest. Thank You for giving them to Me!"

The two brothers walked away from their newfound wealth without a backward glance. As they pointed their footsteps toward the city of Capernaum, Jesus challenged James and John in the same way. Their response to His invitation was even more enthusiastic, and there was much rejoicing as the five men walked away from the shore, leaving the nets, the boats, and the fish behind.

A great shout went up from the cluster of holy angels around them, echoed by an even louder shout of joy in the citadel of heaven. The foundation of twelve stones shook as Tarik joined his voice with ten thousand times ten thousand, and thousands of thousands of angels, all singing in triumph unto God. Not only one, but four, had answered the supreme call, shunning worldly riches for earthly affliction and an everlasting reward.

Tarik still remembered well the day Moses had had to make the same choice, there in the palace of Egypt. All the gold and power in the world beckoned to him, and the temptation to grasp it and use it—only for good, of course—had been almost overwhelming. But a small, quiet voice, which the man had come to know as God's voice, came to him and called him in another direction.

All he could see at the time was poverty, servitude, and an anonymous death. That was probably the hardest to bear—the thought that his name would perish from the earth. Although he did not share his Egyptian mother's beliefs in the multitude of gods, the ka, and the Egyptian view of the afterlife, he still yearned to have his name live on. He could envision the name of Moses carved onto pylons, etched in temples to the One God, his face carved on a stone mountainside. And upon his death, he knew the best embalmers in the land would prepare his body for the glorious tomb that already was under construction. His name, his legacy, could have remained for thousands of years.

Moses could even picture men, thousands of years in the future, traveling for miles to view the things he had built and speaking his name in hushed tones. All that could have been his, and yet he gladly turned away. The way of God, instead of being dreary and sorrowful, was the way of peace. Oh, yes, he had his moments of stumbling—Tarik could remember them all. They were all faithfully recorded for future generations to read, just as Peter's were being inscribed too. But through everything, Moses knew God was with him, and he never regretted his choice.

Pharaohs have come and gone, their palaces and temples buried beneath the relentless sands. But Tarik knew that Moses, safe in the Paradise of God, cared nothing for that kind of fame; he had found eternal value in the crown of life that will never pass away. Another crown of life now awaited Peter, as well, if only he followed the course he had chosen that portentous day.

Predictably, this did not sit very well with the enemy of souls, who immediately plunged into a critical planning session with his top lieutenants. Set and Ares were called, as were Eidolon and Gillulim, the demons newly assigned to oversee the cases of James and John. To their great disgust, Oreb and Zeeb were left out of the summons.

Swiftly, the meeting came to order. "As you can see, our enemy is beginning to gather about Himself a group of men whose every weakness we can exploit. From my careful observations of the crowds, as well as every look and gesture of the enemy, I have prepared a list of names of all those I consider to be likely candidates. They are even now being assigned first-level tempters.

"So far, out of the four who have just been called, I judge Simon to be the weakest, the most productive for our purposes. And he is very close to the enemy, at the center of everything. Set, put his impulsiveness to work. You know what to do. The rest of you, keep on with your regular duties, but be available to assist Set in any way possible. In order for us to reach Jesus," he almost gagged on the name, "Simon must fall."

Chapter 11

Keren rounded the corner of the house, surprised to see her husband's boat left unattended next to two huge piles of fish. Usually by this time, Rimona was selling their share of the fish at the market. Then, too, when she and the girls had been down by the lake after Andrew had returned from his night of fishing, she hadn't seen even one fish then. Where had they all come from?

She stood at the doorway and called inside, "Rimona, what about the fish?"

"Who is it?" Rimona called impatiently. "And what fish?"

"It's Keren, and there are fish all over the place."

"No there aren't; I checked not too long ago."

"Maybe you ought to come out and look again."

Rimona shuffled over and stuck her head out of the door, not looking at Keren or the little girls. Her red, watery eyes widened when she saw all the fish. Suddenly, she burst into tears. "I can't take it anymore," she sobbed. "First there weren't any fish. Now there are fish, but Mother is sick, and I can't help her, and those men go off and leave me with all the work, and it's almost Sabbath, and I just don't know what to *do*!"

Much softened after spending several hours listening to Jesus, Keren reached out and touched the older woman's arm. "I'll take Elhanan his portion of the fish, and carry the rest to the market for you," she impulsively offered. "Just let me leave the baby with you long enough to carry them into town. Jered and Seth can help us."

Still sniffling, Rimona took the baby. "Thank you," she managed through her tears.

Even with the children helping, it was hard work to transport the fish to Elhanan, the wealthy agent of Herod who owned all the fishing rights for that section of Galilee. And after the first load was brought to the market, Keren had to leave Jered there in case any customers came by. When she returned with the second load, nearly all the fish were gone. Jered smiled proudly, showing her the pile of coins in his lap. "And I didn't let them cheat me!"

"That's good, Jered. Your abba will be so proud. Let me take the money you've gotten so far back to your mother, and then I'll bring more fish."

Keren took Abelia, Adalia, and Seth with her to the house. All three of the little ones could scarcely keep their eyes open. When Rimona saw the coins she relaxed for the first time that day, and when Keren offered to bring the doctor, now that they could pay him, she even offered to watch the girls while they napped.

"I'll hurry as fast as I can," Keren told her. "Jered is doing a fine job with the selling, and as soon as I can carry the rest of the fish to him, I will find the doctor and ask him to come."

The rest of the afternoon passed in a haze of sweat, backache, and the sharpening smell of fish. At last Keren carried the last load into the city, squeezing her way through the crowd of visitors who clustered around Jered trying the buy fish before the Sabbath arrived. She had never looked or smelled worse.

Doctor Bakbukiah's wife took one look at the mud-streaked young woman with frizzy hair straggling about her face, before wrinkling her nose and saying, "He can't help you."

"But I have money," Keren protested, jingling the coins in a cloth bag.

"My husband has his reputation to consider. It's out of the question." And she slammed the door in Keren's disbelieving face.

Desperate, the normally shy and quiet woman banged on the door with her fists. "Let me in," she yelled, her mouth up close to the wood planks. "I can pay, and a woman may die if you don't help."

There was no answer, and the door would not yield. Finally Keren had to concede defeat. "Come on, Jered," she said hoarsely to the wide-eyed boy, "let's go home."

All afternoon Rimona had worked frantically, trying to get a few chores done, but most of her time had been taken up dribbling broth and the fever remedy down Batia's unresisting throat. By the time the sun hung low in the western sky, most of the housework was still unfinished, and Batia was no better. When the children woke up, she had sent them outside to play, telling them supper would soon be ready. She had no idea what she was going to fix and fervently hoped that Keren would hurry back.

"Overall, that went well," Igal congratulated himself. "Goiim integrated the doctor's wife flawlessly into our plan, so that all Jesus' efforts to provide them with enough money to seek medical assistance were useless. It was a nice try, but it didn't work."

Hamath hunkered down next to Batia, a fiendish light in his eyes. With his wings trailing behind him in the dust, he looked like an oversize vulture waiting for its meal to perish. "This is more enjoyable than I can say, even though Batia has provided me with so many lovely hours of entertainment that I'll almost miss her when she's gone."

"Look who's coming. Hey, Bozkath, we were just talking about you. Seems like your sinner has had as good a day as ours." Igal smirked.

Bozkath emitted a rasping laugh. "I'll admit I was a little worried when she listened to all that preaching, but she certainly isn't paying any attention to that wimpy Zohar now."

"Just a little word of advice from an old tempter," Hamath said. "When one of your assignments who has previously been downtrodden and mouselike suddenly begins to assert herself—even though things are going well—you should move with extreme caution. The Great Dictator often tries to use such times to His own advantage. Change can be tricky, but keep them ours through it, and they will be ours always."

"Almost always," amended Igal, mindful of a few stinging failures.

Softly Meraioth began to sing. Though the women could not hear the music, Batia seemed to rest a bit easier, and Rimona lost just a fraction of her tension. The song was Meraioth's favorite, his own composition, and its words urged all human beings to go to Jesus, to love and trust in Him.

Nissim never stopped trying to convince Rimona. "Ask Jesus to come. He can heal your mother, and He can heal you too. In your own way, you need healing just as much as she does. Jesus will bring love, happiness, and peace into your home. Don't you want that? It's yours for the asking. Just call for Jesus, and He will be here to help you."

"He's not coming, is he?" Rimona took one look at Keren's face and guessed the truth. Anger flashed through her. "Then I'm just going to go get him myself."

"Here," said Keren wearily, handing her the money. "I brought some olives, cheese, and bread already made so you wouldn't have to cook anything, and I brought some more medicine for your mother. I'm sorry."

"Don't worry about it." Rimona talked fast, her fingers almost a blur as she tried to make herself more presentable. "Stay with Mother and feed the children." Her nose wrinkled as Keren came closer. "I'll try to be back in time for you to bathe before sundown. Here, let me show you what to do for her."

As Rimona started for town, Keren felt rather alone and helpless. "I guess I'd better feed you little ones. Come sit down and eat nicely. Don't forget your prayers." While the children quietly chewed their evening meal, Keren bent over Batia, shocked at how sick she looked. The old woman burned with fever, her eyes sunken into their sockets. She looked nearly dead. Keren shuddered.

"Mama, Adalia just had an accident."

Keren looked up to see her toddler sitting on the floor, a puddle spreading out around her. "Adalia, shame on you," she scolded. "You're a big girl now, and Mama is very busy. Abelia, you're going to have to bring me some water so I can wash her."

"I don't want to."

"Don't you use that tone with me, young lady! You'd better do it—and quickly too." She efficiently stripped off Adalia's wet garment and tossed it outside. Abelia sullenly brought the water and set the jar down with a clunk.

"All right, let's get you cleaned up as fast as we can." She hurried to sponge off the little one and scoop up the mess on the floor. "I'm going to wrap you in your blanket for right now, until I can wash your clothes. Listen carefully. You must not wet on your blanket. Do you understand?" Adalia nodded tearfully, and Keren's face softened. "Good girl."

"Mama, Grandma Batia had an accident too."

Keren stiffened, willing herself to look. "You probably did that on purpose," she muttered, glancing around the one room. "Jered, I need you to be in charge again. Take the other children outside and play for a few minutes while I take care of your grandma. Adalia, you stay here. You're not dressed."

By the time she had removed the soiled clothing and bedding, she was once again drenched in sweat. Now the only thing she had left to do was to bathe the sick woman. Gritting her teeth, she set to work. The odor was overpowering as it blended with the stench of fish, and over and over again, Keren had to swallow hard to keep from gagging.

She took clean bedding from Rimona's mat, rolling Batia carefully to smooth it in place, and covered the nude form with another blanket. "Your daughter can get you dressed!" She walked over to the door. "Children, you may come back in now."

Rimona saw Keren and the children down by the lake almost as soon as she left the city gate headed for home. Wrathfully she descended on them. "What do you think you're doing? You left my sick mother all alone in the house so you could come down here and do the wash right at sundown? It will be Sabbath in just a few more minutes, and what will people think, seeing you down here working?"

Keren stood, holding a sodden bundle of linen. "Do your own wash then. I'm too tired to argue." With a great heave, she tossed the whole mess to Rimona.

Reflexively, Peter's wife caught it, getting liberally soaked in the process. Too late she recognized her mother's bedding and realized what must have happened. Her mouth twisted into a sour shape, not wanting to form the words she knew must be said. "Keren, wait." She gulped hard. "I was wrong. Would you finish these for me so I can check on Mother?" Keren stopped, but made no move to return. "Please?"

It wasn't quite an apology, but Keren held out her hands for the laundry and returned to the water's edge. Her curiosity finally got the better of her as Rimona began to hurry toward the house. "When is the doctor coming?"

"He's not." Rimona didn't turn around. "He said now it's too close to Sabbath, and he would never defile the holy hours with his work." Her slumping posture spoke of unaccustomed defeat.

It's not fair, Keren thought to herself as she sloshed the blankets up and down in the water to rinse them. *Why would Adonai make all these rules that don't make any sense? Why would He let anyone, even someone like Batia, die just because she happened to get sick too close to the Sabbath?* She broke off abruptly, shocked at her own daring. Another thought came to her. *Jesus would come; He isn't like that doctor. Maybe He could even help Batia.*

"What are you doing?" Her husband's voice behind her startled Keren.

She whirled around. "So you've finally decided to join us, have you? Are you sure you're not too busy?"

Andrew was taken aback by the aggressiveness of his normally docile wife. "I . . . we . . ."

"I'll have you know we have been doing a lot of very important things," Peter interrupted haughtily.

Keren turned on him next. "You stay out of this, Simon. I already know exactly what your idea of 'very important things' is. It's leaving a whole mess of fish all over the beach without a thought of who's going to take care of it. It's going off to town while your wife tries to save someone's life, except that she can't because the doctor will never come out just for a couple of women, and there are no men around to make him do it. It's sitting in the square listening to stories while I wash your family's blankets. So don't think you can talk to me about 'important.' Here!" She thrust the dripping wad of bedding into his arms. "Spread it out to dry if you want to sleep tonight." And with that she swept majestically up to the house, leaving a trail of water in her wake.

Peter and Andrew watched her with their mouths hanging open. "What's gotten into her?" Andrew asked in bewilderment.

Peter shook his head. "I don't know."

Andrew shivered. "I'll help you hang that stuff up before we find out."

Rimona said nothing to them when they entered the humble dwelling; she just leveled a long look at the two men before turning back to her mother.

Peter started toward his sleeping place, but stopped short at the sight of the denuded mat. "Hey, what happened to my bed?" Comprehension dawned. "Ah. That must be what Keren was talking about."

Andrew also looked around in confusion. "Where am I supposed to sleep?"

Keren's eyes sparked. "If you have any complaints, talk to your daughter—in the morning. Of course," she went on, "if you can wait another two or three hours, it will be all dry for you, and then you can get it yourself—if you don't mind bearing a burden on the Sabbath!"

"Never mind. We'll just sleep on the boat. Come on, Simon." The two brothers headed toward the shore for another uncomfortable night.

"Can't you stop twisting around?" Andrew's voice broke the stillness.

"Are you kidding? These seats are killing my back."

"Well, I'm just as miserable as you are. And I'm not twisting and turning every few seconds."

Peter managed to lie quietly for a while then said, "You know, I thought I would feel different tonight. I mean, this morning we walked away, just walked away from it all. We were ready to follow Jesus anywhere, into battle, or even into death if need be. And here we are, right back in our boat again. It's like nothing has changed—almost."

Andrew didn't answer for so long Peter thought he was asleep and was surprised when his brother finally spoke. "We really have changed, even if no one else knows it. It doesn't matter what anyone else thinks. It doesn't matter how we feel. We know it, and Jesus knows it, and that's enough."

Peter chuckled. "When you put it that way, I feel so much better." He thought a moment. "Not, of course, that it matters."

"We'd better try to get some sleep. We want to find Jesus as early as we can."

Tarik sat with ageless patience beside his charge, guarding him through the night. Up the slope he could see the dim light that shone from inside

Peter's house as Rimona ceaselessly tended her mother. He knew, too, what Peter had forgotten—that a madman prowled many nights around the humble dwelling, seeking desperately for some relief from the demons that tormented him. He was there now, hiding in the shadows, the man once known as Nahshon, but now known only as a fright and an embarrassment to the people of Capernaum.

Certainly the demons afflicting Nahshon would have brought harm to Peter and his family had they been permitted, but the vigilance of Tarik and the other Guardians was unfailing, and Nahshon was forced to keep his distance. He, too, saw the light inside Peter's house and felt drawn to it. For so long, all had been darkness in his life. More than anything else he longed to somehow walk once more in the light.

A cursory search of the ground revealed no food, but he hadn't really expected any. Many hours later he left, looking back often at the beckoning light. Tarik watched him sadly, pitying his wretched condition. As the man skirted the walls of Capernaum, Tarik looked down at his charge, a smile slowly finding his lips.

Ever a restless sleeper, Peter now tossed and groaned and mumbled. The seat of the boat, with its unnatural slant, obviously caused him much discomfort. Faintly, Tarik heard the strains of his favorite Sabbath hymn coming down, like a benediction, from heaven. He patted Peter on the back as a mother caresses her baby. "Shabbat Shalom," he murmured. "May you have a peaceful Sabbath."

"Where are we going to sit, Abba? Mama always makes sure we get here early."

Peter wiped his bleary eyes and tried again to smooth down his flyaway hair. "We *are* early, Jered. All these people have come to hear Jesus."

"Will I get to hear Him too?"

"Of course. Now go find a place to sit down by Auntie Keren."

"But I want to sit with you." Jered's voice grew plaintive.

"No more arguing. You know you have to sit with the women until you're twelve."

Jered sighed and rolled his eyes. "Yes, Abba. Come on, Seth."

"You'd better be good," Peter called to them. "You don't want me to have to come and take you out of the service."

"You know, he had a good question there. Where *are* we going to sit?" asked Andrew.

"It looks like there might be room for both of us over next to that pillar."

In the synagogue of Capernaum that day, there was certainly no sign of the cool morning outside. So many people had crowded into the building that it felt like afternoon in the sunlight. They kept coming, too, even after every spot was filled, pressing in close around doors and windows, hoping to hear a few words from the visiting Teacher.

Kenan, the town priest, stood at the appointed time to lead the people in prayers. He droned on interminably, his chest swelled with importance to be addressing such a crowd, and his eyes raised boldly to the heavens. When at last he finished, a hum of expectation swept through the people. Surely now he would call on Jesus to speak.

But no, Kenan decided on the spot that such an opportunity as this ought not to be wasted. He drew himself up and took a deep breath. "We are the chosen ones, the true seed of Abraham." Those in front jumped, startled at his sudden shout. "Abraham was our father, as was Isaac and Jacob. As such, we have great moral responsibilities. People are watching us, to see if we uphold the beliefs we claim." He paused dramatically. "Do not talk to idol worshipers! Stay away from those who work iniquity! Avoid the Samaritans! The Lord has forsaken them all!" His voice rose louder and louder.

Gratified to be able to demonstrate his talents as an orator to so many people and thinking wishful thoughts about word of his prowess reaching Jerusalem, the priest outdid himself. He whispered, he shouted, he begged, cajoled, and pleaded. He laughed, he sobbed, he thundered. Upon reaching his cataclysmic finale, he slumped in exhaustion, surveying with pleasure the stunned faces before him.

Hoarsely, he finished by saying, "We have a visiting rabbi among us today. As is our custom, we would like to ask him to say a few words." He smiled smugly, secure in the knowledge that no itinerant preacher could ever hope to match his eloquence.

Chapter 12

Jesus stood and walked to the front of the synagogue. In addition to His customary homespun robes, faded from many washings, He wore a white prayer scarf to cover His head humbly before God. The people, curious, watched every move He made. Many had already heard Him speak the day before, and the rest had listened as Elhanan, local representative of the Tetrarch, had gladly published the story of his little son's healing.

Jesus reached for the sacred scrolls, selecting Isaiah and balancing it reverently in His hands. Before so much as opening it, He bowed His head and said a simple prayer, asking for the guidance of Adonai as the Holy Scriptures were read. Every man, woman, and child sat transfixed as He began to read.

"In the past He humbled the land of Zebulun and the land of Naphtali, but in the future He will honor Galilee of the Gentiles, by the way of the sea, along the Jordan—

The people walking in darkness
  have seen a great light;
on those living in the land of the shadow of death
  a light has dawned."

His mellow voice was so sweet that Peter decided that if he had to listen to Jesus speak every day for the rest of his life, he would never grow tired of it. Judging by the faces of the crowd, most of them felt the same way. A few frowned when some uncomfortable conviction was borne in on them, but none could remain unmoved.

"The poor and needy search for water,
　　but there is none;
　　their tongues are parched with thirst,
But I the LORD will answer them;
　　I, the God of Israel, will not forsake them.
I will make rivers flow on barren heights,
　　and springs within the valleys.

I will turn the desert into pools of water,
　　and the parched ground into springs.
I will put in the desert the cedar and the acacia,
　　the myrtle and the olive.
I will set pines in the wasteland,
　　the fir and the cypress together,
so that people may see and know,
　　may consider and understand,
that the hand of the Lord has done this,
　　that the Holy One of Israel has created it."

Earnestly scanning the upturned faces before Him, Jesus told of the living water which Adonai longed to pour out upon His people. Free to all, rich and poor alike, it satisfied in a way that no earthly treasure ever could. Carefully enunciating each word, He said, "I am the Living Water. If you receive Me, your hearts will no longer thirst after the things of this world."

A whisper of surprise went up but quieted almost immediately. Jesus rolled the scroll nearly to the end, to the same passage He had read the week before in Nazareth. There, the people had been ready to stone Him for applying these words to Himself. But here the reaction was different. Joy overflowed Him as the people received His words:

"The Spirit of the Sovereign LORD is on me,

because the LORD has anointed me
  to preach good news to the poor.
He has sent me to bind up the brokenhearted,
  to proclaim freedom for the captives
  and release for the prisoners,
  to proclaim the year of the LORD's favor."

Jesus closed the scroll. "Today," He said, meeting the gaze of each person there, "this scripture has been fulfilled in your hearing."

Suddenly the familiar prophecy of the promised Messiah took on a new depth of meaning, and as one the congregation erupted spontaneously with a loud "Amen."

I understand now, Peter thought to himself. *The Galileans are so much more independent than the rest of the Jews; it must be that here Jesus is hoping to gather the support He needs to establish His kingdom. And to think, I'm a part of it!* At this happy thought, his mind began to wander from what Jesus was saying to dreams of glory to come. He had no idea what he was missing until a commotion in the back of the synagogue jerked his attention to the present once more.

"Peter, you're not listening again. Pay attention to Jesus. If you would only listen, you would understand that His kingdom is not yet coming in triumph, but in sacrifice. Put aside your pride, your dreams of pomp and grandeur, and listen to what is actually being said. I just want to save you from a great disappointment."

"He isn't listening to you, Tarik." Set's deep-set eyes gleamed. "Only yesterday he was ready to give up everything to follow your Master, and now he's right back where he started, full of his own importance. He is mine."

"He belongs to Jesus now," Tarik answered bravely. "By his own choice he is now a child of the King, even if he still makes many of the same mistakes."

Set opened his mouth to reply when he heard an urgent summons. "Believe me, I'll be back. Oreb, cover me."

He vanished, reappearing in a flash a half mile away, and bowed deeply. "Yes, my lord Lucifer? You called me?"

Chapter 12

"Get up. There's no time to waste," Satan snapped. "They're all listening to Him and falling under His spell. If we don't do something, and I mean now, all of our carefully laid plans could come to nothing. What assets do we have here?"

"Excuse me," Set fawned, "but when you called, I had already distracted Simon so that he didn't hear even one word Jesus was saying."

"Do you want a medal? Pay attention to the big picture for once. We're losing them all!"

Set cringed. "Never mind, then. Apparently there is one man there who is completely ours, to the point of being indwelt. I believe his name is Nahshon, but everyone calls him the Madman of Capernaum."

"Go bring him here. Have whoever is in him break up the service and distract the people from what they are hearing. Make sure the only thing they remember is the Madman. Quickly now!"

They all heard him coming. He was screaming and howling like a wild animal. "It's the Madman," they whispered. As he got closer, those sitting outside the synagogue took only one brief look at the foaming saliva running down his beard, jagged, still-bleeding cuts all over his naked body, and the glassy eyes staring terribly at them, before they turned and ran.

Oblivious to the people scattering before him, he ran up the steps leading into the place of worship to stand, dripping and growling, in the doorway. Those inside froze, afraid if they moved that he would turn on them and tear them to bits. Mothers closed their eyes and hid the children's faces in their laps, horrified at the sight.

"It's all right." Jesus calmly held up His hands. "There is nothing to fear."

Right then, the evil spirits that were driving the Madman seemed to suddenly reconsider the strength of their position; they turned to flee. But the power from those upraised hands held them motionless. They writhed in torment, unable to free themselves from the power of His hands. The Madman's features and limbs twitched and contorted with them.

Finally, in desperation, one of the spirits screamed out, "What are You going to do with us, Jesus of Nazareth? Are You here to destroy us? I know who You are—the Holy One of God!"

"Be quiet!" Jesus' voice was stern and left no room for argument. "Just come out of him!"

The man shook and shivered like a palm tree in a gale, a frightful scream issuing from his mouth. Abruptly, he fell to the stone floor, his head thudding dully against the pavement, and lay senseless. Peter craned his neck for a better view as Jesus walked to the back of the room, bent over the nude man, and covered him with His own cloak.

On many occasions, Set had indwelt the humans who served him, but never before had he been cast out. The evil spirit who usually dwelt in the man cowered, whimpering, down by his victim's feet, leaving Set alone to face Jesus.

Not since the great fall from heaven had he been so close to the One who had created him. He had thought he was ready, but nothing could have prepared him for the power that enveloped him, a power much greater than his own. He felt himself being squeezed out of the man before Jesus ever said a word—and screamed in defiance. If he couldn't master Jesus, he could at least create some problems for Him.

Understanding his purpose, Jesus commanded him to be quiet, and although Set struggled with all that was within him, he had no choice but to obey. Then came a stunning pressure, and he found himself blinking dizzily on a hillside some distance away. Next to him, the little demon who had made his home in Nahshon sobbed pitifully. Set turned from him in disgust. Obviously he had reached the stage where he was uncomfortable, almost panicky, if he couldn't find a human to inhabit.

After about an hour, when his arms and legs had stopped trembling, Set flew back down to the city, landing heavily by Peter's house. Any other time, Oreb and Zeeb would have laughed at him, trying to take advantage of his temporary weakness, but they were just sitting silently outside with Bozkath, Hamath, and the others. All of them looked very dejected.

"What happened here? Why aren't you working?" Then his ears belatedly told him what his numbed senses had not. Set gasped. "He's in there?"

They nodded mutely. Overwhelmed, Set sat down with them, resting his aching head in his hands. "There's nothing we can do then. Nothing at all. Just wait until He leaves." He groaned. "What a terrible, terrible day!"

Gently Jesus lifted the man to his feet and turned to the crowd. A smile split His face. "I have someone I want you to meet. People of Capernaum, this is Nahshon. Nahshon, your family is right over there."

Nahshon turned just as a weeping woman threw herself into his arms, covering his battered face with kisses. "Serah, is it really you? You're so beautiful! I thought I'd never be with you again." He looked at Jesus, tears on his cheeks. "Master, I don't know how to thank You enough. I've wanted for so long to be saved, but I'd almost given up." He looked all around him, holding out his arms as if to embrace the world. "Look," he exclaimed in amazement, "I am in the light!"

Jesus beamed at him. "I *am* the Light."

"What is going on here?" Peter and Andrew looked at each other in amazement. "Jesus gives orders even to evil spirits, and they obey Him!"

Andrew looked over to where Jesus embraced the man He had just healed. "Don't you wish we had that kind of power? And the way He talked—He had such presence, such authority. Not like the scribes." He looked over at a man who stood alone in the front of the synagogue, a black scowl on his face. The priest kicked bitterly at an imaginary fleck of dust, all that was left of his hope for greatness. Jerusalem would hear of this day, of that he was sure, but somehow he didn't think his name would find glorious mention in the telling. Now his throat hurt, and it was all for nothing.

Peter could look only at Jesus. "We'd better get over there where the action is." He was half way to his feet when he heard Jesus calling for attention.

"Wait a minute, everyone, we need to have the benediction." Jesus readjusted His prayer scarf. With one hand on Nahshon's head and the other reaching trustingly toward the Father, Jesus asked for a blessing on each person there, especially Nahshon as he started his new life apart from the demon that had imprisoned him for so long. When He finished, scarcely a dry eye remained.

In the confusion that followed, with everyone eager to talk to Nahshon and ask him questions, Jesus quietly slipped outside. More familiar with His methods by now, Peter and Andrew were waiting for Him.

Peter stepped forward, arms outstretched. "That was wonderful! Where are we going now?"

"As soon as Keren and the children get here, we are going to your house."

"My house?" Peter forced a welcoming smile onto his face, frantically catching Andrew's eye the moment Jesus turned His head. "I mean, that will be nice."

"Here they are now." Jesus helped the frazzled Keren down the steps, the baby making the descent awkward. The other four children followed like lambs. "We need to go right now."

He led the way, with Peter and Andrew making dire faces at each other as they walked behind Him. Neither thought to help Keren with their children, but she came almost as fast as they did, so eager was she to see what was going to happen. Seth broke away from her, running as fast as his short legs could go, to catch Jesus by the hand. "You came," he said shyly.

"Of course I did," Jesus told him. They came to the worn, shabby little house, where Jesus climbed the stone step with Seth still holding tight to His hand, and knocked on the door. "Who is it?" The voice that came from inside was tearful and without hope.

"Rimona, this is Jesus. I came to see you and your mother."

"I didn't ask for You," she said crossly. "Go away!"

Peter thought that he would die of humiliation at any moment. He was just about to take Jesus by the arm and lead Him away when Jesus said, "Someone asked Me to be here." He winked at Seth. "May I have a cup of water?"

With that simple request he had gained an entrance into many a home and heart. Rimona was no more immune than the rest. "I suppose I can at least do that much," she said grudgingly, leaving her mother's side to tug at the heavy door.

The instant that Jesus stepped in, Rimona could feel something different. In spite of the high window in the stone wall, the air had been stifling all morning until she thought she would scream with the closeness of it. She had felt so burdened with the weight of trying to save her mother that she could hardly stand. All that changed in the blink of an eye. Suddenly, the air seemed pure and fresh, and a tiny seed of hope unfolded in her heart.

Chapter 12

"Are you ready, Nissim?" Meraioth asked, drawing his sword and standing just outside the house where Batia had nearly lost the struggle for life.

Nissim drew his sword, as well. "I have been ready for this my whole life!"

"It will be like old times. You and me, side by side with Michael, battling the forces of evil."

"And winning too. Today's battle will certainly go in our favor."

"Let us pray to the Father of all that it does."

Inside the house, the sounds of wild partying died away to a faint scrabbling. "He's coming," Igal said softly.

"Here? He can't come here—this place is ours! I thought I told you to make sure she didn't ask for Him." Hamath was furious.

"I did. I watched her every second, and I would swear on my left wing that the thought never crossed her mind. Or that if it did, she rejected it. She hates Him, you know. There must be some other explanation."

"Well, I can guarantee it wasn't Batia; she's been unconscious."

"He's outside! What are we going to do?" Igal's courage evaporated, and his interior support structure turned to water.

Hamath's eyes glowed in the dim light. "We fight!"

"But she's letting Him in," Igal wailed, almost dropping his sword.

Hamath held his sword out, sighting along its length. Like all the demonic weapons, it shone like obsidian and appeared at first glance to be perfectly straight. But right at the base there was one inconsistency that left the rest of the shaft ever so slightly skewed, making an already-dangerous weapon even more deadly. "Don't be a coward. We have owned these women, their grandmothers, too, for all their lives, and . . ."

Nissim and Meraioth burst into the room, one on either side of Gabriel, shining with the light of heaven. Igal and Hamath covered their eyes, trying not to scream. They stumbled backward through the wall, not stopping until they were a safe distance from that brilliant, blinding light.

"I think we lost this one," Igal commented.

"Do you really think so?" Hamath oozed with sarcasm. "Maybe we just won—backwards."

"At least Set lost too."

Hamath shook his head. "Quit looking on the bright side," he muttered glumly. "We're not supposed to do that."

Rimona busied herself finding a cup, hastily wiping her eyes while her back was turned. She picked up the water jug, surreptitiously inspecting the inside for dirt or leaves. As she turned it up to pour, only a few drops dripped out—just enough to wet the bottom of the cup. She ducked her head down to hide the fresh tears that welled up.

"I'm sorry, it will take just a minute to run out and get some more. Please sit down and take Your ease. I'm sure Simon will keep You occupied until I get back." She started to squeeze past the rest of the family standing just inside the door and watching with fascination.

Jesus' voice stopped her. "Rimona, I didn't actually come here for water."

Slowly she turned around, meeting His eyes for the first time. "Of course I was going to offer You food too."

Jesus removed the water jug from her arms. "I didn't come here for food, either. Tell me about your mother."

Rimona darted a glance at the mat upon which her mother lay. The old woman's lips and hands were turning purple; her breathing had become almost indiscernible. "She's going to die." Peter's wife began to sob. "I can't lose her; she's the only one who ever loved me."

"You don't have to lose her, you know." Jesus put his arm around Rimona's shoulders and drew her to stand next to the mat where Batia lay. "All things are possible for those who believe."

The anguished woman looked up at Him. "But I haven't believed in You. In fact," she averted her eyes from His searching gaze, "I even hated You. Until now, that is."

"Mama." A small boy tugged insistently at her robe. "Jesus can make Grandma well. I know He can."

"Oh, Sethie, it's just not that simple."

"Yes it is, Mama. In the synagogue today Jesus made that bad man well right in front of everybody. He can help Grandma, too, if you ask Him."

Rimona nodded, submitting at last. "Please," she said softly to Jesus, not knowing what He would do, but knowing somehow that He would help her.

Jesus knelt beside the dying woman and took her hand. At His touch, a healthy radiance flooded the dark fingertips, spreading up her arm and across her body. "Batia, wake up."

She opened her eyes and saw Jesus. "Who are You?" Her gaze traveled the room. "Why is everyone looking at me?" She saw her daughter and visibly started. "Rimona, what happened to you? You look terrible!" she exclaimed. Her eyes finally came to rest on Peter and Andrew. Peter winced and held his breath, anticipating the outburst he knew would come. But suddenly Batia became painfully aware of her recumbent position in the presence of a guest. Embarrassed, she exclaimed, "What am I doing lying here while there's company? There you are, Simon, and just in time to help me up so I can serve our Guest something to eat." She laughed, an unfamiliar, but not unpleasant sound. "Come to think of it, I'm hungry too."

Laughing and crying at once, Rimona dropped to her knees and hugged her mother tightly. "Mother, our Guest is Jesus. He's the One who made you well."

"Was I sick? I'm sorry, but I don't remember." She saw the warm smile on Jesus' face and felt unfamiliar gratitude welling in her heart. "Well, thank You, I appreciate it all the same. Come, Rimona, time's wasting, and we're not getting fed any faster. Simon, I asked you to help me up."

Peter shut his mouth with a snap and hurried to do as he was bidden. He bent over and picked up the old lady, setting her on her feet. "There you are, Batia."

"What a good boy!" She patted his arm. "So strong! Please, call me Mother. We're family, after all." Batia deftly pulled her untidy hair back and fastened it, oblivious to the shock on every face except that of Jesus.

Rimona turned to Keren. "Do we still have any of the food left from yesterday?"

Keren nodded. "There's plenty. I'll help you get it."

Batia insisted on serving Jesus with her own hands before sitting down herself to eat. She was so hungry, and at the same time so desperate to talk more with Jesus that she ignored every convention she had ever been taught forbidding men and women to eat together. Jesus didn't seem to mind, gladly answering the questions she asked Him, one after another.

Seth took the place of honor in Jesus' lap, wanting to be as close as he could to his new Friend. Once, while Batia was chewing and unable to speak, he whispered to Jesus, "Thank You."

Jesus leaned in close, whispering back, "You're welcome. I did hear you, you know."

Seth smiled up at Him, cheeks dimpling. "I know."

At the end of the meal Jesus thanked Batia for her graciousness and stood. "You're not leaving already, are You?" Peter asked Him.

"Not yet," Jesus replied, scooping up Seth and handing him to his father. He leaned down and picked up the baby where she lay sucking on her toes. "Here, Andrew. Now you two take your children out and spend some time getting to know them. It will be good for all of you. I have some things to discuss with these dear women. All right, the rest of you children, you go for a walk, too, and I'll tell you a story later."

"How far do you want us to go?" Andrew was ever practical.

"Not far. The only reason no one has come here yet is that they are afraid the priest may make trouble if they ask for healing on Sabbath. You may be sure that as soon as the sun goes down many will find their way to your house. We have a great deal to discuss before that happens."

Peter called back from the step, "Does that mean You need to talk to us too?"

Jesus just smiled and leaned heavily on the door to push it shut.

Chapter 13

"What do you do with a baby, anyway?" Andrew held his infant daughter in stiff, awkward arms.

"I don't know. I've never done anything with them. Ever!" Peter shuddered. "You know I don't do women's work."

"No one ever told me how this was supposed to be done," Andrew fretted. "Come on, children, let's go for a walk."

Jered jumped up and down. "Oh, good! Abba and Uncle are taking us for a walk!"

"I was just going to say the same thing," Abelia informed her cousin, "except that when I said *Abba* I would have meant *my* abba, and when I said *Uncle,* I would have meant *your* abba."

"That's not how it goes," Jered pouted.

"Does too."

"Does not!"

"Abba, tell him that—"

"Children! Enough of this! I don't know how your mothers do this all day. Let's go—and no more arguing." Peter turned to Andrew. "Did you hear anything about what happened to Jesus in Nazareth?"

Andrew nodded. "Someone mentioned it to me yesterday, but we were all so busy I didn't have a chance to ask Him about it. What did you hear?"

"Probably the same thing you did. After He got up and read in the synagogue, just like He did here, the people started shouting to kill Him."

"I heard that they dragged Him all the way to those steep cliffs to throw Him over, but He just disappeared. Nobody knew where He went."

Peter shook his head. "I guess they were saying that Jesus' followers hid Him somehow in the middle of the crowd and helped Him escape, but that would have been you and me, and we weren't there. Not even close."

"James and John were here the whole time too. I don't know if it's true or not, but apparently some of their own people were accidentally pushed over the edge and died. Can you imagine it? I mean, this is Jesus' own town we're talking about here!"

"Jered! Not so far ahead! You bring your brother back here right now! I think Jesus needs a new home town."

"You're right—like Capernaum. Girls, stop it! I saw that! If I see you pull your sister's hair once more, there will be trouble. I mean it."

Just then, Atalia began to wail. "When do you think we can take her back to her mother?" Peter asked. "You're carrying her all wrong, you know. The women jiggle the babies somehow."

"Here," Andrew stopped walking and thrust the squalling babe at Peter. "If you think you can do so much better, you're certainly welcome to try."

Peter held up his hands in mock dismay. "I didn't mean it. You're doing fine. Just fine. Hold her closer, though; I don't think she likes being dangled like that."

Gingerly Andrew held Atalia upright against his chest. The baby reached up and filled both tiny fists with handfuls of hair, her cries fading away with a sobbing little sigh. Andrew let out a long breath. "That's better; she's stopped crying." He held the warm baby closer, putting one arm protectively around the little girl.

"Not only that, she's asleep. What did I tell you?" Peter looked pleased with himself. "Say, where is everyone?"

Just then a dreadful scream rent the stillness. Shriek followed shriek, interspersed with a vicious growling. Both men raced toward the sound, spurred on by panic. Peter, unburdened by a baby, reached the scene first; Andrew pounded up just behind him. Abelia lay still on the ground, dirt and twigs tangled in her curls. Jered stood over her, both hands raised. Adalia and Seth just watched, hands clamped over their mouths, eyes wide with shock.

Andrew rushed forward, picking up Abelia with his one free arm. "Honey, are you all right? Did that boy push you?" He looked sternly at Jered.

Abelia opened her eyes and smiled up at him. "Silly Abba, of course not. We were just playing."

"What were you playing?"

"Couldn't you tell?" Abelia giggled. "We were playing Madman. I was the Madman. Jered was pretending to heal me."

Andrew slumped in relief. "So you're sure you're all right, then? Next time warn us before you do something like that. We were scared to death. I was worried that my little girl was hurt."

All the commotion had awakened Atalia, but instead of crying she arched back to where she could see her abba's face. Her fingers crept up through his tickly beard and into his mouth. "Gack!" Andrew said, spitting them out. She gave him a big smile that featured her one tooth before breaking into a hiccupping laugh. Andrew was so surprised that he had to sit down before his legs gave out. "Does she always do this?"

Abelia cleared her throat importantly. "Sometimes, yes. Sometimes she just smiles. But sometimes she cries too. It all depends on what kind of mood she is in. That's what Mama says."

Adalia leaned close to his ear and confided, "Bee-bee cwy tum-time. Me make waf. Wook." She tickled the bottoms of Atalia's feet, and the baby let out a fresh laugh.

"Abelia, did you understand what she just said?"

"Of course, Abba." She looked at him to see whether he was deficient. "She said that the baby cries sometimes, but she can make her laugh. She can too."

Andrew looked up at Peter. "I had no idea they were this smart. Why, Abelia is just like a little adult. We're never with our children, so we haven't realized how clever and funny they really are."

"Don't forget imaginative," Peter said. "That was some play they put on. But you're right. Maybe we should do this again once in a while. It hasn't been as bad as I expected."

Andrew smiled down at his girls with the fleeting thought that he might have missed out on something by not being a bigger part of their lives. "I guess we should start heading back so we can hear when Jesus calls us." With some reluctance, he staggered to his feet and headed for home.

Jesus walked forward to meet them. "You're just in time." Behind Him, the three women stood with their arms around each other, traces of tears on their faces. The children ran to them, all talking at once about the things they had seen and done with their abbas. Andrew's arms tingled with relief as he handed Atalia back to his wife.

"How did she do?" Keren was a little concerned.

"Fine, fine," Andrew said nonchalantly. "She cried a bit, but it was nothing I couldn't handle."

Keren's eyebrows twitched up a little, but she kept most of the doubt from her face. "And the girls?"

"Oh, they were wonderful! At one point I did think Abelia had been hurt, but it turned out she was just playing. I can't believe how intelligent she is—I wish there was some way we could have her educated like a boy. I bet she would be smarter than any of them. And Adalia is so cute; she was trying to help when Atalia was crying."

Keren listened to the gush of enthusiastic praise for the daughters she had always feared were unwanted, and her heart warmed. *I can't believe how different he is,* she thought.

Jesus put his hand on Peter's shoulder, interrupting a vivid description of Jered's cleverness and Seth's winning charm. "Let's go; there isn't much time left."

They sat nearby in a grassy spot under a tree. Peter picked a blade of grass and twisted it in his fingers. "I can't believe how different the women are. What did You say to them, anyway? You must have really given it to them."

Jesus chuckled. "Ah, Peter, always so eager to know someone else's business. You need to be thinking about what I have to say to you. Do you remember that story I have mentioned several times about the man who had a plank stuck in his eye and who tried to take the speck out of his brother's eye? You should always remember it."

"What do You mean?" Peter wasn't sure what to make of the strange remark.

Chapter 13

"Let me tell both of you men something you may not have realized." Jesus was very tactful. When it came to their wives, there was absolutely nothing that the brothers understood. "The wife sets the tone for the family. She is the one the children look to for clues as to how they should feel. She is the one who rises early in the morning to meet the needs of the family, often continuing to work until long after dark. Solomon spoke of this in his description of the virtuous wife."

Peter and Andrew nodded, waiting expectantly for Jesus to continue. "The husband sets the tone for the wife." Just in case they missed it the first time, he repeated it again more slowly. "The husband sets the tone for the wife." Peter and Andrew looked completely baffled. "Your kind words, compliments, little gestures of affection, and help with the burdens they carry every day will set a new tone in your wives, one that you will like much better than what you've known in the past. Gratitude to Adonai is important, and after that, gratitude to those who are kind to us, even for something simple like cooking or cleaning."

The brothers were stunned at this revolutionary notion. Imagine, thanking their wives for something they were supposed to do as part of their duties! The thought had never occurred to them. Peter asked, "What about those 'gestures of affection'?"

"I remember how it was in the beginning," Jesus said. "I can still see the look on Adam's face the first time I brought Eve to him and placed her hand in his. Even though I had to explain some basic functions to them, they knew already that they were to love and care for each other. It was a delight to them, not a chore.

"Sin has changed many things, but not a woman's need for love and, yes, affection, from her husband. And whether you know it yet or not"—of course, they didn't—"you need that same love from your wives."

Peter made a face like a little boy in school. "How do we do that? It just seems so, so . . ."

"Odd?" Andrew suggested.

"*Different*, I was going to say. Rimona and I have been married for nine years now, and I've never done anything like that."

Fear crept over Andrew's face. "Suppose You're right, and these are all things we should be doing. What if we try, and our wives don't want us to?"

"Trust Me; they do." Jesus radiated glad assurance. "I've already talked to them, but even if I hadn't, it's how I made them. They need you, and they very much want your love. If you will share it with them freely, you'll have the chance to make a new start. You can have a home that angels love to visit."

"I have one more question," Peter spoke up. "You haven't said anything more about helping them with their work. That doesn't seem quite fair. We don't expect them to help with our work, and they shouldn't expect us to help them with theirs."

"Peter, Peter, haven't I taught you anything yet?" Jesus gently chided. "Marriage is not about how little you can do or trying to be sure that a line is drawn exactly halfway down the middle of the labor. Marriage is supposed to teach you something of the closeness you are to have with Adonai, the same closeness I have with My Father. It's about giving everything you can, your whole life, soul, and strength, without worrying what you'll get back in return. When the love of the Father is in you, you'll be generous with your love and with your time."

"Of course there will still be problems from time to time. This is a sinful world, and after a while it will be tempting to fall back into your old habits. You must guard carefully against this. Always remember to love your wives as you love yourselves, and your home can become a place of sublime joy and happiness."

"That sounds like an awful lot to work on," Peter said doubtfully. "I hope we can do it all."

Jesus stood and held out His hands to pull Peter and Andrew to their feet. "It gets easier with practice, and you can start now. Besides, I'll always help you when you need it." He smiled. "Come, your wives are waiting for you."

Peter and Andrew came to a stop, suddenly nervous. "Maybe we can go home later. You said people would be looking for You, and it's almost time."

"You're right. There's not a minute to spare." Jesus took them by the arms and led them briskly down the hill. As Rimona and Keren came out of the house and stood shyly waiting for them, Jesus stopped them for a moment. "There is just one more thing. Remember to fix your door."

Tarik and Nadiv watched through a mist of joyful tears as their Lord and Master took Rimona and Keren, leading them forward to meet their husbands. Jesus took Rimona's hands, placing them in Peter's. Then He had Keren and Andrew join hands. Placing His own hands over the clasped hands of each couple, He pronounced a beautiful blessing as the last rays of the Sabbath sun washed over them.

"Peter and Rimona, Andrew and Keren, I have called you to do a special work for Me, and each of you has your own part to carry out. Love and care for each other with the love that flows from the throne of Adonai. Together you will be better able to resist the enticements of the evil one. Together you will be able to walk more faithfully in the paths of righteousness, for if you stumble, each may hold the other up. Together you will receive a great reward for your work and make your home a foretaste of heaven. Begin anew, and Adonai will daily shine His face upon you."

Cheers burst forth from the watching angels as Peter and Andrew, spellbound by the look in the eyes of their wives, slowly, hesitantly, bent and kissed them. Even more shocking to the men was the fact that their wives kissed them back. Tarik couldn't help laughing when Jesus quietly repossessed His hands and tiptoed silently away. The newly besotted men didn't even notice.

The stream of sufferers had already begun to flow out of the village as the last tiny wedge of sun disappeared over the western hills. Tarik called greetings to many of his dear friends who walked beside their charges who were coming to see Jesus. Some of the Guardians bore the full weight of their feeble humans; they wouldn't have made it otherwise. Jesus had time for each one, to speak a word of encouragement, to touch them and banish their maladies, to show them living proof of the love of the Father. How the angels rejoiced to be in His presence! How the poor mortals loved Him and reached out to Him.

Nothing evil could long abide so close to that outpouring of power, and Peter's humble home became the center of a heavenly oasis, a bustling hub of celestial activity. Satan himself trembled, for the very foundation of his realm was under heavy attack.

Not until the last person had departed during the small hours of the night, singing praises for his healing, did Jesus seek His bed. A few hours later, as was His custom, He rose before sunrise and went, alone, to pray.

"Simon, are you still awake?"

Her whisper startled him just as he was almost drifting off to sleep. "Mm . . . hmm . . ." Peter drew Rimona closer, stroking her soft, dark hair with one rough hand.

She nestled her head into his shoulder. "Today has been the happiest day I've ever had. First with Mother being healed, and now," she blushed in the darkness, "everything that has happened with us. Jesus is just what our family needed."

Peter roused himself enough to ask, "What did Jesus tell you, anyway?"

"We talked for a long time. I'll never forget one of the things He said. He told us, 'I know every burden you have to carry. I understand each one of your cares, your discouragements. Adonai draws very near to you whenever you feel the most alone, and He looks down in tender pity upon your tears.

" 'He has given you a vital work to do, that of raising your children to know Him. In many ways your calling is even more difficult than that of your husband. Adonai knows all that has happened and each trial you will face. He will help you and reward your faithful efforts, for you are everything to Him.' "

Rimona raised her head to see why Peter made no comment. The steady rise and fall of his chest gave him away. "My, aren't you the tired one," she whispered, kissing him on the corner of the mouth. A smile of tender amusement spread over her face as she laid her head back down against her sleeping husband and closed her eyes.

Chapter 14

"Simon, you have to get up. They're here." Batia gave Peter a stern shake.

Peter tried to open his eyes. "What are you talking about? It's not time to get up yet. Go back to bed, you . . . uh . . ." Just in time he remembered that he was not talking to the spiteful woman of before, " . . . dear Mother."

"Where is Jesus? They are here to see Him, and I don't know what to tell them."

Groggily Peter tried to sit up, but an unaccustomed weight held him down. Ever so gently he detached his wife's clinging arms and slid away from her. Recalling what Jesus had said about gestures of affection, he kissed her cheek before he stood. She might not have been aware of it, but for some reason he felt better about leaving that way.

Peter took perverse pleasure in waking his brother, knowing he had slept little more than himself. Still, he was careful not to disturb Keren or the girls, who had piled themselves like puppies all over their parents. With minimal complaining, Andrew agreed to accompany Peter in search of Jesus.

Already the line of people waiting for Jesus had grown a great deal; their little house was nearly engulfed, and the crowd was growing every minute. "Where is Jesus? We want Jesus," went up the cry as Peter shuffled out the door, scratching his head and smoothing his robe.

Enjoying his new role as an official agent of the New Kingdom, Peter held up his hand for silence and addressed the swelling crowd. "Don't worry, everyone. We'll get Jesus for you. Just wait here, and we'll be right back." As he eased his way through the people, he scanned the faces around him for anything suspicious, anyone that might constitute a threat. After all, he reasoned, there was no reason why he couldn't be a fisher of men and still lead the palace security detail too. Almost to his disappointment, he didn't see anyone who needed to be questioned.

Peter and Andrew found Jesus some distance outside the city wall among some trees, still bowed in prayer. Peter coughed to announce their presence. "Master, there are a lot of people waiting for You back at my house. What shall I tell them?"

Jesus jumped to His feet, seemingly full of boundless energy in spite of His lack of sleep. "That's all right; I'll tell them Myself. Come on!" He set off at a brisk pace.

Peter and Andrew followed more slowly. "How does He do that?" Andrew asked softly. "How does He stay up half the night, get up an hour or two later to pray, and still look so cheerful?"

"I have no idea." Peter shook his head. "If we watch Him, though, we may eventually figure it out."

By the time they reached the house, James and John had arrived and were helping the people form an organized line with those who were the sickest at its head. Rimona and Keren went from one person to the next with a pitcher of water, offering refreshment under Batia's supervision. When the crowd saw Jesus, the people started to rush forward, but Jesus stopped them.

"Don't worry; there's time enough for everyone. Let's begin our day with prayer." He prayed a short but earnest prayer, asking Adonai's blessing on each person who had come. At its close He held out His arms to the first person in line, a mother holding a crippled child. "Hello, little one." He carefully lifted the small boy. "Would you like to run and play again?"

On full alert, Peter marched up and down, watching for the first sign of danger. He didn't expect trouble right here at his own house, but it never hurt to be careful. Anyway, it was good practice in case Jesus ever visited Judea.

Glad shouts filled the air, as they always did when Jesus was around. Out of the corner of his eye, Peter caught a flash of movement in some bushes just up the hill. He watched closely. There it was again. Without taking his eyes off the spot, he walked over to his brother. "Andrew, come right now. Something is in those bushes, and I don't think it's an animal."

Andrew and Peter approached stealthily, each gripping the handle of the knife that hung at his waist. Peter motioned for Andrew to take one side while he tiptoed carefully up the other. In perfect coordination they leaped into the bushes, a fearsome yell burning their throats.

A few people on the edge of the crowd saw them backing away the next instant, hands slack at their sides, and a look of abject terror on their faces as they turned to run. "What are they saying?" several people asked.

"I don't know," another said with a shrug. "I couldn't quite make it out; they were shouting something about the sea."

"Leprosy! Leprosy!" One woman screamed the warning again and again. All who heard her craned their necks to see.

Limping down from the bushes, Hezron, the leper, paid no heed to the commotion he had created. Forgotten were all the rules of conduct concerning his disease. No cry of "Unclean!" came from his ulcerated lips. No thought of the proper distance he was to keep from all human habitation crossed his mind. His eyes gleamed brightly in his ruined face, and there was room in his heart for only one overwhelming desire. He had to see Jesus.

His eyes fixed on Jesus' face, Hezron came on steadily, heedless of any obstacle in his path. The crowd parted miraculously before him as the people scattered indiscriminately, covering their noses against the overpowering odor of decay. Most stopped to watch once they reached a safe distance; overwhelming curiosity warred with their fear and disgust—and curiosity won.

Jesus had not moved. He continued sitting on the stone step in front of Peter's door, the same welcoming smile on His face. As He watched the people, a hint of amusement warmed His eyes at the humorous similarity to the parting of the Red Sea.

Hezron came near and knelt on the ground. "Lord," he murmured, his eyes lifted trustingly to Jesus, "I know that if You want to, You can make me clean again."

Jesus stood then and walked toward him. The look of love on His face did not flicker as He took in the rotted face, missing one ear and most of the nose. Hezron did not try to hide the dreadful condition of his hands and arms, although one leg was wrapped to protect the infected sores from the dirt as he walked. Pitiful though he was, he threw himself on the hope of divine love.

Jesus had tears in His eyes as He reached out and touched the grey, scaly skin of the leper. "Of course I want to. Go your way and be healed."

The decayed flesh under Jesus' hand took on a natural color, a smooth covering of skin appearing before the eyes of the crowd. In the blink of an eye, Hezron, the man whom many years before they had given up as dead while he still lived, stood before them once more in the bloom of perfect health.

As the exclamations of the people finally penetrated Hezron's consciousness, he looked around in joyful bewilderment. He gazed down at his arms in wonder, stroking the new skin to be sure his eyes did not deceive him. His hands moved up to his face, and when he felt the new nose that had appeared so suddenly, he burst into tears and fell at Jesus' feet in worship.

Jesus raised him to his feet and held him until the sobs subsided. Not an eye was dry by the time Jesus took the man aside and gave him some very practical instructions. "Hezron, it is very important that you follow My directions exactly." His tone was solemn. "The first thing is that before you do anything else, go straight to the synagogue and show yourself to the priest so he can declare you clean. Make the sacrifice as the Law of Moses requires, *but do not under any circumstances tell them who healed you.*"

Peter, ashamed of his momentary cowardice, eased his way back toward Jesus, trying to pretend he had been there all along. As Hezron hurried off to see the priest, jumping for joy and trailing the loosening bandage from his healed foot, Peter asked, "Why did You tell him not to tell anyone? I can see why You wouldn't want him to tell the priest beforehand; I saw how he looked at You during the services. But why not after the priest declares Hezron to be clean? It doesn't make sense."

But the crowd had closed in again, and not until the quiet of the evening did Jesus have a chance to explain. He sat with Peter and his family inside the house, eating the delicious pottage Batia had prepared. James and John were there, too, much to the disgust of their father.

"So," Peter asked again, "now can You explain what You told Hezron earlier? He didn't follow Your directions, by the way. I heard that as soon as he was pronounced clean that he started telling everyone in sight that You had healed him."

"I know." Jesus sighed. "But I still had to try. You were right as to why I told him not to tell the priest ahead of time. I know Kenan and the other Pharisees are against Me, and I didn't want their prejudices to affect Hezron. As to the rest, his choices mean that our stay here will be cut short, at least this time."

"Why?" Peter was quick to ask.

"You mean we're going to have to leave?" Andrew was startled.

Jesus chuckled. "I wasn't sent just to Capernaum, you know. I need to go and preach in many other cities, as well." He could tell from the looks on their faces that this was a genuine revelation to them. "Now that the Pharisees are so angry, we'll have to leave here very soon. I was trying to avoid that by asking Hezron to keep silent, though I knew it would be very hard for him."

Peter stared blankly as Jesus reached down and picked up a small stone Seth had left on the floor. Jesus weighed it in His hand, holding it up to show them. "Do you see how tiny this stone is?" They all nodded. "What happens if you throw it into the sea?"

"It sinks," Peter guessed. Jesus shook His head.

"It splashes?" Andrew sounded unsure. Jesus shook His head again.

John bit his lip, concentrating. "It might make a little ripple in the water."

"That's right," Jesus exclaimed. "If you throw a stone this size into the water, the ripples immediately begin to spread. Even after you have walked away and have forgotten about ever throwing this stone, the ripples keep spreading and spreading, farther than you can see or know.

"Hezron's choice today will have effects he could not have foreseen. He is the first leper set free from the disease since the days of Elisha the prophet. Suddenly there is hope for those who had no hope. That doesn't sound too bad on the surface, but what would happen to the work I am carrying out if hundreds of lepers start crowding in?"

A picture flashed into Peter's mind of many people running, screaming, and shouting, trampling on each other in their haste to get away from Jesus and the hordes of lepers descending on Him. "I can see that could cause problems," he said slowly. Then his face brightened. "But all You would have to do is make all of them well, and everything would be fine again."

Jesus sadly shook His head. "It's not that simple. It does no good to heal the body and not the heart. Many who came would desire only physical healing, and if I gave it to them, they would waste their new-found health on living, once again, for self. Some would even become dangerous criminals."

Peter's eyes were wide. "I never thought of that. Someone could get hurt or even worse."

"More than that," Jesus added, "their names would be linked to Mine. I, and all who follow Me, would be in jeopardy. It's not time for that yet."

Stunned, Peter put his arm around Rimona and drew her protectively to him. "We must leave this very night!"

Jesus just smiled at him. "Peter, Peter, always so impulsive! It's true we'll have to go soon, sooner than I'd like, but not for at least another week. In the meantime, rest and enjoy your family." The abrupt tension that had filled the room relaxed slightly but did not altogether dissipate.

Their fears, though not forgotten, seemed remote and unimportant bathed in the warm light of the next morning. Jesus sat on Peter's doorstep meeting with those who had come to see Him, telling stories to illustrate the mysterious ways of His Father, and working miracle after miracle. About midmorning Peter hurried to His side, exuding anxiety.

"Jesus," he whispered loudly, "Kenan is coming here, and he's got a whole bunch of the other Pharisees with him. What are we going to do?"

Calm as always, Jesus stood. "Let's find out what they want."

Kenan led the way, his dour face wrinkled and brown. He looked around to make sure his companions were still behind him. He cleared his throat, "Rabbi, Teacher." After several hours of discussion, they had decided to use this title for Jesus. It conveyed enough respect that the common people wouldn't be offended, yet stopped short of the humiliation of calling Him 'Lord' or 'Master,' as many did. "We have seen the things you have done, and there are a number of questions we wish to ask you." The priest dabbed his sleeve against his perspiring forehead. "Perhaps we could talk indoors, where it is cooler."

"Of course." Jesus stepped graciously to one side while Peter remained speechless with surprise. The priest had certainly never before expressed the slightest interest in the interior of the humble fishing cottage of his parishioner. "Peter, show these men into your home."

Rimona hovered in the doorway, nervous as she saw the importance of her guests. She wiped her hands quickly on the back of her robe, smoothed her hair, and put on a smile to greet them. "Welcome to our home. Would you like something to drink?"

The priest waved his hand irritably. "Maybe later. We need to get started." Even standing still, he managed to give the impression that he was a very busy man.

Two of the other Pharisees deigned to accept a drink as they entered. The younger smiled at Rimona and thanked her as she held the door open firmly, lest in its freshly lubricated condition it should slam upon any of her guests.

"You're welcome," she said, returning his smile with a simple courtesy that slowly faded to bewilderment at the near stampede that followed him inside. Kenan and his cohorts had seated themselves on the floor beside Jesus and the sons of Zebedee, over against the far wall. Visiting scholars from all over the province of Galilee—Peter firmly believed they were spies—mingled with them. The crowd surged forward, and within moments curious men and women filled every bit of space, standing tightly packed to fit as many as possible into the close confines of the small house.

Outside, Peter was just about to push his way through the crush of people gathered around his door when he saw four men making their way painstakingly down the hill. Each carried one corner of a crude stretcher made of a woolen blanket. He recognized them immediately and hurried to ward them off. "Get out of here!" He shooed them with his hands. "We don't need your kind here. Go on!"

One of the men asked, "Is Jesus here?"

"Are you deaf?" Peter gritted his teeth. "Go away! Don't think I don't know all about your friend's accident. Anyone who goes through town yelling and drunk deserves exactly what he gets, never mind the part about that woman. He's lucky God didn't strike him dead, instead of just paralyzing him. You're just as bad, too, still associating with him after all the things he's done." He made a threatening gesture at the men, still coming steadily toward him. "Didn't you hear a word I said? Why are you still here? I have my reputation to consider now."

Another of the four interrupted Peter's tirade to say, "Look at all the people. Jesus must be there somewhere—in the house by the look of things."

Plainly, all the attention was centered on whatever was happening inside Peter's house. Ignoring Peter, the roughly dressed men shifted their burden and continued on down the hill. The leader walked right up to the crowd and tapped someone on the shoulder. "Excuse me, please; we have someone here who really needs to see Jesus."

Getting a rude response, he tried another person and then another. "All right, men, if they won't move on their own, we'll make them move. One, two . . ." They charged in at full speed, colliding with the colorful wall of robes blocking their way. No opening appeared for them. Instead shouts and curses were hurled at the abashed men, who retreated in discouragement.

Peter walked past, smirking. "I tried to tell you. Nobody wants you here. Just leave." He moved into the crowd, lifting the nearest man bodily and stepping into his place. Next he grabbed a woman by the arm and forced her to squeeze behind him. At her angry outburst he said brusquely, "Look, I live here, all right?" She glared, but fell silent.

With fresh vigor, the four men picked up their friend and prepared to follow Peter's path into the house. The man Peter had pushed aside saw them coming, however, and doubled up his fists. "Don't even try it. I know who you are."

"Take me into the shade, if you would, please," the man on the stretcher requested meekly. "Maybe we can figure out something else. There must be another way."

"Go home. No one wants you here," Set sneered. Since he dared not follow Peter into the very presence of Jesus, he patrolled the edges of the crowd to see what trouble he could cause. Now he added his voice to the discouragements of the demons who accompanied the five men. "You might as well just give up. It's no use. There is no help for you here." He leaned in close to the paralyzed man. "No forgiveness!"

Angels surrounded the men protectively. "This is just where you need to be," they whispered. "Jesus has everything you need. He is everything you need. He holds healing, and, yes, forgiveness in His hands. Don't give up."

One angel whispered in the ear of the paralyzed man, pointing to the side of the house. How well the man was listening! He followed the direction of the outstretched arm, his eyes brightening at what he saw. He turned his head from one side to the other in his excitement, deluging his friends with instructions. Taking hold of the four corners of the blanket, the men hurried back down the street, pausing at a flight of stairs.

Peter sat as close to Jesus as he had been able to shove, nearly sitting in James's lap. Much of what Kenan and the scribes asked Jesus was too complicated for him to completely understand, though he did admire the easy manner with which Jesus fielded the barrage of questions. The close, stuffy air made him sleepy, and he had to pinch his arm several times just to stay awake.

Finally his head nodded forward, the point of his chin just resting against his chest. He had not dozed for long when a strange sensation jerked him back to full consciousness. Something slithered down his neck and into his robe. Peter sat bolt upright with a strangled yell, remembering his surroundings just in time to contain the familiar oaths that still tried to creep out in unguarded moments.

". . . and so, according to the Law, if the debtor is unable to pay," Jesus was saying. He kept talking and didn't appear to notice anything amiss, ". . . then comes the year of jubilee."

Peter groped around behind him, finding nothing but a fine, gritty dust. The cascade that struck him a moment later, covering his hair and spilling down his shoulders, was not so mysterious. His roof was falling in! He flushed dully at the ill-concealed smiles of his guests and turned snappishly to Andrew. "I thought you said you fixed that a long time ago, after the last rain." Before Andrew could protest his innocence, a third shower of earth, much bigger than the others, covered everyone inside with a fine layer of dust.

Peter coughed, waving his hand in front of his face in a vain attempt to clear the air. More dirt slid off the top of his head, building the mound in his lap still higher. He looked up fearfully, expecting to see a swath of blue sky above him. A quiet curse did slip from his lips then.

Through the gaping hole he could see the heads of four men pressed together, peering in at him. His teeth bared in a snarl. "I thought I told you . . ."

They paid him no more heed than before. "There's Jesus," one man exclaimed.

"I told you this would work," the leader gloated. "We'll just have to make the hole a bit bigger, that's all."

The third man waved to Jesus, while the fourth tore vigorously at the branches that supported that section of the roof. "Look out below!"

As the dust particles slowly settled, Peter could take some small comfort from knowing that he was no longer the only one half buried in a pile of dirt. He wiped his eyes, blinking grittily as a shadow fell over him.

The paralyzed man, still held by the same stinking blanket, was descending slowly through the hole in the roof, suspended by four securely tied ropes. Peter squinted, seized by the sudden feeling that something was wrong.

In a heartbeat, he knew what it was. Trapped by the crowd, unable to so much as stand, he shook his fists at them and yelled. "You stole my ropes! You ripped apart my fishing nets, and cut up the ropes that I wove with my own hands! Thieves! All of you!"

Jesus leaned over and laid His hand on Peter's arm, shaking His head ever so slightly. "Let him come to Me," He said, softly so the Pharisees could not hear. "Don't turn him away."

He stood in the crowded space, waiting as the stretcher dropped lower. Every eye was fixed on Him as He took hold of the wasted hand, looking tenderly into the pale, thin face. The man stared at Jesus with tears in his eyes, satisfied by what he saw there.

Jesus read his hunger, the deep need of his soul. As if the two of them were alone in the room, Jesus said lovingly, "Riphath, don't be afraid any longer. Your sins are forgiven."

The man sank back against the supporting blanket, his eyes closing in rapture. Just then a ray of sunlight shone squarely on his face, bathing him in radiance. "Thank You," he said softly. The desire of his heart was satisfied at last; he didn't ask for more.

Chapter 15

The Pharisees sputtered as if they had just fallen into an icy stream. None were bold enough to speak aloud, trapped there in the small room by dozens of Jesus' followers, but the same thought filled each mind. *This man has committed blasphemy! No one but Jehovah can forgive sins.*

In the silence Peter looked from Riphath, who was just opening his eyes to see what was happening, to Jesus, who turned and impaled Kenan with an all-knowing look. The priest shrank back, unable to break that powerful gaze. He seemed terrified. Peter found himself holding his breath when Jesus finally spoke.

"Why do you think these evil thoughts in your hearts?" Jesus shook His head sorrowfully. "Which is easier for Me to say, 'Your sins are forgiven' or 'Get up and walk'? But just so that you will know that I *do* have the power on earth to forgive sins," He turned to the paralyzed man, "get up, Riphath, pick up your bed, and walk!"

Riphath blinked slowly, taking a moment to absorb the stunning command. A huge grin slowly spread over his face, and he strained his muscles to sit up. For the first time in eight years, his body responded. He sat there in his blanket bed, legs dangling over the side, holding his arms up in the air and watching with fascination as his fingers wiggled.

Above, from the hole in the roof, one of his friends gasped, "We can't hold on much longer. We're going to let you down the rest of the way."

Amid a rain of debris, Riphath descended into Peter's lap. Laughter broke out from all who could see. Reluctantly, Peter had to laugh too.

Riphath teetered to his feet, trying hard not to step on anyone. "Sorry about your nets," he said to Peter, causing fresh laughter to erupt. "We'll fix them before we go."

Peter smiled weakly. "That's all right. Andrew and I need the practice."

A few wobbly steps and Riphath stood before Jesus, holding his blanket and the ropes. There were wet streaks on his dusty cheeks. "I don't know what to say. 'Thank You' just isn't enough. I never thought I would walk again. All by itself, that would've been wonderful enough! But who can understand what it means to me to be forgiven too? You can't possibly know how my sins have pressed in on me over and over again these last eight years." He hung his head. "So many times I wanted to kill myself and end my shame and misery, but I couldn't. It's really very hard to kill yourself when you're paralyzed."

Riphath smiled up at his four friends, framed in the newly formed "window" above. "My friends never gave up on me, no matter how hard things were. I owe them a debt I can never repay, but, even so, they couldn't give me the one thing I needed most."

Jesus nodded. "Forgiveness. You know, I have waited a long time for this day. I do understand how your sins have burdened you, and I've been looking forward for eight years to setting you free. Your shame is gone now. Go, My friend, and live a new life in Adonai."

The man threw his arms around Jesus then turned to the crowd. "Let me out," he shouted. "I want to run!"

This was rather difficult to manage at first. Those inside did try to pull back and give him some room, but when those outside heard the excited cries coming from the house, they pressed even closer, trying to catch a glimpse of what was happening. At last word passed through the crowd, and the people opened a space to allow Riphath to come out. As soon as he got through the crowd, he began to run, leaping and shouting praises.

Four angels on the rooftop laughed and sang for joy, marveling at the Father's ingenuity in planning this meeting. Let the demons beware—when

God purposed for something to happen, all the powers on earth couldn't stand in His way!

Gabriel and Tarik chuckled as they watched Riphath make his own way into the sunlight and stretch exuberant arms toward the sky. Gabriel put one hand companionably on Tarik's shoulder. "I enjoy it so much when we have days like this. The face your charge made when he saw what had become of his fishing nets will stay with me a long while."

Tarik threw back his head and laughed heartily. "I have tried for years to help Simon Peter learn the art of unselfishness, but Jesus taught him more in one afternoon than I have in his whole life. And you're right. His expression was beyond price."

"I hope you're ready to take Peter's instruction in sharing to a whole new level."

"What do you mean?"

"Well, how do you think he would feel about having to share Jesus? Or, more specifically, having to share his position near Jesus?"

"But he already has to share his position with Andrew, James, and John."

"Exactly. If he struggles for power even with his brother and two best friends, how will he react when his honor must be divided with a tax collector?"

Comprehension flashed into Tarik's eyes. "You mean Levi? He is one of the chosen?"

Gabriel nodded. "You've been so busy with the situation here that you didn't even notice when Levi received his extra guards. I can assure you that the matter didn't escape the attention of Satan, and he'll use every means at his disposal to cause conflict over the publican." For a moment the general of the host of heaven looked sad. "Actually, he will probably have to do very little—except let events take their natural course. These humans care so much about externals, and yet they show so little concern about what is in their hearts."

"I'll do everything I can to help," Tarik promised.

"I know you will. I just wanted you to be prepared; our Master is going to make His next call in just a few minutes."

Jesus stood and stretched, His muscles stiff after many hours of sitting in such a cramped position. Peter jumped up, wanting to be sure that he was included in whatever activities Jesus had planned. As Kenan struggled to rise, Jesus reached down and helped the hostile priest of Capernaum to his feet. The elderly man took his surly leave, followed by the delegation of Pharisees, scribes, and spies. Though Kenan had not changed his opinion that Jesus was little better than a rebel, he recognized that the people would oppose any action he tried to take against Him and wisely decided to bide his time.

As the last of the visitors filed out and Peter could once more locate his door, he remembered his nets. Eyeing the huge hole in his roof, he stomped outside and around to the back of the hut where his fishing nets lay.

Riphath's four friends sat on the ground, putting the finishing knots into the net they had "borrowed." Their work was not quite as smooth and straight as Peter's own, but still sturdy and serviceable enough. "Thanks again," they chorused, holding up their hands in greeting.

"You're welcome," Peter muttered grudgingly. "At least you put it back." *Unlike my roof,* he complained to himself.

"Don't worry about your roof, either," one spoke up. "We'll fix that next."

"I wasn't worried." It was not precisely the truth, but Peter was beginning to feel ungracious in the face of their determined courtesy. "Thank you."

Many of those in the crowd waited to follow Jesus into the small town. Peter ran to the head of the column, scowling when he saw John already standing at Jesus' right hand and James at His left. Andrew had pressed in close, too, until there was scarcely room for Peter. *Not again!* His frown deepened, and all the warm thoughts he'd had for Riphath's friends vanished. *If it weren't for those men, I would've been here to take my rightful place. It's not fair!*

"You were right, Gabriel." Tarik shook his head as he watched Peter squeeze to the head of the column and gesture imposingly for everyone to follow him. *"He is definitely not going to have an easy time with this."*

Gabriel sighed. *"Sadly, I'm expecting it to get worse as our Master assembles more and more disciples as His apprentices."*

"Are there going to be that many more?"

"Yes." Gabriel nodded. "He's looking for twelve in all."

"Well, that does make perfect sense. Twelve stones in the foundation of our city, twelve gates leading into it, and here on earth, twelve sons of Israel, twelve tribes, and now twelve apostles to spread the news of His heavenly kingdom."

"That's the idea, anyway. What actually happens will depend on the Spirit, as well as upon their own choices." Gabriel looked at each of the four fishermen with Jesus, reading their deep jealousies and prideful ambitions. "I don't know what the future has in store for them, but I predict they will have a difficult path ahead if they do not change—and soon."

Tarik pretended not to notice Oreb, arms folded across his chest, smiling at Peter with malicious satisfaction. Plainly he had guessed what was going to happen. Tarik turned to Gabriel. "Get ready for trouble."

Gabriel smiled sympathetically, saying in his deep voice, "And also get ready to welcome Levi into the ranks of the saved. His name will be written in the Book today."

Simon Peter looked pointedly to his right as he proudly led the crowd through the gate into Capernaum. Levi Matthew, sitting on the left side, paid no attention. As the appointed tax collector in the region, he was accustomed to being regarded as something lower than vermin. Oh, the scorn, contempt, and outright hatred had bothered him a little at first, but the money soon made up for it. Sweet money! He loved to dig his hands into the piles of coins and let them trickle through his fingers. He adored the feel of money, the smell of money, the sound of the tuneless clanking it made as it poured into his overflowing coffers.

It had been a good week too. Capernaum always had camel trains and merchants passing through, but in the last several days there had been more activity than usual, and all the caravans seemed unusually laden with luxury goods. Locally, there had been an increase in business, too, including one particular catch of fish that had broken all previous records. And the crowds following that new Teacher everyone was talking about brought hundreds of shekels' worth of provisions in the marketplace, generating even more tax from the sellers. It was wonderful! Levi thought he might even throw a party to celebrate and invite all of his publican friends. Lots of women, too, of course. That went without saying.

His pleasant reverie was interrupted with the abrupt realization that a crowd had surrounded his tax booth. Half guiltily, he pulled his hand out of a secret pocket in his striped robe, a little embarrassed at being caught fondling several silver coins. The tax collector looked up at a seemingly ordinary man, immediately recognizing the Teacher.

"Rabbi!" Levi laughed nervously. "I didn't see You at first. Do You owe some taxes?"

Jesus shook His head and took a step closer. Levi's gaze traveled up slowly to meet His. Jesus didn't say a word of reproach, but Levi suddenly had an almost overwhelming urge to hide his ill-gotten money. To hide himself. Anything to block those all-knowing eyes. Every penny he had ever wrongfully taken came to his mind. In that moment of despair he saw himself for what he really was—unholy—and he knew himself for a liar, a thief, a cheater, a criminal in the sight of a holy God.

Strangely, though, there was no condemnation in Jesus' face as He looked at the abject sinner before Him. There was only love and a joy that could not be held back. Jesus reached out His hand. "Come, follow Me."

An answering joy spread over the face of the publican. "Of course!" He scrambled eagerly to his feet, stepping over his abandoned treasury and out into the stony street. "I'm ready. Where are we going?"

Jesus smiled at Levi's enthusiasm, His teeth showing white against His beard. "To the ends of the earth, Levi Matthew, to the ends of the earth!"

Just then Peter pushed his way through the people, having at last realized that he was leading only himself. "What is going on here? Oh no!" He grasped Andrew's arm. "I just left Him alone for a second—what is He doing? Has He taken leave of His senses?" Peter stifled a groan. "The new King touching a tax collector—what will people think?"

Andrew himself looked less than pleased. His lips were tight as he answered, "Jesus seems to have invited him to join us."

"Join us? For the afternoon? For a few minutes to listen to some stories?"

Andrew shook his head. "I think Jesus means to keep him."

"No, no, no. No!" Peter clutched his curly hair. "That isn't how it works. You keep orphaned children. You keep lambs when their mothers can't take care of them. You keep a portion of the fish you catch. You don't keep a tax collector!"

"Jesus kept us," Andrew pointed out practically, noting that Jesus was moving away, arm-in-arm with the publican, as He started again down the street.

Peter gritted his teeth. "All the more reason He shouldn't even have spoken to that man. What are people going to think of us when they see us with that person?" He scowled fiercely. "I, for one, will have nothing to do with him. I'm going to pretend he doesn't even exist. I hate him! How many years now has he been cheating us out of huge shares of our rightful profits, never caring if our families went hungry or not. He's not going to lose that greedy, money-loving heart overnight. If a leopard can't change his spots, then a tax collector can't change his stripes!"

"Maybe we can beat him up when Jesus isn't looking," Andrew suggested.

"Tempting, but no. He would just tell Jesus, and then we might lose the positions we already have." Peter dropped his voice to a whisper. "Psst. James, John, over here."

While Jesus sat in the marketplace, telling a few stories before the time of the evening meal, with Matthew beside Him on the right, the four fishermen gathered in a spiteful huddle, just out of earshot. James and John were nearly as angry as Peter.

"Look at the cunning way he slithers into the Master's good graces," James complained, "while the rest of us are left out here in the cold."

"But it's hot," replied the literal-minded Peter.

"And he's in my spot," John said. "We've got to do something fast."

"Maybe we should just wait and see what happens," Andrew said hopefully. "Maybe he will get tired of Jesus and go away."

"Get tired of not having anyone to steal from and cheat is more like it!" Peter snorted. "We'll get rid of him somehow. When he sees we don't want him along, he'll go running back to his little tax booth, and we'll never have to see him again. Unless, of course, we come back for some reason and catch some fish, and our share's big enough that we have some to sell and we have to pay him the tax on our profits, and . . ."

"Will you be quiet?" Andrew rolled his eyes. "You've made your point. We're all with you. We'll find a way to get rid of Levi Matthew."

"That went better than I expected," Tarik said brightly.

Across the marketplace, Gabriel laughed. "That's what I like about you, Tarik. You're so good at finding something encouraging in every situation."

Nadiv, Arion, and the others looked as if some of the shine had come off of their optimism. "Cheer up," Tarik told them. "Jesus knew exactly what would happen when He invited Levi to join Him. I'm sure that even though He would much rather our dear fishermen had displayed the same loving spirit He's been trying so hard to teach them, He'll still take the wrong choices they're making and weave it into His perfect plan. This is just a temporary setback. Trust me, I know how it works. After all, I've been a Guardian almost from the very beginning."

Nadiv smiled tremulously. "It is a little disappointing to have this happen after what's gone before. Andrew was making such good progress—and now this. Naturally I trust what Jesus is doing; I just thought—hoped—that my charge would be more ready for this test."

Tarik flashed his friend a quick smile. "Don't worry, you'll have another chance to see him succeed. The Spirit will lead them around and around again, testing them in their weak areas and helping them to grow, until they realize the Father can make them strong enough to do what's right. Andrew will pass this way again, and so will his brother. They'll all have many opportunities to show the love they're supposed to learn."

"But in the meantime, all we can do is stand around and watch for a chance to reach their minds. It's hard not to act. It's so frustrating!"

"Don't worry. Though we may seem idle, the Spirit never is. We'll have our chance soon. He'll see to that."

"You know, Tarik, I've always wanted to ask you what it was like when you were with Cain," Arion said, darting a quick look to where the demons lounged off to one side, laughing and cheering as they listened to Peter lead the plotting against Levi Matthew. Only Ares and Set stood upright, doing

little but call an occasional suggestion that was immediately incorporated into the planning of the small assembly. The Galileans gave no heed whatsoever to the urgings of their angels or the pleading of the Spirit.

Tears filled Tarik's eyes. "You know how hard it still is to live and work in the midst of death. But that first time was the most awful—because it was so totally unexpected."

"None of us have ever really gotten used to it," Arion agreed. "But I think in some ways it's even harder now. This whole planet reverberates with death and dying."

"My assignment with Cain was the first time I had faced Set since he was Jothan, our dear friend and comrade. The change in him was startling; it went far deeper than his new name. He looked so much older—and so sad. I think even then he was beginning to feel the first stirrings of decay as he separated himself ever further from the Almighty."

"Set and the others focused all their evil attentions on the little family after the General barred the way to the Garden, and those first days were very bitter for them. The moment Cain was conceived I was assigned to him."

"I have gotten a man from the Lord," Nadiv said reminiscently. "Eve really thought Cain would be the One, the Deliverer, when she named her new son."

"Well, while he was still a little boy she could see she was wrong," Tarik continued. "He was extraordinarily willful and rebellious, even by our standards now. Of course, Michael had already explained to us that when the time came, He was to be the Seed that would crush the serpent's head." His voice broke a little. "The serpent, our friend. I wish things could go back the way they used to be, and he would come to lead us again."

"Who would've thought everything would turn out like this?" Arion commented. "I'm sure none of us pictured what it would be like for Michael to leave behind His throne, His power, His glory, the perfection and peace of the City, to become Jesus, the Savior. Look at Him over there, surrounded by sinners, covered in sweat, dirt all over His feet, precious—but smelly—little children sitting on His lap. That's how much He loves them, all of them, from Adam and Eve right down to little Abigail leaving that streak of mud on His beard. Incredible!"

"He has changed, no doubt about it," Tarik said, "but only on the outside. Our former friends are different inside and out. Look over there at Satan, how

he seems to swallow the light wherever he moves. And his forehead is slowly receding after thousands of years of choosing only wrong. He's still handsome in a way, but I can hardly believe he is the same angel who used to lead us in our songs of praise."

Nadiv shuddered. "Just think what he will look like by the time of the next Coming, when Jesus returns for His people. I don't know when it will be, but surely long enough for Satan to look even more dreadful than he does now. I'm so glad we didn't take his side in the war."

"I am too," Arion said. "But Tarik, you never finished telling us about Cain."

"There's not much more to tell that you don't already know," replied Tarik. "Almost the only discipline Cain ever received was from our realm. Every time Adam and Eve tried ever-so-gently to correct him, he would display a defiant attitude toward them and say, 'If it weren't for your stupidity we wouldn't even be out here; we'd be inside enjoying the good life!' He cast their sin up to them over and over again, and they didn't stand firm with him. In fact, soon they didn't say anything at all to him; they just let him do whatever he wanted."

Arion nodded with understanding. "Some of the parents I've guarded have been like that. They didn't understand that their own sins made it even more crucial that they denounce the same tendencies in their children and proudly wear the badge of a hypocrite if that is what their foolish offspring dare to call them."

"Later Adam and Eve blamed themselves to a large degree for Abel's death," Tarik went on. "Rightfully so, for although the choices Cain made were his own, his character was what they had allowed it to become. Their permissiveness brought about what was surely the hardest day in my life as a Guardian. So far."

The angel took a moment to compose himself. "I knew there would be trouble when Cain piled his altar high with fruits and vegetables. He knew, or should have known, that the sacrifice of a lamb pointed to salvation through the grace of Elohim. Instead, he tried to buy his way back into heaven with the works of his own hands. In his enormous pride, he really thought Elohim would send the fire of acceptance to devour his sacrifice.

"Abel tried to warn him, his words an echo of the warning the Spirit and I both tried to give. Set worked to inflame Cain's temper to greater heights

than usual, but even he was surprised when Abel's sacrifice was accepted, but not Cain's."

Tarik closed his eyes over the tears that sprang up at the memory. "Set's prodding pushed Cain over the brink into insanity, and he swept his rejected offering to the ground. When he picked up the first stone, I shouted, I pleaded, but he was too far gone to hear. The first blow knocked Abel to the ground, and I wept for his courage—and distress. Gurion stayed right there beside him as the rocks came faster and faster.

"Finally a stone struck Abel squarely in the head, and he felt no more pain. Still, Cain continued to throw the stones until his altar was completely dismantled. His mind began to clear, and he crept close to his brother, shock starting to set in as his sanity returned. Aghast, we all listened together as Abel's heart slowed and then stopped. Cain ran away then, taking nothing but his wife. He was never to see his parents again. I went with him into exile, east of the Garden, and watched over him the rest of his sad, lonely, miserable years.

"The mark of the Lord that saved his life also tormented him day and night until he couldn't bear to look at himself and ordered every reflective surface in the house destroyed so he never had to see his face. He had asked Jehovah to spare his life, and he died cursing God for letting him live." The tears ran freely down Tarik's face. The other angels wept at the memory.

Gabriel flew over. "One of the things I remember about the day Abel died is the way it affected Satan. I'm certain he didn't anticipate that he would feel anything but pleasure, but I saw him actually wipe away a tear. I could tell by his face that a struggle was going on. I think he even wanted to come back to us at that point. It was probably the last time he was able to hear or feel any call from the Spirit."

Tarik wiped his eyes. "I can't wait until this is all over and our last enemy—death—is destroyed."

Gabriel smiled. "I'm eager, too, but there's still much work to be done in the meantime. Jesus, unlike Adam and Eve, will discipline His children and help them to root out the undesirable traits in their characters."

"Like selfishness and pride." Tarik nodded at his charge, who, temporarily abandoning the topic of Levi Matthew, was leading an ever angrier discussion on the merits of his being first in the New Kingdom.

"Among many others," Gabriel said wryly. "They don't know it, but their discipline has already begun."

"Men, I need your attention for a moment," Jesus called, to no avail. Then louder, "Men!" James, John, and Andrew turned and looked at Him. Peter carried on for several more sentences before trailing off in the middle of a word. "Peter, take the others with you, and go let the women know that we'll have an additional guest with us at the evening meal," Jesus instructed.

Peter felt as if he had just been slapped. *A publican? In my house? A vile tax collector eating my food? Oh, no! As if it's not enough for Jesus to give that sinner my place of honor. Now He wants to make him a guest in my home? Not while I am alive to stop it!* Peter gave a sickly grin as he looked up and met Jesus' steady gaze. "Of course, Master."

Chapter 16

Rimona was not nearly as upset as Peter had hoped. "An agent of the King coming to our little house? Right now?"

"In a few minutes," Peter said sullenly.

"Then I have to hurry and get ready! Keren, come help me for a minute," she said as she whirled away. Peter frowned at his toes. Clearly the women were going to be no help.

He looked up into the stern faces of his brother and friends, shrugging helplessly. "Batia, where are you? Did you know Jesus is bringing a publican here for supper?"

Batia shuffled in the door carrying a few small sticks of firewood, all the older children following her. "A publican, you say? Yes, that's what I thought. Excuse me, Rimona will need my help to get ready for our important visitors."

Peter slumped in defeat. "I guess it's up to us."

"Get ready," Andrew said. "Here they come now."

It was only Jesus and Levi. All the others had gone to their own suppers. As they walked toward Peter's house, the two men appeared engrossed in their conversation. Whatever Levi said must have pleased Jesus, for He smiled broadly and clapped the former tax collector on the shoulder. A bad taste filled Peter's mouth, and he turned his head to spit.

Jesus looked up then and called a greeting. Andrew, as if reading his brother's mind, stepped forward. "Master! Judging by the smell, supper will be wonderful. Let me help You inside." He took Jesus by the arm and swept Him inside, leaving Levi alone with his brother.

Levi took a hesitant step forward, to find a large angry fisherman barring the door with one muscular arm. The Sons of Thunder stood on each side of him, looking as if they were about to live up to their name.

Peter shot a quick look over one shoulder to make sure Andrew still occupied Jesus' attention before hissing at Levi Matthew, "You won't come in if you know what's good for you. There's no room for your kind in my house."

The once-proud man fell back humbly, without an argument. "I didn't mean to offend anyone," he said quietly, lowering his gaze to the ground. "I just wanted to be with Jesus."

Peter sneered. "So do all the other common people. It's our job," his nod included James and John, "to make sure that only the right sort of people have access to our Master."

James cleared his throat significantly, and Peter turned to see Jesus close by, His face pleasant as He asked, "How are things coming along, lads? Matthew, come get something to eat. I know you're hungry."

Matthew darted a quick look at Peter. "Uh . . . , air is so fresh out here that I, um . . . I think I'll just eat outside."

"That's a good idea," said Jesus happily. "I'll join you." He looked knowingly at Peter and Andrew, James, and John, each in turn, then smiled at them and said, "There's nothing like good air to whet a man's appetite."

In the end, the four ate alone inside, nursing their anger and jealousy. Even the women and children had left them to their own devices, casting aside tradition to stay close to Jesus while He ate. At last John threw his bread down dramatically. "This won't work, you know." The others stared at him. "All we've accomplished so far is to distance ourselves from Jesus and allow that usurper to take our places."

"What do you suggest we do?" Peter turned on him angrily. "Just let him join us without a protest? Next thing we know, you'll be the one sitting by the gate robbing anyone who passes by."

"You take that back, you . . ." John raised his fist.

Peter leaped to his feet in a fighting stance. "Come get me, you publican lover!"

"Boys, boys." Andrew stepped between them, holding his hands up for peace. "John is right. I don't like it, but he is right. Let's sit down and discuss this again—without our fists." Suddenly much subdued, the two men lowered their hands to their sides and sat down. "Now, John, maybe you could share with us what made you change your mind."

"That's easy," John said. "I just looked around your house. All of us inside bickering, and everyone else outside having a nice time. Whatever I may feel about tax collectors in general and Levi Matthew in particular, it is not important enough for me to lose any more time with Jesus. Besides, He's the One who's going to be King. He has the right to decide who is going to join Him, not us."

Peter, forced into agreement by this unanswerable logic, responded grumpily, "I guess if I have to go along with it to keep the first position in the kingdom, I will. But that doesn't mean I have to like it!"

"I think you mean second position," Andrew shot back, heading for the door in an attempt to get outside before the others.

In a tangle of elbows and knees, all four of them tried to fit through the opening at once. Jesus looked up at them and smiled, pretending not to notice the scrambling and jostling. "I'm glad you could join us. By all means, sit down. There's plenty of room."

Still feeling a bit ill-used and neglected, Peter sat with the other three on Jesus' left hand, as close to the Master, and yet as far from Matthew, as they could get.

At the end of the meal, Matthew rose reluctantly, his expensive robes rumpled from sitting heedlessly at Jesus' feet for so many hours. He straightened his head covering and brushed the crumbs from his lap. Bending first over Batia, he held out his hand courteously. "Thank you, kind ladies, for an excellent supper. I wish my cooks knew half your secrets. Your men are truly fortunate, indeed."

Batia smiled with pleasure. "It was nice having you. Please come again."

Matthew hesitated, the sudden silence growing uncomfortable. He looked appealingly at Jesus. "Teacher, would it be all right if I came tomorrow—just to listen again?"

"Of course, Matthew. Today and every other day. As long as you are willing, I want you to follow Me, now and always."

Andrew jabbed Peter in the ribs. "See?" he hissed. "Didn't I tell you? He *is* keeping him."

Joy too great to be contained filled Matthew. "Thank You," he said in a near shout, then more quietly, "Thank You." He started to walk away, but turned back with a wave. "I'll see all of you tomorrow! And it was surely nice meeting you, James and John, you, too, Peter and Andrew."

Peter bared his teeth in a clenched imitation of a grin, waving back halfheartedly. "Tomorrow, then. Heh-heh. Heh." Hardly moving his lips, he leaned a little closer to his brother. "Can you believe the nerve of that man?"

"Get used to it," Andrew replied fixedly. "We're going to have to put up with him every day. Every minute. From now on."

"He's not so bad," John put in softly. "Look how hard he is trying to be polite, even though he knows we don't like him."

"I'd be polite, too, if I didn't want to get beaten up," James added. He jumped, startled, and flushed when he saw Jesus listening with great interest to their conversation. The four men looked like little children caught with a jar of honey, sticky liquid still dripping from their fingers.

"What we meant to say . . . ," Peter stammered, as embarrassed as any of them. "What we meant to say was that we are grateful to have this chance to get to know Levi Matthew."

"Why, yes," said John in his most pleasant tones. "It is quite an experience to have the chance to talk with someone we normally wouldn't be able to learn anything about."

James recovered his power of speech. "One could even say that we're very grateful to You for giving us this opportunity."

"Yes, one could say it . . . if it were true," Batia commented shrewdly.

Jesus paused for a long moment. When He opened His mouth, the men braced themselves for a lecture. "Let me tell you a story," Jesus said.

The children squealed with delight. Abelia and Adalia scrambled into Jesus' lap, Jered and Seth each leaned on one of Jesus' knees, and little Atalia cooed in her mother's arms. The men lifted their eyes, grateful for the unexpected reprieve.

Jesus took a moment to caress each child, love warming in His eyes. "Many years ago, there was a great city named Jericho. It was a very big city surrounded by a huge wall."

"Da wall fall down!" Adalia interrupted excitedly, pounding her hands on her chubby knees.

"Yes, it did." Jesus chuckled at her enthusiasm. "The people of Jericho thought that no army, even a very big one, could defeat them. But the children of Israel obeyed Adonai, and He gave them the victory."

"Da wall fall down!"

"But after the wall fell down, something very sad happened. One man didn't follow Adonai's instructions." Jesus' eyes filled with tears. "The children of Israel already had much gold, silver, and precious stones from the Egyptians, and the land they were entering was filled with even more wealth. Thus the riches of that first city were to be given to Adonai as a special thank offering, much like we do today when we offer a sacrifice of the first fruits at harvest.

"All the children of Israel obeyed Adonai, except for one man. His name was Achan. He stole a Babylonian robe, two hundred shekels of silver, and a piece of gold worth fifty shekels." The children's eyes widened at this princely sum. "He dug a hole in his tent and buried it all, covering it with a rug so that no one knew except his family.

"Adonai instructed Joshua to give the guilty man several chances to repent, but Achan would not admit what he had done. Each time the lot was cast, it drew nearer to Achan, but he still would not confess. Not until he had been singled out of the millions in Israel did Achan confess what he had taken and where he had hidden it. But by then it was too late."

Jesus looked at His first four disciples very seriously as He finished the story. "Achan made two very serious mistakes. First, his selfishness led him to take a treasure that rightfully belonged only to God—a treasure that was to be used in His service. He attempted to hide it for his own use and pleasure in order to secure what he thought would be a better position." The fishermen squirmed uncomfortably. "Then, even when he saw that God knew his secret deeds, he would not admit his mistake.

"Solomon once said, 'He that covers his sins will not prosper, but whoever confesses and forsakes them will find mercy.' So, ah, children, always remember the lessons of unselfishness that we can learn from the story of Achan." Jesus turned casually to His disciples. "Would you men care to take a walk with Me?"

"He is good!" Tarik shook his head admiringly. "I never would have thought of that. He is so clever with His stories, driving home just the point He wants to make, but without embarrassing anyone publicly and making them more likely to resist His leading."

"Jesus' corrections are always as gentle as it is possible to make them," Nadiv commented. "I have noticed that although sometimes He can be quite stern if that is the only way He can reach someone, usually He is so subtle that only those to whom He is speaking understand His message."

"Our charges have made some good progress today, but I wouldn't count on this being the end of the problem," Tarik cautioned. "Not only do they have the natural human cycle of highs and lows, but you remember Gabriel said there would be seven more chosen."

Aitan and Jabir grew excited. "So that's how this is going to work!" Aitan said eagerly. "I wonder who the others are going to be?"

Jabir scratched his head thoughtfully. "I think I know who at least two of them will be. Philip and Nathanael will probably be next. After that, I have no idea."

"Yes," Tarik said, "and so far they have all been from Galilee, but there may be at least a few from Judea. We'll just have to wait and see. Well, it looks like it's time to get into night formation. We'll have to talk about this again later."

Peter held Rimona close, the predawn breeze cool on his cheeks. "I'll be back as soon as I can. Take good care of our sons for me, just like you always do."

"Goodbye," Rimona choked out, wiping her eyes with the back of one hand. "Jesus was right when He said that the harder duty would be to stay behind. I wish I could go with you."

"So do I." Peter kissed her and reluctantly pushed her away. "I have to go; the others are waiting. I love you."

"I love you too." She still sounded surprised as she said it, as if she could hardly believe it was true.

Peter ran to join Jesus where He stood with the small group on the roadway, looking back only once to see his wife wave in farewell, a brave smile on her face as she held tightly to Keren's hand for support. He waved back, trying to swallow the lump that rose in his own throat.

"Sorry to keep you waiting." Peter blinked rapidly and tried to wipe his face clean of emotion as he joined the men. "My wife, she uh . . . just didn't want me to go. You know how women are."

"I know exactly what you're talking about." Andrew winked at him, and Peter hung his head, embarrassed to have had anyone glimpse the depth of his feelings. "But don't worry," Andrew went on, "with so many things to keep them busy, I'm sure the *women* will be just fine."

Peter noticed Matthew and John exchange a worried glance, and John looked over his shoulder at the dim outline of Capernaum, seemingly relieved that all was quiet. Jesus saw them and laughed. "Don't worry," He reassured them. "I really don't think anyone will come after you now."

Peter snickered. "Not after what You said to them yesterday, they won't. I've waited a long time to see Kenan taken down like that. He'll think twice before he tangles with us again." To himself, he thought, *And maybe now You and John will see what happens when You associate with publicans. They're nothing but trouble!*

"Peter, Peter!" Jesus sighed. "First of all, My purpose was not to 'take Kenan down,' as you put it. He has much to learn, but then, so do you. I didn't make the Sabbath to be a burden on mankind, something that children and adults alike dread each week because of all the nonsensical restrictions they have been taught. When I made the Sabbath in the very beginning, it was a day of joyful togetherness, of rest from the labors of the week. Even though I could no longer meet face to face with the children of Adam and Eve, I still drew very near as their thoughts turned toward Me on that holy day."

Peter frowned thoughtfully. "But the Sabbath is a miserable day, or at least it always was until You came to Capernaum. There would be all the long services, hundreds of rules to remember, and having to stay home with the women and children all the rest of the time. Andrew and I would count the minutes until the sun went down and we could go fishing again."

"That's what I mean," Jesus stated. "The rules of men—not Adonai—are what turned My day of blessing into a day of cursing. Those responsible for this blasphemy will stand in judgment before the Almighty unless they repent. It is a very serious matter to attempt to change the laws of Adonai. For Kenan, his response to My message will be the difference between life and death. How I pray he chooses life!"

Peter grew sober. He'd never thought of it that way. "He hates You now. Some of the spies wanted him to bring You, John, and Levi to trial to answer the charges. I heard them talking. Kenan promised them that he would hand You over after he had talked to You, but that was before You jumped up and down on all his arguments." Peter just couldn't help it as his lips curved up at the memory. "You really were good."

"Personally," James spoke up, "although I agree with everything You said, Master, I would recommend that none of us pick any more grain to eat on the Sabbath, at least not where anyone can see us. It might be all right in the eyes of Adonai, but I don't want to have to live through another day like yesterday ever again."

"Me either." Matthew walked even faster, hoping to put the city behind him even more quickly. "I'm sorry; I just didn't think about it. I didn't mean to make trouble."

"That's all right." Jesus laid His arm across Matthew's shoulders. "It all turned out for the best. We had to leave anyway, and it gave Me a chance to show you a little more of what the Sabbath is meant to be like."

Peter had a sudden thought. "You never told us where we are going."

"All over." Jesus' smile lit the morning with its glory. "I'm not trying to tease you. We really are going just about everywhere. First, though, we are going to make a brief stop in Bethsaida. I have an appointment to keep there."

"What is it?" Peter was curious. "I was born in Bethsaida, You know."

Matthew frowned thoughtfully. "You're going to call someone else to join us, aren't You?"

"Two someones, actually." Jesus was very pleased at Matthew's perceptiveness. "Philip and Nathanael will be coming with us, if they choose."

Peter was surprised, but not too unhappy. He counted on his fingers. "Seven of us," he told Andrew quietly. "So that's what He's been trying to do. They say seven is the number that symbolizes Adonai's perfection, so it makes sense that there would be seven of us. That won't be too bad."

Andrew shrugged. "I guess not. I liked it better when it was just the four of us, but Philip and Nathanael will be better than getting another tax collector."

"You were right," Tarik laughed. "Philip and Nathanael it is. That leaves five more. Does anybody want to guess who they will be?"

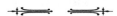

The flames jumped and crackled in the waning darkness of the early morning. Sparks floated heavenward, mingling with the smoke as their light faded and went out. One man threw another armful of sticks onto the fire, stepping back hastily to avoid the sudden blaze. The surrounding trees, barely visible, seemed to lean in toward the warmth.

Thirteen men circled the fire, twelve with wary—even hostile—looks on their faces. The haunting melody of a reed flute hovered over the mountaintop, finding a poignant place in each heart. Jesus sat with head bowed until the song's end. "I have called you all here tonight for a very special purpose," He said as He stood and looked around the circle. "Most of you have, before tonight, answered My call and have followed Me. Some of you have been with Me for only a few days, some for several weeks, and a few for many months." Peter sat up straighter, filled with pride at hearing his group mentioned. "During that time you have seen and heard many things, witnessed the power of Adonai, and had the opportunity to grow closer to one another." A distinctly unfriendly Peter glared at the newcomers as Jesus went on.

"This day has been chosen by My Father as the time when you are to be dedicated for His service, when you will leave behind your old lives and begin seeking to win souls for His kingdom."

Always ready with an interruption, Peter asked, "When are You going to set up the New Kingdom?" The other men nodded, murmuring their desire to know the answer to this question as well.

"You are going to help me establish it," Jesus answered, "but the time is in My Father's hands. From now on, you will be preaching, teaching, healing, and even casting out demons in My name."

That got Peter's attention! Eyes wide, he leaned close to Andrew and whispered, "Can you believe it? He's giving us His power! It's what I've always wanted."

Andrew replied softly, "I'm still trying to picture what the kingdom will be like—with all of its princes doing miracles. There's never been anything like it!"

Jesus paused, smiling at the excited voices that broke out all around Him. When the noise faded away, He went on. "This is a wonderful time for Me, as well. I have waited so long for this day. Thank you for choosing to help Me by becoming My messengers.

"I would like for us to spend a few minutes getting to know more about each other. Of course, some of you are already well acquainted, but some of you have met only in the last few days. My plan is that in the coming years you will all grow as close as brothers, for you have been grafted into the family of Adonai. This should be a little easier for My first four disciples, who truly *are* brothers. This is Simon Peter, and his brother, Andrew." Jesus laid a hand on each of their heads, affectionately tousling their hair. "They were the very first to answer My call. They were born in Bethsaida, but now live in Capernaum with their families. They are both fishermen, like their father before them."

Peter's grin was an odd mixture of self-consciousness and pride as he waved to the group. "Hello, everyone."

Tarik and Nadiv, shining with parental pride, stood with Gabriel and the others as they encircled the fledgling apostles. Aitan and Jabir, with the other newly assigned Guardians, formed a second ring around the first, the gleam of their outstretched swords holding the darkness at bay.

The demon horde swirled thickly, too far away to hear what was being said. Satan was present as well, sensing that a momentous event was about to occur, trying to anticipate and counter it. The instant he realized that any hope of eavesdropping was futile, he called for a summit with his top lieutenants and issued a special summons for the tempters of each disciple. The evil strategists laid out clearly every strength and weakness of each man and updated their reports; in seconds, Satan was able to formulate any necessary alterations to his plans.

Gabriel stayed by Jesus' side as He went to stand between the two sons of Jonas and placed one hand on each dark, curly head. Peter's lips curved into a self-satisfied smile at the mention of him and Andrew before all the others. He sat up straighter and swelled his chest, unobtrusively flexing his arms, hoping everyone would notice how very strong he was.

"These two," Jesus continued, moving to the next pair of brothers, "are James and John, the sons of Zebedee, and also fishermen. Some of you may have heard them referred to as the Sons of Thunder, and rightfully so." James and John laughed heartily at this, and the newcomers chuckled with them, if somewhat nervously.

James spoke up jovially. "If any of you haven't yet found a spouse, I have a sister at home who is of marriageable age. You can meet her the next time we go through Capernaum."

"Levi Matthew is from Capernaum, as well." Jesus refused to become distracted. "He has chosen to grasp the heavenly reward that comes from service to Adonai, leaving behind a life of ease and prosperity in exchange for the hardships and poverty that await us. After all, foxes have dens, and birds have nests, but the Son of man has nowhere to lay His head."

Peter had heard Jesus say this several times. As he had always done before, he mentally added, *For right now, that is. Later, He will have a palace fit for a king.* Peter understood that Jesus naturally didn't want to do or say anything that might upset the Romans—at least before He staged His revolt.

Matthew ducked his head shyly at the praise from his Master, crimson flooding his smooth face. "It was nothing. I was glad to answer the call," he said. He ran one hand across his chin, wishing he had a beard, then spread his hands apologetically. "You will all find out soon enough, so I might as well tell you now. I was a publican."

An ugly murmur sprang up. One fiery young man turned to his neighbor, an older man with thinning hair, and said, "I suspected all along he was nothing but a puppet of Rome. He, and everyone like him, should be stoned!"

"All of you stop it!" Peter was surprised to hear himself speak. "I don't like tax collectors any better than the rest of you, but he's not one anymore. He's one of us, and if there's a problem with that, you can answer to me!"

Hardly able to believe his ears, Matthew mouthed a silent thanks to his unexpected champion. Peter nodded in acknowledgment and waited for Jesus to continue.

Jesus smiled, moving to stand behind the first man to follow him at Bethabara, although after months of hard labor and much walking he was considerably less plump than before. "Philip is from Bethsaida, where he used to work as a scribe for Shillem. He loves children and will soon have his ninth." Philip groaned good-naturedly as the men laughed. "His methodical attention to details will be helpful to all of us."

Turning to a tall, slender man seated next to Philip and clutching the reed flute, Jesus patted his shoulder. "Nathanael of Cana, it's been over a year and a half since you prayed under the fig tree. Do you regret leaving your life as a musician?"

Joy infused the thin, flushed face. "Not for an instant! I miss my sons when I am gone, of course, but they are fine with their grandparents. Following You brings all the happiness I could ask for, and the only regret I could ever have is if I had stayed." Nathanael did not speak of the wife who had played him false, abandoning her family and moving to Koraea with her Samaritan lover. In spite of the tragedies in his past, he meant every word he said.

Jesus was clearly pleased with Nathanael's answer as He moved on around the circle. "We have two men with us who are named James." He rested His hand on the older man in front of Him. "As well as two Simons." He indicated the young man on His left side. "This James is the son of Alpheus, and he knows what it means to work the soil and watch for the latter rain. Young Simon here has much need to learn of the patience a farmer must have, and yet he is overflowing with enthusiasm and zeal. We can learn much from each of them.

"And Thomas, for all that the boys at the rabbinical school must wish to have you back, I am glad you have chosen to join us. Keep studying the natural world around you, for in it you will learn much of My Father's ways." Thomas blinked twice and smiled a small, crooked smile, appearing very scholarly.

"We also have two Judases, one the son of James ben-Alpheus, and one the son of Simon Iscariot. We won't have any trouble telling them apart, though. This Judas—" He touched the sturdy youth whose rugged frame showed the hours he had spent working his father's farm— "prefers to be known as Thaddaeus. And for this Judas—" He looked with solemn tenderness at the handsome, worldly wise man before Him— "so much lies ahead." Perhaps it was only a trick of the firelight that made Jesus' eyes suddenly glisten, as if filled with tears. "So much lies ahead."

The sun had just crested the horizon when Jesus turned to the little band of men, arms spread to include them all. "Come, kneel with Me. I must ask My Father to bless you."

As Peter knelt, he looked once more at Judas—suave, handsome, self-assured, obviously a sophisticated city man instead of an uneducated fisherman like himself—and felt a sharp pang of inadequacy for the task that lay ahead. Leaning over to Andrew, he said quietly, "I can see why Jesus picked Judas, but why did He choose the rest of us?"

Standing by Peter's side, Tarik frowned in bewilderment. "I can see why Jesus picked all the rest of them," he said to Gabriel, "but why did He choose Judas?"

Chapter 17

"Technically, Jesus didn't choose Judas," Gabriel replied, "but I know what you mean. He could have refused him, but He didn't."

Tarik couldn't help but scratch his head. "I suppose He did it this way because of the others, since they wouldn't have understood why He would turn away such a prominent, talented, cultured socialite. They think He needs that kind of support for His kingdom, which is ludicrous, of course."

"I hate to bring in a note of gloom on this remarkable occasion," Arion joined in, "but I have the feeling that Iscariot is going to bring trouble to our Lord sooner or later. I guess it's going to be another one of those times when we just have to trust that He knows what He's doing."

"I couldn't help but hear what you were saying." At the meek voice beside them, they turned as one to their friend, his short brown hair swept back, a look of appeal on his face.

"Why, Taberah, I haven't been able to work with you for almost four centuries," Tarik exclaimed. He smiled sympathetically. "I can see you have a real challenge."

"You've got that right." Taberah nodded. "He's had just about every disadvantage there is in life, from his mother ingesting toxins before he was born, to being born into wealth and privilege, to having every whim indulged from day one. He is prideful, spiteful, cruel, and, I regret to say, dishonest."

"Doesn't he have any good qualities?"

"A few. He speaks very persuasively, with a great deal of power that could be used for good or ill, and deep down he has a longing for something more substantial than his life of excess has brought him. I expect that he will make a very loyal disciple, as long as everything goes his way. But . . ." Taberah's voice trailed away into silence.

"But if it doesn't, it will be like stepping on a viper," Tarik finished.

"Yes." Taberah sighed heavily. "As much as I love Judas, I fear for our Master. He explained before He left heaven about all the things He would have to suffer, but I tell you, it would nearly break my heart if Judas should turn out to be the one who brings it about."

"We will watch and pray with you," Tarik promised. "In the meantime, we're so glad you have joined our little company."

"Not so little anymore." Jabir flashed a quick grin. "Perhaps you haven't noticed, but there are nearly two score of us on direct assignment, and many more standing by. Look around—this is our finest hour." His triumphant words stirred them all, and they burst into a spontaneous hymn.

The morning sun melted over the hilltop, warming the men as they still knelt. Bright as it was, it was overpowered by the glow of the swords that surrounded them on every side. As Jesus knelt with each disciple, laying His hands on their heads as He prayed, the current that flowed from the throne grew so strong it was nearly visible in the human spectrum. The angels beamed with delight at the blessing of their charges.

Last of all, Jesus knelt with Taberah's charge. Taberah knelt, too, overcome to be once again in the direct presence of the Majesty of heaven. Jesus placed His hands on the wavy black hair and lifted His gaze to the sky. "My Father, I ask that You would also bless this man, who is beloved in Your sight. Draw near to him and help him as he begins the work You have planned for him. Thank You for this special gift, this new servant of the kingdom. Father, thank You so much for Judas Iscariot."

Peter walked down the mountainside toward the shore of Galilee, silent for once. Mingled with the awe he felt at the solemn commitment he had just made was a soaring elation. It seemed his patience had finally paid off, that events were finally speeding toward the establishment of a new order, free of the Romans. He looked down at his dusty robe, worn and patched, with thin spots in the elbows. Soon now he would exchange it for soft linen—a new garment every day! And food, all the food he could ever eat. His mouth watered.

Along the narrow strip of beach, a huge crowd waited for them, larger than ever before. *This is it,* he thought, *this is what we've been waiting for. All Jesus needs is more support from the people before He can act.* Peter looked at the diverse men around him. *And, as much as I hate to admit it, Judas will probably help Him even more than the rest of us, at least in getting Him crowned King. He must know just about everybody that's worth knowing.* Peter couldn't help feeling a twinge of envy. None of the leaders of the nation had ever heard of Simon the son of Jonas. Taking a deep breath and straightening himself, Peter resolved that within two years they would all know his name.

There was just not enough room on the sliver of shore for everyone to hear Jesus, so He led them back the way He had just come, until each had a place to sit. The people pressed as near as they could to Him, but the newly dedicated disciples pressed nearer still, not wanting to leave His side for even a moment. Somehow, they sensed that each word He was about to speak was meant just for them—that in them they would find the direction they needed in order to fulfill the immense task that lay ahead.

Jesus smiled in the peculiar way they had come to know meant that they would have to think very hard to understand what He was going to say. "Happy are those who are bankrupted spiritually—and know it. The kingdom of heaven belongs to them."

Well, I'm pretty close to bankrupt, Peter thought. *That ought to count for something. And I know a lot of Romans that I'd like to see bankrupted!*

"Those who are proud," Jesus spoke again, "work and try their hardest to buy salvation with their own efforts. Those who are humble hold out their empty hands and beg Adonai to fill them. Such a prayer the Father is delighted to answer." Many who listened nodded in dawning comprehension.

"Happy are those who are sad," Jesus chuckled, knowing He had startled them with His apparent contradiction, "for they shall be comforted."

Nathanael felt the tears come to his eyes. Surely those words were intended for him! For many nights after his wife had left him, he wept silently, fearing to wake his young boys. The pain and sense of failure had been almost crushing. Jesus' words brought hope and healing to his lonely, discouraged heart.

"There are many kinds of sorrow," Jesus said. "Some drive us away from Adonai; others bring us closer. If a thief is caught and sentenced to death, he will certainly feel sorrow, but only because he was caught. Unless a sinner is sad *because he has sinned,* his sorrow will do no good. True sorrow leads to repentance, which means turning away from the sin. This is what is pleasing to God."

Looking right at Nathanael, He said, "Others are tested with great trials and suffering. At times they wonder if God has forsaken them. But even during their suffering, when they cannot feel His presence, the Father is very near. He loves each one of you as His own child, and in His time He will cause you to rejoice." Nathanael was not the only one who surreptitiously wiped watery eyes.

"Happy are those who are gentle and humble. The whole earth shall be their inheritance."

Judas couldn't believe what he was hearing. *This Man is so naïve. I didn't know anyone still believed this stuff. I'll have to help Him see the truth—that the only language the Romans understand is force. The only thing the humble inherit is an early grave!*

Peter squirmed a bit too. Who had ever heard of a gentle head of security? The very idea was preposterous. Of course that couldn't be what Jesus was talking about.

Jesus suppressed a sigh, reading every word His friends thought. "The world sees gentleness as weakness, but which is harder—to show anger to those who are cruel or to show love? To be gentle, you must have the greatest strength there is, which is the love of God. If His love finds a place in your hearts, you will be like He is. If you are to have a part in My kingdom, you must accept My peace under all circumstances and in the face of any abuse.

"Happy also are those who are hungry and thirsty for the righteousness of Adonai. They will be filled."

Did my stomach just growl? wondered Peter.

I hope that noise didn't come from my brother. No, wait; I can tell by his face that it did. Honestly, Peter, we're in important company now. Andrew wished he had sat somewhere else.

Matthew leaned closer to Jesus, a shy smile on his face. *That's so beautiful! I'd never thought of it quite that way before. When I was still rich, I had all the food I could eat, all the wine I could drink, and all the women money could buy, but I was never satisfied. I never guessed it at the time, but I was hungering and thirsting for righteousness, and Jesus has truly filled me.* That thought led to another: *I wish I had the chance to tell someone what Jesus did for me.*

"Happy are those who show mercy to others, for mercy will be given to them. I know this is hard for some of you to understand. You have been brought up to believe in revenge and retribution; you've been told that mercy is yet another sign of weakness. But if God rewarded His people according to their sins, who could stand before Him?"

"No one," Andrew admitted.

"Not even one," Jesus confirmed. "It is only through the mercy of the Father that anyone feels his spiritual poverty or comes to repentance or becomes gentle or develops any part of a character that is pleasing in the sight of heaven. And if the Father shows you such mercy, of course He wants you to show mercy to others as well."

"Except to the Romans," Simon said loudly enough for all to hear.

Amid the general laughter, Jesus said soberly, "Don't you think the Romans are in even more need of mercy than you?" The coarse laughter died on suddenly somber lips as Jesus' words bore in at them. "The Scriptures say, 'For I desired mercy, and not sacrifice; and the knowledge of God more than burnt offerings.' More than anything, Adonai desires to extend mercy to every human being—Jew, Samaritan, Roman, and Greek, alike. The greater the sin, the more the sinner needs his heavenly Father's mercy.

"Happy are those whose hearts are pure, for they shall see God face to face."

See God? Had they but known it, Philip's and Thomas's thoughts ran along the same course. *No one can see God. I don't even know where He is.* It was so much easier to understand the sea, the grass, the trees, and the sky, than to grasp the idea of a God so real that someday He could be seen—by them. It didn't cross their minds that heaven was a real place, a real city with real streets, where someday they would walk if they were faithful.

"Sadly, many believe that as long as they don't perform an impure act, they are right before Adonai, but that is not enough. Our hearts must also be pure, and every thought holy. Anger, cherished in the heart, leads to hatred and even murder. Lust, cherished in the heart, leads to adultery. Greed, cherished in the heart, leads to theft. Every evil act springs from evil thoughts and imaginings. Whatever is plentiful in the heart will overflow through the mouth and spill into the hands."

Peter could hardly comprehend the full scope of what he heard. He had always thought of himself as a good man, far above a heathen or a publican. What Jesus said convicted him that many of the things that went through his mind were not at all pleasing to God. Despairingly, he thought, *There's so much more to being good than I realized. How can anyone ever measure up to this? It's impossible, that's what it is.*

"Happy are the peacemakers, because they will be called Adonai's children." Jesus smiled down at John, sitting raptly at His right hand.

James—the other James—smiled wryly to himself. *You can't have a family with seven children—hers, mine, and ours—without learning plenty about being a peacemaker.*

Peacemaker? That sounds just like Abba, Thaddaeus decided. *Anyone who can make my sisters get along deserves some kind of prize.*

There He goes again, talking about peace as if everyone will be happy if they just love, love, love. A frown was the only sign of turmoil on Simon's face. *Jesus just doesn't understand that sometimes the path to peace leads directly through war.* He allowed himself a small smile, feeling very profound. *The Roman tyrants rule by force, and nothing will ever change that except a show of greater force.*

Jesus patiently continued His explanation. "Man often makes plans for peace that are based on force. But the absence of war does not make true peace. These efforts are doomed because they do not bring about a change in the heart. You can make laws against fighting, but no law can make you have peace. Only Adonai can give you this gift. Only Adonai can change your hearts."

He looked at the Twelve, His precious harvest, and for a moment, time opened up before Him. He saw what the future held for each of them—hunger and sword, arrest and crucifixion, torment and betrayal of every kind. Only one would reach his full years, dying a natural death, alone and apparently forgotten, an elderly prisoner on a desolate island. Jesus would have wept but for the vision of their glorious reward, as eleven of the original company entered into the City, clothed in white robes, radiant with everlasting youth.

"Happy are those who are persecuted for obeying the truth. The kingdom of My Father belongs to them." Silently Jesus flashed a prayer to heaven that His dear ones would stand firm when the test came upon them. His gaze lingered on James and John, knowing that one brother would be the first of His faithful eleven to sleep in death, the other the last.

"You will be happy when men speak evil things of you and do everything they can to harm you because of Me. They have done these things to each of the prophets who has gone before, and they will do it to you also, but be glad! Your heavenly reward will be wonderful, beyond imagination.

"Those who seek honor and approval from the world may receive it, but that will be their only reward. If you seek honor and approval from Adonai by following His way to happiness, your reward will never fade away or be destroyed. You are the light of the world."

As Jesus continued speaking, Peter's thoughts remained on the idea of a reward. What Jesus had mentioned sounded so different from what Peter had expected, and yet enticing on a whole new level.

Unused to such abstract thinking, Peter felt awkward as he mentally turned the problem every which way, trying to figure out how to make two opposite views harmonize. Dimly, he heard Jesus say animatedly, "No, don't think that I came here to destroy the law and do away with the prophets. I didn't! I came to fulfill them—to complete them. I tell you truly, that until heaven and earth pass away—" He gestured to the sky above and the ground beneath—"not even the dot of an *i* or the crossing of a *t* will be removed, until all things are made perfect. So, as long as you see the sun come up in the morning and feel the grass under your feet, God's law still stands." Eventually, Peter gave up trying to understand right then and just let the words wash over him, trying to remember and treasure each one.

"Do not swear by anything—not by heaven, because it is God's throne, nor by the earth, for that is His footstool.

"If someone hits you on the right cheek, let him hit your other cheek, as well.

"Love your enemies.

"Save up your treasures in heaven where they will be safe, because wherever you place your treasure, that is where your heart will belong."

By the time Peter laid down that night, he thought his head must be swollen, so filled was it with information and instruction. Only that morning, he had been so overwhelmed and felt so inadequate for the task that had been laid on him. The brief, whispered prayer for guidance had been answered beyond every expectation. As his eyes drooped closed, he prayed silently once more: *Adonai, I know You heard my prayer this morning, so thank You. Now I have another favor to ask. Please help me to understand all the things Jesus said today, and help me to be able to follow them. It sounds like so much, and I know I can't do it without You. Be with my family too. Amen.*

In the stillness, he thought he heard a soft voice speak to his heart. *"Of course I will help you. Rest in Me."* Confidence restored, Peter slept.

"I hate it when he smirks like that," Oreb growled, glaring at the spot where Tarik smiled beatifically as he kept his unsleeping vigil. The demon ground his teeth, not looking away until he heard his commander's voice calling the meeting to order.

The rebel leader was in fine form, pacing to relieve his overflowing energy. "At last the enemy has laid out His plan of attack, and we can begin to counter it. The part where He laid out, commandment by commandment, how He expects these weak little humans to keep the law was priceless. Never before has He given us such a far-reaching tool to use against Him."

Oreb tried to hide his bafflement, stretching to see around the huge form of Set, who was seated directly in front of him.

"Don't look so disheartened," Satan said jovially. "Don't you see? The more wide-ranging the commandments are—the more ways there are to

break them—the better off we are! Even I, with all my study of the Scrip-tures, had never realized the full extent of the commandments. It should be almost too easy now to tempt every human into doing something—any-thing—wrong, even the men in the Inner Circle. Also, don't neglect their families.

"One last thing to keep in mind . . ." His gaze flicked over Oreb and Set, Zeeb and Ares, before he continued ominously. "I know how ambitious you all are. But those who are assigned to the Inner Circle had better not let any personal views interfere with our ultimate objective of winning full control of earth and ensuring our survival. Unite in your hatred of the great foe and leave the squabbling until after we have declared victory. Success will be re-warded appropriately. So will failure. That is all."

Chapter 18

Jesus led the winding procession through the streets of Magdala, a city filled with such vice and blatant wickedness that many from the cities to the north considered it to be like Sodom and Gomorrah of old. In fact, Peter privately thought of the place as "Little Sodom" and wished he had never set foot there.

In an aside to Andrew, he said, "Please don't tell me we're doing this again."

Andrew gave no reply; there was no need. Obviously, they were doing this again.

You'd think He would have learned by now, Peter complained silently to himself. *Both times before, she promised she would stop too. And where is she now? Right back where she started, that's where. I hope Rimona never finds out I was here.* He shuddered at the thought. *She wouldn't understand. I mean, I don't understand. I just hope this time He's here to tell her how wicked she is.*

By now, the route was familiar to many of those with Jesus, and they pressed as close together as they could. Peter spotted their target up ahead, reclining on a bench outside her small but luxurious apartment. He looked away, trying not to notice her heavily shadowed eyes, artificially bright cheeks, and the sheer veil over the lower half of her face. Her clothing was worse—what there was of it. The tips of his ears turned as red as the woman's lips, and he blushed like a schoolboy. He had never seen anything like this in Capernaum.

The woman turned toward them and turned suddenly pale as she recognized Jesus. Terror filled her eyes, and her face was contorted; she tried frantically to get away. As Jesus came silently nearer, her feet scrabbled against the bench, and she pressed her back tightly to the wall.

He didn't touch her—not yet. But He stooped low and looked into her face. Peter could only see Jesus from behind, but he could tell the Master was not angry or even indignant. "Come out of her," Jesus said loudly enough for everyone to hear. The woman shuddered, her eyes rolled back into her head, and she slid from the bench and lay very still upon the ground.

Jesus took her hand, then, and whispered her name. Her eyes fluttered open, fixing on the kind face in front of her. The hardened prostitute dissolved in tears, her cosmetics flowing in a colorful, grotesque river down her cheeks, as she tore away her veil and flung herself at Jesus' feet.

"I'm sorry, so sorry," she sobbed over and over again. "I didn't mean to. It was just the one time, and then I couldn't get away. They had me again. Thank You for saving me from them; I'll never do it again—I really mean it this time." Jesus' feet and ankles were liberally smeared with black, green, and red.

You promised last time too, Peter thought irritably. *I hope Jesus isn't going to fall for your empty vows, because they sure don't fool me!*

Just then a small hand grasped his arm and pulled hard. Reluctantly, Peter pulled his gaze from the scene as the tugging became more insistent. The sight of the sweet face down near his elbow nearly undid him. "Mother Salome!" he gasped. "Do James and John know you're here?"

"Am I too late? Did Jesus heal her again? Let me get up where I can see." Zebedee's diminutive wife was practically jumping up and down in her effort to see over the shoulders of her tall sons.

Peter used his elbows to open a space between his friends. "There you are, Mother Salome. You missed most of it, though."

Angrily, James and John looked down, ready to make short work of the rude person who was shoving against them so insistently. Both leaped back in unison as if the woman standing there had been a snake. They came down hard on the feet of Matthew and Andrew on either side. "Mother!" they cried in unison. Peter couldn't help laughing to see the two large men flounder and stammer.

"Don't worry, boys." She took their shaking hands. "I'm not the only mother who came. Now be quiet; I want to listen!"

If Jesus had any doubts about Mary's sincerity as she continued to pour out a flood of assurances, He kept them to Himself. Lifting her to her feet, He said softly, "My dear sister, you should go home."

She shrank back. "I can't do that. I know You don't understand, but I just can't. Not yet, anyway. May I just follow You?"

No, no, no. Absolutely not! Tell her no! Oh, this is worse than the last time. What will people say? Peter held his breath, waiting for Jesus' answer.

"Of course you may come with us," Jesus welcomed her. "We'll wait here a few minutes while you wash your face and change your clothes."

Peter could see by the dismayed looks the other disciples gave each other that they were as unhappy as he was, and none more so than James and John. All the married ones were wondering what their wives would think, and the rest were worried that no decent woman would have them if she knew they were spending weeks, maybe even months, walking around the countryside in company with the now notorious Mary of Magdala.

James and John reached for their mother, but it was too late. She had already slipped past them and stood beside Jesus and Mary. "Oh, you poor girl," she clucked sympathetically. "Let me help you." Turning to Jesus, she said briskly, "I know You do just fine healing and casting out demons, but this is women's business now, and You'd better just keep out of it. I'll take care of everything." Still chattering, she took Mary by the arm and helped her up the stairs to her rooms.

"Thank you, Salome," Jesus called after them, chuckling.

James and John were mortified to hear their mother address the future King with such familiarity—and in front of the crowd too. Their mother had always been such a busybody; they didn't even want to think about what things would be like with her along—pushing, prodding, and coaxing at every step.

A few minutes later the two women were back with everything duly organized and neatly packed. Truly, it hadn't been much of a challenge for someone with Salome's skills, since most of Mary's clothing wasn't fit to bring anyway. "Here we are, Jesus, all ready to go. James! John! My precious boys, I didn't have a chance to greet you properly." Leaving Mary's side for a moment, she kissed them soundly to the amusement of all who could see. "Let's be going, then. Jesus, what are we waiting for? We need to get this poor girl out of here."

There were mixed reactions from the hundred or more people who regularly followed Jesus from place to place. Some were shocked and angry; some were titillated. And a few, who had much faith in the soon-to-be King, were glad, even praying that this time the Magdalene might succeed.

Peter was certainly not in the latter group, especially that night around the fire. Mary, desperate to stay close to Jesus lest her demons return, intruded on the Inner Circle, even going so far as to take Peter's usual place right next to Jesus. That left him with a painful predicament. If he pushed his way close to Jesus, he would be close to Mary, too. But if he stayed away, the others would have a more honored spot than he. Finally he sat as close to Mary as he could stand to be, glaring fiercely at her all the while.

The joy-filled woman didn't even notice. With her face clean and modest clothing covering her body, she looked like a completely different person. Her lips had a hint of a stain yet, but that would be gone in a day or two. She gave Jesus her whole attention as He began to tell His stories. "Once there was a man who had been taken over by a demon," He was saying.

Peter gritted his teeth. "He tells this one every time," he whispered to James and Andrew, "and it never does any good."

Jesus smiled at Mary and the others gathered around Him. "One day, Someone came to him and forced the demon to leave. The evil spirit wandered all over the earth, but soon began thinking about his former home. Finally he went back to check on the man and see what condition he was in.

"To his amazement, he found his house sparkling clean, swept and scrubbed from top to bottom—but empty. 'Hey, look at this, everybody,' he called to his friends. When they came, seven of them, all bigger and more evil than the first demon, he invited them in, too, and the man ended up far worse than he had been in the beginning." Jesus looked intently at Mary. "It is not enough to get rid of the evil inside. To stay pure, you must be filled with the goodness that comes only from Adonai."

Jesus paused, and in the brief silence that followed, Salome's motherly voice, filled with pride, rang out clearly in mid sentence, ". . . those two right by Jesus, yes the good-looking ones, they're my boys!"

James and John blushed and hung their heads as Jesus looked around and then continued His story. "This is a lesson for all of you, as well. Any sin that you have to overcome must be replaced with a wholesome habit. Any void you leave in your life is an invitation for evil to come and fill it. Instead, be filled with God and His love."

He spoke a little longer, and then, as He often did, he turned to the eager young disciple sitting nearby, reed flute at the ready. "Nathanael, would you favor us with some music?"

A few people rolled their eyes, but Peter was pleased. Nathanael had quick fingers and a light touch that coaxed lovely sounds out of the little carved instrument. True, he tended to play the same songs over and over, but he did it so well that most didn't mind. And when Jesus began to sing to them from the Psalms, no one even moved.

"Bless the LORD, O my soul:
And all that is within me, bless His holy name!
Bless the LORD, O my soul,
And forget not all His benefits:
Who forgives all your iniquities,
Who heals all your diseases,
Who redeems your life from destruction,
Who crowns you with loving-kindness and tender mercies."

Nathanael seemed to know just which notes would best complement the familiar melodies, and by the song's end not an eye was still dry. Quietly, reluctant to shatter the sense that this was holy ground, Peter slipped to his sleeping place without a word. Jesus walked to a small clearing and bowed in prayer. It would be very late before He lay down, and long before dawn He would be there again, clinging to His Father to find strength.

Mary's demons waited in a writhing, malignant huddle at the outskirts of the camp. Holy angels barred their path, even though it wasn't strictly necessary. None of the evil spirits would voluntarily go that close to the Only Begotten—not if they could avoid it.

Like a soft, ominous night sound came the oft-repeated complaint. "We can't get her now. Not while He's watching. He's always watching—and praying for her."

"Don't worry," one of the small, shivering figures hissed comfortingly. "She never lasts long. If we just wait a little while, she'll be ours again. She always is."

Judging by the size of the dust cloud that rose and choked them all, Peter guessed there must be more than three hundred people in the crowd by the time they sighted the city where they were to stay that night. He took the surge of popularity as yet another sign that Jesus would soon wear a crown, and he smiled to himself in spite of his aching feet. *That's it, I'll get myself a chariot. Why didn't I think of that before?*

The road curved to the left around a clump of large cedar trees before straightening as it approached the city gate. Not far from the road, several men were digging a hole in the rough earth of the burial ground, pausing now and then to rest as sweat poured down their bodies. "Look, Andrew," Peter nudged his brother, "someone must've died."

"Not only that," Andrew replied, "but they're going to bury him any minute now."

"How do you know? Oh." Now Peter, too, saw the second cloud of dust cloak the procession just leaving the city. "This is Nain, right? I've never been here before."

"That's what Judas said," Andrew nodded, "but I haven't been here, either, so I'm not sure."

Chapter 18

As the two groups neared each other, they slowed, unsure of what to do. Jesus stepped forward and motioned everyone to stop. The residents of Nain stood just as they were, but the followers of Jesus swarmed around to form a wide circle, each trying to see what was going on.

Peter recognized one of the men holding the stretcher as someone who had often sat and listened to Jesus. Searching his memory, Peter seemed to recall that the man was usually with two women, one a servant and one of higher rank. There, that was one of them now, supporting the bereaved woman on the right. And although her hair hid her features as she buried her face in grief, surely that was the other woman on the left. Peter felt quite smug, as he did whenever he made an identification like this. Having a knack for recognizing faces was surely one of his most important skills for serving the King; Peter was sure no one else had made the connection.

Jesus stepped close to the side of the stretcher, and in one smooth movement pulled down the sheet covering the body, laying it open to the waist. Peter grimaced slightly. It was certainly one of the most unattractive corpses he had seen—a young man, most likely the woman's son. Illness had taken its toll, and the boy was hardly more than a skeleton, but the worst part was the wide-open mouth with the jaw dropped down against his throat in a last, silent scream. Whatever dreadful sickness had taken him, he had not gone gently.

Only the mother's wracking sobs marred the stillness. She was almost fainting and obviously unaware of anything going on around her. Tears ran down Jesus' cheeks as He turned to look at her and at the man carrying the stretcher, whose red-rimmed eyes gave him away as a close relative. Jesus touched the man comfortingly, though he was ceremonially unclean. Then He reached down and picked up the stiff, bony arm that had spilled off the stretcher.

"Young man, get up!"

Immediately, starting at Jesus' hands, a blush of color spread up the boy's arm and rushed over his body. The shriveled flesh grew and swelled before their very eyes. The youth's chest rose and fell, and he opened his eyes to look straight up into the sky. Squinting into the bright light, he looked around, puzzled. When he saw Jesus bending over him, he sat up.

For the first time he saw the crowd and the haggard, weeping woman nearby. "Mother?" he said hesitantly, "Where am I?"

His mother didn't move—couldn't move. She stared, unblinking, unable to comprehend the scene before her. One of the women helping her looked up then, and grasped it all instantly. "He's alive!" Her ear-piercing scream was heard by every person there. Overcome with joy, she shook the mother and shouted, "He's alive; Jesus raised him!"

That's definitely the same woman. Peter was intrigued. He had never gotten a really good look at her before, and he wondered if she were hiding something. His curiosity grew when she froze, looking startled, then shrank back, trying to hide her face again. Yes, she was definitely up to something; he could tell.

The young man stood up just as the stretcher crashed to the ground, the pallbearers too shocked to keep their grip on the handles. Ranon, as Peter later learned the boy's name was, walked slowly to his mother, trying to make sense of why she would be standing in the middle of the road, shaking from head to foot and weeping violently.

"Mother, what's wrong? Did someone die?" He clutched the sheet more tightly around his waist, belatedly aware that he was in a most unusual state of undress. Looking down at the trailing cloth, he finally understood. "Did *I* die?"

It hit Peter then. Distracted by his sleuthing, he hadn't really been paying attention until now. His jaw dropped open in amazement. This boy had been dead, and now he was alive! Jesus had raised him from the dead! The ramifications were stunning. *I don't need to be afraid to die anymore. If someone kills me, Jesus will just raise me to life again.* Then a picture flashed into his mind. Jesus led a small army of only a few thousand against a vast sea of Romans. The two forces collided, melded, and the Jews began to fall. Within minutes it was plain that Rome would have an easy victory. Then Jesus walked through the melee, perhaps even glowing a bit. Of course, no weapon could touch Him. Going from one of His dead or dying soldiers to the next, He touched them, and they stood, ready to fight once more. No matter how many times the Romans killed them, they just kept coming back, until the field was littered with the red plumes and shining armor of the ruined foes. The way to the throne was clear, for none could stand against such a glorious King and His awful power.

This talent will surely come in handy, Peter thought, watching the widow, Ornah, as she wept in joy, thanking Jesus again and again. *He's going to be the greatest King Israel has ever had.* The boy joined his mother to express his gratitude, and the enormity of what had happened overwhelmed Peter all over again. He trembled as he looked at Ranon, now at the pinnacle of health. And when Ornah reached out to touch Jesus, thanking Him yet again, all traces of her age faded away, and she looked as radiantly young as a girl.

"Mother, I think I'd better get some clothes on," Ranon said dryly. "This is getting rather embarrassing."

"Oh, son!" Fresh tears welled up as Ornah laughed. "I've been so happy I haven't even thought of it." They walked by Jesus' side back toward the city. Behind them, the freshly dug grave sat open, abandoned, and forgotten.

Chapter 19

"*M*ove aside! I'm taking personal charge of the situation," Satan snarled. "What part of 'move' don't you understand?" Viciously, he kicked his underlings aside. "He's coming this way, and we've got to be ready."

Ever since his stunning defeat at the temple, Satan had organized an information network to send an alert every time it appeared that a needy human might try to intersect with Jesus. At the slightest indication that someone was merely thinking about coming to Jesus for help, every effort was made to discourage, or failing that, to prevent a meeting from actually taking place. The task-force leaders handled this part, sometimes succeeding and sometimes failing, but their standing orders were to notify Satan himself if any cases of particular importance seemed to be taking shape. An imminent death in a city less than five miles from Jesus and in His direct path, certainly seemed to qualify as important.

"Delay Him. Do whatever you have to do, but make sure He doesn't get here in time. I'll be waiting right here. I needed a break anyway." A nervous subordinate from the lowest order produced a comfortable chair, seemingly from nowhere, and the rebel leader settled into it, a terrible smile on his face.

He could smell the rank odor in the little room if he chose, and he did. Watching a death, especially an agonizing one such as this, afforded him intense pleasure. The suffering of the lonely widow on the brink of exhaustion as she tended her only son inflamed his sadistic passions still further. The unfortunate woman had no idea what had caused the sudden heaviness in the room, but she bowed even lower in her sorrow.

Each of the frequent reports were encouraging. Efforts to slow the crowd had borne fruit, and now Jesus would never make it in time, even if He ran the whole way. Yachne, the town busybody and the only one who might have helped, had been away and would arrive too late. The neighbors would know nothing until it was over. Perfect, just perfect!

The underling who had brought the chair cleared his throat and stammered a few times before nerving himself to speak. "Er . . . your excellency, I couldn't help but thinking . . ."

"And that's one of your main problems too," Satan snapped, but only halfheartedly. He was enjoying himself much too much to be very petulant. "Very well, what is it?"

"I was thinking that even if our enemy came too late, maybe it wouldn't make any difference. Remember M—" A giant hand shot out, reached around his neck, and squeezed hard, so that he finished with a squeak, "—oses?"

"Don't speak that name in my presence! Do you think I'm so stupid that I haven't considered that possibility? But have you seen Jesus raise any dead people yet? Have you? Well, neither have I. Could He? I'm sure He could. But for whatever reason He hasn't, and I'm sure He's not about to start here, today, with an unimportant, unknown teenage boy!"

Terrified beyond belief, the smaller demon sought obscurity in an even deeper dimension. In the raucous laughter pursuing his unceremonious retreat, no one marked, less than a minute later, the trio of humans turning onto the street, nor realized their destination until they were right outside the door.

For a long while after that, every word Satan uttered was even more vile than the one before. Apparently he hadn't known that the man, Oded, was Ornah's brother. It wouldn't have mattered anyway, for the boy was nearly gone, and there was nothing any human could have done to delay his final breath. The Guardians did nothing, either. They only stood by solemnly without interfering, their somber faces giving nothing away.

Once Satan calmed down and realized that the prayers of the big man were having no apparent effect, his pleasure returned. Though Oded couldn't hear him, Satan mocked him in a way that had every wicked spirit for a mile *rolling with laughter. And when the end finally came, the heavenly citizens could not help but shudder at the explosion of evil glee.*

With an effort, Satan composed himself and stood. "All right, we've had our fun. Now get the old busybody in here to hurry things along. It will take careful timing, but we can still have him buried and be gone well before our enemy arrives. Places, everyone." The nervous assistant crept out of hiding, folded the chair, and vanished again.

It was rather odd. While the efforts to delay Yachne had worked just fine, once on the scene, she resisted all attempts to rush her. By the time she even found out she was needed, time was very short. It was getting late in the afternoon, and although her greatest concern was to see the body buried that day and not have to wait until morning, she insisted that the boy still be thoroughly cleaned. Unseen spirits cursed and tugged on their hair, nearly dancing with impatience as she supervised the preparations, careful that no step, however small, was left out.

"Hurry up already, or I'll have to bury him myself," Satan half shrieked. And when he saw the tiniest hint of a smile appear on the face of Ranon's Guardian, he went absolutely wild. In the end, prohibited from meddling with the humans, he could do nothing except wait, nursing the growing fear that once again he had been caught up in a plan much larger than his own.

As Ornah finally left the house beside the body of her son, the two visiting women holding her lest she fall, word came from the lookout that Jesus was at last within sight of the city. There was no other choice now. Satan strode along grimly at the front of the procession, followed by as many of his troops as he could muster at a moment's notice.

Demons pressed close to the grieving family, filling their minds with doubts and questions. "If God is fair, why did He let this happen? Doesn't He care about us? Jesus has healed so many other people. If He is really God's Son, why didn't He come in time? Is God listening? Is He even there?"

Such doubting words found fruitful soil in those broken, aching hearts, and as their mistrust grew, so did the power of the demons, who swelled and stretched, more confident with each passing second. If, by their timing, they could not avert even the possibility of a blessing, there was still an excellent chance they could cause the humans to doubt, robbing themselves of their only hope of a miracle. As long as no one had any faith with which to receive Him, Jesus would be as powerless as if He were bound.

Chapter 19

The two companies came to a confused stop, facing each other. Satan folded his arms defiantly, and stood ready to challenge any display of divine power. Jesus did not even acknowledge his presence but walked straight to the covered form on the stretcher. Gabriel was at His side, and none of the rebels dared enter a dispute. They just held their breath, hoping that Jesus was not going to do what they thought He was going to do.

Carefully, Jesus pulled back the sheet, not brushing against the boy in any way. No trace of sin or sickness—not even death itself—could endure the touch of the Son's hand. He paused, and Satan knew He was searching the hearts of the boy's family for a shred of faith. The rebel signaled his tempters to continue pushing their thoughts of disbelief, but they could only remain forcibly mute in the presence of their former Commander.

The mother was in turmoil and nearly out of her mind from the depth of her loss. Jesus looked on her with pity. Then He turned His gaze to Oded, the boy's uncle, and met his eyes knowingly. Oded, in spite of the many times he had seen Jesus heal others, had given place to the evil whisperings of the devil, and the sin of his doubting was far greater than that of his sister.

Then Jesus bent over Ranon, love showing in every movement, and Oded began again to weep, but this time in repentance. It was enough. "Young man, get up." Jesus' voice was quiet, but the effect on the unseen world was tremendous. What a flapping and wailing went on as the forces of darkness fell back before the mighty shout of the heavenly host!

"Mother, what am I doing here?" Tears sprang to the eyes of those watching at the wonder and confusion in the boy's face. How amazed he must have felt, to sleep in death and awake face to face with the Creator.

"Use your gift well, dear boy," Tarik said to himself. "Few have such an opportunity as this."

Of course Peter, aided neatly by Set, wasted no time deciding how this wonderful power of God could be used to further his erroneous ideas of the kingdom. Most of the tempters were still fearful and held at bay. Set, however, snarled at the Guardians, claiming the right to mingle among the holy messengers because of the sinful pride Peter cherished. And since that was the rule, reluctantly they let him pass.

Tarik was not idle, but it took him several minutes to turn Peter's mind back to the essence of what he had just seen. Without the work of the Spirit, it would have been impossible. And when Peter finally prayed silently, thanking Adonai for letting him see this great event, Tarik smiled broadly. "Move back," he commanded Set, stepping between his charge and the towering demon. "It's my turn again."

As the two groups merged and turned toward the city, Tarik noticed something strange. The human assigned to his good friend, Deron, was behaving in a very peculiar manner. As an enemy of the Teacher, the highly placed servant often wore disguises in order to better spy on Him and went to great lengths to avoid calling attention to himself. Yet now he was weaving back and forth through the crowd, peering closely at the faces of all the women.

Peter saw him right away, and it took him but a moment to connect him to the suspicious beggar he had seen in Cana, as well as several middle-class businessmen who had come to hear Jesus for a day or two each. Yes, he looked different now, but the noble nose and hooded eyes were unmistakable, at least to someone with Peter's abilities. I knew it, I just knew it! *he gloated.* I'll be watching you, my friend.

Tarik laughed, calling to Deron, "What is he doing, anyway? He usually tries to be so sneaky."

Deron chuckled. "He's looking for his wife. It's a long story."

"Maybe you'll be able to tell me next time. I'd love to hear all about it."

"I don't want to hear any more. Enough!" Andrew scowled at his brother.

Peter scowled back. "But he's here again. That same one I told you about all those times before. He's right over there."

"Shhh! I want to listen." Andrew very pointedly turned his back and refused to look.

"The kingdom of heaven is like a treasure that was hidden in a field. A man found it, hid it again, then went and sold everything he had to be able to buy the field." Jesus raised His voice slightly to cover the interruption. "The kingdom of heaven is also like a merchant, a seller of fine pearls. One day he found a pearl that surpassed all others—the pearl of great price. It cost him everything he had, but he was well satisfied."

Peter's thoughts wandered back to the suspicious man. For at least the hundredth time, he wondered why no one would pay any attention to his warnings. Didn't they understand that this spy would do Jesus harm if he could? He, and a dozen others like him, were probably in the crowd right now, examining every word and gesture Jesus made, hoping to find something to use against Him. Peter sank back, feeling trapped and helpless. He didn't dare do what he wanted to do—stand up right there and denounce every person he thought was a spy—but obviously no one was going to listen to him when he tried to handle it quietly, either.

I know—as soon as I get a chance I'll ask John. Peter immediately felt better at the idea. *He spent all those years at the school in Jerusalem and met a lot of people. If anyone will know who this suspicious character is, it'll be John.*

"The kingdom of heaven is like a fishing net." The homely illustration of the judgment, with fishing boats nearby and nets spread out for all to see, made a subject clouded and complicated by the priests and scribes easy enough for even a child to understand. In fact, the children caught the deeper lesson missed by many of the adults—especially the disciples—that the great sorting of the saved and the lost would be carried out by heavenly hands and not their own. Their task was merely to gather all who would come and leave the act of judging to the Father.

At the close of the story, as the sun grew low in the sky, Jesus stood shakily to His feet. During the last several days in Capernaum, He had eaten little and slept less. In spite of the willing hospitality of Peter's household, the Master had been so busy teaching and healing that there had been no time for anything else. Now, near collapse, He called Peter, James, and John over to Him.

"I'm so tired," He said weakly. "We need to go somewhere I can rest for a little while."

"Where?" Peter asked, eager to help. "My boat is still here. I can take You anywhere You want to go."

"Please go the eastern shore. It will be quiet there."

The eastern shore? Peter shivered involuntarily. *Who would want to go there?* The far shore of the lake was barren, populated mostly by a few scattered heathen inhabitants. And then there were the demon-men. Stories had traveled far of the evil creatures that ranged up and down the shoreline and slept in the cemeteries, broken chains hanging from their ankles and wrists, and clanging against the stone memorials. Countless murders had been attributed to them, and any sensible Jew avoided the whole area.

Still, Jesus was very tired, and almost no one would dare follow Him where He now planned to go. Peter decided that for once he would obey first and ask questions later. Reflexively, he checked the weather around the lake. Everything seemed fine, so he called Andrew, and the two men began to go over the boat as quickly as they could in the waning light, checking for leaks or other damage.

Peter jogged down the beach to his house to say goodbye to his wife. The whole family had been in the crowd around Jesus that day, but it was Rimona's turn to prepare the evening meal. When Peter told her he had to leave, she was disappointed but not surprised.

"Jesus looked so tired today that I'm surprised He didn't leave yesterday. Just give me a second, and I'll fill a basket to take with you. I don't think either of you have been eating properly." She smiled at him. "It's been nice having you home, even if only for a few days."

Once again Peter marveled at the treasure he had won and had been too blind to see. "You're wonderful, Rimona. Thank you. And I, um . . . I love you."

"I love you, too, Simon Peter. Take good care of my husband while you're gone."

The door swung open easily as he reached for the food. "Thank you. Really, I mean it. Tell the boys I said Goodbye."

"Come back soon," she said softly. Suddenly afraid he might cry, Peter waved with determined good cheer and ran back to the boat just in time to help Jesus find a seat near the steering oar. "Here, Master. Rimona sent some food for us. Why don't You eat a little and then take a nap? Andrew and I have everything under control."

Jesus meekly took the food, managing to eat some bread and fish before He lay down. He closed His eyes and was asleep before the boat reached deep water.

"It's been a busy day," Matthew commented, sitting nearby, "first with Jesus' family coming to visit and then a whole day of teaching and healing."

Peter had long since given up ignoring the former tax collector and hoping he would go away. "I could hardly believe Jesus wouldn't stop what He was doing and go see them." He made a small adjustment to the steering oar.

Andrew and John strained against their oars, glad they were nearly far enough from shore to raise the sail. "I don't have any trouble believing it," Andrew said. "Did you hear the way His brothers were talking about Him?"

Matthew snorted. "At first I thought they were a delegation of Pharisees. You should have heard the way they criticized Him and everything He did, as if Jesus somehow needed to receive their wisdom." He was openly scornful. "The Messiah needing to learn from them, sitting at their feet to hear the precious gems falling from their parted lips! Nothing could be more ridiculous! They tried to turn His own mother against Him too."

Peter whistled in amazement. "Sounds like I should be grateful for *my* brother. No matter how annoying he gets, he's never done anything like that. But I still don't understand what Jesus meant when He said that we're His mother and brothers."

"I'm sure He didn't mean it literally," Matthew answered. "I think He just meant that our relationship to Him is even closer than family, because we look to Him to save us."

Andrew rested the handle of his oar on the floor of the boat and loosened the sail. "Amen to that."

Peter cast a pained glance at his sleeping Master. "Yes, but I still wish He would make more of an effort to win over the Pharisees and not just insult them all the time. It would really smooth His way to the throne if they put their power behind Him. But it seems that the more tired He gets, the more He goes out of His way to make them angry. I worry about Him."

Andrew and Matthew exchanged an amused look. "That's just what one of His brothers said."

"Well, then, at least that much is true," Peter snapped, more indignant than usual. "Jesus is making more enemies than you realize, and if He's not careful, He might get hurt. I suppose you don't care about that."

Andrew's heated reply dwindled away in the sudden ominous hush that spread over the lake; he had felt something like this only once before.

Then a strong gust of wind hurtled down on them from out of nowhere, catching the sail and driving the boat from its course. Peter braced himself with both feet, holding the steering oar as steady as he could without causing a devastating break in the wood. Matthew joined Andrew in the struggle to lower the sail.

"Hold on tight everyone; this is going to be a bad one," Peter shouted above the nonstop thunder crashing about them. Lightning flashes lit up the foaming water that threatened to engulf the little boat.

With tremendous effort, John and Andrew succeeded in releasing the sails, but they couldn't secure them. In seconds the thick fabric splayed out in tatters. Both men clung to the mast with all their strength, determined not to be swept overboard. Later, John remembered holding to the wooden beam and looking up into the sky, vaguely surprised to see the stars still steady in their ceaseless journey overhead.

"Help me, Andrew! I can't hold on by myself!" Peter struggled with the almost useless steering oar. In all their years on the lake, they had never seen a storm like this one. *Not even the one that killed Abba,* Peter reluctantly admitted. That storm had been vicious enough. An unpredictable gale-force wind had come on them without warning. During the few seconds of unnatural calm preceding the storm, their father had tied his two boys to the mast and gripped the steering oar for all he was worth. As the boat began to fill with water, he abandoned all attempts to guide it, frantically bailing until he was swept overboard by a wave that nearly swamped the tiny craft. And then, as quickly as it had come, the storm was gone, leaving young Simon and Andrew to wriggle loose and bring the foundering vessel to shore in the darkness.

This time, though, the lightning flashed in an unending show around them, almost seeming as if it were aimed directly at them, so close did it come before turning aside at the last instant to sizzle into the water. The air felt strange—so thick Peter could scarcely move or breathe. He worked feverishly with Andrew to keep the boat turned to face towering waves, larger than any he had ever seen, looming above them. With each successive wave, the boat tipped crazily, creaking and groaning as it mounted the tower of water, slowing—almost stopping—at the cusp, before plummeting into the valley and up the other side again.

James sat too far forward to help as water sprayed everywhere, drenching the fishermen and filling the bottom of the boat. "Bail," Peter shouted at the terrified men. "Bail, or die!"

Matthew was the first to respond, and the others followed his lead. They used everything they had—Matthew's favorite turban, Rimona's food basket, even their hands if they had nothing else. In the end, nothing mattered. They still could not keep the sea at bay, and Peter could see that the other boats, blown nearly close enough to touch, were succeeding no better as the wind swirled around them.

As the noise grew shattering, the boat listed sharply to one side, no longer tossing so violently. Alarmed, Peter saw that they were headed across the face of a huge curved wave. Then the full horror of the situation burst on him. It was not a wave at all, but a massive whirlpool, drawing his boat and its fragile human cargo down into the very depths of the sea.

Peter looked frantically for a way of escape, but there was none. His mind could not even accept what his eyes tried to tell him. Even if they could break away from the deadly grasp of the water, they would still be trapped by the raging whirlwind above.

God forgive me, he moaned. *I have failed them all. My brother will die, Matthew will die, even Jesus will die, fast asleep, never knowing anything was wrong. Jesus! What am I doing?* He reached forward and shook Jesus desperately. Andrew must have had the same thought, for he, too, bent over the sleeping Man. "Lord, save us! Don't You care that we're going to die?" The words were torn from his lips by the wind, shrieking as if it were the voices of a thousand demons surrounding them.

Actually, the number was well over a million demons, and there would probably have been more except that Satan felt unusually confident. As the boats left the shore by Capernaum, Gabriel signaled all the angels to retreat, leaving the convoy entirely unguarded and, Satan thought, vulnerable. No one was there to care for the disciples except Jesus, but He was exhausted and fast asleep.

Surely, such a tired Man posed no threat, and without their Guardians to guide them, the disciples would be easy to manipulate into sinful thoughts that would remove any lingering protection they might have had. The more he pondered the idea, the more the deceiver realized this was a grand opportunity to kill not only Jesus, but all His closest followers.

"Lead them into doubt," he barked to the tempters. "Distract them with anything you can and make them forget about our enemy. And you," he addressed his top generals, "muster as many of your troops as you can manage, and every weathermaster, too, whether you think you can spare them or not. I want at least half a million here in the next two minutes."

The message went out over their telepathic communications network, and it took a mere ninety seconds before the requested reinforcements, and more besides, arrived. At their leader's signal, a large portion swarmed over the boats to begin their campaign of whispering. At first the insensitive humans noticed nothing amiss, continuing to converse as usual, but by the time they reached the middle of the lake, most were nervous and on edge, though unsure why. Then the storm struck.

Reserve forces rode the cold front over the mountains surrounding the lake, pushing and guiding the violent wind so feared by Galilean fishermen. But this was to be no ordinary storm. Satan laughed to himself as he watched the tiny boats scatter before the onslaught. "Cue the lightning," he snarled.

At his signal, the weathermasters went to work, gathering charged particles from the air and hurling them gleefully at the panicked humans. Satan noted with passing concern that none of the lightning bolts actually reached their targets, passing harmlessly into the water at the last instant. Suspicious, he checked for any angelic guards that might have tried to slip in unnoticed, but there were none that he could see. "It must be some type of residual power," he said to himself, before turning his attention back to his troops. "Keep that lightning coming; it's frightening them, if nothing else. Let's see how He does when He gets wet!"

The demons powering the unnaturally tall waves saw to it that plenty of water sloshed over the sides of all the boats, saturating everyone, including Jesus, in bone-chilling spray. Still, the Son of God slept on.

"We've got to get to Him!" Satan was screaming by now. "If we can awaken Him with even one tiny bit of fear, He's ours. Work harder! This is life or death for us!"

As grand weathermaster, the fallen general had reserved the right to orchestrate the storm's stupefying finale. A flick of his hands sent the wind spin-

ning violently around him—a savage funnel that surrounded the boats and cut them off from the world outside. And in response, the fluid warriors in the deep turned their waves around and about until the very sea itself danced to the tune of the unseen piper of the whirlwind, holding the flotilla in its lethal embrace.

Somehow—it could have only been by the leading of the Spirit—several of the disciples suddenly, simultaneously, remembered their precious Passenger. Even now they bent over Him, pleading for Him to save them. Their words, their hearts, were full of disbelief, yet under all their doubt gleamed a tiny, golden grain of faith, and it was enough.

Jesus opened His eyes, taking in the situation with a single calm glance. Unhurriedly, He stood in the slanting vessel and looked squarely into the sky at His unseen opponent. Those in the other boats felt a sudden surge of hope as they watched the confrontation, though they little grasped the true nature of the battle being fought on their behalf.

Stretching out His arms, Jesus addressed not only the rampant storm, but the evil force behind it. "Peace! Be still!" He commanded.

Chapter 20

Peter exhaled slowly, releasing the breath he hadn't realized he was holding. For a long moment, the only sound was water dripping from the tattered sails. Cautiously, he took an experimental breath and discovered that the heaviness that had plagued him earlier was gone.

Jesus lowered His hands and slowly sat down, looking around at each of His disciples in turn. Peter felt foolish and embarrassed, as if he had been fearful for nothing. He scanned the peaceful night and the soft path the moon made on the glassy water. He *had* been fearful for nothing. Bowing his head with shame, he waited for the rebuke that was not long in coming.

In a gentle voice that nonetheless was filled with disappointment, Jesus asked them, "Why were you afraid? After everything you have seen and heard, do you still have so little faith? I was right here with you the whole time."

Peter almost wished He would just have yelled at them. Or something. That would have been easier to take than knowing the sadness they had brought their beloved Master. He didn't feel any better, either, when from one of the other boats, an awestruck voice floated out into the night. "What kind of Man is that? Even the winds and the seas obey Him!"

Adonai, Peter thought grandly, *I promise that from now on I will never be afraid. I will have faith. I will obey. I will be strong!* Such a good heart this fisherman had, but still unaware of the most important lesson of all—the true Source of his courage, faith, obedience, and strength.

All was silent for some time. Andrew and John laid into the oars mechanically, each lost in thought. Finally, John spoke the question on all their minds. "Master, what was that?"

"The prince of the power of the air," Jesus answered after a moment. "He comes again and again, but each time finds nothing in Me."

That riddle kept them occupied until the distant shore grew close in the first light of dawn. Between lack of sleep and the rush of relief at his narrow escape, Peter was quite giddy by the time the bottom of the boat scraped on the shore. James, nearest to the beach, jumped over the side and pulled the boat in closer.

"Just a moment," Jesus stopped Andrew and James from stepping into the water to help. "We must take full advantage of this little respite. In just a few days I will send you out two by two, throughout the whole land of Palestine, to spread the good news of the heavenly Father's great love."

"Just like the animals went into the ark," snickered Peter, bursting with even more than his usual confidence. He had survived the storm. He could do anything!

Jesus ignored his levity, only saying solemnly, "You have Me with you for such a short time. You must learn to depend on the Father, and not only on Me." Unspoken, but just as clearly understood, was the message, *You don't even depend on Me when I am here. How can you hope to run with the horses when you can't even keep up with the footmen?*

A man clambered out of the boat next to theirs, his rotund belly hanging low, grossly outlined by his wet, clinging robe. Peter sat up straight, reaching for his brother's arm. As subtly as a man of his straightforward nature could, he drew his brother around, hissing in his ear, "Now do you believe me? There he is again—the one I keep telling you about, but you never listen."

Andrew squinted at the portly man just stepping onto the beach. "Are you sure? He looks too fat to me."

"Of course I'm sure! Wait till he turns sideways and you see his stomach. It's nothing but padding, or my name isn't Simon Peter."

But the man didn't turn. He seemed intent on several of the other passengers who were already quite a bit farther along on their way to the small nearby town. Andrew rolled his eyes. "You're imagining things again. This idea of you being in charge of security has gone to your head. Hello—" he tapped his fist against the side of brother's skull, "—you're just a fisherman."

Anger flamed in Peter's eyes. "I'll show you my imagination," he growled. "I'm going to drag him back here and prove it to you in front of everyone!" He splashed noisily overboard and stalked off down the shoreline, offended dignity vibrating almost visibly.

There was an awkward hush at the boat as Andrew turned and noticed eleven pairs of eyes focused interestedly on him. He grinned sheepishly. "Welcome to Gergesa, everybody."

Peter became more and more furious the closer he got to the man who was responsible for everyone else, even his own brother, thinking he was crazy. The man had almost caught up to the woman he was pursuing—why, Peter could not fathom—when he reached out to take hold of her and drag her back. Peter ran the last few steps ready to leap on the man and bring him crashing down.

Just as he was about to spring on the man's shoulders, a horrible, unearthly laughter froze him where he stood, arms still raised. It hadn't come from the man in front of him—he was just as surprised as Peter, crouching down and producing a long dagger from beneath his robes.

The fearful sound came once more and echoed along the shoreline, seeming at once to come from behind, ahead, and both sides. Trapped, Peter started backing ever so slowly toward the boats, ready to take refuge in the sea if need be.

The undergrowth on the hill above them shook as a large creature passed through it. Directly ahead, a rustling noise confirmed the presence of a second—whatever it was—coming right at them! Peter glimpsed the top of a man's head and started to relax. At least it was human, and not some wild animal.

With a piercing shriek, a hairy, naked man leaped out of a patch of bushes up the hill to the right, running down the slope amid a slide of rocks. Peter could take no more. He turned and ran just as another madman charged forward to stand by the side of his companion. Both were covered with terrible wounds, some old and beginning to heal, others so fresh they still bled. Broken chains dangled from their arms and legs.

Through matted hair, dully gleaming eyes shone with hatred and malice, malignantly intelligent in spite of their ruined appearance. Working as one, they stalked forward, sniffing the scent of their prey.

Peter had forgotten the man he had been following; now the man pushed his way in front of the others, dagger held ready. "Get the women out of here," he ordered a large man behind him, preparing for a fierce battle. "Take them to the boats." The man obeyed without question, although he had to drag one of the women away by brute force.

Peter slowed for nothing as he raced for the boats. Even when he passed by Jesus, headed the other way, he didn't stop. "Get in! Get in," he cried in panic as he reached the first vessel and began single-handedly shoving it away from the shore. The frightened passengers made no protest as the fisherman seized the oars and dug them deep into the water, almost lifting the boat in his haste to be gone from that evil place.

Well away from the shore, Peter's frenzied energy suddenly deserted him. The full extent of his cowardice bore in upon him, and he slumped forward, trying not to cry in front of the others in the boat, one of whom was trying unsuccessfully to figure out how to use the steering oar.

They drifted a long time while Peter tried to gather himself together. At last, along with the crushing despair, came a curiosity to see what had happened. Now that he was himself again, Peter had no fear for Jesus or His safety. If the worst storm in twenty lifetimes couldn't touch Him, then neither could two puny men, inhabited by demons or not.

"All right folks, let's go back," he announced matter-of-factly to cover his own embarrassment. The man sitting farthest back clumsily picked up the steering oar again and jabbed it into the water, wiggling it back and forth as fast as he could. "Tell you what," Peter suggested, "why don't you row, and I'll steer?"

That didn't go much better, and Peter fought back annoyance that there were no other experienced sailors in the boat. It took some time to draw near the eastern shore again.

Something large and brown and very dead bumped against the side of the boat. Peter looked to see what it was. "A pig!" screamed the woman next to him. She started to point then yanked her hand back to avoid any contamination from the unclean beast.

Peter leaned around her to see ahead. "Pigs, actually." Thousands of carcasses floated on the water, spreading out from a point near where the boats had first landed. Peter fought back his revulsion and his fear of ceremonial defilement. "Stay calm—all of you—just stay calm. We're going to turn the boat around and try to stay ahead of them."

The woman who had screamed closed her eyes and let out a little moan. "Storms, madmen, pigs—what next?"

"Madmen?" Peter muttered under his breath, not wanting to upset the woman by openly contradicting her. After all, women were emotional and didn't observe things as well as men did. "What is she talking about? I was much closer than she was, and I only saw one madman."

The two possessed men faced Jesus, civil war breaking out in their ravaged bodies. More than anything, they wanted to be close to Jesus, sensing somehow that He was the only One who could save them from the unending torment they had once entered of their own will. The years since their first foray into spiritism had been a blur of blood and mayhem, hunger and pain, and sleeping amongst the markers of the dead. With the last small fiber of their beings that still belonged to them, they yearned for freedom from their curse.

More than anything, the devils that indwelt them wanted to be somewhere else, especially after seeing so many of their number so recently routed by only three small words. All together they wailed, "Jesus, Son of God Most High! What are You going to do with us? Did You come to torture us ahead of time?"

The cruelest irony of all was that they were forced to stay not only by the power of Christ but by the orders of their own commander. "Get ready. He's going to cast you out, make no mistake. Ask to go into that herd of pigs. Destroy them, and the people will beg Him to leave. We may still be able to salvage something out of this miserable day." With no other choice, they did as they were ordered.

Truly, even Satan was surprised when Jesus immediately nodded His agreement to their request. "Go."

There was no disobeying that order, vested with full authority from the throne of heaven. Faster than sound can travel, they left their human hosts and entered the pigs feeding on the bluffs above, hating the empty moment between. When they thought of it afterward, which was as seldom as possible, they were never quite sure whether the catastrophe came because they had followed their instructions, or because the pigs were obeying a silent command from their Maker. All they knew was that, despite their orders, they played no part in the mayhem that followed.

Either way, a shrill, frantic squealing filled the air. The entire herd of more than two thousand pigs, writhing with unfamiliar and uncomfortable sensations, stampeded over the edge of the cliff and plunged into the sea. There they thrashed and fought, inflicting terrible gashes on each other in a futile struggle to live. Soon nothing remained of the wealth of the Gergesenes but scores of bobbing corpses, scattered as freely across the lake as a handful of leaves thrown by a child.

By the time the delegation arrived from town, the two men wore borrowed outer robes, one of them provided by Jesus and the other by John. They had tried to clean themselves and to straighten their hair the best they could before they sat down to hear Jesus. Peter might have had a caustic thought or two when Jesus began the now-familiar story, but the two men listened as if their very lives hung in the balance, which of course, was true. "Once there was a man who had a demon . . . ," Jesus began.

"Peter, Peter, Peter." Out in the lake, Tarik sat down next to his charge and wrapped one wing around Peter's shoulder, wondering what Oreb was thinking. It was not like the small demon to waste an opportunity like this, when he had worked so hard to persuade Peter to swear that unholy oath. Why wasn't he here, trying to get Peter to kill himself? Had he even told Set? Undoubtedly he was up to something, but just as surely, the Father's plans were already in place to counter those of the rebels.

Tarik spoke aloud, half to himself. "Oh, Peter, you put yourself in such danger by being impulsive, and you miss so much, too. You could've been there by Jesus' side when even the demons acknowledged Him as Son of the Highest, or watched Him throw the armies of the wicked one into disarray—again—or seen Him minister to the bruised hearts that have opened to Him for the first time. Now He will have to leave. It will be a long time before He passes this way again—and you missed it all."

"Oh, Simon, I missed you so much. You don't know how worried I was!" Rimona clung to her husband in joy and relief. "The storm came, and all I could think about was you out on the lake. . . ." Her voice died away into a choked sob as she hugged him again and again.

"I would've been worried about you, too, but by the time I had the chance to think of it, I realized Jesus would keep you safe, as well."

"At least I found out you were still alive before you even got back."

"How? Did someone in one of the other boats tell you?"

She nodded, pointing to a woman just about to enter Zebedee's property. "She told me."

"What do you know about her?" Peter grew intent as he recognized the same mysterious woman the mysterious man had been chasing. *Oh, this is getting so complicated!*

Rimona rubbed his arm soothingly. "Don't get all upset. You don't have to worry about her."

"Well then, what did you find out? It could be important."

"First of all, her name is Alona. Her parents are both dead; she is married, has no children, and her uncle is a priest. Her husband serves Caiaphas, but she is a firm supporter of Jesus. Her husband doesn't know she's been following our Teacher all over the countryside, and now she's got to get home before he finds out. She's on her way to start building support for Jesus in Jerusalem."

Peter's eyes widened at this amazing recital. "How long did you two talk, anyway?"

Rimona shrugged. "Just a moment, really. She came by to check on us before she went to pick up her mare at Zebedee's."

"Her mare at Zebedee's? Is there anything you don't know about her? You're going to have my job, at this rate!" Peter told her, only half joking. "I have been trying to find out about her for weeks and haven't even seen her face. I suppose this means you know all about the other two who always travel with her?"

"Of course. Alona's maid, Erith, refused to be left behind, and Oded is a servant of the uncle I mentioned."

Peter appeared mollified, but now even more questions churned in his mind. Yes, he supposed he trusted his wife's judgment that the woman was harmless; after all, Rimona had a knack for figuring people out, but what about the woman's husband? What exactly did he do for Caiaphas? Was he the man who chased that woman down the beach, or was that still another spy? Either way, it seemed certain to Peter that the man upon whom his suspicions rested was connected somehow to Caiaphas, and whatever connection there was made him suspicious of Alona. Round and round it went, getting more confusing at each step. Peter determined to sort it out somehow.

"Oh, I almost forgot. I'm going away again. Jesus said He was sending us out two by two. I guess He'll tell us more about it when He gets back."

Rimona peeked over his shoulder to scan the shoreline. "Where is He? I don't see Him yet. Wasn't He in your boat?" She frowned, puzzled. "Where *is* your boat?"

Peter turned the deepest red he had ever been in his long, embarrassing life. "He was . . . That is, we, er . . . got separated on the other side of the lake. He should be along any time now, I think." Suddenly, Peter realized that he had no idea at all where Jesus was or where He would be going. When he saw all the pigs, he assumed Jesus would be going somewhere else rather quickly, but he hadn't really stayed around long enough to be a part of any revised plan. No, indeed! For neither the first time nor the last, he mentally cursed his tendency to act before thinking. What was he going to tell Rimona?

"You're right—there He is now." Rimona pointed behind her husband to the three boats just coming into view. "Now, what were you telling me about getting separated?" Her curiosity only increased at the length of time it took him to answer.

"Separated? Yes, well, we were. That is, we became that way. Somehow. Um, nobody who was in this other boat knew how to sail, and I wanted to be helpful to them and make sure they got back safely. That's right, I was just thinking of them."

Rimona eyed him suspiciously, but said nothing. She turned and walked slowly down to the waterline to wait for the others.

When they came within hailing distance, Andrew called loudly, "Brother! Where were you? You missed all the excitement."

Behind his wife's back, Peter gestured to his brother to keep quiet, but it was no use. Rimona stepped forward and used her most carrying voice. "He was just telling me about that, but hadn't quite gotten to the part where he lost his boat."

"Did he mention how he ran like a scared gazelle?"

Rimona held her sides as she laughed. Andrew was stepping onto shore before she recovered enough to say, "He must have forgotten that part. I was hoping you could tell me."

Andrew was only too happy to oblige, drawing out each part of the story with comical exaggeration until even Peter was forced to laugh with the others. When Andrew finally brought the tale to an end, Matthew cleared his throat nervously and tried to speak. "I was hoping, that is, you're invited, all of you, to a feast. At my house. Tonight." His words trailed shyly away as he mumbled, "My friends and all. Not the usual sort of thing, I know, but I was just hoping."

"Of course we'll be there," Jesus answered heartily. "We all will. Thank you for your hospitality, Levi."

Despite grave reservations about entering the house of a publican, not to mention eating at the same table with sinners, they all came. With Jesus so enthusiastic, they didn't feel that they had much choice. Of the disciples, Peter, Andrew, James, and John knew the former tax collector the best and were the least hesitant to attend. But several of the others, Judas among them, barely veiled their hostility. After all, if Jesus was to become King, He would have to stop associating with such undesirable people and cultivate the friendship of the more socially prominent.

This frame of mind didn't lend itself very well to a festive atmosphere, and even the more tolerant of the disciples looked and felt out of place. For this momentous occasion Levi Matthew brought his whole family together and had issued a special invitation to all the tax collectors from Capernaum, Bethsaida, Chorazin, and Magdala, too. His former lady "friends" made an especially colorful addition to the assembly and were accompanied by numerous other individuals of shady backgrounds.

There had also been a more general invitation to the townspeople of Capernaum, and many decided to come. Some came to be near Jesus. Some came for the chance to see one of Matthew's famous entertainments. Some were just curious. The Pharisees wanted to be shocked and to stir up some trouble if they could. They were. They could. And they did.

Naturally they went to Judas first, where he sat sullenly next to Simon the Zealot about halfway down the first table, both concentrating on their food and pointedly ignoring the excess of joy swirling around them.

Kenan knelt at their side, deliciously horrified by the goings on. "Judas—is that right? Yes? Ahh. Well, Judas, I couldn't help but wonder something, and you seem like the kind of man that would know just about everything there is to know, so I thought I'd ask you. Oh, no thank you. I can't eat anything right now—I'm fasting, you know. Anyway, can you explain to me just why it is that your master feels the need to eat with these people? Tax collectors, gluttons, and—" He paused to shudder ostentatiously as one of Matthew's "friends" walked by, her pungent perfume trailing behind, "—sinners of all kinds."

Judas was just opening his mouth to thank the priest for expressing so well the concern they both shared when Jesus held up His hand for silence. Within seconds, the attention of the whole room rested on Judas and the unfortunate priest still squatting awkwardly beside him.

"I couldn't help but overhear your question," Jesus informed Kenan in carrying tones. That alone was enough to cause the priest a pang of fear. With all the noise of the party, he'd been quite sure no one could hear what he said except Judas and Simon.

Jesus held Kenan pinned under a steely gaze as He went on, "Tell Me, who visits Doctor Bakbukiah—those who are well or those who are sick?" Kenan squirmed, but didn't answer. "Anyone knows it is the sick who need a physician," Jesus answered for him. "And to whom do you think the call to repentance should be given? To those who are already righteous or to those who are sinners?" The priest stood creakily to his feet, easing over toward the security of the other Pharisees, but Jesus wasn't through with him yet. "Go back to the sacred scrolls you claim to know so well, and study them until you understand the meaning of 'I desire mercy, and not sacrifice.' What should this tell you of the priorities of Adonai?"

Fuming, Kenan retreated with what little dignity he still had. His fellow priests and Pharisees followed. As soon as he was out of earshot of the partygoers, he stopped abruptly. "We've got to do something. You can see how he steals the hearts of the people from us with his new teaching, and now he's making us look like fools, besides." Just then, his stomach growled loudly, and a sly look suddenly crept onto his face. "Hmm.

Fasting. Now that gives me an idea. Who among you knows where to find some followers of the Baptist?"

A few hours later, the feast was once again interrupted. Matthew, especially, cringed when he saw the plainly dressed disciples of John the Baptist regarding the lavish spread with revulsion, the hungry Pharisees standing smugly behind them, trying to ignore the mouthwatering aromas. Matthew had tried so hard to prepare something nice for Jesus. It hurt him to see how others might view his offering, and he wondered if perhaps he had been excessive.

"Jesus," one of the Baptist's disciples exclaimed, when he could force the words out, "why do we fast, and even the Pharisees, but Your disciples do not?"

Peter froze with a large bite halfway to his mouth, suddenly feeling guilty. The idea of fasting had never occurred to him until just then. How impious to feast, and with John in prison, too! He set his food back down and swallowed hard.

Jesus paused in His story, unruffled by the interruption. "Welcome," He said, smiling warmly. "I can understand why you're sad, but can you really make the children of the Bridegroom fast while the Bridegroom Himself is with them? The day will come soon enough that He will be taken away from them, and then they will fast. But right now, they cannot. Would you care to join us?"

Sensing that they were on the edge of a great mystery that only Jesus might solve, the men hesitantly accepted. Matthew motioned his servants to bring more couches and put them near Jesus so the men could hear Him. After several more stories, they even unbent enough to accept a light repast. No one even noticed when the Pharisees left again, hungrier than ever, and in an even blacker mood than before.

Peter chewed slowly, trying to think what it was about Jesus' words that had so disturbed him. *The Bridegroom will be taken away? What can He possibly mean by that? Taken where? Jesus must be trying to teach us some hidden lesson, because obviously He doesn't mean that like it sounds. He couldn't be King if He were taken away, and then He would never be able to save us.*

Chapter 21

"Jesus! Wait for us!" The two men caught up with them just outside the small city of Bethabara, where the Baptist had so often preached. Jesus stopped, and the crowd opened to make way for the plain, impoverished travelers as they jogged the last few steps. Their appearance marked them as followers of the Baptist. Tears glistened in their earnest brown eyes as they bowed respectfully and repeated the message from their imprisoned master. "Are you the One we are looking for, or is someone else coming after You?"

Peter saw that their words grieved Jesus in some way; he didn't understand that the hurt stemmed from the disbelief and doubt of the one man sent to prepare the way of the Lord. Fearing these men might be spies, the rough fisherman stepped forward and said harshly, "The Teacher is tired. Leave Him alone."

Jesus patted Peter gently on the shoulder. "It's all right," He told him. Then stepping in front of Peter, He said to the followers of the Baptist, "I know what you're asking." His sympathy flowed out to them. He knew full well how hard it had been for His cousin, shut up in a dank, gloomy cell with no release in sight. He knew how the demons had pressed in with their doubts and fear, seeking to break John's connection to heaven. He saw how tenderly and faithfully the two men before Him had cared for their master, taking him food and giving what comfort they could, at great risk to themselves. Jesus saw in them sincere truth-seekers, and He opened His arms in welcome.

Just then a woman pushed her way through to Jesus. "Please help me, Master. My daughter is blind, and they say You can heal anyone."

Jesus knelt right there in the road, gently drawing the thin little girl out from behind her mother. Her face was a horrible sight, one eye gray and protruding, so badly infected that the lid would not close completely. The other eye was red and swollen, in danger of losing what sight it had left. "What happened?" Jesus lifted the hair away from her face and tilted her head up for all to see.

"She fell, and a stick went into her eye. We don't know what else to do for her. The doctors said they can do nothing." The mother dabbed at her tears.

Jesus passed His hand over the girl's face. Surprised, she blinked her perfect eyes in unison, threw her arms around His neck, then hid shyly behind her mother. After a moment she peeped out, whispered, "Thank You, Sir," and giggled.

Turning to the two men, Jesus said, "If you want to know the answer to your question, just come with Me." Irresistibly drawn to the light and love that shone from His face, they joined the glad procession as it flooded through the gates of Bethabara.

All that day, Peter watched the men as they watched Jesus. The wonderful healings they witnessed left them too amazed to speak, and finally, humbled by their awe, he admitted to himself that his suspicions were unfounded. Still, at the end of the day when Jesus called them to come near, Peter made sure he was within a sword's length of them.

Jesus read their faces with satisfaction. He did not need to ask if they had found what they had been seeking. "Go tell John what you saw today. The blind can see, the lame can run, the lepers have been made clean," He told them. And then, knowing how much John hoped for a personal word from Him, He added, "Blessed is anyone who does not stumble because of Me." Clearly the men didn't quite know what to think of that last remark, but nodded in acquiescence.

"We will tell him," one said. Both bowed themselves to the ground as if before a king. With obvious reluctance, they started the long journey back, wishing they could stay longer—and yet wanting to fly to comfort John with the glorious news: "We have found the Messiah!"

Jesus watched them stride out the gate. When they were no longer close enough to hear, He turned to the crowd around Him, His eyes searching out each person there. "Almost all of you went to listen to John preach, didn't you?" Nearly every head nodded in agreement. "What did you go out there to see—a reed shaking in the wind?"

Peter immediately thought of the reeds that lined the Jordan River, bending their supple stems whichever way the wind was blowing. No matter what each man's opinion was about the Baptist's message, there was no denying his strength of purpose. Unlike the Pharisees, whose main concern was their social status, John preached boldly, as steadfast as the mighty mountains.

As Jesus went on, every eye fixed on His face. "Or, perhaps, you went out to see a man in soft clothing? You know, you can always find men in gorgeous apparel in the king's court." Jesus joined in the ripple of laughter. In keeping with his austere lifestyle, John was well known for his coarse garments woven of camel hair. The contrast between his untamed appearance and that of the mincing, prancing court officials was supremely ridiculous.

Jesus' expression grew tender. Softly He said, "But what did you go out to see? A prophet? Yes, and even more than a prophet. John was the one of whom it was written, 'Behold, I send My messenger before Your face, which shall prepare Your way before You.' John was the greatest man ever born." A collective sigh went up. The people were gladdened to hear such a strong affirmation of the wilderness preacher from One they had quickly come to love.

"If you are able to understand and receive it, John is the Elijah the prophets said would come, carrying the message of repentance and announcing the coming of the Lord." Jesus smiled. "And to what a generation he came! They were like a bunch of children sitting in the marketplace, doing nothing. Their friends said, 'We played songs for you, but you didn't want to dance. We were sad, but you didn't cry. What exactly do you want?' "

Unsure whether or not to laugh, Peter waited for the rest of the story. "When John came, living simply and fasting often, they said, 'He has a devil!' But when the Son of man came, eating and drinking like a regular person, they wrinkled up their noses and said, 'Look at that Man—He is a glutton and a drunkard, a friend of tax collectors and sinners!' " Peter did laugh then; he had heard Kenan say just that to several other Pharisees. Jesus put His hand on the tax collector from Bethabara sitting next to Him; the man had followed Him eagerly since the night of Matthew's feast. "They can't make up their minds what is right, but true Wisdom is shown by the results of her actions. And all who hear the words of the Son of man have an even greater share in the New Kingdom than John."

Matthan shared the lonely cell with John, ever vigilant to keep Zuar as far away as possible. During the nights, the demon was able to creep closest, whispering poisoned words of discouragement. Matthan, for his part, kept up a litany of hope, but as the months of John's imprisonment wore on, he had to work harder and harder to keep Zuar at bay.

At his lowest point, the Baptist sent two of his followers to find Jesus, to ask Him if He was truly the Messiah. Though John remembered the Voice from heaven, it now seemed faint and far away. When so much time went by with no word or sign of the New Kingdom, he began to think perhaps he had somehow misunderstood what was to happen. Rome still ruled the land with its iron fist, and no deliverance from on high had come to loose the bonds that held him fast. John was discouraged and weighed down by questions; his fear grew that what he thought was his life's mission might have been only a vain obsession.

Through a narrow grating barely above ground level, he could just see the faces of his disciples when they returned. Hope swelled as they told him all they had heard and seen on that marvelous day. Faithfully they repeated Jesus' final mysterious words to His wavering prophet. "Blessed is anyone who does not stumble because of Me."

"Adonai, forgive me! Can it be true? Did I stumble because of Him?" John sobbed in his repentance. Not until the following day were his disciples able to learn what had so wounded their leader. For as John lay on the cold stone floor, for the first time he finally understood. The New Kingdom would not come with violence and the clash of sword against sword. It would come when the Spirit of God found a home in the hearts of His people. In meekness, humility, and love it would spread to the ends of the earth.

Just as clearly, John also realized for the first time that he would die, the first of many to give their lives in the service of the New Kingdom. Even then, he still did not grasp the magnitude of what lay ahead as Jesus would take upon Himself the sins of the world, becoming the Lamb of God. Still, of any human living at that moment, John came the closest to heaven that night. And there in the darkness, heaven drew very near to him.

"It's time." Jesus' voice woke Peter much too early in the morning to suit the tired fisherman. The others of the Inner Circle were already up and followed Jesus outside the encampment, quietly, so as not to wake the rest who traveled with them.

"What are we doing now?" Peter asked, yawning, when they reached the crossroads.

"Remember, I said I would send you out two by two? Well, My friends, today is the day. I just wanted to spend a little time with all of you first, to give you some instructions and ask the Father's blessing on your ministries."

Peter came wide awake at that. "Today? But we're not ready to leave You. Where will we go? Where will we stay? How are we going to support ourselves? What if someone doesn't want us to come? Who is my partner going to be?"

"Wait just a minute!" Jesus laughed and held up His hand to slow down His eager disciple. "I said I had some instructions for you, and I do. I'm sure by the time you're done *listening carefully*, you will have found your answers. First, though, let's say a short prayer."

The men bowed and covered their heads as Jesus asked the Father to help them take His words into their hearts and to have a right spirit as they prepared for His work. When He finished, the men gathered in a circle around Him, sitting on the cold, hard ground. Peter pulled his cloak tighter, but used to the nighttime chill as he was, it didn't bother him much. Nathanael, Judas, and several others who had been accustomed to a more genteel life, shivered and found themselves hard pressed to pay attention.

"Don't go to the Gentiles yet," Jesus said, drawing a sigh of relief from many throats. "Travel through Israel to the same cities we have already visited. Preach to them and let them know that the kingdom of heaven is here. In My name, heal their sick, raise their dead, cast out their demons. You have been greatly blessed by Adonai; now you are to bless others in return."

"What are we supposed to do for money?" Judas asked, repeating the question nearest to his heart. "We're starting out with nothing but our staves. How are we going to live? Eating would be nice too."

"You won't be taking any money with you or even an extra change of clothes. You will be staying in the same house for whatever length of time you're in that place, and your host will be glad to provide you with sustenance in exchange for your services."

"Services?" Judas's voice came out in a squawk. "Do You mean manual labor?"

"Of course." Jesus hid a smile. "You will have so many more opportunities to share that way."

By the time He had finished giving His advice to the disciples, it was nearing sunrise and the camp was just beginning to stir. "You will need to go soon. Some, even in our little family group, might try to interfere if they knew what you were doing."

"Like Mother." James chuckled quietly with John, who made a face in response.

Peter opened his mouth to ask another question, but Jesus spoke up first. "Have a little patience, Simon Peter. I didn't forget. You will travel with your brother, and John with his brother. Philip and Nathanael, you will be together, and Thomas with Matthew. Thaddeus, you will go with your father, and Simon with Judas."

Jesus laid His hands on each one and blessed them as He had the day He first appointed them to minister, but this time He asked for a special outpouring of the Holy Spirit to come upon them as they went out as sheep among wolves, to be wise as serpents and harmless as doves. He lingered the longest over Peter and Andrew, then sent them all on their way in the direction of the four winds.

"This is a fine missionary journey so far," Tarik commented to Nadiv as they walked along the road to Judea. "Very quiet."

Nadiv shook his head. "If they won't speak to each other, they may have the shortest trip of all. I seem to be saying this a lot, but while I trust that Jesus knows what He's doing, I don't understand why He is handling things this way. It's almost like He's trying to make problems between the two of them, but that can't be true."

"Keep your distance," Set reminded the angels menacingly, floating with Ares directly over the two disciples. "And don't think your little plots are going to succeed—we're a bit too smart for that."

"Was he talking to us?" Zeeb raised his head from his whispered huddle with Oreb.

"I don't think so." Oreb looked around nervously. "I think he just meant Tarik and Nadiv." A hint of wistfulness crept into his eyes. "I wish . . ."

"Stop it! It's too late for any of that—we've come much too far. Besides, would you really rather be back with those poor creatures, to be little better than a robot automatically obeying everything your precious Father tells you? Don't be silly. At least we're free."

"I guess so." Oreb gingerly felt his neck, still tender from the last time Set had choked him. He knew it was too late, and deep down he didn't really want to go back. Still, if he were to lapse into temporary honesty, he'd have to admit that his old friend Tarik didn't look like he minded his lot in life. In fact, even with the tide turned against him, he still looked, well, happy. Oreb could almost remember being happy.

"Snap out of it, will you?" Zeeb grew impatient. "We have work to do."

Their journey had started out well enough—two men walking along the road to unknown adventures side by side, brother with brother. But within a few miles, one of the darts of the enemy hit a tender spot, and all the smoldering resentment Andrew had felt for several days burst into flame with a speed that surprised them both.

"Don't you dare talk to me like that! You think you're so great because Jesus let you watch that resurrection and not me."

"All I said was . . ."

"I know what you said, and I don't like it. I don't like the way you said it; I don't like what you meant by it; and right now I don't even like you very much!"

A flock of sparrows flew up, spooked by the loud angry voices of the two men who faced each other in the middle of the road, each yelling at the other, and neither listening. Long after most people would have concluded the argument was pointless, Peter finally threw up his hands in disgust and stomped down the road, leaving Andrew to follow, or not, as he chose.

After a moment, Andrew turned and began trudging after his brother. Miles passed, and still they refused to speak, each man choosing instead to cherish the feeling that he had been treated very unjustly by the other. Thus it was that the assignment that had started out with such high hopes now stood in gravest jeopardy. By their anger, jealousy, and pride, they had separated themselves from the Source of their new power before they had a chance to use it even once. Without that divine power, there would be no teaching, no preaching, no miracles, and no new believers to support the cause of the King. There was not much time left, either. The city of Lebonah waited for them over the next rise.

"I really wish I knew why Jesus took Peter in with Him, and not Andrew too." Nadiv had little else to do just then but to ponder the events that had brought about this sorry state of affairs.

"I don't know, either," Tarik replied, *"but this probably isn't the last time we'll have this sort of trouble. Jesus seems to have some special plan for Peter, James, and John—and something different in mind for Andrew. Even after all my years as a Guardian, being involved with humans, I still can't begin to guess what it is."* A satisfied smile came over Tarik's face, and he added a little louder, *"That's two resurrections, though, just in case anyone's counting."* Set and Ares, flinched in unison, but managed to avoid looking at the Guardians.

Nadiv laughed, cheered at the memory of what had happened. *"That was sure a surprise, at first. When Jairus came and asked Jesus to heal his daughter, of course I knew He would. But I thought it would be no more than that—a healing. Then as the crowd grew thicker, I became more excited, thinking that maybe I would see another prisoner rescued from the grave."*

Tarik nodded. *"Of course I sympathized with that poor father when the messenger told him Zara was dead, but our perspective was a little different than his. When death comes to true believers like Zara, we always think of it as a temporary problem that will soon be cleared up—well, since Moses was raised, anyway."*

"Exactly." Nadiv grinned. "And in Zara's case, the problem was much more temporary than usual."

"Even knowing what was going to happen, I cried a bit when Jesus told her to get up. She was warm yet, and looked almost as if she might awaken at her mother's touch, but I couldn't hear her heart, and I knew she was gone. Then, when Jesus took her hand and she opened her eyes, I just . . ." Tarik dabbed at his eyes, ". . . well, I was happy."

"Andrew wasn't happy, not particularly. That was when he first started to feel resentful. He thinks he is angry only with his brother, but it goes much deeper. Underneath everything, he is incensed at Jesus for seeming to prefer his brother over him. He has all the same questions we do, but without the trust. He doesn't realize that Jesus does, indeed, know what is best for him. What should we do? They're almost to their first town."

"I don't think we'll have to do anything at all. Listen." The Guardians paused. The sound was faint and far away, but they could hear it. It was their Supreme Commander, bowed before the Father, pleading that the forces of evil would be held back from each of His disciples—Peter and Andrew in particular—and that the Spirit would be poured out from heaven to fill them to overflowing.

Set and Ares heard it, too. They tried to fight against it, but some unseen force compelled them to leave, and the holy angels wasted no time filling their places. Though undeserving and thus far unrepentant, Andrew and Peter now had a much better chance of winning their struggle as the fresh, untainted air of heaven surrounded them, replacing the poisonous words of their adversaries.

"We need to talk." The words shattered the icy silence like crockery falling on a hearthstone.

Andrew stopped in the middle of the road. "What do you want to talk about?"

Peter ran his fingers along the folds in his robe and sighed deeply. "I'm sorry. You're right—I was feeling more important, and I guess it showed. I'm not now, though. I just feel stupid for letting this get in the way of what we're supposed to do."

"So do I. And I'm sorry, Brother. I should have talked to you sooner."

They stood there, unsure what to do next. Then Peter's face brightened. "Is it just me, or do you, too, feel we should pray before we go on?"

The two brothers knelt there in the road, offering their prayers as savory incense before God, vowing to trust Him always, even if they didn't understand His ways. After some time they stood, dusted off their knees, and climbed the hill overlooking the city. For a moment they stood, hesitant and uncertain, as the scene of their first test spread before them. Its difficulty had been increased sevenfold by the delay due to their pride. The gates of Lebonah stood open, and they could hear, carried on the wind, the mournful wailing of a funeral procession.

Chapter 22

"What are we going to do now?" Peter's voice came out in a croak. "We were probably supposed to heal that person, and now he's dead." It was like Nain all over again, but this time without Jesus' reassuring presence.

Andrew tried vainly to moisten his suddenly dry lips. "There's only one thing we can do. We have to go down there and meet them."

Why did Jesus send us out like this? Peter, his breath coming in short gasps, had to force his trembling legs to work. *We're not ready for this. What if it doesn't work? We'll look like idiots, and they won't listen to us. And how will we do it? Jesus didn't exactly tell us how to raise someone from the dead. Adonai, please help us!*

He clung to the flood of joy and peace that came in answer to his brief prayer, assured that the events to come had been ordained from on high. Still nervous, but trusting in the power of Adonai, he strode forward with Andrew, ready to teach, preach, and, yes, raise the dead. He was sure the procedural questions would take care of themselves.

"Greetings, people of Lebonah! We have come to tell you more about our good Friend, Jesus, who has already visited here before. He is the One spoken of by the prophets, the Sent of Adonai. He asked us to come here today to tell you more about His kingdom, which will come soon." Peter exuded warmth and love, holding his hands up in blessing as he had seen Jesus do many times. The people looked at him as if he were crazy. "To give you a few examples . . ." A distinctly unhappy murmur increased in volume; the perspiring pallbearers complaining louder than anyone else.

Andrew had made no attempt to interrupt his brother's impassioned sermon. Instead, he slipped unobtrusively through the crowd to stand at the side of the draped body. His lips moved in silent prayer before he reached for the covering, pulling it back as he had seen Jesus do. A woman in her thirties reposed in unending slumber. The erstwhile fisherman ignored the curious stares of those around him and leaned forward to whisper, "Lady, . . . please . . . get . . . up. In the name of Jesus!" Now everyone thought both men were crazy.

"And so this kingdom is like mustard seeds and fishing nets and treasures hidden in a field," Peter was saying. "Whoever finds it is—did you just see that?" Mouth hanging open, he pointed at the dead woman. Except that she wasn't dead now. She stood next to Andrew, looking around in amazement.

"What happened?" she asked incredulously. "I was so sure I was going to die. What am I doing out here?"

Her husband, a widower no longer, scooped her into his arms and buried his face in her hair. "I thought you were gone!" he cried. "I thought I'd lost you!" Tears ran down his cheeks as he told his wife what the two strangers had done. She slid from his grasp and threw herself at Andrew's feet.

"Thank you, sirs, thank you! Oh, how can I ever thank you enough?"

Andrew turned bright red as he detached the woman's fingers from his ankles and lifted her up. "You must not thank us. It was Jesus. He told us to come, and it was His power that saved you. We are just simple people like you."

The woman's husband stepped forward to clasp Andrew's hand. "Where are you going now?"

Andrew looked at Peter for confirmation. "We haven't made our plans yet."

"Then please come with us. My wife and I have plenty of room for you to stay. Would you tell us more about Jesus? I didn't pay enough attention when He was here before."

"Of course." Peter finally succeeded in operating his vocal chords. "We are honored by your hospitality."

"We want to hear more too," shouted a man in the crowd.

"All of you, come!" Their host opened his arms in welcome. "Come to my house for a feast and stories for as long as my guests can still talk." His booming laugh was contagious, and it was a jubilant procession that followed the two brothers into the city.

"They did it!" Tarik spun in elated spirals, laughing with Nadiv. "They allowed the Father to use them, and He did!"

"Did He ever! I wonder if Andrew still minds being excluded from Zara's resurrection?"

"I rather doubt it. And look at all the sick people following them. They will both be busy far into the night—and doubtless tomorrow too."

"Just like Jesus, but then, that was the idea."

It was a new morning in a new town, and Peter stood before the gathering crowd. "Men and women of Emmaus, we have come here in the name of Jesus to tell you about the New Kingdom. First, Jesus has asked us to share His healing power with you, so if there is anyone who is sick, lame, blind, mute, possessed by demons, or in need of anything, please come and line up. Let the most urgent cases come to the front. The rest of you, don't worry. We'll make time for all of you. Looks like you're first, young man. What is your name? Yiftach? Well, Yiftach, in the name of Jesus, you can see."

Peter's kind face was the boy's first sight. He reached out to touch the bearded cheek. "Thank you, sir." As Peter moved to interrupt his thanks, the boy added, "Don't worry, I've been listening for a while. I thank Jesus most of all, but thank you for bringing Him to us. Will you tell me just one story about Him?"

"Of course. Andrew, would you take over for a bit? Thank you. Now, let me see. There was a man working in a field one day, when he found something strange buried in the dirt. He dug down to uncover it and discovered a box full of treasure." Yiftach looked up at his friend, immersed in the story that Peter told very well by now. By the time the tale was ended, a large group had gathered around them.

"If you still have time, sir," the boy asked politely, "would you please tell the one about the storm—just one more time?" To the delight of all, Peter agreed.

At the end of another long day, Peter and Andrew sat together for a few minutes before going to sleep. Their fire had burned down to coals, barely illuminating their bowed heads as they thought through the events of the day and prayed about the morrow. Andrew held still for so long that Peter was thinking he might have gone to sleep, when he spoke. "I think it's time to go back."

"Really?" Peter sounded surprised. "I was thinking the same thing, but this whole trip is going so well I didn't want to suggest it yet."

Andrew rested his chin on his arms. "I'd like to stay longer, too, but I just keep getting this feeling that it's time to go. Maybe it's the Spirit, or maybe I'm just homesick, but I think we need to find Jesus again."

"All right." Peter shrugged. "Then let's leave in the morning, right after we say goodbye to the folks here in Emmaus."

"Don't forget your small admirer."

"Yiftach? Of course I won't forget him. He's a good boy. In fact, he even invited us to stay with him and his family the next time we come."

"I wonder when that will be. I'll miss him—and all the other nice people like him that we've met along the way."

"But at least we'll get to see our families in a few days. Sleep in our own beds, eat our own food prepared by the hands of our own wives."

Andrew grinned. "Which is certainly not as bad as it used to be. A lot has changed since Jesus came, hasn't it?"

"I think the biggest change is in us." Peter looked at his brother with awe, not envy. "I mean, who would ever have thought you would help raise the dead? You had the courage it took to just walk right up there and claim the promise while I was still trying to get the nerve to do anything. You inspired me to be much bolder in asking Adonai to grant His help. Without you, I don't know if I would have been brave enough to try to heal anyone. I probably would have been too afraid of being embarrassed."

"Without your preaching to distract them, I don't know what I would have done. I think I would've obeyed Jesus eventually, but it would have been very tempting to sneak back into the cemetery after everyone had left and try my 'resurrection technique' with no one watching."

"Thank you for all your help. I'm glad now that Jesus sent us together."

"You're welcome, and thank you too. Now go to sleep so we can wake up early. I want to go home!"

The other ten had received a divine summons as well, and from the far reaches of Galilee and Judea they prepared for the return journey to Capernaum. The dark empire had been dealt a staggering blow, and all available resources had been pulled in to cope with it.

How beautifully the ancient prophecy had been fulfilled: "But unto you that fear my name shall the Sun of righteousness arise with healing in his wings." And as the light brightened and grew, beneath its radiance the darkening shadow of a cross stretched the length and breadth of Palestine.

"Simon!" Rimona saw the two weary travelers from afar and ran to meet them. "Andrew, you both look so tired. I thought I asked you to take care of my husband. What have you been doing?"

"That question," Peter caught her up and whirled her around, "would take almost as long to answer as we have been gone. Let us get cleaned up first, and then we can talk while we eat. I've missed your cooking."

"Only my cooking?" she teased. "Well, you'd better hurry. I'm an impatient woman." She walked along between them, pulling on Peter's arm when his steps flagged. "Besides, I have a surprise for you."

"Is Jesus here yet?"

"He'll be here later tonight or tomorrow. Word went around that He was leaving Magdala yesterday."

Andrew rolled his eyes dramatically as Peter groaned. "What do you suppose He was doing there again? Not that I really need to ask."

"It was only a matter of time. What is this, her fourth—fifth—deliverance?"

"I don't know. I lost count after three."

"Who?" Rimona interrupted. "The Magdalene?"

Peter clutched at his head in frustration. "I don't know why Jesus keeps trying to help her. It's obvious she's never going to change—she'll always be a whore."

"Even if she did transform herself, she's not the sort of person He should speak to, or even notice. He shouldn't even know she exists."

Rimona surprised them both by disagreeing. "First of all, how can you stand there and judge her when you don't know anything about her background? You don't have the first clue what happened to make her the way she is. No, you can close those mouths right back up again. I'm not trying to make excuses for her. She has certainly made some bad choices for herself, but I'm positive that a wicked man somewhere was the original cause of all her troubles. If what happened was as bad as I think it was, it's not exactly amazing that she has had a hard time keeping on the right path."

"But . . ."

"I'm not done yet. Second, anyone who has seen the effect Jesus can have on a home like ours has no business doubting His efforts on Mary's behalf. If He could change us, He can change her. It's as simple as that. Don't you have any faith?"

Exercising unusual prudence for once, Peter kept his mouth shut. Andrew adroitly changed the subject. "What surprise did you have?"

She smiled mysteriously. "You'll find out. Just go home. Simon Peter, you come with me."

"Tell me it's not another daughter . . . no, it hasn't been long enough. I would have known." Andrew kept muttering as he followed the shoreline toward the small house.

"Hurry." Rimona was definitely up to something.

"But this is Zebedee's estate."

"I know." Maddeningly, she would say no more, leading him to one of the houses that sat on Zebedee's property. Peter was astounded when she walked right in, not calling out for entrance or waiting for a reply.

"What are you doing?" Feeling distinctly uncomfortable, he waited outside, not wanting to enter without being invited.

"Abba! Abba!" A single blur of motion sped out of the house toward him, sorting itself out into his two sons as they clung eagerly to his waist. "You're home! Come quick! We want to show you where we sleep now. We waited so long for you to come!"

Taking his hands, they pulled him none too gently up the steps and into the house. Rimona tried not to laugh at her husband's bewildered expression, but finally gave in to the mirth that bubbled up. "Isn't it beautiful? How do you like it?"

"How? What? When? Why?" Peter looked around dazedly, attempting to take it all in. This dwelling, though nowhere near as spacious or elegant as Zebedee's, was still a far cry from the shabby, crowded house by the beach. A trace of anger crept into his voice as he said firmly, "I won't take charity from Zebedee."

"Actually, it's Zebedee who is taking charity from us." Peter was taking this far better than Rimona had expected. "His whole household was turned upside down when Salome left to follow Jesus. What meals they had were burned and soggy; no one thought to do wash for almost a week; and by the time Zebedee realized it, he had to wear the same clothes to synagogue that he had sorted fish in the day before. Merchants were lining up to demand the payments that Salome normally sent without having to be asked, and oh, Simon, you should have seen the clutter in that poor, gorgeous house! It was a disaster! How could we refuse when he asked us to help?"

"So now you are running Zebedee's house for him? I'm not sure I like that either, even if he did need it."

"Of course not, silly. Mother is in charge—I just lend a hand once in a while. Keren and I weave linen in our 'spare time' to bring in extra money. Keren has even done a bit of redecorating, as Andrew has doubtless discovered by now."

"I don't know what to say. I really hate the thought of you having to work so hard when I should be here with you, supporting you myself."

Rimona hugged him tightly. "You don't have to say anything. Truly, I don't mind. Remember Jesus warned me ahead of time that by staying here, I would have the harder job. What He didn't tell me is that when I accepted my crowded living conditions and made up my mind to be happy no matter what, He would bless me with everything I had asked for before. We are in our own home now, Mother has a separate room, and when the weather is fair—like tonight—the boys sleep up on the roof."

"Oh." He thought for a moment. "How early do they go to sleep? Can they go now?"

Blushing, Rimona laughed again. "You're awful, Simon Peter. They've missed you just as much as I have." She pulled away from him to pour water into a basin, growing unexpectedly solemn. "Surely you've heard about the Baptist by now."

"Yes." Peter turned his face to hide the quick flash of pain. "I heard the news only a few days ago. I just keep hoping the message Jesus sent him before he died brought him some encouragement. He spent so long in the dungeon—and then to die in that terrible way."

"What message?"

"It was even before Jesus sent us out. Two of John's followers came to ask if Jesus was the Messiah. After they had watched Him heal people all day, they went away very happy. John must have been so glad when he talked to them and found out what Jesus had been doing."

"How did everyone react when they heard John had died?"

"Well, some of the people became more fearful and maybe a little more hesitant to support Jesus in public. A few are always hostile. Still, there was only one town where we actually had to shake the dust off our feet."

"Shake the dust off your feet?" Rimona echoed curiously.

So Peter started at the beginning, forgetting to bathe or eat, not noticing when the sun set, with Jered and Seth nodding in sleep, and unaware when Batia arrived and sat down quietly on her couch. From Lebonah to Emmaus he told them everything that had happened. The women laughed and cried by turns as he shared his experiences.

"Peter, I am just so amazed!" Far into the night, Rimona wiped her eyes at the end of the last story. "Your experiences are beyond incredible, especially where Andrew—our Andrew!—raised a woman from the dead."

"With Adonai's power," Peter reminded.

"Of course, with Adonai's power. Andrew couldn't raise a fish from the deep without help from God. But do you know that you seem like a completely different person? Really, you do. You're so much more confident, and, well, polished. You're not quite as arrogant anymore either. Why are you looking at me like that? You know you've always been rather conceited and very aware of your own worth. But this trip has left you changed."

Peter was thoughtful. "Some of it was the trip. There were so many needy people, needing health, needing life, and ready to take it from my hands. And I couldn't do even one thing for them by myself. I had to receive the blessing first before I could share it with them. That kind of gift changes the one who gives it as well as the one who receives it. The rest of it is just from spending more time with Jesus. No one can be with Him and stay the same old person. Everything seems fresh and new, when you're with Jesus."

Jesus knelt in prayer in an olive grove less than a mile from Capernaum, preparing to receive His disciples the next day. As so often happened, He fell asleep on His knees, and the dew covered His cloak as He slept. The next morning, as He shared a glad reunion with His disciples, the press of the multitude was so great that He was not able to speak with the twelve men as openly as He knew they needed.

Besides Peter and Andrew, James and Thaddeus were the only pair who had been given the opportunity to raise someone from the dead, and they were eager to share their joy with Jesus. The sons of Zebedee had had an experience of climactic victories alternating with stunning defeats, and most of the latter had been brought about by their own volatile natures and lack of tact.

Philip and Nathanael, with his ever-present flute, had moved slowly and steadily, gently winning the hearts of nearly all who heard them. Though their triumphs had not been as stellar as those of their companions, their steady, consistent witness pleased Jesus greatly.

Thomas and Matthew had certainly had an interesting time of it in the area near Jerusalem. Thomas, so very focused only on things he could touch with his hands or see with his eyes, had a hard time reaching out to an unseen God for an unseen power to work unearthly miracles. That the Father could use the poor man at all was a testament to His love and patience. With the addition of Matthew, however, the two made a good team. Matthew freely passed on the blessings he had received and healed everyone who asked, while Thomas gave concise, well-reasoned answers that appealed to even the most learned listener.

All the worst troubles seemed to have been reserved for Simon and Judas. They went to the cities in southernmost Judea, traveling across the forbidding countryside on foot. Simon wanted to offer his fellow Zealots the same chance that had been given him—to become acquainted with the true Messiah—and made the difficult climb to Masada, a nearly impregnable mountaintop fortress near the Dead Sea. Of all the cities whose dust was shaken off the feet of rejected disciples, none was removed faster than that of Masada as the two men ran for dear life away from the deadly rain of arrows!

They didn't look back, and even if they had, they wouldn't have seen the giant angelic warriors standing between them and their enemies, blocking all chances of a stray hit. Little did they know they were as safe at that moment as they were while sitting on the shore of Galilee eating a leisurely breakfast. Neither did they have any inkling of the high price the residents of Masada would someday pay for their rejection of the Savior.

Yes, Jesus had much to talk with them about, but He had to get them away from the noise and the crowds. "Come," He told them quietly, leading them down to the boats on the shore. "Come with Me and rest for a while."

Chapter 23

In the early light, Jesus managed to go ashore near Bethsaida without being seen by the crowds that followed Him so persistently. There in the wilderness, atop a hill greened by a fleeting carpet of grass, He knew He could find the seclusion to teach the Twelve at least some of what they so desperately needed to learn in the short time left before His sufferings.

Before the morning was through, however, He couldn't help taking pity on the thousands wandering on the plain below, searching for Him like lonely sheep without a shepherd. His immense love went out to them, and far sooner than He had planned, He called an end to the solitary rest and walked down to meet the people.

As Jesus talked to them and told them stories, the people were so enthralled they forgot to eat or drink. Many of them didn't even realize they had been there for hours until late afternoon, when Philip reminded Jesus that more than one mealtime had come and gone and that five thousand men, plus uncounted women and children, were exhausted and faint, out in the middle of a wilderness area with nothing to eat.

"At least if You send them away now, they might be able to buy something in Bethsaida or one of the other villages before it's dark." Philip's stomach growled just then, as if in agreement.

"Well, then, let's give them something to eat. You know this area well. Where can we buy bread for all these people?"

Philip scanned the crowd, quickly doing a rough estimate of how many thousands were there, how much bread it would take to feed them all, and how much it would cost for so many loaves. His best guess was that 250 or 350 pennies' worth of bread would provide only a meager meal—perhaps enough to last them until they reached home. He found Judas, the appointed treasurer of their little group, and asked him how much money was available just then to purchase supplies.

Judas squeezed the bag dangling at his waist. "Fifty or seventy-five pennies, I should think."

Philip frowned. "I thought we had more than that; it won't be nearly enough for what we need."

Judas shrugged, not overly concerned. "We had some unexpected expenses. You know, the usual poor folks and so on."

Nothing in his manner was particularly suspicious, but Philip noted that the new sandals and fresh cloak Judas wore were better quality than Philip had been able to afford since the day he answered Jesus' call. Still, there was no sense making trouble. Right now all that mattered was that they didn't have enough money. Philip returned to Jesus to inform Him of the problem.

"Even if we had two hundred pennies, which we don't, it still wouldn't be enough to feed them all."

His discouragement must have shown on his face, for Jesus smiled at him, saying, "Maybe you should have been the one voted to be treasurer. You have a real talent for figures."

Very little cheered, Philip asked, "Should we send them away now?"

"No, no, just have them all sit down. Take the other eleven and have them divide everyone into groups of fifty and help them to get comfortable. See if anyone has any food, and when you find something, bring it here."

A few minutes later, Andrew led a young boy to Jesus. "Here, Master. This is all we could find."

"What is your name?" Jesus asked the boy, gratefully accepting the basket he held out.

The boy smiled bashfully. "Andrew, Sir, just like his." He looked up admiringly at the fisherman.

"That's nice, Andrew. Did your mother fix your lunch?"

Andrew nodded. "She sent plenty and said to share if I found some-one else who didn't have a lunch."

"It sounds like you have a very kind mother." Jesus drew him close. "Now, Andrew, I have a favor to ask of you. Would you be willing to share your lunch with Me—the whole thing?"

Oh, good, Andrew—the fisherman—thought, *if Jesus takes the whole thing, there will be enough for Him, and still some left for the twelve of us.*

The smaller, more unselfish, Andrew didn't hesitate. "Of course. I'd be honored if You ate my lunch." He stoutly pushed aside the thought of the long, hungry walk home.

"Thank you. Adonai will bless your offering." Then calling the disci-ples back, Jesus told them, "Please announce that we will return thanks for the food."

They did as He asked, but not without wondering why everyone had to express gratitude that Jesus and His disciples were to split a few mor-sels of food among themselves. When it was quiet, Jesus bowed His head and prayed a simple prayer, thanking Adonai for the bounty He had provided. Opening the basket with its five loaves of bread and two fish, Jesus began to break the food in pieces and hand them to His disciples to distribute throughout the crowd. Again and again, He pulled out more loaves and fish, breaking them and passing them out. And no matter how many times He did so, there was always more!

Peter surveyed the scene before him—an ocean of satisfied people with their hands and laps full of plain, but delicious, food—and the soar-ing ambitions he had forgotten over the last several months of hard labor and miracle working possessed him once more. Not only could Jesus rally the people beneath His banner and heal the injured or dead on the battlefield with a single touch, but He could feed thousands with a single basket of food!

So this is how He's going to do it. His armies will be invincible! Stronger and stronger grew the conviction. *It's time. We need to crown Him to-night. Before all these people, we will declare Him King and then march on Jerusalem. As we pass through the countryside, more people will join us until our number is as the sands of the sea. We will be unstoppable, and at last Rome will fall before the Messiah and His terrible banners!*

It didn't take Peter long to communicate his exciting dreams to the other eleven disciples as they finished gathering the leftover food into twelve large baskets. They responded enthusiastically to his suggestion and began circulating through the crowd to gather support. With the meal they had just eaten sitting comfortably in their stomachs, the people had never been more ready to make Jesus their King. A sizable group approached the Teacher, determined to crown Him King—by force if necessary, should His natural reticence lead Him to balk at the idea.

Jesus stood and walked forward to meet them, His bearing as kingly as they had ever seen. The forbidding look on His face and the fierce gleam flashing in His eyes reminded Peter of that first trip to the temple; he almost wished he hadn't said anything.

Before anyone had a chance to speak, Jesus said firmly, "No, absolutely not! This is not why I came, not why I am here, and I will have no part in it."

"But," Simon started to argue when a single glance from the Master stifled whatever he had intended to say.

"Go now," Jesus said, slowly and clearly, "all of you. You twelve, get in the boat and head toward Capernaum. I will dismiss the people Myself and talk to you about this later."

To be reproved before everyone like that was nearly more than the disciples' pride could take. To see all their dreams and hopes, seemingly on the verge of fulfillment, crumble yet again, was bitter indeed. Still, something in the way Jesus spoke forestalled any further argument.

Even so, they did not go as they had been instructed. The Twelve returned sullenly to the boat and stayed there, hoping Jesus would change His mind and call them back. When He didn't and they saw the people sadly dispersing, they finally put out from shore and trimmed their sails for the journey home.

Satan stood there in the midst of them, and though Jesus could not see him through human eyes, He still sensed his influence in the rumblings of the crowd. It saddened Him greatly to recognize the voice of the evil one coming from the mouths of His own disciples. Certainly, the human side of His nature felt an attraction to the power available to an earthly king, power which, if rightly used, could change the world, as well as lead Him away from the

Cross. But such a path would also lead outside the will of the Father, and Jesus refused even to consider it.

Every waking moment, He was aware that the fate of the entire world—past, present, and future—depended on the choices He made at any given moment. The destinies of Moses, Enoch, and Elijah were just as closely bound with His, as they watched with keen interest from the City. They loved Him more each day as they saw the terrible risk He took to ensure their place with Him forever.

At the same time Jesus ordered the people to return to their homes, He also admonished the demons to keep their distance. They obeyed as they always did—quickly, but grudgingly.

After the crowd had dispersed and He was alone, Jesus quietly returned to the spot where He had spent those precious hours with His disciples earlier that morning. There He sobbed as He prayed for those who would have crowned Him, who had no understanding of His true purpose in spite of His many efforts to tell them. Even more, He prayed for His disciples, so quick to take offense, so slow to have faith. To them, to these men who were to carry on the work when His time on earth was finished, He had revealed the most of all. How His loving heart grieved that after everything He had told them, all they could think about was their erroneous ideas of the kingdom and who would have the most important place in it.

After months of ministry, of spreading God's blessings liberally throughout Israel, and a day of teaching and miracles that had brought the Twelve closer to heaven than ever before, they had set it all aside in a matter of minutes to grasp vainly at the whispered mirage of the deceiver. That would have been discouraging enough for anyone, yet still Jesus thought only of them and what would become of them when He was no longer present to lead them.

As Gabriel watched His anguish, tears came to his own eyes, and something kept nagging at him. At first, he couldn't pinpoint what was bothering him, but something was definitely wrong. It didn't take long for him to realize what it was. Why wasn't Satan there, pressing his advantage and trying to dishearten Jesus even further? Why wasn't he involved in his usual taunting of Jesus and Gabriel? The huge angel was puzzled and looked around for any sign of his greatest foe.

There he was, just north of the sea among some oak trees and accompanied by every weathermaster and apprentice. He was taking no chances this time *as he executed his deadly plot. Gabriel knew now that this had been Satan's goal all along. He hadn't really thought Jesus would give in to his temptation—not yet. He had merely been trying to separate the disciples from all forms of divine protection.*

It was chilling how well he had succeeded. Out on the lake, midway between Bethsaida and Capernaum, the small ship containing the Twelve had come under heavy attack. The Guardians were compelled to retreat, held away from the disobedient, rebellious humans by a swarm of armed devils. Only the Recorders were allowed to stay, their presence working to the advantage of the rebels. Their pens never faltered as they faithfully wrote down each thought, each word, each expression of disbelief and doubt.

The oblivious disciples, united in their resentment of what they saw as Jesus' unjust treatment of them, criticized Him bitterly, to the boundless delight of the impious spirits. The Recorders were kept busy transcribing their exact testimony. Then, when the sins of the disciples had removed all hope of help, the storm hit.

"I can't believe He did that to us. Who does He think we are, anyway?" Andrew was particularly upset, feeling some entitlement as the Great Finder of the Food.

Judas wrapped himself more tightly in his new cloak. "He humiliated us in front of everyone. I don't know how I'm going to hold my head up in public ever again."

Peter leaned heavily on the steering oar. "Maybe we shouldn't have given up so soon. If we had tried harder, I'll bet we could have made Him King after all. We've been waiting so long to see Jesus take the position He deserves. We could have shown those Pharisees once and for all!"

"I don't know about the rest of you," Simon the Zealot burst out, "but I'm getting really tired of being known as one of the followers of the false prophet. Why doesn't Jesus let us make Him a king—if He's really the Messiah?"

"That's another thing I don't understand," John added. "If He really is the One, why did He let the Baptist die like that? It seems like He ought to have done something about it."

"Just our luck if He is," Thomas joined in.

"Is what?"

"A fraud. A charlatan. A big fake. I don't want to believe it's true—nobody does—but what else are we supposed to think? Every time we try to bring about a coronation, He ruins it for us somehow."

No one argued with him. All were silent for a moment, examining their own thoughts. Finally, Peter spoke. "I think . . ."

There was no warning, just a rapid, ominous chill that settled over them, diverting them from their grievances. The wind seized the boat and shredded the sails before Peter could even remember what he was about to say. Their course turned from Capernaum, out toward the middle of the lake, the boat spinning around dizzily. The waves grew higher, spilling over the sides of the boat.

This time there was no lightning, no whirlpool, nothing to indicate it was anything but an ordinary storm. The wind increased its speed, whipping the clothing of the twelve men struggling frantically to survive. They rowed, they bailed, they steered, but all their efforts were useless. The small craft struggled up the face of one wave after another, plummeting into the trench and rising again, creaking in a most terrifying manner.

How much more can our boat take? We're going to be torn to pieces! Peter tasted sick fear, every muscle and sinew straining to hold the oar steady. Gone was the indignation he had felt only minutes before. Gone were the ambitions to be the leading prince of Israel. All that was stripped away, leaving nothing but a strong desire to live. And then even that was gone. His world had been reduced to wind and water, each breath an unimaginable effort. Man and nature, engaged in a deadly contest that only the sea could win. Unless . . .

"Jesus, where are You? Please help us." He mouthed the words, knowing he would die. Jesus would never come after what they had done, what they had said about Him. It was too late.

"Easy now, don't overdo it. We want it just bad enough to kill them, but not so bad it reminds them of the other storm. They have to think this is just a freak arrangement of the elements." Satan oversaw the crafting of each part of the storm, putting it together with a delicate touch.

The Sea of Galilee, hundreds of feet below sea level, is often blanketed with a protective layer of warm air. The weathermasters ranged over the mountains to gather a layer of very cold air and bring it spilling over the ridges onto the sea. And as the cold air rushed in, warm sea air rose rapidly to meet it, causing violent eddies and fierce winds, with little guidance needed from the demons.

Tarik watched disconsolately as stress fractures widened in the beams making up the little tempest-tossed vessel. The wrenching of the waves opened up a spider's web of tiny cracks. The whole structure was so fragile that one hard blow could shatter it. "Pray, Peter, please pray," he begged, hoping the stubborn fisherman would hear him. "Ask Jesus to help you. It's never too late!"

Finally, as the boat was about to founder, Peter surrendered to the urgings of his Guardian and the Spirit. "Jesus, where are You? Please help us!"

The almost musical rhythm of the storm was interrupted by a single, piercing note, a low, reverberating pulse of energy that encompassed every drop of water in the lake. Jesus stepped from the shore onto the surface of Galilee, knowing it was firm enough to hold Him. His luminous footsteps sent out widening ripples that jangled the nerves of the demons making one last effort to sink the ship before He could reach it.

Satan was so angry he could hardly contain himself. "Why didn't one of you tell me He might walk on the water? You should have prepared for anything! Hurry—He's almost here!" The weathermasters cringed, knowing there would be some rather unpleasant repercussions for the failure that seemed imminent.

Jesus was far from finished with His surprises. Instead of simply rebuking the storm as He had before, He walked near the boat and paused. "Hello," He called, waving to His friends.

Thomas saw Him first. "Ghost!" he screamed in a high-pitched falsetto, pointing with one trembling finger.

When the other men saw the glowing figure gesturing at them, they also cried out in fear. Peter dropped the steering oar, not caring that it floated away beyond his reach. No word in any known human language on earth could hope to match the strangled cry that burst from his lips. A moment before he would have thought nothing would be able to sidetrack him from the storm, but now he scarcely noticed the billows surrounding him on every side. The blood rushed from his face, and his dripping knees clattered against each other.

The apparition gesticulated again, and this time Peter thought he might actually faint. It glided past as if it would continue on, tracing a path atop the white-capped waves. There was something almost familiar about the way it walked, the curve of its cheek . . . "Jesus," Peter shouted in a voice that was ragged and raw. "Wait! Help us!"

The light about Jesus grew even brighter as He turned, smiling His joy. "Don't be afraid. I'm here." And although the waves were as high as ever, the wind seemed to lose some of its overpowering force.

Peter had a sudden suspicion this might be a trick of some kind to lure them into a fatal trap. *How can I be sure? How can I prove it really is the Master?* An idea came to him. "Lord, if it's really You, tell me to come to You. Out there on the water."

He had asked, but still he was taken aback when Jesus simply held out His hand and said, "Come."

All eyes were on Peter as he gulped and stood shakily, grasping the side of the boat for support as he swung one leg over the edge. To his amazement, as his foot touched the water, something wide and strong held it there so he didn't sink. He slid the other foot over and stood, gingerly holding on to the boat. Delighted, he even gave an experimental hop but found that his footing still held.

Jesus waited patiently as Peter started toward Him with the tentative, rolling gait of a baby just learning to walk, arms stretched out for balance. The fisherman easily climbed up one of the waves that had so frightened him a short time before, laughing excitedly. "Do you see? I can do it, too! Are you looking?" He had always thought of faith as vague and indefinable, and yet it was holding him up now, physically supporting his entire weight as he strolled on the surface of the sea.

His pace deepened to a swagger. He had almost reached Jesus when he had to—he just had to—see the faces of his friends as they watched him participating in this flamboyant miracle. He raised his arm in a jaunty greeting. "Hey there, fellows," he cried, "look at me!"

For some reason, the waves looked considerably higher now, and the boat with its anxious passengers very far away. In fact, Peter reflected, the others didn't look so much impressed as just plain scared, as well they should be with such big waves. Big waves! His thoughts stuck there, and the warm, happy feeling vanished. So did whatever was supporting him. With a shout and a splash, he sank into the water, thrashing to stay afloat.

"Help! Help!" A swell broke over him, leaving him coughing and sputtering. His cry rose to a screech. "Jesus! Save me!"

No sooner were the words out of his mouth than Jesus was there at his side, grasping his arm and hauling him out of the water to stand once more on the mysterious, firm foundation of faith. With water soaking him from head to foot, it was impossible to tell if he was laughing or crying, or maybe both at once, as he clung to Jesus. "Thank You—so much! I can't believe I was so foolish!"

"Oh, Peter," Jesus returned his embrace, "why is your faith still so small? Why did you doubt Me?"

It was a thoroughly chastened man that returned to the boat, eyes downcast in embarrassment and holding tightly to Jesus' hand. He was the envy of no one, and his humiliation only deepened when, as they neared the others, Jesus bent down to pick up the steering oar that Peter had so carelessly dropped.

"Here," He said, handing the long piece of wood to the silent fisherman, "I think you'll need this."

Peter didn't feel much better when Jesus stopped again to collect the other oars, released into the tempest by James and John. As Jesus stepped over into the boat and helped Peter inside as well, the storm stopped without a word from Jesus, and the exhausted men found themselves floating on a sea as smooth as glass.

James and John took their oars, prepared to row the long way back to Capernaum, when Matthew tapped them on their shoulders. "Look," he whispered reverently, pointing up.

The ragged sail had apparently mended itself, for it hung in pristine condition, ready to unfurl. As they were to discover later, all evidences of the demonic attack, including the cracked beams, had been completely eradicated in an instant. If it weren't for their sodden robes and pounding hearts, the disciples could have convinced themselves it had all been a bad dream.

Compassionately, Jesus asked them again quietly, "Why is your faith so weak? I am always with you."

Chapter 24

In the furor that followed the aborted attempt at coronation, many scornfully abandoned the Teacher and did all they could to deliver Him into the hands of the Pharisees who wanted to kill Him. As they left behind the truth they had once embraced when they thought Jesus would take over the literal throne of David, the Holy Spirit was shut out of their hearts, and another spirit took control.

With more individuals each day joining the priests and rabbis in their opposition, Jesus turned to His disciples and asked if they were going to leave Him too. Peter, still subdued by his grave mistrust in himself, plaintively asked the question that was on all their hearts. "Lord, if we left You, where would we go? You are the only One who has the words of eternal life." And as much to reassure himself as anyone, he added, "We're convinced that You're the Messiah, the Son of God."

In spite of Peter's frequent instability, Jesus valued the growing faith that had led Peter to the place where he could admit his belief in front of the others. Far too many had turned away at the first hint of opposition; public opinion had swung against Jesus so quickly that He had to retire to Phoenicia in order to postpone the confrontation whose time had not yet come.

His reception in that heathen country put the self-righteous Jews to shame and was a comfort to Jesus in that time of turmoil. The second visit to Gergesa was better still. Following Jesus' instructions carefully, the two men who had been healed of their demon possession had traveled throughout the entire region of Decapolis, broadcasting the good news of what Jesus had done for them. The same townspeople who had once begged Jesus to leave now waited eagerly to welcome Him into their homes.

For most of the next year, Jesus and the disciples spent the majority of their time outside the nation of Israel. Cesarea Philippi provided a refuge from the many Jews who demanded their lives, and in that idolatrous land under the more benign control of Herod Philip, Jesus was able to work many mighty miracles. Here, too, He began trying to prepare the Twelve for the ordeal He would soon face. More plainly than ever before, He spoke to them of His sufferings and death, but they could not bring themselves to believe He meant it literally.

Over and over they searched His words for hidden meanings, but found none. Instead of simply asking Jesus what He meant or accepting what He told them as true, they set the whole issue aside. They reasoned that if He died, He could not become the King of Israel, and therefore He would not—could not—die. Any further statement Jesus made about the cross that awaited Him seemed only an obscure metaphor.

Peter's experience during this time was one of extremes. He was elated at being praised by Jesus for his insight the day Jesus had asked the disciples, "Who do the people think I am?" The men were ashamed to admit it, but even among those who still supported Him, most people thought He was only a good man, possibly a prophet. Jesus was silent a long while, then asked, "What do all of you believe? Who am I?"

There was an embarrassed pause, and none of them quite knew what to say, for all of them had doubted Jesus at one time or another. Then Peter remembered how it felt to have the turbulent waves pass over him and his relief as Jesus' hand grasped his and pulled him up to walk on the sea once more. Humiliated though he had been, his faith had never been stronger than at that moment, and now he felt compelled to speak. "You are our Redeemer—the Son of the living God!"

The other eleven nodded their agreement. They knew they had been guilty of disbelief before, but they had come to trust fully that Jesus was the Messiah, even if they didn't understand His reluctance to ascend the throne. They were glad to hear Peter give voice to the conviction they had not been able to put into words.

Tarik was so happy he cried, even more so when Jesus embraced Peter, saying in a choked voice, "Oh, Peter, you have been so blessed by My Father. He is the One who showed you this." It meant more to Jesus than Peter could have guessed for him to express that encouragement and trust to his Master in front of the others.

The rosy glow he felt then made what happened a short time later all the more shocking to him. Jesus tried again to tell the disciples of what was to occur at the upcoming Passover, when He would become the sacrificial Lamb at a most unexpected coronation. Peter, saddened and angered at the thought of anyone bringing harm to his beloved Master, cut Him off abruptly. "Lord, You're wrong—that will never happen to You!"

Jesus looked Peter right in the eyes, saying sharply, "Leave Me alone, Satan. You are offensive to Me. You have nothing godly in you at all; you are filled with the same wickedness as man."

Peter's mouth dropped open, and his eyes bulged. He could hardly begin to fathom that Jesus had called him "Satan." Completely disconsolate, he had no inkling that he had just been delivered from the commander of the dark forces, who, having ordered Set to step aside, had used Peter's misguided beliefs in the Messiah's worldly kingdom to carefully insert an idea into the fisherman's head.

That thought was a carefully disguised repetition of the third temptation in the wilderness, but if Satan thought Jesus would fail to recognize it if it came from another source, he was sadly mistaken. Jesus knew it instantly for what it was and had no illusions about its origin. As the words left Peter's lips, the former light-bearer stood so close to him that his giant hands touched Peter's shoulders, and his seductive voice whispered soothing reassurances into Peter's willing ear.

When Jesus ordered him away, Satan's sneer turned to a snarl, and he spiraled off into the sky in a towering rage at being unmasked so easily. When at last he could speak again, he shook both fists at the heavens, screaming, "I'll get Him yet—do You hear me? I will get Him yet! I am the ruler of this world. You will never defeat me. I will never give up what is mine."

Peter knew none of this as he found a solitary place to shed a few tears. He wasn't bitter—his pride was at much too low an ebb for that—but he was terribly wounded and had no concept of what he might have done that could have merited such a public rebuke. On his knees he laid out his pain, and on his knees he received healing, though still not understanding that through many trials he was being prepared for the stunning surprise Jesus had in store.

They quietly skirted Gennesaret, keeping off the main roads to avoid calling attention to themselves. Peter caught a glimpse of Capernaum, but no more. That night, as they gathered companionably around the campfire, Jesus took advantage of the intimate setting to once more attempt to prepare them for the future.

"I know you all want to follow Me wherever I go, and I'm grateful for all that you've been willing to give up to be with Me. But if you want to truly follow Me, you will have to completely deny self, pick up your cross, and go where I lead, even into death."

His words, even more solemn than usual, caught their attention, and all Twelve listened in a hush as He went on. "Anyone who tries to save his life will die, but those who die for My sake will live. Which is more important? What good is it if you gain the whole world and lose your hope of eternal life? What are you willing to trade for your soul?"

Peter, wrung with grief, asked Him, "When will we see Your glory? You keep talking to us about crosses and dying, but when will we see Your kingdom?"

Joy stealing over His features, Jesus answered, "Someday, the Son of man will come wearing the glory of the Father and of all the holy angels. When that happens, He will reward each person according to his deeds." Jesus smiled a strange, secretive smile. "Some of you here with Me right now will see Me come into the kingdom before you die."

It was six days before Peter, along with James and John, learned what He meant. For the others, it would be several months.

They were all very tired by the time they reached the outskirts of Jerusalem. It was near sundown, and when Jesus announced they would make camp, a halfhearted cheer went up. Peter slumped against a tree, telling himself he would help set things up in a minute or two.

When preparations were well under way and the smell of a hearty stew tantalized the hungry men, Jesus came over to Peter, James, and John and said softly, "Come with Me."

John tossed Peter a slightly stale loaf of bread, and the four men ate as they walked. As soon as they were out of hearing of the others, Peter asked, "Where are we going?"

Jesus laughed. "You're always ready with a question, aren't you, My friend?"

Peter grinned, momentarily distracted from his sorrow and confusion. "That wasn't really an answer, was it?"

"Some things are meant to be experienced. You'll have to take that on faith."

They made their way across the gently rolling countryside for several miles, growing more exhausted with each step, until they came to a familiar steep trail.

"You're kidding, aren't you?" James regarded the ascent with dismay.

Jesus shook His head and started for the top, and the three men followed Him. By the time they reached the summit, their whole bodies ached; their exhaustion was total as they collapsed to rest. The sun hesitated momentarily in the west before plunging into oblivion, leaving them alone with their thoughts in the deepening night.

After taking a minute or two to catch His breath, Jesus stood slowly. "Watch and pray," He told His friends, then knelt nearby in a clearing.

Obediently, Peter, James, and John rolled over onto their knees and started their prayers, propping their heads and arms on a fallen log. If they had stretched out on the softest cushions in Judea, they would not have fallen asleep any faster. Peter went out first, with James and John following in close succession.

Jesus prayed for many hours, heedless as the cold evening condensed moisture in the air to form a heavy blanket of dew over Him. He agonized over each soul who thought of choosing Him, that they would decide rightly, holding up each of His disciples in turn, knowing each one's strengths and weaknesses and what would be the result of their decision to follow Him.

"Now, Father," He concluded, "I have something to ask You on behalf of these three dear men who have followed Me here tonight. You know they're not as prepared as they should be for the ordeal ahead. Please send them a sign, so that when the time comes they have a chance to hold firm.

"I don't ask this for Myself. I know I'm Your Son and that I'm here to die. I am ready to fulfill Our agreement, but I want to make it as easy as I can for My friends, who are Your friends too.

"This is why I'm asking if tonight You will show them Your glory—and My glory before I came to earth—so they will better understand the kingdom We want to establish and so they will not doubt that I am the One."

When Jesus closed His prayer far into the night, He stood again, chilled to the bone, his knees throbbing with pain. Shaking His disciples, He told them, "Wake up. It's time now—they will be coming very soon. Remember, I asked you to watch and pray with Me."

Peter blinked heavily and wiped a trail of drool from the side of his beard. "Sorry. Must've fallen asleep."

"Watch and pray," Jesus repeated, more insistently.

In response to Jesus' prayer, the Father called Elijah and Moses to Him and told them they had been chosen. He instructed them to travel at the speed of thought to the upper atmosphere of earth, put on their heavenly glory, and meet with their dearest Friend with whom they had not spoken in over three decades. They had missed Him greatly, though in some ways it was hardest those first few years when He didn't yet remember His previous life. Then, as He grew, each time He read the Scriptures, He would remember more and more. A flash of memory here and there became a flood, and at the age of twelve, when He saw His first Passover, Jesus came into a knowledge of His origin.

Chapter 24

Be assured, the Father didn't have to repeat His invitation twice. The two were gone in the blink of an eye, appearing less than a second later at the edge of the first heaven. As they had been told to do, the two men put on their full glory and descended rapidly.

The first thought to cross their minds was how dark it was. In the centuries of unremitting heavenly light, they had nearly forgotten how dreary the earth had become in the years since the Fall. They were accustomed to observing their gloomy planet while still surrounded by the brightness shining from God's throne, and it was different—somehow troubling—to be cut off from that light. If not for the glory they were allowed to keep, they might not have been able to bear it.

The two men had to chuckle, just a little. All across the countryside, people awoke to the strange light and reacted with comical dismay. Some even thought they were still dreaming. Elijah and Moses passed over the city of Jerusalem, their radiance lighting every corner of every street. They slowed as they neared the mountaintop, coming to a stop next to Jesus, who waited with open arms.

Tears flowed freely as the friends reunited and for the first time Moses set foot in the Land of Promise, the land of his people. He took off his crown and laid it at Jesus' feet, bowing before Him to worship as he had longed to do for many years. By the time he rose, Peter was again asleep.

They stood and talked for a long time of the sufferings Jesus would shortly have to bear as He paid the price for all sin. Moses, especially, sobbed as his lifetime of wicked deeds came into his mind, knowing that each one would make the pain of Jesus a little greater. The sorrowing man would have gone through anything to spare Him that, but alas, his life would not atone for even the smallest of his own transgressions, let alone the sins of the whole world.

Elijah kept looking over at Peter and the others, hoping they would wake up and have the chance to hear vital information that would prepare them for the way of the Cross and spare them much disappointment, but they slept on.

As the time grew short, Jesus laid His hand on Moses' arm. "It has been such an encouragement to have you here, My good friends. You have given Me the strength I need to walk through the fiery trial that is coming. When that time comes, I will cling ever more tightly to My Father, and I will be thinking of you.

"Moses, I know you have to go back very soon, but I also know how much you've wished to meet my faithful fisherman. And Elijah, I know you've been drawn to my Sons of Thunder, who are now so much like you were then—bold, fervent, and extremely loyal. Would you like to wake them up?"

"How did You know?" They hugged Him again, awed that even in His human form, He was able to discern so much about them and what they were thinking.

"I can always feel you watching Me, and I know when you're near." It seemed an ironic twist, for they both could remember saying that to Him many times while still on earth and reaching for His presence in a time of need.

Moses walked over to the snoring form of Peter and shook him firmly. The former leader of Israel knew that gentleness would be completely lost on him. "Peter, wake up! Can you hear me? I have to go soon, and I really want to talk with you."

Peter yawned, eyes tight shut. "I had the most interesting dream," he murmured sleepily. "There was a light or something. I'm not sure what it was . . ." He opened his eyes, then immediately clamped them shut at the brightness. "Who are you?" He squinted through one eye at Moses, trying to make out his features.

"I'm Moses," the glowing being said, smiling. "I think you may also have heard of Elijah," and he motioned toward his brilliant companion.

Peter did open his eyes then. On Moses' other side, near James and John, Elijah waved a friendly salute. The astonishment on Peter's face was nothing compared to how he gawked when he saw Jesus.

At the moment of Moses' and Elijah's arrival, Jesus had also received a measure of the Father's glory. His face and clothing were shining to rival the sun. Although he had been waiting and praying for Jesus to come into His rightful inheritance, Peter had never thought it would be like this.

Moses helped him to his feet. "I need to leave, and I'm so sorry to have missed talking to you the way I'd hoped."

"I have an idea," Peter interrupted excitedly. The others were not as surprised as they might have been; if Peter didn't hesitate to interrupt Jesus, why should it be any different for a mere messenger from heaven? "James, John, and I can use some of this brush and build three shelters. Then you won't have to go right away—you can stay and talk for as long as you want—and even be shaded from the sun!"

Moses and Elijah laughed softly, amused by his innocent enthusiasm and touched by his quick hospitality. "We wish we could," Moses took his hand. "Someday we'll sit down to a banquet together and talk as long as we want. In the meantime, no matter what happens, always remember that Jesus is truly God's Son and the Adored One of all heaven. Promise me!"

"Of course." Peter was puzzled by his vehemence, but glad to agree. "I promise."

"Goodbye, my friend. We'll meet again someday."

The night lit up around the clearing for miles. From above, a massive cloud floated down over the mountain, so bright it made the light around Moses and Elijah look like a shadow. Jesus held up His hands, reaching as high as He could. "Abba!" He whispered, unspeakable joy on His face. The thousands of colors in the rainbow around the throne spilled down and wrapped themselves around Him, curling around His outstretched fingers.

A great Voice thundered out of the cloud, echoing in the surrounding mountains. *"This is My beloved Son, in whom I am well pleased. Listen to Him!"* The resonance passed into the earth, shaking the ground as far away as Galilee.

Many saw the great manifestation and fell into fear, having no idea what it meant. The nine disciples who had been sleeping fitfully in the camp saw it too; they knew it had something to do with their Master, and jealousy grew against the missing three.

Oblivious to all else, Peter, James, and John fell to the ground, hiding their faces. As the ground rolled beneath them, every defect of their characters loomed before their eyes, and they feared for their lives. Jesus quickly soothed their anxiety, touching them gently on the shoulder. "You can get up now."

Peter raised his head, eyes darting all around. It was the gray hour before dawn, and Jesus was alone. "Where are they? I know I wasn't dreaming." He reached out and touched the sleeve of Jesus' garment, now the same plain homespun as when it had first been woven.

"They went back where they belong, and we must too."

"What are You talking about?"

Jesus looked off into the valley in the direction from which they had come. "Your brother needs Me, and now our place is back with the others. Don't tell anyone what you saw here until after I have risen from the dead."

How can He do that? Peter wondered. *We've just seen with our own eyes that He is not only the King of earth, but also King of heaven. Even Moses knelt to worship Him. And yet after all that, He's still talking about dying. No matter how hard I try, I just don't understand.*

It was as if Jesus was reading his thoughts, which, of course, He was. "You don't have to understand why I ask this of you. All you have to do is trust Me."

Chapter 25

*A*s the cloud covering the Father's glory lifted the two men back into the heavens, history repeated itself. Centuries earlier, the first time Moses had met with Jesus on top of a mountain, there had been trouble in the camp below. So it was again. Those who were to have been waiting and praying had, instead, turned aside in anger and envy at the privileges given to the favored three. When Jesus descended the mount and drew near, He could hear a babble of noise and confusion.

A crowd surrounded the nine disciples, watching with keen interest and no little amusement as Andrew proved unsuccessful at casting out the demons afflicting a young boy. The attitude of the disciples left no room for God's love or the Spirit's power, so all their own efforts came to nothing.

However, Adonai was merciful to them even in their iniquity, and He commanded Nadiv to organize a formidable barrier around the men so that the demon who possessed the boy could not attack them and rend them to pieces. Satan, himself, made a personal appearance, replacing the boy's usual occupant to further his plan. He would have loved to claw at the hated disciples and feast on the terror in their faces but was held back by the fearsome ring of angelic swords.

When Satan saw Jesus approaching, he ordered his underling to repossess the boy, but the smaller demon couldn't move. Satan would have chased him down and beaten him senseless, if only he himself could have budged. All the *supernatural entities stood frozen in a tableau in which only the humans moved.*

Jesus wasted no time coming to the heart of the problem. He read the dismay and humiliation in the furtive glances of the nine, knowing each part of the story as if He had watched it happen. Upon seeing the confounded, speechless disciples, He walked over to confront the snickering scribes and their near-blasphemous leader. "What questions are you asking them?"

Andrew started it first. When he woke for the third time at daybreak, he looked around and snorted with disgust when he saw his brother still hadn't come back. "Great! Just great! I stay here and work, while my brother goes off by himself with Jesus to watch some kind of cosmic light show. That's really fair . . ."

"I don't like the way things are being run, either." Judas chimed in with his own malcontent. "Just because they have been with Jesus a little longer than we have, they think they're entitled to everything."

"But they haven't been," Andrew burst out, frustrated. "James and John, maybe. But *I* found Jesus before Peter did! If anyone should get to go, it should have been me." He thought for a moment. "I'll bet I know why He picked my brother instead of me—my brother has two sons, and I don't have any. Maybe Jesus wants to make sure that His top three princes," his voice dripped with scorn, "have some posterity to carry on their names, and all I have are daughters and more daughters. I wish I had known before I got married that my wife wouldn't be able to give me sons."

"That doesn't exactly make sense." Nathanael frowned. "James is only engaged, and John isn't married yet. Neither of them have any children at all."

"Don't argue details with me! I just know that however this whole thing was decided, it was unfair to the rest of us. I may be only a fisherman, but I know when something's rotten!"

The discussion among the disgruntled disciples grew only more rancorous as the morning progressed. They were in a decidedly unhappy frame of mind when the forerunners arrived in advance of the crowd seeking Jesus.

"Is Jesus here? We heard He was nearby, and we are bringing a man who needs to see Him."

"He's not here right now." Andrew scowled at them. "He went off somewhere without telling us, and He's not back yet."

"Jesus, where are You? My son needs You—I need You!" An older man with desperation on his face pulled ahead of the approaching throng, leading a teenage boy who clearly had something very wrong with him. His eyes were rolled back into his head, and foam dripped from his slack lips. Bruises and gashes covered every visible part of his body—which was most of it since his clothes were ripped and torn, little better than rags, actually.

As they watched, the evil spirits seized the battered body, and it convulsed, falling to roll wildly across the ground. Horrible, tortured screams came forth from a throat already raw from previous attacks. The boy pushed himself up on one elbow, his eyes rolling down for the first time to stare malevolently at each of the disciples. He screamed again, so fearsomely this time that Andrew felt his insides quiver in fear.

The boy started forward, clawing his way across the ground toward them until he seemed to hit some invisible wall, an unknown barrier he could not pass. Rising up on his knees, the boy stretched as far as he could toward the disciples, trying to reach them for reasons that were anything but benign.

"There. Do you see what I have to put up with? Can't Jesus help me? Where is He?" The poor father wiped the tears from his cheeks, hoping against hope that the Teacher could bring relief to his son's suffering.

Andrew wiggled the fingers on his "miracle hand" to warm it up, swaggering closer to where the boy still snarled at him. "Like I was just telling the others, Jesus isn't here. He went off somewhere yesterday and hasn't bothered to come back." The father moaned softly, swayed, and seemed about to fall. "But," Andrew's emphatic tone caught the man's attention, "even though He's unavailable, we'll be glad to help you out instead."

Pleasantly conscious of the admiring looks from the other disciples and the fixed regard of the crowd, Andrew waved his hand with a flourish and said dramatically, "Evil spirit, I command you in the name of Jesus to come out!" He thrust his hand forward as if he were throwing an invisible ball of magic at the boy, closing his eyes and lifting his face heavenward for effect.

A gasp went up from the crowd, followed by stunned silence. When Andrew thought enough time had gone by, he opened his eyes and looked around with a smile. *That was too easy,* he thought, preparing to receive the thanks and congratulations that would start flowing at any minute.

The boy stood up, head down, and wiped the foam from his mouth. Andrew took a step forward, still smiling. "You're welcome. I was glad to help." He held out his hand.

Slowly the boy raised his eyes to meet Andrew's. The disciple felt a clutching constriction in his chest that surely must be his heart stopping. A concentrated, evil intelligence looked out at him from inside the boy, and a strength greater than his own pulled Andrew in. He was powerless to break away.

With a marrow-freezing scream, the boy launched himself into the air, his hands reaching for Andrew's throat. Just short of his target, the boy hit the unseen barricade yet again and collapsed on the ground, rolling and frothing afresh.

Andrew ran and hid behind the other disciples, to the laughter of the many scribes who had come out that day. "Go away," he yelled at the weeping father. "We can't do anything for you." In an aside to the other disciples, he muttered, "Unless one of you knows what went wrong and wants a chance at him." They shook their heads emphatically. They were embarrassed enough just being seen with Andrew, never mind repeating his humiliation.

"Ha! I knew it!" One of the scribes loudly addressed his companions. "Finally, we have found an evil spirit so strong that even Jesus can't cast it out! I tried all along to tell you that he and his followers are all deceivers, leading the people to transgress the laws of Moses and of God, but now you have seen it for yourselves. He's a fake! A fraud!"

"No, He's not!" The usually placid James stepped forward to defend the honor of his Master. "Jesus is not a deceiver, and it's not right for you to say that He is."

Chapter 25

Thaddeus walked to his father's side. "I don't believe He's a fake, either. We've seen too many of His miracles to doubt Him. He has power over all the earth." His indignation caused a fresh burst of laughter from the crowd, and Thaddeus flushed a deep red.

"Then explain this to us." The scribe motioned at the possessed boy. "Why couldn't you cast the spirit out? You say you're Jesus' followers, but you can't even help this poor lad, can you? Why not? I think I'm being very reasonable by allowing you this chance to explain yourselves. What of it? What do you have to say? That's what I thought—not a word." Carried away by his own eloquence, he turned to face the crowd, ignoring the persistent efforts of one of his friends to get his attention.

"Do you see now why we have warned you of the dangers of this false messiah and his lying disciples?" The tugging on his sleeve became more insistent. "Can you understand now that we have only your best interests at heart when we condemn this Jesus as an imposter—a thief of the respect and high regard you should have for us, your true spiritual teachers?"

This time his companion grabbed his whole arm and pulled on it. The scribe hissed angrily at him, "Don't interrupt me again. Can't you see I'm in the middle of something? We may not have a chance like this for a long time. Be quiet!"

Pasting his beatific smile back on, the scribe went on. "If Jesus were here in front of you now, do you really think the outcome would have been any different? Well, if he gave his power to these men," he gestured at the disciples, "and they can't do anything for this pitiful boy and his dear, grieving father, then do you really think Jesus could have helped? He's not even here!" The scribe's friend whimpered, but with a great effort remained silent. "If he cared so much, if he knew so much, if he really had power over the sea and skies, he would be . . ."

"Here!" squeaked the friend, unable to contain himself any longer. "He's right here!"

The scribe half turned to look over his shoulder, and indeed, Jesus was there, standing directly behind him with terrible majesty. The scribe tried to sidle away, but Jesus fixed him with a steely gaze. "Why are you asking these questions of them? I'm here now. If you want to know something, ask Me."

"No, no. That's all right, no. I mean, yes, I'm all done here. No, no questions." The scribe, shocked into incoherence, stumbled away as quickly as he could.

Jesus motioned for the distraught father to come to Him. "How long has he been like this?"

The father bowed at Jesus' feet, and with hope faintly renewed, poured out his sorrowful tale. "I don't know how he became like this, but my son has had this problem since he was a small child. He throws himself around violently, as you can see, but if I don't watch him every moment of the day and night, he will throw himself into the fire, or walk out into the lake where the water covers his head. I've lost track of how many times now I've saved him from burning or drowning." The sunken cheeks and dark-rimmed eyes gave mute testimony to many years of sleep deprivation.

"What happened here today?" Jesus' voice was gentle, but the look He gave His nine followers was filled with disappointment.

The man began to weep. "I brought my son to Your disciples and asked them to cast out this evil spirit, but they could not. I didn't know what else I could do. I thought maybe if I saw You, that You would heal my son—if You can."

Jesus looked around at the assembly, reading each heart and not liking what He found. The father's unbelief was reflected by nearly everyone there. With pain in His eyes, He asked each of them, "How long am I going to be here with you? Not nearly long enough. The people of your day are completely lacking in faith—what more can I do to help you believe?" He turned to the father. "If you can believe, all things are possible."

Suddenly, the father saw his plea for help for what it was, an expression of doubt. Just as quickly, he understood that Jesus might pass him by, unable to heal his son because of his own sin. "Wait, Jesus, please!" he cried in the same penitent spirit as the father from Capernaum. "I believe, truly I do. I know even that isn't enough—I need Your help to believe even more."

"Of course." Jesus smiled reassuringly. "Any time you ask." His features hardened as he looked inside the boy. Silently, He gave permission for the possessing demon to put on a wild display of its power before demanding, "You mute and deaf spirit, come out of that boy at once, and don't ever return—any of you!"

Released from his momentary prison, Satan erupted from the boy with such great speed that the devastated body gave a great heave and fell to the ground almost dead. Once again the Prince of heaven and the prince of the power of the air had met in direct confrontation, and once again Jesus emerged the uncontested Victor.

Jesus bent over the fallen boy and took him by the hand. "Jacob, get up. There's someone here who wants very much to see you." He led Jacob to his father and presented him, sound of body and mind at last. The father threw his arms around his son and Jesus together, weeping tears of joy.

"Thank You, Jesus," he said over and over, "thank You for making my son well."

Jesus sat down and made Himself comfortable, ready to begin telling stories and parables. Jacob sat right next to Jesus' feet, taking in every word. "Once there was a man," Jesus began, "who was possessed by a demon."

It was a very unusual experience for Tarik to watch while Peter stood silently to observe the whole drama play out and listen without objection to the same familiar story. A residual glow clung to all four men, a dim reflection of the throne of God, but the fisherman was entirely unaware of it, having not thought of himself in hours. Even if he had known, he had been so humbled by his proximity to the Almighty that he still would not have tried to lord it over his brother. And most amazingly, he didn't even have one sarcastic comment when Jesus stood late that afternoon and announced they would head to a certain house in Magdala for the seventh time. Tarik hoped the transformation of Peter's character would last.

As they neared Capernaum, the disciples drifted to the rear of the crowd, talking quietly in little groups of two or three. In part, they were despondent over Jesus' strange insistence that He would soon die and baffled as to how that could be a part of the divine plan. In part, they did not really want to stroll into the town that was home to a good number of them with Jesus on one side and the Magdalene on the other. But mostly, they wanted to stay far enough from Jesus so He couldn't hear them as they argued softly, yet bitterly, about who would hold the highest offices in the kingdom.

Mary clung closer to Jesus than she had any of the previous six times He had delivered her, and it really was getting embarrassing. Jesus didn't seem to mind that she never allowed Him out of her sight, barely allowing Him a few moments of privacy in nature, morning and evening. The disciples were getting tired of it. That, and the way she always sat right next to Him, in one or the other of their spots.

"What are we going to do with her when we get there?" Peter's tone was matter-of-fact, for the sloping section of the path called to mind his wife's scolding the last time he and Andrew had passed that way, and he didn't want to seem judgmental. Rimona was probably right, anyway, that Mary would have quite a story to tell if she chose.

"I don't know, but we'll have to think of something. It wouldn't be proper for her to follow Jesus as closely in town as she's been able to do in the countryside, but she's so afraid of being alone. I kind of feel sorry for her," Andrew admitted.

"Speaking of that, where is Jesus going to stay? So many things have changed."

"We'll think of something," Andrew repeated.

But in the end, they didn't have to think of anything at all. Zebedee waited for Jesus at the bottom of the path leading to his home, inviting Him to stay in a small, unused dwelling near the back of his property, along with any of the disciples who didn't have a home there in the city. Though Zebedee still didn't believe Jesus was the Messiah, he had come to think that perhaps Jesus might be the next king, and as long as that was a possibility, it seemed foolish to alienate Him. Besides, if Jesus were there on the estate, maybe Salome would be content to stay home for a little while. Not that Batia wasn't doing a splendid job, mind you, but Zebedee missed his wife and wished she'd come back.

Rimona waited right behind Zebedee, knowing she would be needed for something. As soon as she saw Mary, she understood what it was. Holding out both hands to the other woman, she said warmly, "And you must stay with us. Mother would be glad to have you share her room.

Please consider our home yours whenever you're here." Mary's tender spirit reached out to Rimona's kindness, and soon the two felt as if they had always been friends.

Jesus had so much He wanted to say privately to His disciples, and Zebedee's offer, regardless of the motives that had prompted it, provided Him the chance to have some time away from the crowd for a while. Batia offered to stay with the children so Rimona and Keren could join the small gathering shortly after noon.

The two women, together with Mary, slipped into the small house, concealing several neatly folded bundles of cloth. Mary knew all about the secret by then, having found something of her own she could add to it, and watched with interest as Rimona and Keren knelt on either side of their Master.

Jesus put His arms around them, welcoming them with delight. Rimona blushed as all eyes turned to them, straining to see what they were doing. "Here," she said, laying the bundle in His lap, "we made this for You."

Keren smiled. "You wouldn't believe how many times we had to practice before we got it right, but Zebedee was kind and let us use as much material as we needed, once he found out what we were doing."

Jesus fingered the smooth cloth, the fibers catching lightly on His calluses. "Did you weave this yourselves? It's very soft."

Eyes shining, Rimona nodded. "We thought it would be more comfortable than the one You have now. Do You like it?"

Jesus carefully unfolded it and held it up. His men gasped at the sight of the flawlessly woven, snowy white, seamless robe. It was a garment fit for a king. "It's beautiful." Tears filled His eyes. "Thank you—both of you."

"But that's not all," Keren burst out. "What use would a robe like that be if You still had scratchy cloth against Your skin? We made You an undergarment of the same material."

Mary stepped forward shyly. "I brought a length of purple cloth I would like You to have too. It would make a nice sash."

"I'll be right back." John jumped up and ran out the door.

"Thank you," Jesus repeated in a choked voice. "I will need these very soon—much sooner than you realize."

Peter was thrilled. *Oh good—it's almost time for Jesus to come into His kingdom! Hmm . . . He sounds a little sad. I wonder why? Oh well. I guess it doesn't matter. Now, what should I wear to the coronation? Maybe Rimona will have time to make me a robe like that, unless Jesus is planning to do something sooner than she could finish it. Of course, Andrew will probably want one, too, and whose should they make first, mine because I'm older, or Andrew's because his wife does more of the weaving? There's so much to worry about!*

Jesus must have been reading Peter's mind again, for He looked right at His friend as He said, "Yes, it is almost time for Me to set up My kingdom. When we go to Jerusalem, a man will betray Me. I will be put to death, then rise again. When it is done, My kingdom will last forever."

Rimona rocked back on her heels in shock. Jesus spoke of His death so plainly, so matter-of-factly, as if it were already accomplished. Her gaze shot to her husband to see if he was surprised, too, but he only squirmed uncomfortably at the supposed figure of speech, which was getting rather wearying in its repetition. After a few seconds, Peter's eyes grew unfocused, and he stared dreamily into space, a hint of a smile on his lips.

How can he be so unfeeling? Rimona wondered. *Jesus just told him He's going to die, and my husband, the father of my children, sits there looking like he's listening to soothing music at an outdoor feast!*

Could she have known it, Peter's thoughts had wandered back to the robe. Of course, that led to thoughts of coronations, which led to thoughts of high-ranking princes in the kingdom, which led to thoughts of palaces, which led to thoughts of more fancy robes, by which time he had forgotten everything else Jesus had told him.

Just then, John came back in with a pair of thin ornamental sandals and a leather bag. "Here, I bought these just before You called me to follow You, and I never wore them. They ought to look nice with the robe. And this satchel ought to be the right size to carry them all until You're ready for them."

"You're so thoughtful, John." Pleased, Jesus embraced His beloved disciple. "One of the things I have always appreciated about you is how you think of others before yourself."

Chapter 25

John winced, thinking of the way he had argued just that morning about how he should be the greatest of the princes because Jesus favored him more than the others. "I'm always glad to help, Master," he muttered under his breath, hoping he wasn't too transparently hypocritical.

Peter looked down at his dirt-encrusted feet and shuddered, picturing the worn, crudely made sandals protruding from beneath his new robe. A man in his position would need new shoes—not for the sake of pride, naturally, but only so he wouldn't embarrass the new King. He didn't have to get them today, but it couldn't hurt to look and see what the merchants had to offer. He slipped out the door, a faraway look on his face. Thinking of sandals reminded him of robes, which reminded him of coronations, which reminded him of . . .

The sandal maker's shop boasted a much greater variety than it ever had before. Perhaps because of the additional traffic through the town now known as Jesus' own city, the man had been able to hire a young apprentice to do most of the tedious labor, leaving the craftsman himself free to experiment with new designs and techniques. Absorbed in a study of the more expensive styles, Peter started when a man standing next to his elbow spoke to him.

"So you're one of His followers," the diminutive scribe sneered. "Maybe that means you know why your master doesn't pay the yearly coin for the temple tax like the rest of us. Either he thinks he's better than we are, or he just doesn't value the temple as much as we do."

"He does too," retorted Peter hotly. "You don't know what you're talking about."

"Really?" The scribe feigned surprise. "I suppose you could be right, and I just forgot to record when he paid it. Do you know when he turned it in?"

But Jesus hadn't paid the tax, and Peter well knew it. "He didn't pay the tax yet, but I'm telling you, it will be taken care of by day's end," he promised rashly.

The scribe sailed away, satisfaction fluttering out of each billow in his robes. "Don't forget your own tax," he called back over his shoulder.

Peter gritted his teeth. He *had* forgotten. Biting back a string of curses for the scribe and his ancestors, he muttered, "Great! Just great! Why didn't I think that one through? I guess I'd better go talk to Jesus."

Jesus was alone in the house, and as soon as He heard Peter's step at the threshold, he called him to come in. "I'm glad you came along just now, Simon, because I have a question for you."

Peter hung his head. "I have a question for You too."

"I've been thinking about taxes," Jesus said casually, "and there's something I've been wondering about. When a country here on earth has a king, and the king wants to collect the taxes that are due, where does he go to collect them?"

Peter gulped. "I'm not sure what You're getting at."

"Well, just think about it." Jesus frowned thoughtfully. "When a king collects the taxes, does he take them from his own children or from his other subjects?"

"Um . . . not from his children, that's for sure."

"You're right. He taxes his subjects, but not his sons. The king's children go tax-free."

Peter was not a man of nuance, but this simple illustration showed him how easily he had been tricked by the clever scribe. The question was not whether Jesus had paid the tax, but whether He even should. The sons of Levi, devoted to the care of the temple, were exempt, so shouldn't God's Son be exempt as well? The prophets were exempt, and Jesus was greater than any of them. Too late, Peter realized his hasty answer had given the scribe a weapon to use against Jesus and that by agreeing to pay the tax, Peter had practically called Jesus a liar.

"Oh, no! Not again!" The contrite man slumped to the floor and buried his face in his hands.

"Peter, Peter, what am I going to do with you?" Tenderly, Jesus put His arm around His most impulsive disciple and drew him to his feet. "Here, stand up, and let Me tell you what to do."

Chapter 26

The instructions sounded bizarre to the experienced fisherman, but he was in no position to protest or question. Hoping he wouldn't meet anyone he knew, Peter took some of his old fishing supplies and walked down to the shore of the lake.

Impaling an insect on the sharp point of a hook, he girded up his robe and waded out into the water. Peter looked both ways to make sure no one was watching then tossed the hook out as far as he could. Slowly, patiently, he drew the cord back in. Several times he felt the hook snag on something, but each time he tugged on the line, it pulled free.

Then he saw the hook a few feet away in the clear water, most of the insect still attached. His shoulders drooped. *Maybe I'm doing something wrong. Maybe I just don't have enough faith. Adonai, please help me.* As he pulled the line in the last few feet, a large fish darted forward and seized the bait. Oddly enough, it didn't struggle at all as Peter reached down and lifted it by its gills from the water.

Reflexively, he held the fish up with one hand and reached into its mouth with the other to remove the sharpened, curving bone that served as a hook. But it fell out into his hand before he even touched it. Puzzled, he looked into the fish's mouth for some sign it had bitten down on the hook at all, when he saw something gleam inside where it caught the light.

Knowing what it would be, Peter reached reverently for the coin, which was enough to pay the tax for Jesus—and for him as well. He stood a long time looking at it, until an insistent flapping along his arm reminded him of the fish he still held. Briefly, he contemplated the idea of taking it home for supper, but couldn't bring himself to do it, not when it had come to him at the Lord's command. Lowering his hand into the water, he watched as the fish flopped about, righted itself, and swam away into the deep water that meant freedom.

"Go ahead. You've earned it," Peter whispered, closing his hand over the hook and the coin. "I need to go straight to the priest, anyway."

His step was light and his heart happy as he entered the house where Jesus was staying. He had made a mistake, to be sure, but Jesus had fixed it for him in such a way that, although the tax had been given in order to avoid any controversy, it was clear that Adonai was the One who had actually paid it for His Son. Given a second chance to explain, Peter had made that very clear.

Upon walking in the doorway, even such an obtuse man as Peter could sense the tension in the room. While he was gone, Jesus had called the others together, and pinning them with a look they could not escape, had asked, "What were you arguing about on the way here?"

The whole sordid story came tumbling out, and a shamed silence descended as Peter entered. Not one to broach anything delicately, he boomed, "What are you all talking about without me? You look like a bunch of Pharisees on a fast!"

Jesus answered, "We were just discussing who would be the greatest in My kingdom, when it is set up."

"Really!" Peter looked around, wondering why that would make the others look so glum. "That's a good question—who *is* going to be the greatest, anyway?" Having already chosen what he wanted to do, he was less involved in the dispute than the others.

The disciples looked to Jesus for a reply that was not long in coming. "If any of you want to hold an important place in My kingdom, you must put yourselves last and others first. If you want to rule over all people, you must be a servant of all people.

"Once, there was an angel of heaven who wanted a higher position than the one he had, but even if it had been possible to give it to him, he didn't want the responsibilities that came with it—only the power. In his quest for supremacy, he lost even the position he had, altering the peace and happiness of God's city forever. And the rival kingdom he set up here on this earth is still marked by the same yearning for dominance and control."

A racket by the door distracted Peter, especially when he realized his children were the ones making most of the noise. "All right, you two, be quiet out there! We're having an important meeting right now!"

"Abba!" Seth burst into the room at the sound of his father's voice. "I missed you!"

"Jesus!" Jered was right behind his brother, but bypassed Peter in favor of Jesus. "I was wondering when You would come back, and Seth and I have been learning to fish, and sometimes we pretend to heal people like You do, and we want to hear more stories, so please tell us some more, and then maybe You can come play with us for a while and we can show You our special fort we built, but we help our mother out a lot, too . . ." he finally had to take a breath, and sputtered to a stop.

"Boys," Peter said sternly, "how very rude to come barging in here like this. Tell Jesus you're sorry and then go back out."

Jered looked disappointed, and Seth's lip began to tremble. "We're sorry, Jesus."

"Oh, Jered," Jesus hugged the small boy tightly, "I'm actually glad you came right now. I need you for just a minute. You stay, too, Seth."

"Really, truly?" Jered's eyes shone.

"Really, truly." Jesus settled Peter's eldest son onto His lap and turned to the disciples. "Unless your hearts are changed, so that you become like these little children, you won't be able to have any part of My kingdom. Just look at them." Jered snuggled against Him, patting His beard. Seth laid his head contentedly against his father's broad chest. "So loving, so trusting. They are satisfied simply to rest in the love of their father. That is exactly what each of you needs to learn."

As Jesus spoke, John had grown troubled, finally blurting out, "Master, I didn't think anything of it at the time, but now I wonder if maybe I made a mistake. While James and I were traveling near Meiron, I think it was, we met a man who was using Your name to cast out demons, and I told him to stop. We thought it was an insult to You because he wasn't one of us. But what You just said made me think maybe we were afraid he would take our places, instead. What should we have done?"

"You're right about one thing, anyway," Jesus said kindly.

"Which one thing?"

"Realizing you were mistaken." John smiled in spite of himself as Jesus explained, "You shouldn't have told him to stop, because if he was working miracles in My name it was because the Father was with him and he was carrying out the work he was called to do. Even if that man didn't know some of the things you know, the Spirit will guide him into all righteousness—or rebuke him if need be. Judging whether a man is or is not My disciple isn't what you are supposed to do. I came to look for the lost sheep and to save them, and I've told you to do the same. With each person you meet, you should pray that you'll be able to lift him or her closer to heaven."

John took this mild correction very much to heart, sending a prayer winging heavenward that Adonai would undo the effects of his selfish pride and send encouragement to the miracle-worker of Meiron. *Please, Father, don't let him stumble because of me. Don't let my sin turn him away from Jesus forever. And please, please help me to be more sympathetic and understanding to others. I am willing to be anything—to do anything—for Jesus' sake, and for His kingdom. Amen.*

For some reason John felt better after that. The others felt some relief, as well, however temporary it might prove to be. The quarreling had, to a large degree, fractured their unity, and it was a welcome respite for them to set their worries aside and simply enjoy their time with Jesus, knowing that all too soon this time would be over, and they would begin another journey with a whole new set of labors.

A few days later as Rimona tearfully kissed her husband goodbye yet again, he swept her up in his arms, saying quietly in her ear, "How would you like to go to the Passover with me?"

She threw her arms around his neck. "Do you mean it? I've always wanted to see it."

"Get the boys ready when you hear that we're coming back. And you might as well bring your mother too." He grinned. "That way we'll have someone to help watch the children."

"When do you think you'll be here again?"

"I'm not sure—maybe a few months from now. I was hoping you could come along on the Grand Tour and see some of the cities I've been to." Secretly, he hoped she might have the chance to see him perform a miracle or two, as well. Even though she'd believed him when he'd told her some of the things he had done—with Adonai's help, of course—it would still be nice if she could witness it for herself, nice that she'd know what a special man she'd married.

"Is Jesus going to the Feast of Tabernacles too?"

Peter shrugged. "I don't know. I haven't seen Him getting ready to go, so it might just be the twelve of us."

"That makes a lot of sense." Rimona nodded understandingly. "From what I've heard, so many of the priests in Jerusalem are against Him that it would've been too dangerous for Him to go to some of these feasts."

"That's what I think, too, but there are a lot of people who disagree, including His own brothers. They were really harassing Him, trying to get Him to go this time. I would never dare to say half the things they've said."

"They must have been pretty bad, then." Rimona bit back a smile. "You'd better go, dear. It's getting late. Besides, the sooner you leave, the sooner you will come back again."

Peter set her down abruptly, teasing, "I know you just want to get rid of me, and don't try to pretend you don't." One more quick kiss, and he headed south, striding briskly down the well-traveled road to Jerusalem.

During the Feast of Tabernacles, all Israel spent a full week living in small shelters constructed from freshly cut branches, as a reminder of the years they had spent with no homes but their tents. Coming at the time of harvest, the feast was also an opportunity to bring a thank offering for a bountiful season and the blessings of the past year. The name of Jesus was on thousands of lips, everyone wondering if He would come to the convocation.

Caiaphas took full advantage of Jesus' absence, spreading the rumor that He had retreated in fear before the rightful leaders of the people. Still, he hoped Jesus would come after all, so he would have the opportunity to attack Him. Satan had personally assisted the high priest in the preparation of a host of snares, though Caiaphas knew him only as Zarad, a brilliant tactician and advisor loaned to him by his father-in-law, Annas. All their efforts would be wasted if Jesus simply didn't attend, and after several days with no word of Him, Caiaphas had just about given up hope.

It was hard to tell whether the priests or the disciples were more surprised on the third day of the feast when a plain, humble man who had quietly attended each service since the very beginning, straightened up, threw back His cloak, and walked to the front of the temple court. In ringing tones, He spoke to the assembly, basing each talk in His series of messages on the prophecies of the Scriptures.

The entire company of priests and rabbis was dumbfounded by the unarguable logic of everything Jesus presented and by His incredible knowledge of the Word of God. "How can he know so much?" many of them asked. "Where did he learn all this? He's never been to one of our schools."

Jesus pitied the foolish prelates. He had attended a much different school from the one they would have offered Him. While the other boys were shut in a classroom, memorizing the dry traditions of the priests, Jesus sat beneath the trees He Himself had made and memorized the very messages which He had once sent His own prophets, treasuring each word in His heart.

During those years of patient service to His earthly father, years most of the rulers would consider to have been wasted, Jesus was systematically learning the Scriptures in their entirety, from Genesis to Malachi. After many years of study, He had come to the concluding words. "Behold, I will send you Elijah the prophet before the coming of the great and dreadful day of the Lord: And he shall turn the heart of the fathers to the children, and the heart of the children to their fathers, lest I come and smite the earth with a curse." And at this heavenly promise and command, He had carefully rolled the scroll again, returned it to His mother, and left for the heaven-ordained meeting with John the Baptist.

That verse again came to His mind as He spoke at the Feast of Tabernacles, delivering a tearful warning to the cherished nation that disaster would soon overtake the people if they did not accept the opportunities He now offered them. Some listened, most did not, but His heart yearned after them all.

Each day of the feast brought new attempts to trap Jesus, but each failed. Every morning Satan materialized into the tall, brooding form of Zarad for his daily briefing with Caiaphas. The name he had chosen for his human manifestation was no coincidence, for it meant "ambush," and his domination over the high priest was nearly complete.

The most sinister ambush of all came near the end of the feast, when an unfortunate woman caught in the very act of adultery was dragged to the temple and thrown down at Jesus' feet. It was no accident that the priests and rulers had found her in such dishabille, as one of their own was the other person involved in the assignation.

Othniel, who had attended the rabbinical school in Jerusalem as a young man, stood among the woman's accusers—several rows back. No one realized that he had been the other party in this disgraceful episode. He smirked as one of the priests gestured with a dramatic motion toward the cowering woman and turned to face Jesus. "Moses, when he wrote the Law, said the penalty for this sin should be stoning. What do You have to say about that?"

He brought the name of Moses into the middle of his argument with such defiance that the angels cringed. It was difficult to stand by silently while those inspired words—words given by the very Lord now being accused— were used to bludgeon Jesus in the hope of driving Him into a fatal trap.

What could He answer? If He said, "Stone her," they would execute the woman, then report Jesus to Pilate for usurping the authority of Rome, for only a Roman official could sign a death warrant. Jesus would be arrested and tried, convicted and killed as a revolutionary. But if He said to send her to the Romans, the priests would stir up the people against Jesus because He had rejected the Law of Moses. Either way, by day's end they hoped to be rid of the Teacher from Nazareth. It was as neat a ruse as any, and everyone—human and angelic—wondered how Jesus could possibly extricate Himself.

The Spirit surrounded Him, filled Him, whispering many things thought to be secret. Jesus didn't answer the question; He didn't act as though He had even heard it. Instead, He bent down and began to write in the dust on the marble tiles. Those who were closest crowded forward to read His words: "Murdering your opponent to gain a position of power at the head of the people." The high priest stiffened with anger and fear then stormed away in a rage.

Unruffled, Jesus wrote on. "Stealing the priests' portion of the sacrifice from other priests." Several more left in haste. "Cheating a widow on the sale of her property three days ago." One of the men blanched and all but ran for *the gates. "Committing adultery repeatedly, trapping a woman in sin, attempting to kill an innocent Man."*

The ranks had thinned by this time, and Othniel felt suddenly exposed and vulnerable. His sin was etched there for all to see, and the woman's face as she glanced at him told the tale all too clearly. From the moment the idea had first occurred to him, he had thought of this plan as his, and this unforeseen defeat struck a huge blow at his pride, to say nothing of threatening his reputation for ingenuity. Teeth clenched, he slunk away with the others.

He was not the only one gnashing his teeth. Satan was nearly hopping up and down as he tried to restrain his ire at being so easily bested. "How could He have seen through it so easily? The adultery ruse should have been foolproof!"

Jesus looked around before asking the woman, "Where are the men who accused you? I don't see anyone left." Turning to the crowd, He announced loudly, "Any of you who are sinless may cast the first stone against her." For some reason, no one volunteered.

The woman began to cry. Jesus took her hand and lifted her up. "You're free to go, but don't do this ever again." And as the woman sobbed out her thanks, a stray breeze playfully sifted the dust on the floor, lifting and erasing the letters as if they had never been there.

Jesus had time for only one more trip to Galilee, the place where He had spent so much of His time in ministry. True to his word, Peter helped Rimona prepare to accompany them, though warning her of the rigors of life on the road. Rimona didn't mind; she was too happy to be able to stay by her husband's side to bother with a few trifling inconveniences. Batia was there as well, hovering over Keren to make sure she didn't work too hard. For the fourth time, Andrew hoped for a son, and in spite of his protests, Keren would not be dissuaded from the trip, insisting she felt fine.

But after only a few short weeks, Jesus led His disciples away from the sea, turning for a last look at the place and the people He loved so much. Unimaginable trials awaited Him, and many months would go by before He again walked along the familiar shore.

Chapter 26

Unlike times past, when Jesus avoided every attempt to give Him the honor and glory due a king—often waking His disciples in the middle of the night to travel secretly away from a place where the sentiment of the masses was rapidly becoming uncontrollable—this time it seemed to His disciples that He did everything possible to attract attention. Though Jerusalem was His ultimate goal, Jesus made no hurry to get there; He traveled slowly and by the most public routes.

As the multitude that accompanied Him entered Samaria, Jesus called seventy of His most loyal followers to Him, among them a young man named John Mark, and Luke, a physician. Laying His hands on them and praying as He had done when the Twelve were ordained, He called them into His service and sent them ahead of Him to tell everyone they met that Jesus was coming. In Jesus' name, they worked miracles of healing, cast out demons, and proclaimed the arrival of the Messiah until it seemed that the whole world must know.

During their lengthy visit among the Samaritans, Luke and John Mark returned to James and John with the dismaying news that the city of Gitta had refused Jesus admittance, even for a single night. "We tried to tell them what they would miss if they turned Him away," Luke said sadly, "but it made no difference to them. They closed and barred their gates at noon, shouting that if He kept the Passover in Jerusalem, they wanted nothing to do with Him."

"So we shook the dust off our feet, just like Jesus told us," John Mark added.

Unfortunately, that was not enough to allay the anger that kindled in the Sons of Thunder at this grave insult to their Master. Brimming with wrath, they hurried to Jesus and indignantly told Him what had happened. Seeing Mount Carmel in the distance gave James an idea.

"Master, do You want us to call down fire out of heaven and burn them all up? I think we need to make an example of them. How dare those dogs treat You like that after everything You've done for them!"

John laughed spitefully. "Nobody else would try it again, that's for sure. People would trip all over themselves just to make You welcome."

Peter bounded up, noticing that he had been left out of an important looking discussion. "What did I miss?"

James flared his nostrils. "We were just deciding to incinerate a den of wickedness. The fine citizens of Gitta decided they were too good to have Jesus contaminate their city, so we're going to call down fire like Elijah did."

"Sounds like a good idea to me." Peter shrugged. "The rest of those dogs would bark to a different tune after that."

John opened his mouth to say something more, but the look on Jesus' face stopped him. "What? Was it something I said?"

Pain filled Jesus' eyes as He said, "You don't know which spirit is in you when you speak like that. I didn't come here to destroy lives; I came to save them." And without further protest, He walked away, preparing to stay at another village.

Satan was just plain disgusted by this time. No matter how carefully he concealed his temptations under mounds of high-sounding scriptural rhetoric, Jesus instantly knew them for what they were, and identified the source. He shouldn't have been so surprised—the foundation of his kingdom was so much in opposition to the one Jesus brought that any variation from unselfishness and service to others jarred the sensitive nature of the Son of man.

Jesus had not come to earth to call down fire upon His enemies. Those times when flames had consumed the enemies of God—even then it was only when every last opportunity for mercy had been exhausted and every plea for repentance spurned. The Samaritans, grievous though their sin was, still would have another chance to accept their Savior after He rose from the dead. Then many who now hated Him and tried their best to keep Him away would be saved.

How little the disciples understood of all this. Peter, James, and John, having seen Jesus in His glory, should have known better than the others that the Son of man had not come to destroy the lives of men and women; He had come to save them.

Chapter 27

For many weeks Jesus worked in Samaria and Peraea, on the east side of the Jordan. Jews and Gentiles alike flocked to His side, and He accepted one as readily as the other. Rimona had never been so happy, listening to Jesus for hours at a time, storing up His parables to repeat over and over to the children.

While staying in Beth-haram, in the southern end of Peraea, Jesus told the Twelve that they had an appointment to keep in Jericho, only a short distance away.

"Who's going to be there?" Peter asked immediately.

"We're meeting with a lawyer," Jesus said, eyes sparkling.

Within sight of the city walls, Peter saw something strange, possibly even suspicious. Earlier, three men had passed through Jesus' little procession, trotting on donkeys. Now Peter saw them again, acting very peculiar. One of the three rode his animal almost to the city gate before jumping off and pulling the donkey's halter to make it run in circles.

The other men, their red hair visible from afar, seemed to find a great deal of amusement in this, clutching their middles and slapping their knees. Something about the man responsible for all the merriment seemed familiar, but Peter couldn't think why.

When they finally reached the city, Peter walked beside Jesus through the main gate. Jesus stopped next to a beggar and bent down to talk to him. Eyes downcast, the man held out a rough, dirty hand, saying in a practiced whine, "Alms! Alms for the poor!"

James and John, busy with their own conversation, didn't hear what Jesus replied, but Peter did. "I have something that you need far more than money, Malchus."

The man gaped up at Jesus in surprise, and Peter, catching an unobstructed glimpse of his face, suddenly recognized the familiar stranger on the donkey. Gasping, he ran after Jesus. "Master, wait! He's the one I've been trying to tell you about—the spy. The one who's always coming around in some new disguise." He pulled frantically on Jesus' robe. "Why won't anyone believe me?"

But the crowd pushed them steadily forward, frustrating Peter's efforts to drag Jesus bodily back to the beggar. Jesus took Peter by the arm and led him forward again, saying quietly, "I already told you; he's one of Mine. Leave him to Me."

But Peter had seen the man's face clearly, even if only for an instant, and the joy that always spread across the features of a true follower of Jesus was missing. What this spy was doing riding donkeys and begging in Jericho, Peter couldn't guess, but he was sure it was not from any outpouring of charitable fervor. The two red-haired men were nowhere to be seen, but that didn't make Peter feel any better.

In the town square, Jesus settled right down and began to talk, without even trying to see if anyone was waiting for Him. More and more people crowded in, squeezing and jostling each other to hear the famous storyteller. As Peter scanned the faces in the crowd, looking for one in particular, he saw just about the last person he would have expected. There in the midst of a delegation of priests and Levites was the stern, hawklike profile of Joseph Caiaphas.

The shock of seeing the high priest of Israel deign to join the audience around Jesus distracted Peter enough that he didn't notice at first when the two red-headed men, most likely brothers, edged their way into earshot.

All the players were assembled. Right on cue, a young lawyer pushed his way carefully through the multitude until he stood before Jesus. For some time, he had studied the sacred scrolls and had found them a contrast to the many forms and displays of his unsatisfying religion. One of the priests, trying to stir up controversy, sent him to Jesus with a difficult question, but the lawyer discovered he truly wanted to hear the answer. With a humility rare for one in his position, he waited until Jesus acknowledged him before asking, "What do I need to do to be sure of having eternal life?"

Tarik took a few moments to greet his good friend, Deron, while Caiaphas's servant waited in concealment, not wanting to risk another run-in with the keen-eyed fisherman. "So, how is Malchus doing? It looks like he's having to run even faster than before to try and ignore our Master's voice."

"You're right, as usual," Deron agreed. "His current mission has occupied enough of Malchus's attention that he thought Jesus didn't matter to him any longer, but when he found out Jesus was going to be here, he just couldn't stay away."

"What is his mission, anyway? The last I knew, Jesus was his only priority."

"Sirion must have decided Malchus was getting a bit too personally involved, and at his request, Satan, or perhaps I should say Zarad, convinced Caiaphas to reassign Malchus to another case. The situation called for the unique talents of my charge, since he had to infiltrate the camp of a murderous revolutionary, then capture him and hand him over to the Romans."

"Do you mean Barabbas?"

Deron nodded. "Those two over there, Elan and Arnon, are some of Barabbas's top men. They think they are here only to keep an eye on Malchus, but the Almighty arranged to have them in Jericho on this day and at this time."

"It was pretty funny to watch Malchus when we got here." Tarik laughed.

"Wasn't it though? He didn't know which way to go or where to hide. Poor Malchus, just barely able to arrive ahead of Jesus—with your clever fisherman watching for him behind every tree—and then having to dodge Caiaphas, too, was almost more than even he could handle. Of course Caiaphas knows what Malchus is doing, but since Elan and Arnon don't, Malchus had to pretend he was afraid of being exposed by his 'former' master, when he was really far more worried about your Simon Peter."

"And the look on his face when Jesus called him by name was priceless! I wouldn't have missed it for anything."

"Did you notice the others are all here? The priest, the Levite, Samuel of Samaria, and Tobias—you remember the man who was injured. Now even some of the robbers have arrived. It's just like a reunion, and I'm sure it's not an accident."

"Nothing ever is."

Jesus gave the young man before Him a kind look, reading his thirst for righteousness and his desire for eternal life. "What do you believe about it? What does it say in the law?"

For a moment the lawyer was tempted to launch into a detailed explanation of the entire Jewish legal system, flashing his dazzling knowledge in a way that would impress the many bystanders. He was acutely aware that Caiaphas was listening and had to resist the urge to show him what a fine addition to the Sanhedrin he would be. But then, for some reason that he, himself, didn't even understand and contrary to his first impulse, the lawyer reduced every rule of law into two statements any child could understand.

"Love the Lord your God with all your heart and soul, with everything that is within you," the young man said simply, "and love your neighbor as yourself." All the priests, even Caiaphas, gave nods of approval at this ready reply.

"Aha!" Jesus' shout startled all those near Him. The priests, leaning forward breathlessly, ready to denounce Jesus the instant He uttered heresy, could never have predicted His next words. "Did all of you hear what this man just said?" Jesus was more excited than Peter had seen Him for a long time. "This is wonderful, just wonderful! Love God, and love your neighbor. That is the foundation for all the law and everything the prophets have written. And this man—what is your name? Raphu?—Raphu understands it! All of you must do just what this man said, and you will live."

Raphu felt a bit silly standing there in front of everyone. He had answered his own question, and the enthusiastic endorsement from Jesus left nothing to argue about, so he said the first thing that popped into his mind. "But *neighbor* can mean different things to different people. Who is my neighbor?" He cringed as the words left his mouth. They were such a flimsy covering for his inadequacies regarding obedience to the law.

Jesus sat back, a satisfied expression on His face. He had led Raphu right to where He wanted him. The children wiggled closer, knowing there would be a story. When every eye was on Him, Jesus began. "Once there was a man who was traveling from Jerusalem to Jericho. Along the most dangerous stretch of road, halfway through the narrowest part of the valley, a band of robbers attacked him and beat him without mercy. They stole everything he had except his underclothing and left him for dead.

"Tobias wasn't dead—not quite—and he groaned feebly for water as he saw a priest approach. The priest not only ignored him, but passed by on the other side of the road, fearing that he would be defiled." Next to Caiaphas, the priest in question winced and tried to look very interested in his fingernails.

"The next to come was a Levite, fresh from ritual purifications at the temple. He walked right up close to Tobias, bent down, and squinted at him to see if he still breathed. When the man he thought was dead opened his eyes, the Levite was startled and leaped back, clutching his robes tightly about him."

This brought a roar of laughter. Many had already heard the story from one or another of the participants and could picture only too well the reaction of the supposedly religious men to a dirty, bloody near-corpse. The flushed Levite, grateful he had not been called by name, carefully examined a bustling anthill in the ground near his feet.

"The sun grew low in the sky," Jesus continued, "and Tobias grew steadily weaker. He knew he would never survive the night, exposed as he was to the cold and any predators that might happen by. Barely able to move his lips, he whispered three words. *Adonai, save me.* The next instant, he felt an arm slide under his shoulder, lifting him to drink a few mouthfuls of refreshing water. Nearly unconscious, he couldn't see who had come to his rescue; he thought it might even be an angel."

Tobias chuckled from his position near Jesus, clapping his good friend, Samuel, on the shoulder. "He wasn't the angel I was expecting, but I was glad to see him, all the same." Samuel ducked his head shyly.

"No, it wasn't an angel," Jesus agreed, smiling approvingly at Samuel. "In fact, it was a Samaritan. The Samaritan man tended the wounds the robbers had made. He put his own cloak around Tobias and lifted him onto his own donkey. As carefully as he could, not wanting to cause the man any more pain than he could help, the Samaritan slowly led his beast down into Jericho.

"Already, he had done more than most people would have, but he was not content. The Samaritan took Tobias to a fine inn, paid for him to stay several weeks, and promised the innkeeper that if any additional charges were incurred, that he would take care of them personally the next time he came to the city.

"Now," Jesus asked the lawyer, looking him squarely in the eyes, "what do you think? Which of those three men was a true neighbor to the man who fell among the robbers?"

The lawyer could not bring himself to force the sibilant of that hated name between his teeth, but finally answering grudgingly, "The man who showed compassion to him."

"Very good, Raphu; you've done it again. Now you go and do the same thing as he did." With much to think about, Raphu drifted away, not back to the priests he had forgotten about impressing, but to a quiet place outside the city walls where he could sit and think.

Meanwhile, Peter eyed the two red-headed brothers as they argued heatedly about something. One of them kept gesturing at Jesus, and the other motioned forcibly away from the city toward the desert. It appeared that the one in favor of Jesus was winning, until Caiaphas slid beside them and spoke a few words. Whatever he said must have been persuasive and very hostile toward the Master, for both men looked shocked, darting little glances over at Jesus before leaving hastily for their rendezvous with destiny.

At the urging of the innkeeper, Jesus spent the night in Jericho. Peter was very gratified to taste at last the luxury to be found at the Comfort Table Inn. He was a bit disconcerted to have to share a meal with the ceremonially un-clean Samuel—the good Samaritan, as he was rapidly becoming known. All in all, though, Peter was quite pleased with the experience and even happier

when he realized their next destination was the home of Martha and Lazarus in Bethany.

A year and a half before, after the third time Jesus passed through the ill-reputed seaport, Peter first became aware of the connection between the lovely, elegant, hospitable Martha and the ravishing backslider of Magdala. Their brother, Lazarus, had done much to support Jesus and His work, but this was to be Peter's first visit to the spacious home.

Martha and Lazarus had been overjoyed to see their sister the first time she came back to them, but they were the only ones in the village who felt that way. Mary quickly tired of the whispers, giggles, staring, and pointing. With the best of intentions, she returned to her home in Magdala, determined to hold herself above her former lifestyle. It didn't work then, nor any of the other times she tried it, either.

This time, she not only vowed to lean on Jesus rather than depend on her own strength to keep herself pure, but she sold the apartment in Magdala, keeping nothing to remind her of her former life but a heavy purse. She didn't know what to do with the money—that awful, tangible reminder of the hundreds of men she had known. She couldn't bring herself to throw it away, but she didn't feel right dropping it into the offering at the temple, either. In her confusion, her Guardian impressed her to hold on to the coins a little longer. This, too, was a part of God's plan.

Mary was so weak, that dear child of the light, and when Jesus came to stay at the house in Bethany, she could not bear to leave His presence. No matter how many times Martha walked through to serve platter after platter to the ravenous men and their families, stomping as delicately as only that fine lady could, Mary only sent a pleading look her direction and leaned a little closer to Jesus.

Finally, Martha could take no more and appealed directly to Jesus. "Lord, don't You understand how much I have to do? It's more than I can finish by myself, even with the servants. And here Mary sits listening to stories. Something has to be done! Will You make her come and help me?"

Tarik nudged Peter, hoping to call his attention to Jesus' reply, but Peter was so busy stuffing his mouth full of dates, apples, and raisins that he missed it all. "Martha," Jesus said tenderly, "I appreciate all that you do for Me and how hard you work, but Mary has chosen something better that will never be taken from her. Your house will still need care long after I'm gone, but Mary will have My words with her."

Could Peter have seen the room then as heaven saw it, his eyes would have been dazzled by masses of angels hovering protectively around the woman most people regarded as an incorrigible sinner of the worst kind, but who, by the redeeming grace of Christ, had become a cherished daughter of the kingdom.

Following the disaster at the Feast of Dedication, where Jesus had inflamed the priests by speaking more plainly than ever before of His relationship with the Father, Jesus and all who followed Him returned with some haste to Peraea. Peter strongly suspected that without unseen intervention, Jesus would have been stoned that day.

In the relative safety of Peraea, the miracles poured out like a flood. Jesus was not frantic, trusting as He did in the Father's care, but worked longer and harder than ever, knowing that His time was short. Peter did all he could to help, carrying out as many of the healings as he could so that Jesus could spend more time talking to the people and, Peter hoped, gathering their support.

The encampment covered a large plain; thousands had come to search out Jesus in the wilderness. Never had Peter been more glad of Rimona's presence. After a hard day of ministering, he would always find her with a bowl of hot stew ready for him and eager to listen as he talked enthusiastically about the soon coming of the New Kingdom.

With such a large crowd following Him, Jesus and His disciples traveled slowly. The messenger found them only a day's journey from Jericho. Peter quickly recognized Salathiel, a manservant from the household of Lazarus. When he heard the man's urgent message, Peter rushed him to Jesus, unhesitatingly interrupting a parable about a lost coin.

"Master, You really need to hear what Salathiel has to say." Peter took the slightly built manservant by the shoulders, practically lifting him over to Jesus.

Exhausted, Salathiel bowed before Jesus, his eyes red from weeping. "Lord, Your good friend, Lazarus, is sick. Martha sent me to ask You to come as quickly as You can."

Jesus did not appear troubled, saying reassuringly, "Don't worry. This sickness won't end in death. This has happened to show the glory of God and to bring glory also to the Son of God."

Salathiel's face lit up. "So may I tell them You will come?"

Jesus smiled, giving no hint that He knew the dead body of Lazarus was already growing cold on its pallet. "You may tell them just what I told you."

Peter couldn't believe Jesus would be so cold-hearted, especially toward His friend. Especially toward His friend who had a sister who could make challah bread that just melted in your mouth. For two long days, Jesus gave no further sign He even remembered the desperate plea from Bethany, pretending not to notice as the Twelve grew more and more agitated.

"It's like what happened to the Baptist all over again," Peter exploded that night as he talked to Rimona. "Someone dear to Jesus is in trouble, and He doesn't care. There's nothing that important keeping Him here, but He just dawdles along doing His own thing."

"But Simon, dear, why don't you just trust Him? So far it seems like He's done a very good job of working everything out for the best."

"Except for the Baptist," Peter insisted stubbornly. "If Jesus would let His own cousin die in prison and let His best friend waste away on a sickbed, how do I know He won't do the same to me? To any of us? How would you feel if you were in Martha's place right now?" Rimona didn't have any answers; she just held her arms open, and her husband walked into them.

The morning of the third day, it was a great relief to everyone when Jesus announced that they would begin moving toward Bethany. Those who followed Him quickly packed their things and hurried to catch up. It seemed that, having at last decided to go, Jesus was in something of a rush.

The throng spread out for miles, and the people traveling with Jesus clogged the streets of Jericho when they reached the city. Masses followed behind, and hundreds from the city mingled with the procession until movement was almost impossible. Peter roughly forced his way around in front of Jesus and went to work trying to clear a path.

"We should have gone around this awful city," he muttered, swimming against the heavy current. "At this rate we'll never get to Lazarus before it's too late."

Jesus didn't seem bothered at all by the delay, stopping to greet a man here, a child there, or to bless a whole family. Several agonizing hours later, Peter finally saw the gate leading to the Jerusalem road. *At last! Once we escape this selfish crowd, we can make better time. If Jesus keeps going after dark, we'll be there by morning.*

Just short of the gate, an ancient sycamore tree grew by the side of the road, its branches spreading far out across the highway. Peter paused to rest a moment in the long shadow the late afternoon sun cast on the pavement. Jesus stopped, too, and Peter thought He must be tired. The weary, perspiring disciple pressed on the rest of the way to the gate before he realized Jesus was no longer behind him. Instead, He still stood beneath the tree, squinting up into the foliage.

Dimly, Peter could make out the figure of a man, sitting on one of the lower limbs. Fearing the man might be an assassin, Peter reversed direction as fast as he could, sick with the knowledge that he would be too late.

"Zacchaeus, come down out of that tree!" Jesus held His sides and laughed heartily as the small man, less than shoulder high to most of the women, slid down from the fig tree, tearing his silk robe in the process. Jesus embraced the man, who couldn't help laughing too. "Well, Zacchaeus, I'm coming over to your house. What are we having for dinner?"

An assassin would have been better, Peter thought bitterly. *Why, why, why does Jesus always have to associate with people like that?* He shot a black look at Matthew, guessing that if one of their number hadn't been a tax collector, too, this Zacchaeus fellow wouldn't have had the nerve to ask Jesus for dinner. Except that he hadn't, really. Jesus had invited Himself. But He wouldn't have if Zacchaeus hadn't wanted Him. Now Jesus would probably want Peter and the rest to go along, and then there was Lazarus! How could he have forgotten already? How could Jesus have forgotten? Heavyhearted and full of doubt, Peter followed his jubilant Master and the ecstatic tax collector to the feast.

Chapter 28

Early the next day, Jesus woke Peter to tell him it was time to go. "Finally," Peter snapped before he was fully awake. "Oh, good morning, Jesus. I mean, of course, that is fine with me."

Jesus led them away from Jericho quietly, before anyone from the never-ending crowd could miss them. When they had gone far enough that no one could see or hear them, Jesus motioned for the disciples to walk closely about Him. "Lazarus fell asleep," He told them, "but I'm going to wake him up."

Peter's temperature began to rise. First, Jesus couldn't be bothered to go to Lazarus when he was very sick, needing Jesus terribly, and now that he was sleeping peacefully, Jesus was planning to wake him up. Peter tried to keep silent, but lasted less than two minutes before blurting, "Why are You going to wake him up now? If he's asleep, it means he'll get better." And to himself, *Some days Jesus just doesn't make any sense!*

Jesus stopped where He was in the road and turned to face His disciples. Gravely He informed them, "Lazarus is dead."

Peter clutched his chest, trying to break the iron bands that kept him from breathing. *Dead? Dead!* The word hammered repeatedly into his brain. If Jesus couldn't even keep Lazarus alive, what would Caiaphas be able to do to them when they all arrived in Jerusalem? Most likely they would all be killed—and in a variety of unpleasant ways, too, no doubt. After all, Jesus had almost been stoned the last time He was there.

The other men took the tragic news just as hard, somehow not questioning how Jesus knew it. It seemed ominous, a sign from above that death waited for them, lurking in the capital city. The thought flashed into each of their minds that it would be far safer to turn back and leave Jesus to go on alone.

Jesus shocked them still further with His next words. "Actually, I'm glad Lazarus died." Twelve horrified gasps went up in unison from twelve gaping mouths. "I'm glad for your sakes, so your belief in Me will grow stronger."

But the only thing that grew stronger right then was a deep-seated fear that they were following a man who was rapidly becoming unhinged. It must have shown on their faces, for Jesus asked, "What are you waiting for? Let's go to Bethany now."

Their hesitation was broken by the ever-gloomy voice of Thomas. "We have to die sometime. We might as well go to Jerusalem and die there with Jesus as anywhere else."

This courageous, though pessimistic, speech, coming as it did from such an unexpected source, galvanized the others into action. Without looking back toward home, family, and security, they set their faces toward Jerusalem and stepped bravely forward into the unknown.

Of course, it really shouldn't have been the unknown. Jesus had certainly tried to tell them enough times and to prepare them for what would happen. He spoke so plainly, but their pride stopped their ears, and they heard only what they wanted to hear. Someday, all His words would surely come back to them and comfort them, but not before they suffered a crushing—and completely avoidable—disappointment. As time wore on, the angels worked harder than ever, adding their voices to that of the Spirit, pleading with the disciples to listen and believe what Jesus told them.

Four days earlier, Satan had paced, baffled, wondering what his enemy was doing. Originally, the plan had called for a messenger to reach Jesus two days before Lazarus would die. In Satan's scenario, Jesus would come at a run to heal His friend, be arrested before He could enter the town, and then executed swiftly before the crowds massed for the Passover. Caiaphas's men were in place, and minions of the dark lord surrounded them, ready to give them any assistance they needed.

Chapter 28

But then the messenger was delayed. As closely as Satan watched, he could not see any direct interference from the host of heaven, but from start to finish Martha's servant ran into every possible difficulty. He arrived two days behind schedule. Satan cursed, but readjusted his plans accordingly.

The victory over Lazarus had been easy, much too easy. Satan had grown exceedingly suspicious of any ground gained without opposition, and two days later, when Jesus suddenly picked up everything and started toward Bethany, he understood. The conflict he had orchestrated was coming, but on Jesus' terms, not his. He massed his troops, preparing for the biggest clash yet. Any fool could see that Jesus planned His most spectacular resurrection thus far, and Satan was no fool.

"What can He possibly be thinking?" Peter grumbled to Andrew as they approached Bethany. "Lazarus is dead, and an army is probably waiting to arrest us before we have the chance even to taste Martha's cooking. I'm no fool, but if Jesus has any plan at all, I can't guess what it is."

Andrew shook his head in disbelief. "I don't know, either. If we'd gotten here a few days ago, I'd think maybe Jesus would just raise Lazarus from the dead, but it's a little late for that now."

Peter sighed. "I guess we'll find out soon enough."

Jesus stopped outside the town and sat in the shade of a terebinth tree. Two young boys chased each other through the grass, laughing and shouting. Smiling, Jesus watched them for several minutes before calling to them.

"Jehiel, Mattithiah, would you like to do something for Me?" Both boys nodded vigorously from their place of honor on His lap, delighted to help their favorite storyteller. "Would you go in very quietly to Martha and tell her I'm here? Make sure no one else is listening."

Moments later a servant brought her the news that two boys urgently needed to see her. And shortly afterward, Martha bowed in sorrow at Jesus' feet, cheeks dry and eyes emptied of tears. As He bent over her, holding out His hand, she looked up at His face to see the same love and tenderness as always. "Lord, I know if You had been here, my brother would not have died." It was not a question, but her heart badly wanted to hear an answer.

"That's very true," Jesus told her. "Lazarus couldn't have died if I had been with him, but surely you know that your brother will rise again."

Finding the comfort she needed, if not the explanations, Martha said, "Lazarus was a wonderful brother, and I believe with all my heart that I will see him alive again on the resurrection morning."

"*I* am the Resurrection. *I* am the Life." Jesus cupped her face gently in His hands. "If anyone dies believing in Me, he will live again. And anyone who lives believing in Me, even if he falls asleep in death, will never perish." His gaze was earnest, intense. "Do you believe this?"

Martha's eyes filled with fresh tears. "Yes, I believe," she whispered, setting aside the questions she wanted so much to ask. "I believe that You are the Christ and the Son of God. I know You have the power to do anything it pleases You to do."

She thought Jesus was comforting her, but actually, she was comforting Him. Deeply moved, He kissed her forehead, saying, "Why don't you go get Mary?"

Mary, not as restrained as Martha had been, leaped to her feet and rushed from the room when she heard that Jesus had arrived. A large number of the mourners followed her, thinking she was going to her brother's tomb and knowing that their task was to give voice to the grief she was too spent to express. The rest of the mourners followed her as well, quite sure she must be going to see Jesus and knowing that their task was to arrest Him by any and all means necessary.

Peter scarcely recognized the woman who knelt at Jesus' feet, her eyes swollen and her usually flawless skin blotchy and red. Overcome by the shrill wailing of the mourners, she began to sob. Unaware of what her hands were doing, she wiped her eyes and nose with the sleeve of her robe. "Oh, Lord, if You had been here, my brother would not have died." Concern for Jesus' safety kept her from saying more.

Peter swallowed the lump in his throat, pretending he had a speck in his eyes that needed to be wiped away. Lazarus had been a true friend to them all, and it was so hard to believe he was gone. Harder still to believe was that Jesus had let it happen. *How could Someone who is supposed to be so loving and kind let something so dreadful befall His friends? If Jesus has so much power, why must Mary and Martha suffer so?* There was no answer that he could see.

"Where is your brother's grave?" Jesus asked, supporting Mary as she stood.

Mary hid her face against His strong arm. "Come with me, and I'll show You."

The path to the tomb was dusty and well-traveled, and a choking cloud rose under several hundred feet. Peter no longer had to pretend to have something in his eye; the tears flowed freely. He was far from the only one, for all his companions felt the loss just as keenly.

As they came near the tomb, Jesus sagged under the weight of a sorrow inexplicable to anyone else there. Mary and Martha all but carried Him the last few steps, so weak had He become. Fierce sobs shook Him as He stood with them in front of the grave that had been carved deep into the rock.

Jesus was sympathetic to the sisters in their loss, but His grief was far deeper and larger than theirs. His divine heart broke for those throughout history who had died, lost and without hope of the life He longed to give them. Well He knew that some of those standing there with Him, a false sadness masking their hatred of Him, within hours would swear out an illegal death warrant, not only for Him but also for Lazarus. The fate that awaited some of these men, starvation and slaughter at the hands of the Romans, was not what He wanted for them even yet, but they would not accept the life He tried to offer in so many ways.

One by one His divine gaze wordlessly singled them out of the crowd—these men who sought His life. It made no difference whether they were priests, rulers, or covert agents of the high priest disguised as mourners, He knew them all. One by one they squirmed under His regard, frantically wondering how He knew their very thoughts. But they would not repent.

His strength returning, Jesus called loudly, "Roll away the stone."

Martha was more horrified than anyone else at this gruesome request. Her hands flitted nervously from her mouth to tug at her belt. Her manservants hesitated to comply, looking to their mistress for permission. "But, Lord," she finally protested, "Lazarus has been dead four days already." She gulped. There was really no genteel way to explain her predicament. "He . . . well . . . he stinks!"

Jesus smiled at her, almost blinding her with His radiant joy. "Didn't I tell you that if you believed, you would see the glory of the Father?" Then, with such authority that no one else dared object, He commanded the men, "Roll away the stone!" They scurried to obey, shuddering to think what they would soon reveal to the curious gaze of the morbid crowd. The round stone scraped its way along the trough that held it in place over the mouth of the cave.

A light breeze came up just then, carrying the heavy odor of decay to the nostrils of all who were present. Mary and Martha trembled, fighting the bile that rose in their throats. Martha, especially, was determined to avoid the shame of being sick in public. Women covered their faces with their scarves, and some of the men couldn't help but retch. That seemed the hardest of all for poor Martha to bear just then, for she always went to such lengths to present only perfection to the members of her community.

All those who had attended the burial several days before could see that the sepulcher had remained untouched in the intervening time. Unlike the elaborate burials of the heathen, where the tomb was filled with articles to be used in the afterlife, Lazarus had been laid tenderly on a simple shelf carved into the rock. His swaddled form lay exactly the way they had left it, resting in the grave with his parents and grandparents. The body had bloated grotesquely, its tension against the spice-soaked wrappings clearly visible to all, and the sickly sweet aroma unique to decomposing human flesh left no one with any question as to whether or not Lazarus was truly dead.

Jesus took a step forward, raising His hands to heaven. The stench did not seem to bother Him in the least as He took a deep breath. "My Father, thank You for always hearing Me when I talk to You. I know You would hear Me even if I didn't speak out loud, but I want the people standing here to listen, so that they might know that You are the One who has sent Me." There was a long, painful silence, shattered at last by a shout. "Lazarus, come out!"

Peter froze, his gaze fixed on the body of his friend as it shrank instantly to its usual proportions, the noxious odor immediately dispersing. The wrapped head moved first, then the legs. Wriggling about like an insect larva, Lazarus managed to reach a sitting position. The bindings had loosened somewhat, but he still couldn't disengage his arms from their folded pose across his chest. He rocked forward unsteadily onto his feet, turning his head about in an effort to see. Ever so slowly, he began to shuffle blindly toward the light.

Jesus looked with amusement at His petrified friends. "What are you waiting for?" He shook Martha gently, squeezing her arm to bring her out of her stupor. "Go let him out."

With Mary at her side, Martha hurried to obey. Beginning at the top, they unwound yards and yards of the linen strips, finally freeing their brother from his fabric prison. When they uncovered his face, dancing with mischief and life just as always, they began to weep, laughter breaking through their tears.

Lazarus embraced them fervently, kissing their moist cheeks before gently detaching himself and kneeling before Jesus in worship and gratitude. Words failed him as he tried to express his devotion. All he could say, over and over again, was, "Thank You! Thank You!"

Mary and Martha joined him, not caring if their expensive garments trailed in the dust. The language of earth seemed so inadequate to tell of the deepening of their faith and love and of the appreciation they would carry into eternity for what Jesus had done for them.

As they stood, the crowd pressed about them, everyone eager to see and touch the man who had risen from the dead. Their voices, which a short time before had been lifted in sorrow, were now lifted loudly in praise. Such excitement filled the air that no one, not even Lazarus, noticed when Jesus quietly signaled the Twelve to follow Him and slipped out of sight, traveling quietly along obscure paths around the city of Jerusalem.

Within minutes, two of the spies gasped out the account of the incredible occurrence to none other than Caiaphas, the high priest. Within the hour, an emergency meeting of the Sanhedrin came to order, Gamaliel, Joseph of Arimathea, and Nicodemus conspicuously absent. Only three nonmembers were present: Malchus, Othniel, and Zarad.

Still burning from the humiliation in Bethany, Satan watched with malicious satisfaction as Malchus and Othniel testified before the court. The

Spirit of God was present as well, seeking an entrance to any heart there, but to no avail. Satan smiled an awful smile, sure now that they would listen only to him.

For the first time the Pharisees and Sadducees found unity in their determination to stop Jesus. The Pharisees had hated the new Teacher from the beginning, because of the way He exposed their hypocrisies and diminished their power over the people. Until now, the Sadducees had been much more tolerant, yet without favoring Jesus in the slightest. But now that He had shown their most cherished belief—that there can be no resurrection—for the lie it was, they were incensed. Even so, Caiaphas knew he would need to tread very carefully to bring the learned body of legal experts to the point where they would be willing to disregard every facet of the law, violate every tendency toward justice, and hand down the informal verdict he sought.

When Zarad, speech already in hand, walked into the spacious chamber in Caiaphas's palace just before the start of the meeting, it seemed positively providential. It may well have been; unfortunately, Caiaphas did not stop to question whose providence it was. There was time for Caiaphas to receive only a few hasty instructions from the diabolically clever advisor before he had to hurry to admit the members of the Sanhedrin.

Normally the court met in the Hall of Hewn Stone, but only during the hours of daylight, so Caiaphas called them to his own residence, where there would be fewer questions afterward as to why the highest court in the land had convened well into the middle of the night. Fewer questions, too, about why a trial of any sort should be held without the presence of the accused and with only the testimony of the two spies to convict Jesus.

The reaction of the court was just as Zarad had predicted to Caiaphas. The Pharisees were more zealous than ever before about putting Jesus to death, but the Sadducees, though in agreement, still advised caution. "There is a great danger," one of them urged, "that if we harm Jesus, the people will rise against us. And if there is any kind of rioting or revolt, Rome will penalize us and take away what little power we still have left."

While many gray heads nodded their agreement, several Pharisees at once began shouting their dissent. The ensuing dispute went on for hours, growing ever more heated, until tempers were frayed past repair and the debaters were exhausted. Zarad motioned to Caiaphas. The time had come.

Caiaphas stood, holding up his hands for silence. Gradually the room quieted, and the men waited to hear what their leader had to say. He paused dramatically, waiting until every eye was on him. "My fellow Israelites," he said smoothly, "we are the children, the seed of Abraham. Many times in our history we have been taken prisoner, scattered, and nearly obliterated from the earth. Yet that is what we again face if we do nothing.

"Our wives, our sons, and our daughters depend on us to save them from this imminent and very real danger. This Galilean has stirred up the people so that many want to crown him king. The news of this latest magical working is even now racing across our fair land. Once Jesus' followers learn that his evil power can turn back the unrelenting tide of death, there will be no stopping them. And when they revolt, Rome will do everything necessary to regain control. We will be killed, our sons sold as slaves, our women violated and forced to live in the homes of pagans." The men nodded in assent. This was one of their great fears, as well.

Demons stood by each one, whispering thoughts of the bloodshed that would come and massaging their fears.

"It is for us here, today, to save our families, our temple, yes, even the whole land of Israel. This Galilean who cares nothing for us or for our safety must be stopped." Caiaphas paused, looking around the room at each one to gauge if they were ready to receive the radical idea he was about to present.

"If Lazarus be the bond that brings together this man's followers, then Lazarus must die first." Though initially shocked, no one spoke up in favor of justice or the due process of the law. Zarad, watching closely, could see the moment the idea took hold and began to send its deadly roots into their minds. Just that easily, they were his.

"Believe me, I have thought this through," Caiaphas continued. "My servant, Othniel, will see that it is done quietly, without involving any of us." Othniel jumped when he heard his name and turned pale when he realized what he was supposed to do, but dared not voice an objection to his master. "With Lazarus out of the way, it will be a simple matter to sway public opinion in our favor and arrest Jesus." Caiaphas paused, then continued, carefully emphasizing each word. "After all, it is far better that one man should die than that an entire nation should perish."

The murmur of agreement following that shocking statement was drowned out by evil laughter and raucous merriment as the demon horde celebrated a complete victory of wickedness over justice.

Chapter 29

For more than a week Rimona was unable to find her elusive husband, but she finally traced him to Ephraim, north of Jerusalem. Some women might have fought the temptation to feel annoyed at being virtually abandoned in unfamiliar territory, without a word about where their spouses might be, but not Rimona. Possessed of wit and understanding far beyond what Peter had yet come to appreciate, she knew Jesus had led the way out of a potentially dangerous situation. Among those seeking Jesus as the Messiah, more spies mingled than ever before, growing bold in their pursuit, and she knew Jesus had acted to keep Peter safe, as well as Himself.

The reunion, when it took place, was all she could have hoped for, and Peter amazed her by kissing Batia's wrinkled cheek in greeting. Tears came to her eyes as she saw him return the eager embraces of his sons. Yet again, she whispered her thanks to Jesus for blessing her with the love of a real family—and friends, besides. In the past months, Keren and Salome had become even closer to her, until they seemed like true sisters.

In the atmosphere of heavenly joy that surrounded Jesus, it was easy to forget His dreadful prediction of death, though the sense of foreboding never quite went away. After a few idyllic weeks, when the Passover was close at hand, Jesus gathered His closest followers around Him. They knew by the solemn look on His face that He had something very important to say.

"It is time to go to Jerusalem, but this trip will not be like all the others. All the things the prophets have said about Me will come true. I will be betrayed into the hands of the Gentiles, mocked, treated cruelly, spat on, whipped, and at the last killed, but on the third day I will rise again."

Rimona put her hand into Peter's and squeezed it hard, terrified at the vivid picture Jesus painted. The sick feeling didn't leave her the rest of the day, and she wondered how Peter could still be so calm. That night when he came to the tent, she fell into his arms. "How can you bear it? That's the second time now Jesus has said He's going to die, and it sounds like He really means it."

Peter brushed the tears from her cheeks and kissed her resoundingly. "He's said it a lot more than twice, but it's just His way of talking. He doesn't mean it literally—there's no reason to get so upset."

"How do you know for sure? He didn't sound like He was just telling a parable."

"Simple." Peter grinned. "For months now, He's been sending us out to tell everyone that the day of His kingdom is here. He promised that any of us who followed Him would have a place in His kingdom. Let's see, He also said the twelve of us would sit on thrones and judge the twelve tribes of Israel, and all the prophets speak of the Messiah's glory when He rules over the whole earth. Do I need to go on?" He didn't speak of it, even to his wife, but Moses and Elijah were very much in his thoughts just then. They had confirmed what he already believed, that Jesus was the Christ.

"It sounds so logical when you explain it like that." Her tone was doubtful, but she began to feel a smidgen of hope.

Just then, Keren burst into the tent, so upset she didn't give them any type of warning first. Andrew ducked down and came in right after her. "You'll never believe what she just did! I can't even believe it myself!"

Andrew ground his teeth. "Those backbiting ingrates, just waiting until none of us were paying attention to try and worm their way in and claim the best spot all for themselves."

Keren rushed on without a pause. "That horrid, encroaching woman went right up to Jesus, and pushed them forward, and she asked Him—"

"—to let those two ravening wolves sit on thrones at His right and left hand," finished Andrew.

"Who?" chorused Peter and Rimona.

"Salome," snapped Keren.

"Our so-called friends, James and John," Andrew added sourly. "It's not fair of them even to ask. We've been with Jesus just as long as they have."

Rimona's eyes were wide with outrage, and Peter's normally ruddy face turned an alarming shade of red. "What did Jesus say?"

"I didn't stay long enough to hear," Andrew admitted. "But it's too late for us in any case. If only we'd thought of it first!"

How grieved their Guardians were that James and John, on the eve of the most important journey of their lives, approaching the scene of the greatest sacrifice of unselfish love they would ever see, should display such unremitting self-absorption. As always, Jesus dealt with them far more kindly than they deserved.

Knowing as He did how much these brothers loved Him, He simply asked, "Are you able to drink the cup that I am about to drink and to be baptized with My baptism?"

Even remembering what Jesus had just said about His fate, John readily replied for them both with the assurance, "Of course we are able."

Their future was an open book to Jesus. He searched their faces silently for several seconds, then nodded slowly. "You will have what you ask," He told them sadly. "You will certainly drink of My cup and be baptized with My baptism, but the rest is not Mine to give. It is only for My Father to decide who will sit at My right and left hand."

Demons scattered in search of the other ten and their families, whipping up their indignation against the brothers. The other mothers and wives who had followed Jesus for many months were furious with Salome, and the other disciples were livid with James and John. Gabriel drew as close as he could to his Commander, giving Him the comfort that should have come from the companionship of His unified disciples. Ever watchful, the General spread his wings over Jesus all through the long night.

It was a seething and sullen group that followed Jesus to Bethany the next day, arriving a few hours before the Sabbath began. The day of rest descended on hearts that were anything but restful. Lazarus, Mary, and Martha gladly welcomed Jesus into their home, showering Him with every possible luxury and the best accommodations in an attempt to show Him their gratitude.

Peter certainly enjoyed their hospitality, unwilling to let his resentment toward James and John spoil his appetite or his appreciation of this treat. At the synagogue services the next morning, he was even more gratified when Jesus accepted an offer for them to dine that evening with the most important Pharisee in Bethany. Unlike most of his fellow Pharisees, Simon freely proclaimed himself a follower of the Teacher from Nazareth and was just the sort of influential man that Peter felt they were fortunate to find.

Simon had once been a leper, an outcast from society. Jesus had healed him the same day He first met Lazarus, and Simon thought he had found the perfect way to repay Jesus—by honoring Him with an invitation that any Jew, even one from the highest social stratum, would be proud to receive. It was to be a feast that rivaled all other feasts, and Simon hoped that if Jesus really did turn out to be the Messiah, that he, Simon, would enjoy a prominent place in the government once the Romans were overthrown.

Rimona was excited to hear that she would accompany her husband to the special dinner, and for the first time in a long time the sun seemed to drag its way across the sky to signal the end of the Sabbath when she could make her preparations and beautification. Peter's eyes bulged when he saw her.

"You look amazing! I'm going to have the prettiest wife there!"

Rimona patted her shiny black hair and smoothed the dark green material of her dress. Its simple lines and jewel-like tone became her, and she knew it. "Thank you, sir." She peeped up at him. "If you are going to sit on a throne, you will need to have a hostess as well as a wife, and I might as well start practicing now so I can learn how it's done."

They walked arm in arm behind Jesus the short distance from the home of Lazarus to Simon's mansion. Rimona noted idly that the view of Lazarus's courtyard was excellent from the vantage point of their host for the evening and wondered if Simon could be the man Mary had mentioned, the one who first led her into sin.

"Welcome." A servant dressed all in white nodded deferentially and led the way down a long hallway filled with mosaics of colored tile, carefully arranged to suggest the sea and the sky. Potted grapevines trailed above marble benches, giving the hall the appearance of a restful arbor. At the end, a marble archway led into a massive dining area filled with rows of tables and reclining couches. Jesus didn't seem to be unduly impressed, but Peter had to take himself firmly in hand to keep from gawking.

"This is just what I want our palace to look like," he whispered to Rimona before they separated. She watched in pride as her husband followed Jesus to sit in a high place at the host's table.

Platters piled high with melons, grapes, pomegranates, and apples, were everywhere, while servants walked beside the tables to replenish the olives, leeks, and cucumbers. Many of the delicacies Peter had never even seen before, and the sweet, fresh wine flowed freely. Jesus turned to thank Simon on behalf of them all, although He Himself ate very little. Lazarus, seated on the other side, noticed that Jesus seemed subdued and thought He must be tired.

Martha served the host's table, rolling her eyes and sighing pointedly whenever she walked past her sister, who had taken her usual place, sitting right on the floor at Jesus' feet. Martha was not yet aware of the struggle Mary faced that night in her quest to stay close to Jesus.

For a very long time, throughout her recurring battles with demon possession, Mary thought she would never be able to face Simon again. Rage and humiliation surged in her breast whenever she thought of the man who had so vilely used her, only to turn from her in disgust once her honor was ruined. Now her need of Jesus was so great that nothing, and no one, could stand in her way if she could be close to Him. She did nothing to draw attention to herself; she just crept in quietly between her brother and her Lord.

Hidden under her cloak was a translucent blue alabaster box filled with spikenard. No sooner had Jesus' words about His impending death pierced her heart than she knew what she must do with her money, the fruit of her sin. She would give it to Jesus. Sparing no expense, she bartered away every last one of the hateful coins to buy the very best spices to embalm Jesus when He died.

Mary was still not sure what had driven her to bring the box tonight. Certainly she did not want to be noticed, especially in this household. Besides, she was saving the ointment for when Jesus died. Still, everyone talked as if He were about to be made King, and she wanted to honor Him for everything He had done. She fingered the box, unable to decide what to do with it.

Her gaze traveled down the Master, coming to an abrupt halt at His feet. Tears filled her eyes at the sight. Those dear feet had walked so many miles on her behalf, coming from far off to save her seven different times. But now they were dirty, the outline of sandal straps making a lighter pattern against dusty brown skin. Simon, in his insolence, had not even given Jesus water with which to wash His feet. She burned with the indignity of it.

Tears welled up as she drew out the box, determined at last. As quietly as she could, she tapped it on the floor until it broke then poured every drop over Jesus' outstretched feet. Holding in the sobs, she looked for a cloth to wipe away the dirt, but none was at hand. Pulling her long, wavy hair loose from its bindings, she smoothed the strands over Jesus' feet, cleansing away the dirt and spreading the costly oil.

The perfume was more fragrant than she had expected, enclosed as they all were in the crowded room. The conversation died away to a hush as everyone looked up and down for the source of the sweet aroma. Judas spotted Mary first. "Look," he said to the others, whispering loudly and pointing at Mary, "she wasted at least three hundred pennies to buy that stuff, and then just dumped it all over the place! Why wasn't the money given to me—for the poor?" he added hastily, patting the moneybag around his waist.

"You're right," Peter responded. "Just think how many people we could have helped with that money."

"Three hundred pennies would have fed approximately . . ."

"Not now, Philip," Peter grumbled. "We don't have time for all your calculations. It's too late now, anyway; it's all wasted."

"Wasted, wasted," echoed around the table.

Mary hung her head, her long hair falling forward to hide the agony on her face. She meant no disrespect to Jesus, and it had never occurred to her that her gift might slight the poor. She slipped back into the shadows, eyes lowered so she wouldn't have to see His condemnation as He looked at her. Sobbing brokenly, she looked about for a way of escape.

"Leave her alone." The voice of Jesus cut through the murmuring of His disciples with a severity that had previously been reserved only for the Pharisees and priests. "Why are you troubling her? She has done something wonderful for Me."

"What about the poor?" Judas muttered to Peter. "I guess nobody cares much about them."

"You will always have the poor who need your care, and yes, you should do all you can to help them, but I will not always be here." In contrast to His stern tone, Jesus smiled lovingly at the trembling woman. His voice softened. "Mary has done what she could. The Spirit brought her here tonight to anoint My body for burial. From this day forward, everywhere the good news about Me is told, her deed will be remembered and commended by those who hear it."

Judas went white about the lips. Never before had Jesus spoken to him like this, and to be scolded like a dog in front of the cream of society was more than he could bear. Blackness filled his mind, and white-hot anger flooded his heart. Judas bowed his head in shame and rage, vowing to himself that Jesus would pay dearly for every humiliating pang he had just suffered.

As the disenchanted disciple stepped away from his place at the banquet, vowing at least to gain some monetary profit from his association with Jesus, he saw his former Master turn to the host. "Simon, I have a little story to tell you. Once there was a creditor who had two debtors. One owed him five hundred pennies, and the other owed him fifty. The creditor forgave them both. Which do you think loved him more?" Judas was sick of stories. Clenching his teeth tightly together, he walked out into the night.

Simon answered Jesus' question. "The one who was forgiven the most will love the most." Suddenly, he realized he had condemned himself with his own mouth. His transgressions loomed ominously before him, and he understood for the first time that he, not Mary, was the greater sinner, that instead of cherishing the forgiveness Jesus offered him, he had puffed himself up in his own pride.

Turning abruptly from the table to hide his tears, Simon silently thanked Jesus for not uncovering his wickedness before the multitude. He deserved public shaming, he saw now, but mercy he would never again take for granted had spared him.

Two men were rebuked by Jesus that night. Two men had their souls laid bare before the searching gaze of the righteous Judge. One, resentful and angry, hurried away to arrange the most notorious betrayal in history, while the other found true repentance at last.

Peter was still snoring the next morning when Jesus awoke. He picked up a jug to draw His own water, but a servant waited outside the door with a small bronze tub, and several more servants followed with pitchers of warm water. Jesus sat down in the tub with a sigh of contentment. This unasked-for extravagance was a far cry from His customary morning dip in frigid streams or lakes, and He stored up the comfort against the trial that would soon come.

Drying with a long strip of yellow linen, undoubtedly prepared personally for Him by Martha, Jesus opened the leather pouch and drew out the new robe Keren and Rimona had made for Him. Its softness felt strange against His back and arms, and He smiled again at the thought of the love that had gone into its making.

The thin leather sandals had a rounded sapphire on the arch strap, surrounded by a ring of jasper. The stones, though not as pure, were like the ones which composed the first two foundations of the City of God. A single tear fell onto His palm at the thought, and homesickness threatened to overwhelm Him. The hardest part was knowing that all He had to do, at any time, was to speak the word, and He could go home.

Gabriel stepped back to allow Satan full access to Jesus. The rules had changed, and each day the angel would have to withdraw a little farther, leaving his sacred Charge at last unprotected before the buffeting of His enemy.

Satan had waited a long time for this, making sure every plan was in place to optimize this ultimate opportunity, for he knew without a doubt that it would never come again.

"They're not worth it," the arch deceiver said slyly. "Even the ones who like You don't have any idea who You really are, and the rest are going to torture You and kill You. Are You ready to deal with that? Your blood falling, wasted, to the ground? All heaven is waiting to receive You, to adore You, to call You Lord. Gabriel is right here—call him, and he will come, whisking You away from this earth to where You will be forever safe from my power. Turn back while You still can!"

Jesus steadfastly ignored the seductive whispers, sliding the sandals on His feet and reaching for the wine-colored sash Mary had thoughtfully provided. An emblem of royalty, it was a more apt gift than she had known, for it indeed heralded the coming coronation of the King of all creation—not on a royal throne, but upon a cross.

Chapter 30

"Peter, wake up, I have a job for you." Jesus vigorously shook the sleeping man by both shoulders. "Peter, can you hear Me? Wake up!"

Peter groaned and rolled over. "No jobs. Ask my servants."

Jesus shook him again. "I need you to get Me a donkey."

"No, no, no! Not another donkey in the palace!" Peter pulled the covers up over his head.

"I had hoped you would help Me, but if you're not feeling up to it, I can ask your brother instead."

Peter sat bolt upright in bed, eyes glazed and staring. "I'll help, I'll help. What kind of palace do You need?"

Jesus laughed and offered His disciple a cold cloth for his face. "Donkey," He enunciated slowly. "I need a donkey."

Peter shook his head, trying to clear it out. "Where am I going to get a donkey?"

"Take John with you and go to Bethphage." The little village near the crest of the Mount of Olives was well known to them all. "As you go through the main gate, you will see two donkeys, a mother and her colt, tied out in front of the corner house. Untie them and bring them to Me."

"That's it?" Peter thought maybe he was still asleep. "We just walk up to the house and take both animals, without so much as a by-your-leave?"

305

"That's right. If anyone asks what you are doing, just say that the Lord needs to use them. That's all you'll have to do."

"You're kidding, aren't You? We don't tell the owner our names; we don't give him any money—and he'll just let us walk away with two donkeys?"

"Exactly!" Jesus beamed at him. "Oh, and one more thing. The colt has never been ridden before. Don't try it."

"Then I guess I have only one more question. While we're there, do you want us to go to Baram and purchase the lambs we need for the sacrifice?"

"No." Jesus' voice turned suddenly hoarse, weighed down with some unearthly sorrow. "God Himself will provide the Lamb."

Peter felt chills run up and down his spine as he walked with John through the gates of Bethphage and saw the animals tied in front of the corner house just as Jesus had said. Peter looked around furtively, but no one seemed to be paying any attention. "Come on, John. Let's get this over with."

Each of them untied one rope and turned to lead the donkeys away, the colt following docilely after its mother. Just then the door of the house swung open with a bang. "What do you two rascals think you're doing with my donkeys?" The deep bass voice belonged to a giant of a man who must have been nearly seven feet tall. Peter gulped, his muscular frame dwarfed by the owner of the beast he was all but stealing. His hand, acting reflexively, started to throw away the lead rope. Just in time he remembered his instructions.

"Um . . . sir," his voice cracked embarrassingly, "the Lord needs these donkeys."

The man's frown melted away. "Why didn't you say so? Of course you may have them," he boomed. "Be careful, though, that colt's never been ridden."

"I will, and thank you." Peter shook his head in amazement. All of it had happened just the way Jesus said it would. Still carrying a grudge over John's selfish behavior at Ephraim, Peter hurried on without speaking to his equally silent companion.

They had no trouble finding Jesus, for before they reached Bethany they could see the crowd surrounding Him. Already it looked like there were twenty thousand or more, with more arriving every second. People came from every direction, flocking to the Man they believed would lead them to freedom from Roman tyranny.

The noise was astounding. Shouts and songs of praise rang out, giving homage to the King. Jesus smiled and waved to them, doing nothing to discourage them as He always had before. Peter joined Him at the front of the procession, surprised that the nervous colt didn't bolt and run when faced with such a horrendous racket.

"Thank you!" Peter could barely hear Jesus as He shouted to be heard above the voices of the crowd. "John, would you take that donkey to my mother? She just arrived from Nazareth and is too tired to walk all the way. I appreciate it!"

Peter looked critically at the donkey, sure it was missing something. That was it! It needed some cushioning for its bony young back. No sense having the King so sore He couldn't walk up the steps to His throne. Whisking off his cloak, Peter laid it over the donkey's back, arranging it with care. Andrew did the same, then Matthew, James, and Simon. Judas had returned, as charming as ever, and he was the last to lay his bright azure garment with its tan trim over the young colt.

Peter and Andrew took Jesus by the arms, lifting Him bodily onto the donkey. Though inexperienced, the donkey didn't move as the unfamiliar weight came down on its back; a tremendous shout went up when the people saw Jesus in the traditional posture of a king about to enter His city in triumph. A verse Jesus had read in the Bethany synagogue only the day before sprang into Peter's mind, filling him with exultation.

Rejoice greatly, O Daughter of Zion!
Shout, daughter of Jerusalem!
Behold, your king comes to you,
Righteous and having salvation,
Lowly and riding on a donkey,
On a colt, the foal of a donkey.

John returned just as Lazarus took hold of the colt's bridle, preparing to lead Jesus to victory. Unfastening his cloak, John spread it out before the donkey's hooves, and others followed his example. Those who had no cloak to lay in Jesus' path broke palm branches and olive boughs from the trees nearby to carpet the way of the King. Little children danced in delight, shouting, "Hosanna! Hosanna! Hosanna to the Son of David!" Their mothers chorused in reply, "Blessed is He that comes in the name of the Lord! Hosanna in the highest!" Their exhilaration and anticipation rose high.

Grim and determined, the angels of heaven marched along in the crowd, accompanying their beloved Commander to the scene of His execution. The tramp of their feet beat out martial time as they assembled at the scene where the final outcome of the war would be decided in only five more earth-days.

Tarik was too spent for tears as he accompanied Peter along the road. He ached for his charge as he watched Peter bask in the atmosphere of glory and adoration. Peter waved jubilantly to each person he recognized, preening in delight as he passed Rimona and Batia.

"Look, boys, there's Abba!" Rimona was nearly excited as Peter.

Batia blew kisses as her son-in-law walked by. "That's my daughter's husband," she shouted, in case anyone could hear.

Tarik was pleased to see that Peter didn't gloat or feel smug, as he had once thought he would if Batia witnessed him coming into his place of honor, but that small relief was far overshadowed by concern for how Peter, so grievously unprepared, would take the coming disappointment.

Tarik shook his head sadly as Peter grabbed a handful of leaves and threw them in the air, holding up his hands in unrestrained exuberance. "It won't last," he told Peter, knowing he would not hear. "He tried to warn you, but you wouldn't listen. Jesus is going to die, and you're not ready."

The crowd was filled with familiar faces. Jairus was there, Zara blooming with health at his right side, and Nahshon, the former madman of Capernaum, at his left. A little farther along, Ranon and his mother vigorously waved their palm branches, and there was the woman of Lebonah whom Andrew had raised from the dead.

Riphath, the man whose friends had forever changed the shape of Peter's roof, ran ahead of Jesus, leaping and shouting, "Make way for the King! The King is coming!"

The crowd was filled with people who had been blessed by Jesus, and their excitement exploded in an outburst that echoed off the nearby hills. Thousands more poured out of Jerusalem, swarming up the incline to the Mount of Olives, not looking back at the nearly empty temple behind them.

"Master, You must not allow Your followers to demonstrate in this unseemly fashion." The leader of a group of Pharisees blocked the road, his orange-and-black robe fluttering in the warm breeze. "This kind of noise is unlawful. Besides, the authorities will never allow it." Peter noticed that Kenan, the priest from his own synagogue, stood behind the man, whispering conspiratorially.

Suddenly it seemed as if the sun were not so bright, and the flowers' luster had dimmed. Many of the people began to wonder if they had done something wrong, after all. "If these people kept silent," Jesus said solemnly, "the very stones will cry out." If the rulers wished to say anything further, it was useless. Their vain protests were overpowered by the renewed shouts of the glad crowd. The sullen men fell back, and the unstoppable tide of exuberant humanity flowed past them.

When they reached the brow of the Mount of Olives, Jesus motioned for Lazarus to stop. This exalted sight of the temple was the best-known view in the land. Every child of Israel wondered how the temple of Solomon could have been any fairer. From where they stood, the white marble dome gleamed blindingly, reflecting the crimson rays of the setting sun. An immense vine adorned the main gate leading into the temple. With grapes worked in silver, tendrils of gold, and leaves of bright green, it was a fitting symbol of the nation of Israel. The only blot on its perfect beauty was the row of Roman banners lining the outer wall. In spite of that, all who saw it fell silent, spellbound by the sight.

In the hush, Peter heard the trumpets signal the commencement of the evening sacrifice. At that very moment, a lamb was being led through the Sheep Gate and up the stairs to the altar of sacrifice, just as had happened for many centuries. Sacrificed on the altar, it would exchange its life for the guilt of the people, its innocence and perfection for their sins. The lambs had never struggled or cried out as the high priest slit their throats, draining the blood into a cup to carry to the altar. It was a mysterious, awful ritual that never failed to impress those who partook in it. None of the ecstatic crowd knew yet that its full meaning, obscured for centuries, was now to be brought forth at last.

Suddenly, Peter heard the sound of a sob, a cry so filled with agony that at first he didn't think it was human. He looked around, seeking the source. Jesus still sat on the young donkey, the coats of the disciples pillowing His ride. Both hands covered His face, and He swayed as if He would fall to the ground from grief. Gradually words, heartbreaking in their anguish, began to emerge from the sobs.

"If only you had known, today of all days, what would bring you peace, but it is hidden from you." A fresh storm of weeping rocked Him. "Oh, Jerusalem, in the days ahead your enemies will build an embankment around you and surround you on every side. They will dash you to the ground and kill you, and not you only, but the children who seek safety within your walls. Not one of your stones will be left on top of another, because you did not acknowledge the time God came to you."

Peter put his hand up, feeling, for the first time, tears he had no memory of shedding. The premonition of disaster that had hung over him much of the past several months returned with force, and he looked down at the lovely capital city with revulsion. It seemed dark, brooding, and ominous. For just a moment he thought he could see it encircled by the Roman legions, the starving children of Israel trapped inside. But when he blinked, his vision cleared, and the same familiar city was all that appeared.

Jesus straightened up at last, wiped His eyes, and signaled Lazarus to move on. The people followed, far more subdued. The little children, unaware and unconcerned, still laughed and shouted, but much of the liveliness had gone out of the day. Broken palm branches littered the path after they passed, and hundreds of forgotten coats lay trampled in the dust as the procession quietly made its way toward Jerusalem.

At the base of the mountain the road divided, its paths leading to different gates of the city. Jesus, seemingly absorbed in the glowing panorama that towered above Him, chose the northernmost way, which ran alongside the temple for a time.

Turning toward the center of worship for the Jewish nation, Jesus sat even straighter as the donkey carried Him inside the siege wall at the Sheep Gate. Sliding to the ground, He gathered His precious Twelve around Him and walked regally into the temple, His measured stride following the path worn smooth by the hooves of countless lambs on their way to the place of their death.

Peter waited hopefully for Jesus to rally the people and declare Himself King, but Jesus was far more interested in architecture that day. They wandered about the courtyards, admiring the arches and pillars, talking to those attending the Passover, and trying to avoid the hostile stares of the priests.

After a whole hour, when Jesus still had made no effort to bring about the expected uprising, the crowd drifted away in twos and threes into the gathering darkness, the blazing torches of the temple lighting their way. All were acutely aware of the close scrutiny by Roman soldiers stationed in the Tower of Antonia and all around the outside of the sacred walls. Pilate was in residence, too, as was his custom during the feasts. The Roman's increased vigilance was unnecessary, though, much to Peter's dismay; he had expected to see the blasphemous banners torn from the walls before nightfall.

It was a disappointed little band that walked with Jesus back to Bethany, finding their way by the light of the waxing moon. Peter sought out Rimona at the encampment, hoping for someone sympathetic to talk to, but she was already sleeping. Taking comfort from his wife where he could, he curled up beside her warmth and fell quickly asleep.

When Jesus came for him early in the morning, Peter could tell at a glance that Jesus had not slept. He guessed Jesus had spent the night praying, as He often did. "Are we going back to Jerusalem today?" His eyes were bright with hope.

"Yes, there is still much that needs to be done. The others are ready."

Peter kissed his sleeping wife and put on his sandals. "I'm ready, too."

His stomach growled as he walked along, and he started scanning the sides of the road for something to eat. "Look, there's a fig tree! Is anybody else hungry?"

"It's too early for figs," Thomas sighed. "They probably wouldn't be any good, even if there were any."

"But there are lots of leaves on the tree," Nathanael pointed out hopefully.

"Come, then, let's take a look." Jesus searched the tree from top to bottom, but no sign of any fruit could be found. "What hypocrisy," He exclaimed. "Here it is, covered with enough leaves to promise ripe fruit, and not even a bud on the whole thing! No one is going to eat the figs from this tree ever again." Still hungry, the men resumed their walk to Jerusalem, entering the temple through the Court of the Gentiles.

Chapter 31

For three years the merchants had cursed themselves for fleeing in unreasoning fear before an uneducated carpenter from Galilee. For three years they had sworn that if He ever came back, they would be ready—no more running. But still as they spoke their grand boasts, they glanced nervously over their shoulders, afraid He might be there again.

Peter could hardly believe the state of the temple courtyard when he entered. The night before, a vast army of servants had come through to clean the straw and animal waste from the marble floor, but now a fresh influx of sheep, cattle, and goats filled the outer court as far as he could see.

Obviously, business had expanded since Jesus had driven out the moneychangers and animal dealers; an even larger area was now devoted to the exclusive use of the sellers. The din of the frightened animals, the clinking of the moneychangers, the shouting and fighting of men trying unsuccessfully to secure a bargain—it was all more awful even than the vast marketplace in Joppa. Peter patted the sheath strapped to his left thigh, quite sure from the set of his Master's spine that there was going to be trouble. That was fine with him; he was ready.

At every waking moment since his sixth birthday, Peter had worn a large knife. As a fisherman, he could never be sure when he would need a sharp blade at the ready, whether for preparing breakfast on a distant lakeshore or cutting a snagged piece of line. Having it there was second nature, and a few months ago when he had replaced it with a curved sword, it hardly felt any different. Simon the Zealot, whose swordplay was little short of astonishing, had taught anyone who was interested how to use their new weapons, until the hillsides rang with the clash of iron. Peter fingered the sword now, taking comfort in its solid strength.

Jesus strode along the four rows of columns in the Royal Porch, coming to an abrupt halt at the edge of the milling confusion. A ray of sunlight illuminated the place where He stood, and every eye turned in His direction. He waited until there was complete silence, until the last coin had fallen with a clink, spun around on the pavement, and circled to a stop. Then His power flashed out in a brilliant display of might, and His voice resounded throughout the sacred precincts.

"It is written, My house shall be called the house of prayer, but you have made it into a den of thieves!" The masses quailed before the devouring anger on the face of the Man they had scorned. "Take these things away!"

The merchants and their customers ran toward the far gates, their sandaled feet scrabbling in haste. All boldness forgotten, the one thought that consumed them was to find somewhere—anywhere—to hide from the wrath of Jehovah. Coins sprayed everywhere, and animals pressed against the walls in terror as the people fled, taking nothing with them.

Methodically Jesus walked along the rows of heavy wooden tables just as He had before, upending each one with a ringing crash. Soon the courtyard was empty, piles of brown rubble the only sign of the confrontation. A sweet peace infiltrated the compound as Jesus, appearing as an ordinary human once more, sat down on the steps and once again surveyed His house with satisfaction.

Peter crept from behind the pillar he had shared with Andrew, James, and John. Hostility all but forgotten, he let out a shaky breath. "That was really something—almost as amazing as the night when . . ." Intercepting a warning glance from John, he finished lamely, ". . . He did it the last time."

Andrew looked quizzically at his brother. "It wasn't night the last time. What are you talking about?"

"Er . . . hem . . . look! Here come all the people to be healed, just like before. Everyone back to work." Chuckling nervously, Peter was gone so fast that his brother couldn't question him any further.

Early the next morning, as the Twelve followed Jesus once again to the temple to teach the people, Peter stopped so suddenly that Andrew bumped into him. "That's the tree, the same fig tree that Jesus cursed yesterday! Look, it's dead already."

Andrew squinted, unable to believe his eyes. "You're right, that's the one. Well, it got what it deserved."

Jesus had tears in His eyes as He walked past the once-beautiful tree, the embodiment of His own special people. Intended to be a source of blessing and nourishment to the nations around them, they were instead like this tree, having the appearance of good works but without the fruits of a changed heart. And, like the fig tree, their time to bear fruit was nearly over.

The day before the Passover, just before Jesus left the temple for the last time, He pronounced a withering curse on His people. Not with ringing denunciations did He condemn them to the death He knew was coming, but with tears. Hands outstretched to them, pleading with the hard-hearted leaders one last time, He wept. "Oh Jerusalem, Jerusalem, you have killed the prophets, and stoned all those I sent to you. How often I longed to gather your children together just as a hen gathers her chicks under her wings, but you would not!"

His tears flowed as Jesus walked through the arched doorways and out of the temple for the last time. "My children," He exclaimed mournfully. "My poor children, look. Your house has been left to you desolate." He turned back toward the sacred courts for one lingering look as He spoke the divine sentence on His fruitless tree. "For I tell you, you will not see Me again until you say, 'Blessed is He who comes in the name of the Lord.'" And with terrible resoluteness, He turned His back on His beloved temple and went out to meet His fate at the murderous hands of those He had come to save.

Peter fingered his sword as he walked, trying hard to imagine what it would take to destroy a temple so massive that it reached into the heavens.

It seemed so permanent, as much a part of the earth as the mountains themselves. A portion of it even remained from before the attack by Nebuchadnezzar, yet Jesus had said that not one stone would be left on top of another.

Peter was deeply troubled, and as soon as they had reached the safety and seclusion of Gethsemane, he asked Jesus, "Please tell us, Master, when are all these things going to happen to our city? What are the signs of the end of the world?" As Peter looked at the temple, the only possible explanation that came to mind for its destruction would be such cataclysmic events that the planet itself could not hope to survive.

Jesus looked at His dear ones, gauging their strength and finding it lacking. They would not be able to bear it if He revealed the full truth—that the destruction of the city and the destruction of the world would take place separately, many centuries apart. They still couldn't even grasp that in only two days, by this time in the afternoon, He would be dead. In His mercy, the prophecy He gave them was twofold, its meaning equally as important to the disciples as to those on whom the end of the earth would come.

"Be careful that no one fools you," Jesus warned first, "for many will come, using My name and claiming to be the Christ. Many people will be deceived. There will be wars, and rumors of wars, but don't be alarmed, for much will still happen before the end. Nation will rise against nation and kingdom against kingdom. There will be famines and earthquakes all around the earth, but that is only the beginning of the sorrows yet to come."

"How much more can there be?" Nathanael asked, his mind boggling at the thought.

"Plenty," Thomas said. "There always is."

"It's better to know ahead of time so you can be warned," Jesus cautioned. "Because you believe in Me, you're going to be tortured and killed. All nations will hate you for My sake, and many will turn back from following Me. Betrayals and hatred will be commonplace. False prophets will appear and deceive the multitudes. Because of the abundance of iniquity, the love of many will grow cold; but whoever endures to the end will be saved.

"The good news of My kingdom will be preached throughout the whole world, as a witness to all nations. Then the end will come."

"Could you be a bit more specific?" Philip asked anxiously, worried—as always—about the details. "How will we know for sure when Jerusalem is going to be destroyed?"

"Very well, when you see the abomination of desolation standing in the holy place, just the way Daniel described, those in Judea must flee into the mountains. I cannot emphasize to you strongly enough how quickly you must go. If you are in the city, standing on the roof of your house, do not go into the house to get any of your possessions. If you are in the fields, do not go back for your clothing.

"It will be very difficult for those who are pregnant or nursing, and you must also pray that your flight will not be made even harder by coming in the winter or on the Sabbath day."

"But how will we know when the abomination of desolation is about to come?" persisted Philip. "You still haven't told us that part."

"Trust Me, you'll know it when you see it, if you study the prophecies of Daniel. You can tell it is near when you see Jerusalem surrounded on every side by great armies."

Subdued and sober, they did not interrupt again as Jesus finished pulling back the curtain to allow them this glimpse of a frightening future. "After that, there will be a time of terrible trouble, worse than anything this world has ever known before or will ever see again. If those days weren't cut short for the sake of My people, no one would survive.

"So if anyone says to you, 'Look, here is the Christ,' or 'He is over there,' don't believe them. There will be false christs and false prophets who will work great miracles. The deception will be so clever that, if it were possible, they would even deceive My very own people. I am telling you this ahead of time so you can be ready.

"If anyone says, 'Look, Jesus is in the desert,' don't go out to see who is there. If they say, 'He is in a secret room,' don't believe them. When I come, it's not going to be a secret at all. Just as the lightning shines from the east and flashes to the west, so also My coming will be, and the eagles will gather around the carcasses that remain."

The men shuddered.

"Just after the tribulation I told you about, the sun will grow dark, and the moon will not give its light. The stars will fall out of heaven, and the powers of the heavens will be shaken. Then the sign of the Son of man will appear in heaven, and all nations of the earth will mourn when they see the Son of man coming in the clouds with power and great glory. He will send His angels with the sound of a loud trumpet, and they will gather His children from all directions, from one end of the heavens to the other.

"I have a story to teach you about the fig tree. When its branches are tender, and its leaves begin to grow, you know that summer is near. In just the same way, when you see these things happen, you will know that My coming is near—right at the door.

"Truly, your generation will see the fulfillment of these things. Heaven and earth may pass away, but My words will always remain. No one, not even the angels in heaven, knows the day and hour that I am coming; only My Father knows.

"The time before My coming will be like the days of Noah. Just before the Flood, people were eating, drinking, getting married, living their lives as usual, until the day Noah went into the ark. They didn't realize that their time was almost over, until the Flood came and swept them all away.

"It will happen again when I come. Two men will be working in the field, and while one is taken, the other will be left. Or two women will be grinding at the mill. One will be taken, and the other left."

Jesus looked into the faces of each of His followers, now strained and pale under the burden He had to lay on them. "Watch, because you do not know just when your Lord will come."

Satan carefully wrote down every word Jesus spoke for detailed study later. Much about the final days of earth was still a mystery, not only to the enemies of God, but even to the holy angels, as well. By putting the words of Jesus with the writings of Daniel, anyone who wished to know more could now gain a clearer picture of the destiny of the Israelites and of the earth.

True, the future Jesus had just shown His disciples was filled with doom and destruction, persecution and death, but they had the assurance that someday all would be put to rights. Someday, the King would say to His people, "Come, you whom the Father has blessed. Come, inherit the kingdom prepared for you since the foundation of the world." And joyously, all suffering behind them, the righteous would enter into the joy of their Lord.

What a beautiful picture of hope! It was to give them much comfort during the coming hours, when the sins of the world would rest on the Lamb and the price of entrance into the kingdom would be paid.

The Day of Unleavened Bread dawned sunny and clear, when the Passover lamb was to be slaughtered and prepared for the feast, and still Jesus had made no move to arrange for the ceremony. Finally Philip felt he must interrupt his Master's preoccupation by asking, "What do You want us to do for the feast? It's almost time, and we haven't done anything to get ready. We don't have a lamb, and all the rooms are probably already taken."

"You're right; it's time." Jesus turned wearily to Peter and John. "Would you two make the preparations for us to eat the Passover?"

"Of course," John said after only the briefest hesitation. "Where do You want us to go?"

Jesus explained what He wanted, and they were too well trained by now to express skepticism, though Peter raised his eyebrows a trifle. Still a little uncomfortable, neither of them had much to say as they went down into the city. Entering into the Ophel Gate, they looked around for the man Jesus had described.

He wasn't long in coming, and he was every bit as conspicuous as they had imagined. With the hem of his robe girded up and a water jar on his shoulder, the muscular young man waited with the women at the spring above the pool of Siloam for his turn to draw water. A few suppressed giggles turned his cheeks bright crimson, and when one of the unmarried girls cooed, "Oh, how sweet! I wish someone would draw water for me," the young servant turned such a dark red he looked as if he might almost burst into flame. Suppressing their smiles at his discomfort, Peter and

John quietly followed him as he clenched his jaw and started back up the hill once he had filled his jar.

The house he entered was near the temple wall, and the two disciples went up to the door. "Hello," Peter called, sticking his head in through the opening. "Is anyone here?"

A heavyset man with black hair and a gray beard appeared almost instantly. "What is it?" He appeared distressed, the strain visible in his eyes.

Peter thought for a moment, trying to remember the exact words Jesus had told him to say. "The Master wanted me to ask you where your guestroom is so that He can eat the Passover with His disciples." He paused, for the man seemed stunned. "Do you know what He's talking about?" Peter asked anxiously.

"How many of you are there?" the man replied after a long silence.

"Twelve," answered John, "no—thirteen, counting Jesus."

"Come with me," his voice was hoarse. "I want to show you something."

He led them to a large upstairs room dominated by a central table. Thirteen places were set, and thirteen couches ringed the table. "Will this do?"

Peter was far more surprised than he should have been. "It's perfect."

"It's just like He said it would be," John whispered.

The man turned to them. "Just before you came to the door, I received word that the group, thirteen in number, who planned to rent the room for the evening would be delayed. I thought all our work, and all the food we had prepared, would go to waste. Now I see that we were just preparing it for the King. What an honor!"

"He knew it would work out," said Peter earnestly. "That's why He sent us."

"I have an idea." John looked at his fellow disciple. "Why don't you stay here and see if they need help with anything, and I'll go back and get the others."

Peter shrugged and turned away as John hurried down the stairs. He found himself feeling angry all over again at the way John always tried to push himself in ahead of everyone else in the kingdom. The less he had to be around that irritating man, the better.

Chapter 31

"You're better off without him, anyway," Set insinuated, one arm placed confidingly across Peter's shoulders. "You'd be better off without all of them, for that matter, and you know it."

"There is strength in unity," Tarik countered.

"Think of the thrones."

"Think of Jesus."

Peter thought of the thrones.

"Think of the palaces."

"Think of Jesus."

Peter thought of the palaces.

"The others are trying to rob you of your rightful place. Oh, yes, Andrew too. They all want to see you in a lower place than themselves; it's just not fair."

"It's not an earthly kingdom," Tarik offered, but by that time Peter had given himself over to resentment and self-pity too far to hear even an echo of his Guardian's voice.

Similar arguments were going on with each of the disciples, and sadly, the other Guardians succeeded no better than Tarik. In fact, as the eleven traveled together ahead of Jesus, the contention between them grew so heated that they walked faster and faster, trying to leave Jesus behind so He couldn't hear them.

Judas was the most vocal, calling down recriminations on James and John for their continuing closeness to the Lord. "If you think for one minute that just because you were the first ones called that you're going to be first in the kingdom, let me be the one to disillusion you. I am smarter, better dressed, and have higher connections than either of you. And, as an added bonus, I don't stink of fish!"

James doubled up his fist and almost punched Judas for that, but John held his arm, reminding him that although Jesus might not be able to hear them, He certainly could still see them, and even if He couldn't, He would be sure to ask why Judas came to the feast with a fresh black eye. So James relieved his frustration instead with several foul curses involving Judas's ancestry.

Shihab and his cronies shrieked with laughter at the irony. Here was Jesus, staggering into the city for the Passover at which He Himself would *become the Lamb, with Satan on one side and Gabriel on the other, and all the while His chosen disciples could hardly complete a ten-minute walk without violently attacking each other. Pretending not to hear the amusement of their enemies, Nadiv, Bahir, and the other Guardians kept silent, biding their time.*

John led the stampede up the stairs. James lost precious seconds when he started to turn down the wrong corridor, and Judas was quick to jump in ahead of him. John had the advantage of them all, though, since he knew just where they were going, and he entered the chamber first, skidding across the room to throw himself down on the bench in the place of honor at the right hand of the Host. Judas, right behind him, hurled himself onto the couch at the left hand. James complained bitterly at this heavy-handed maneuvering, but he didn't dare take the seat that was reserved for Jesus. He stomped around to sit next to Peter, halfway down the table.

Peter eyed the basin, towel, and pitcher of water that one of the servants had left for them. Courtesy demanded they all have their feet washed, but there was no one to do it. True, Jesus had sent John and him to prepare for the supper, but if John wanted his feet washed, he could do it himself. Peter wasn't going to do it for him; that much was sure.

"What, all this time, and you didn't arrange for someone to wash our feet?" James asked snidely—and loudly enough for the others to hear.

"Of course, you could've done much better," Peter sneered back. "Perhaps you could show us how it's done—you or your conceited brother."

"Take that back!" James raised his fist.

Just then, Jesus entered the room, alarmingly pale, and James subsided. None of the men would rise from their seats to help their Master, lest someone in a lesser seat take advantage of their absence to move up. An uneasy hush fell as Jesus took His place. He looked around sadly at the discontented faces, knowing the cause of their strife and wishing He could do more to prepare them for the storm about to break over their heads.

With unsteady hands, Jesus picked up the cup of fresh wine and held it up as He gave thanks. He lifted the vessel to His lips and sipped, savoring the rich flavor. "Take this," He passed it to John. "Share it among yourselves and drink it all. It is My blood, which I have shed for you. Do this in order to remember Me."

Surprised, John took the cup. This wasn't how they had celebrated the Passover before. He drank and passed the cup on. Jesus swallowed hard before He spoke. "I will not drink this again until the day I drink it anew with you in My Father's kingdom."

When the cup came at last to Judas, who drained the last drops, Jesus took up several pieces of unleavened bread. Again, He lifted the bread as He prayed. Breaking the flat loaves in pieces and passing them around, Jesus told them, "This is My body, which is broken for you. Take it and eat it all. Do this to remember Me, for as often as you eat this bread and drink this cup, you will show My death until I come." The men chewed silently, glaring at each other when they thought Jesus wasn't looking. Judas was nearly unbearable in his smugness, smirking at those in lower positions, which meant everyone but John. Not one man had room in his selfish heart to ponder the words of Jesus. *This is My body, which is broken for you.*

Chapter 32

The meal ended in silence. The pitcher of water seemed to grow steadily larger as they repeatedly cast furtive glances at it, each wondering angrily why someone else didn't just get up and wash everyone's feet, like they were supposed to do. Jesus waited a long time, looking sadly from one to the next around the circle, before standing and stripping off His seamless white robe. Tucking up the end of His undergarment, He quietly picked up the basin and towel and turned to the disciples.

With great dismay they watched as He knelt, first of all before Judas, and began washing his feet. The task they considered too degrading for themselves, Jesus was doing for them. With shame on their faces, one by one, they put their feet into the lukewarm water.

When it was Peter's turn, he found he just could not put his feet into the water as the others had. It grieved him to see the Son of the Highest kneeling before him, a towel spread across His royal lap. "Lord, are You really going to wash my feet? I should be washing Yours!" Peter impulsively blurted out what he had been thinking.

Jesus looked up at him and smiled. "You don't understand now why I need to do this, but someday you will."

"No!" Peter exclaimed. "I'll never let You wash my feet!"

Jesus held out His hands to receive Peter's foot. "If you won't let Me do this, you will not have a part in My kingdom."

With comical haste, Peter thrust both feet at once toward Jesus. "Don't wash just my feet then, wash my hands and my head. Wash everywhere—please!"

"Ah, Peter, you've bathed already, and that was enough. You need only to have your feet washed to be completely clean."

Humbly, Peter submitted, ashamed of his spiteful attitude. He wasn't the only one. Except for Judas, all the disciples felt themselves drawn once again to the love and harmony they had lost. At last they could comprehend Jesus' words as He rose, put aside the towel and the pitcher of water, and asked them, "Do you know what I did for you tonight? Do you really understand? You say I am your Master and Lord, and I am. But if I, your Master, have washed your feet, don't you think you should be willing to wash each other's feet? What I did was an example for you. It is what I want you to do for each other. After all, the servant is not more important than his Lord, is he? Whoever wants to be the greatest must be a servant, the same way I have served you. You will be so much happier if you follow My instructions."

"I know I feel better!" The relief in John's voice made them all laugh.

Jesus embraced His beloved disciple and took His place at the table once more. "That's because you're clean now—or at least most of you are."

Peter felt as if a great weight had been lifted from him, and he ate heartily of the meal that followed the Passover supper. His bite of bread dipped in herbs and olive oil was halfway to his mouth when Jesus made a most startling announcement. "Now, I'm not talking about all of you that I have chosen, but just as the Scriptures say, one of you that is eating bread with Me has turned against Me for harm."

Peter dropped the piece of bread on his arm, and next to him, James choked and tried to swallow. Fear gripped them all. "What are You talking about?" Peter asked.

Jesus answered the question plainly. "One of you is going to betray me."

Peter looked wildly from one of his friends to the next. He knew them all so well; it was unthinkable that one of them could be a traitor. He saw the amazement on Andrew's face, and his heart constricted. *Please, Adonai, don't let it be my brother.* He ran his fingers through his hair, frantic to know who it was. He looked down at his own hands. *Oh, dear God, don't let it be me!*

Nathanael was the first to speak. "Am I the one?" His voice shook, and he slumped in relief when Jesus shook His head.

"What about me?" Philip was next.

"I hope it's not me." Thomas looked aghast. "I'd never do anything like that—on purpose, anyway."

Peter gathered up his courage and asked, "Lord, is it I?" Again Jesus shook His head.

By now the table had become a scene of distress and confusion as each man asked if he were the one who would bring disaster on them all. Through it all, Judas sat silently, seeming not even to be listening, and Peter came to regard him with suspicion.

Finally, John could take no more. "Who is it, then, Lord?"

Pain engulfed Jesus as He answered, "The one who dips his bread with Me is the same one that will betray Me." All eyes went to Judas, who at that moment was in the act of dipping his bread in the same dish with Jesus. "The Son of man must go to His death just the way it was written," Jesus continued, "but what wretchedness will come to the man who betrays Him!"

Shocked silence filled the room as Jesus' words died away. Judas had been lost in his own thoughts. Now, confused and not sure what had just been said, he asked quickly, "Am I the one?"

Jesus nodded slowly. "It is just as you say."

He was caught! Judas jumped to his feet, determined to fight his way out if need be. To his surprise, no one tried to stop him. Jesus touched him gently on the arm. "What you're going to do, do quickly." Judas put in his mouth the last bite of bread he still held then hurried out into the night.

"Where is he going?" Simon asked the younger James.

"I don't know." Already Jesus' words seemed misty and unreal. None of them could comprehend the reality that one of their tight little band was collaborating with the enemy. "Maybe he's gone to get something else for the feast."

"Simon!" Both Simons jumped when Jesus called their name, but Jesus was looking at Peter. "Simon, Satan wants you." Peter was so surprised to be addressed by his old name it took a moment to assimilate Jesus' words: *Satan wants you.* He stared in shock at Jesus, hoping to see a gleam of humor in His eyes, some indication that this was only an odd jest, but Jesus seemed entirely serious. "He hopes that if he sifts you like wheat, you will be blown away with the chaff. I have prayed for you, though, that your faith will not fail; after you are changed, give strength to these men, your brothers."

Could Jesus possibly have meant that I am the one who would betray Him—not Judas? It can't be! "No!" Peter shouted. "It won't happen that way; I won't let it!" His voice turned pleading. "Lord, I'm ready to go anywhere with You. I would go to prison for you—even death!"

Jesus dropped back into the old familiar form of address. "Ah, Peter, I must tell you that before the rooster crows, you will deny three times that you even know Me."

Cut to the quick, Peter buried his face in his hands, unable to look at any of the others. *No,* he sobbed quietly to himself, *it can't be true! Please, Father, don't let it be true!*

There was little any of them could say after that, and in near silence they finished the meal. Jesus smiled tiredly at them. "Before we go, let's sing the hymn."

Nathanael's eyes lit up, and he whipped out his flute from the bag around his neck. The others sang quietly, not wanting to overpower the awe-inspiring voice of their Master. Nathanael had never played more sweetly, his harmonies blending perfectly with Jesus as He repeated the chorus from the Psalms:

"O praise the Lord, all ye nations,
Praise Him, all ye people.
For His merciful kindness is great toward us,
And the truth of the Lord endureth forever.
Praise ye the Lord!"

Peter thought that his Master's customary animation had been restored, so joyous did Jesus appear as He sang; but as the last notes died away and Nathanael reluctantly slipped his instrument back into its pouch, Jesus leaned heavily on the table, His energy waning quickly.

Peter rushed to help Him, offering a strong arm on which to lean. "I hope you're not getting sick. We'd better get you to the Garden right away so You can lie down." He hoped his tender devotion would show Jesus just how wrong He was in saying that such a faithful disciple would deny Him.

All of them were tired as they worked their way through the festive crowds filling the streets of Jerusalem. Just outside the gate, Jesus stumbled and nearly fell. Instantly John was on His other side, holding Him up. By the time they began the ascent to Gethsemane and the cave that was often their haven, Jesus could barely walk. More than once it was necessary for Him to rest His full weight on Peter and John.

"We'd better hurry." John sounded worried. "He's in really bad shape."

The men clustered around Jesus, concern filling them as they saw how very serious His condition had become. Inside the Garden, at the stone steps leading into the olive orchard, Jesus motioned weakly, indicating that Peter, James, and John should accompany Him. For once, Andrew showed no jealousy.

"You go ahead," he told Peter. "We'll stay here and keep watch in case anyone comes. No one else but Judas knows we're here. I don't think he would do anything, but . . ."

"It's better to be safe," finished John. "Just warn us if you see anyone coming."

Jesus held up His hand for silence. "All of you will stumble tonight because of Me." A new pang struck Him, and He groaned aloud. "The Scriptures tell of it. 'I will strike the shepherd, and the sheep will be scattered.' "

"But I won't," Peter protested. "Even if all the rest of them stumble, I will not!"

"Truly, you will," Jesus corrected gently. "It will be tonight, just as I have told you. Before the rooster crows twice, you will deny Me three times."

"I will not!" Peter exploded. "Even if I die, I will never deny You!" A chorus of agreement went up from the others.

Jesus didn't argue with them. Instead, He quietly requested, "Please pray for Me. Pray for yourselves, too, that you are not caught in temptation."

"We will," Andrew promised forcefully, taking up his post.

The sound of hurried footsteps caused them to hush suddenly as a shape separated itself from the shadows. By the light of the full moon, Peter recognized John Mark. "So this is where you all went," the young man exclaimed as he drew near. "I thought I saw you coming this way, but I wasn't sure. Do you stay here at the oil press all the time? May I stay with you?"

"Andrew can answer all your questions." Peter grinned at his brother. "He has all night."

Peter held his perspiring Master firmly as they climbed the stairs and found the path leading to the rear of the Garden. He advanced slowly, apprehension growing with each step. At the edge of the little clearing just before the cave, Jesus stopped. "Wait," He gasped. "Pray!"

The three men sank down on the cool grass and watched, horrified, as Jesus staggered on a little farther and collapsed. They would have gone to Him then, but He waved them back. Feeling helpless, Peter could only obey, bowing low and beginning a heartfelt prayer.

"Father, You can see there's some kind of problem here. Jesus is having trouble with something or other, and . . ." In spite of himself, he yawned. He shook his head to try to organize his thoughts and continue his prayer.

James and John yawned, too, feeling melancholy as they overheard a little of Jesus' agonized prayer. "Oh, My Father, if there is any way, let this cup pass from Me." His rasping sobs echoed into the night. "It's so hard . . . so hard to feel You pulling away from Me, shutting out the light. Dear God, be with Me—I cannot do this alone!"

Peter tried again. "Father, we need Your help . . . well, Jesus needs Your help, and something's really bothering Him." He yawned again, slipping into the familiar prayer Jesus had taught him. "Your kingdom come, Your will . . . be done . . ." Slowly, his forehead touched the ground, and he let out a loud snore.

"Not My will," Jesus wept, "but Yours be done. I accept Your plan for Me, and I know this is the only way. Just stay close to Me in this awful darkness!" Tears of surrender poured down His cheeks and wet His beard. His features distorted with grief, Jesus crawled painfully over to the disciples and shook them one by one. "James, John, Peter—

couldn't you watch and pray with Me for just one hour?" He desperately yearned for their company, to know that they were supporting Him.

The strained voice woke Peter, and he was shocked to see the change that had come over his Lord. The swollen face, tangled hair, and wild eyes were those of a stranger. "Master!" Peter sat up. "You have to let us help You!"

Again Jesus hoarsely repeated, "Please, watch and pray with Me."

Tarik and Arion stood with Gabriel at a distance. They wept to see the Father withdraw the light of His presence from the Son, one ray at a time, leaving Jesus with no ally, no celestial support, as legions of evil angels pressed in on Him, nearly crushing out His life. The angels could hardly keep from going to His aid as He crept to His friends and awakened them again, begging, "Please, watch and pray with Me."

With fresh determination, Peter started in again. ". . . On earth as it is in heaven. Give us this day . . ." Set sat cross-legged beside him, enjoying all too much the unexpected freedom to toy at his leisure with the susceptible fisherman. He sang a queer little lullaby and stroked Peter's hair gently. ". . . Our daily bread." Set smoothed Peter's eyelids down and eased his head onto the ground once more.

"Sleep, little fisherman, sleep. I have such interesting plans for you when you wake up." When he was sure Peter was well and truly asleep, with no chance of angelic interference, Set gleefully took his place in the swooping, screaming riot of demons swarming over the fallen form of Jesus. The air was thick with them as they came from all around the earth, rabid with evil joy as they tormented the One they had once rejoiced to worship.

For the third time, Jesus prayed the same prayer. "Father, if it is Your will, let this cup pass from Me." He hesitated a long time, His fragile human shell broken nearly beyond repair.

Satan put both hands around the head of his opponent and squeezed with all his might. "Give up! Go back!" He chanted the words again and again, trying to force confusion and despair into Jesus' mind.

Jesus cried out in a loud voice as great drops of blood burst through His skin and trickled down His face and arms, signs of the deep agony of soul He suffered as the sins of the world were laid on Him. The Lord of heaven fell to the earth and lay still. Only His lips moved in the whisper, "Even so, not My will, but Yours be done." The deep-set eyes closed, and the great heart of love slowed. There in Gethsemane, Jesus was dying.

"Back, all of you get back," Satan screamed at his troops. He turned and appealed to Gabriel. "He can't die yet—it's not time!"

Gabriel looked up into heaven and nodded before entering the dark corridor cleared for his passage through the demon horde. He knelt by Jesus and lifted Him bodily onto his lap just as he had that day in the wilderness. With measureless patience he gave Jesus a few swallows of a potent beverage unknown on earth and tipped His head back so He could swallow it. The change followed rapidly. Color rushed back into the pale cheeks, and the unconscious Man opened His eyes.

"Thank You, Father." Jesus rested His head on the broad chest of His friend, soaking up a last bit of love and warmth to carry Him through the trial ahead.

Gabriel handed Jesus a portion of manna, speaking words of encouragement to Him as He ate it. "The Father loves You. See? There is the glory from His throne." Gabriel pointed up through a rift in the sky, through which shone the light of heaven. "If You finish what You have started, Satan will be overthrown. The Father will accept Your sacrifice, and many who believe on You will be saved." Tenderly, the angel wiped the bloodstains from Jesus' face.

Something woke Peter then, and his wild thrashing woke James and John. The three disciples blinked in the bright light, their eyes finally registering the great angel who cradled their Master. "At last," Peter sighed in relief. "God has sent an angel to take care of Him. Everything will be fine now." He gave in to the insistent tugging at his eyelids and fell back to sleep.

"That's it, save Him for me," Satan taunted Gabriel, now that the danger was past. "We wouldn't want Him to die before He finds out what I have planned, now would we? Let me see, shall we whip Him first, or pull out His beard? Beat Him with our fists, or pound a crown of thorns into His head? Tsk, tsk, so many decisions."

Gabriel ignored him, looking instead across the valley to the temple, seeing three spots of flame break away from the city wall and cross the dry wadi before merging into a single fiery tumult. "It's time." He pulled Jesus to him

in a crushing embrace, sobs breaking loose in spite of his best efforts to keep
them back. "Just remember, no matter what, I'll be there." Reluctantly set-
ting Jesus on the grass, he vanished in a trail of glory.

Hearing the tread of the mob as it searched for Him, Jesus again bent over His disciples. "Get up! We need to go. My betrayer is here looking for Me." He walked on, leaving them to follow.

A commotion at the gate caused Peter to jump to his feet. There were shouts and angry voices, then the sound of running feet. He didn't find out until much later that the mob had caught the other nine men sleeping. The disciples awoke in horror to find that the doom they had not really believed possible was upon them. In panic, they all fled without ever remembering the weapons that many of them carried.

John Mark, more than the others, would never be allowed to forget the humiliation of that night. Rich, and somewhat spoiled, he had habitually slept in a most shocking state of undress, a habit he refused to discard even when sleeping out in the open. "But I get so hot," he had querulously explained to Andrew. "I brought a sheet to cover up with, so you don't have to be embarrassed. I just can't sleep well in clothes!"

When the motley crowd awoke him with a start and he saw all the swords and sharp farming implements, he leaped up, filled with terrible fright, and chased after his companions as they ran. As he clutched the sheet, it billowed around him, and many of the superstitious people thought at first that he was a ghost.

"Seize them!" ordered Caiaphas from the front row of the mob, pointing to the fleeing men.

An enterprising agent of the high priest obeyed instantly, darting after John Mark as he stumbled headlong down the hill behind the others. The man caught a corner of the trailing linen and held it fast. Suddenly dressed only in the clothing he'd worn on the day of his birth, the unfortunate boy raced back toward the city!

Caiaphas's men, ringed by Roman soldiers, pushed their way into the orchard. Just inside the gate, Jesus quietly stepped into the glow of their torches and asked, "Who are you seeking?" They all heard Him plainly and wondered at His composure.

Caiaphas lifted his white beard defiantly. "Jesus of Nazareth."

"I am He," Jesus replied, unruffled. Following the signal from the high priest, the mob rushed forward to arrest the supposed miscreant, but as they did, the empty space before their eyes ripped open to reveal a mighty angel, flaming sword held high. The blinding light petrified them, and the terrible look on the angel's face wiped out any thought of what they had been sent to do.

They cried out, trying futilely to block the stupefying radiance with their hands and arms. Unable to move, they all sank unconscious to the ground. When they came to themselves, they didn't know if a few hours had passed, or only a few minutes, but it was night still, and very dark. A number of the lanterns had broken on the ground, and the torches had nearly been extinguished, but when the men held them up and blew softly, flames sparked anew. After gathering the weapons that had fallen in the darkness all around them, the men at last stood huddled together, still belligerent, but afraid to approach Jesus again.

The Man who confounded them at every turn took a deep breath as He faced them. For the second time He asked, "Whom do you seek?"

A peculiar sense came over them that the strange event had never really happened, and they had just come into the Garden, after all. It would have been more convincing if the fresh image of an angel, tinted with a green afterglow, had not danced before their eyes every time they blinked. Not a few wondered if the stark image would ever fade. Even Caiaphas hung back, unsure what to do next.

Malchus, the high priest's chief servant, answered for his master. "Jesus of Nazareth."

"I have already told you that I am He," Jesus said, walking toward them, "but let these others go free." He motioned toward the three men who were all He had left.

The mob fell back before Jesus' steady advance, fearful to touch Him lest something even worse should happen. Greedy Judas, seeing his reward slipping away, pushed through the ranks. He shuddered as he stepped away from the mob, glancing back at them in great disdain. He squeezed as much sympathy as he could into his face before grasping Jesus by the shoulders and kissing Him on both cheeks.

"Greetings, Master," he said, sounding as if he were about to weep.

This attempt at piety did not fool Jesus for an instant. "Where did you come from, Judas? Do you betray the Son of man with a kiss?" At this gentle rebuke, Judas pulled away angrily, but his ploy had worked. When the unruly men saw that Judas had touched Jesus and nothing had happened, they were emboldened to attempt once more to arrest Him.

Jesus submitted peacefully, trying still to turn their wrath from His disciples. Caiaphas motioned several of the Roman guards forward to tie the prisoner's hands, and Malchus was only too eager to help them.

Peter became even more agitated when he saw Malchus step forward. The brokenhearted man half sobbed, "Jesus, I tried so many times to warn You about that man, but You would never listen to me. You said he was one of Yours, so I didn't do anything about him, and now it's too late." He shifted his weight from one foot to the other, and his restive hands came into contact with the sword he had all but forgotten.

Jesus held out his wrists to be bound, and Malchus began winding the rope tightly around them. A shouted warning from one of his fellows made him look up in time to see a sword swinging through the air in a downward arc, Peter's enraged face right behind it. Instinctively, the servant rolled to one side, grateful for the combat skills that kept him from being divided vertically in two.

Chapter 33

*T*arik gladly took up his post again as Jesus stood. Set didn't mind retreating; he had accomplished what he wanted already. He stood with feet spread apart and arms folded, watching with wicked delight as his part in the plan came together. Occupied with weightier matters, he didn't notice Oreb and Zeeb in a quick whispered conference before Oreb approached him ingratiatingly.

"Your highness," Oreb groveled, "I'm not at all trying to imply that you haven't taken care of everything, and you have so much more experience with this kind of thing, but it's almost the right time to use it, and I just want to be sure you are aware of it."

"Aware of what?"

Oreb carefully opened his copy of Peter's record, thumbing back several years. "Right here, where he said, 'I swear in the sight of Adonai that I will forfeit my life before I ever desert Jesus again. And if I ever break this oath, I vow to end my own miserable existence rather than face another day with such treachery on my head.' Now, there were several times you could have taken advantage of this and didn't, so I thought you were probably saving it for an occasion like this. Was I right?"

"You little worm," Set sneered, "you have a lot to learn about being a really good tempter. Why would you even think I wouldn't have allowed for that in my expert calculations? Now get out of here before I forget we're on the same side." Once the little demon's back was turned, Set's expression grew even slyer.

Oreb scurried back to Zeeb, trying to conceal his triumph. "He took the bait!"

"Are you sure?" It was against Zeeb's nature to hope.

"Of course I'm sure," Oreb bragged. "I've studied Simon since his birth, and Set has been with him only a little over three years. That pompous windbag will rue the day he wouldn't listen to me!"

"But are you sure Peter won't take his own life?"

"What if he does? Either way, we can't lose. If he dies, we'll be assigned to someone else. If he lives, which I think he will, Set will face disciplinary action." Oreb smiled. "I've been watching Peter all the time he's been with our enemy, and I think he is still much stronger than Set realizes. All it would take would be one little prayer, and . . ."

". . . and we'd be back in business." Zeeb let out a long breath. "Here we go!"

Gabriel stepped into the fourth dimension, bringing enough of the Father's glory with him to drop every one of the evil men unconscious to the ground. He stood there long enough to make a dazzling impression then stepped back out of view. He had not been sent to protect Jesus, for Satan had now received full latitude over the body of the Begotten. No, Gabriel was the final warning sent by a loving God to the very men who were there to carry off His Son to be killed. In the final day of judgment, none of them would be able to say, "I didn't know—I thought He was just a man."

Tarik laid his hands on Peter, trying to steady him. As Jesus stepped forward to receive the kiss of His betrayer, the angel looked soberly at Deron, who faced him from the crowd. "Are you ready for this?"

Deron nodded. "I'm ready."

Jesus stood quietly, waiting to be bound. As soon as Caiaphas gave the order, Malchus, Deron's human charge, stepped forward, enthusiastically reaching for the rope. Peter clenched his fists in distress. Partly to Jesus and partly to himself, the distraught man moaned, "Jesus, I tried so many times to warn You about this man, but You would never listen to me. You said he was one of Yours, so I didn't do anything about him, and now it's too late." Another anguished cry burst from his lips as he saw Malchus tug roughly on the Master's bonds. Near the end of his self-control, he bent with both hands resting on his thighs. A long, hard, metal object reminded him that he was not entirely defenseless. Rage filled him as he silently slipped the sword from its sheath.

Tarik and Deron tensed. Peter charged forward, his sandals tearing into the sod. Sword lifted high, he swung it down with both hands. Tarik held Peter as he ran, lest a misstep alter the outcome. Deron placed his gleaming sword alongside Malchus's head to deflect the coming blow. The only bit of flesh left unprotected was a single, naked ear, just as he had been instructed.

At the last instant, Deron shoved Malchus to the side. Peter's blade clashed against the heavenly weapon and slid smoothly down its length, neatly slicing off the exposed right ear of the high priest's servant.

In the searing flash of pain that followed, Malchus responded instantly, covering the wound with his right hand and drawing his own dagger with his left. Regal gems twinkled in the torchlight, and the eagles of the hilt looked ready to wreak their vengeance. Blood trickled from between Malchus's fingers and ran down to his elbow as he crouched for the kill. Tarik stepped in front of Peter to shield him from the furious attack.

"Put your sword away." Without any apparent effort, Jesus released His hands from His bonds, and the rope fell unheeded to the ground. Stepping away from the Romans who held Him, He blocked the way between the two warring men. He looked intently into Peter's eyes, though His words were for them both. Reluctantly, compelled by the quiet command, Malchus sheathed his weapon first. "Put away your sword," Jesus repeated to Peter. "Those who live by the sword will die by the sword."

Bending over, He picked up the scrap of flesh and moved to Malchus's side. Each individual in the Garden seemed frozen, holding his breath, as Jesus took the hand that covered the wound and then pressed the severed ear into place. The two men—Malchus and Jesus—gazed into each other's faces for what seemed a very long time. Malchus stared at Jesus as if he had never seen Him before. The tanned face seemed unfamiliar, though he had seen it many times, and in the powerful love that drew him in despite himself, Malchus could read the answers to every question he had ever asked—and to some questions he hadn't even known he had. In those loving eyes, the servant of the high priest saw limitless, fathomless Deity. Filaments of time stretched into eternity as man and God faced each other, bound together in cords of love forever.

A smile flickered across Jesus' face as He reached for Malchus's hand and lifted it to the side of his head. Malchus started in surprise; his fingers closed over the ruined place, only to find it made whole. At the same moment he realized the pain was gone; it was as if nothing had happened to his ear at all! His legs would no longer support him as the enormity of his transgression sank in. Memories of all he had done to this Man rose into his mind, and with awe and dread he admitted to himself that he had not been fighting against a mere human, but against the Almighty, the Creator of the universe.

When the three remaining disciples saw Jesus turn again to the minions of Rome and hold out His hands to be retied, in spite of Peter's attempt to save Him, their last shred of restraint snapped. With shrill cries of anguish, they darted past the mob and into the darkness, a panicked Peter in the lead. The pounding of unknown feet was right behind him at every step. He ran faster, trying to outdistance his pursuers. James and John ran faster, trying to stay close to their friend.

As Peter took the stairs in two long strides, a shadowy apparition emerged from the middle of the road and blocked his path. It was too late to stop. He ran full force into the creature and fell, tumbling end over end in a tangle of arms and legs. At least from his vantage point at the bottom of the heap, Peter could tell the creature was only a man, and that relieved his mind somewhat.

His alarm returned full force when an unfamiliar voice spoke his name. "Peter, please, you must let me speak to your Master." Peter thrust him away and sprinted off, doing his best to catch up to the distant figures of James and John. Behind him, the winded man tried to stand, calling futilely, "Wait!" But Peter was already gone.

He slowed as he came nearer to the city. If he went on, he would be plainly visible to anyone who chanced to look. Nauseated, his teeth chattering uncontrollably, he debated the best course to take.

"Pssst!" The low hiss came from a stand of grapevines off to his right. "In here."

He looked around suspiciously. "Who is it?"

"It's John. James is here too. We want to see which way they go. Hurry, they're coming!"

Peter scrambled into the bushes with them, and the three men retreated deep into the undergrowth, far enough that the searching light of the torches would not fall on them. When the mob passed by, they caught a glimpse of Jesus, surrounded by a ring of iron. He was still as tranquil as if on His way to the synagogue, but the three men had to stifle their sobs at the sight.

"I'm going to follow them," John declared as soon as the rabble entered the city. "I feel bad for running, but I'm not going to desert the Master now."

"Go ahead," James told him. "I'm staying here. Someone needs to survive and tell the others what happened."

"I can't believe you're such a coward! Fine, just stay here, then. What about you, Peter?"

Peter swallowed hard. "I, uh . . ."

"Good, I knew I could count on you. Come on!"

The temple was dark as they hurried past, so they silently continued following the mob at a distance until they reached the palace of the high priest. Its courtyard was shining with light and swarming with people. Peter peeked around the corner of a nearby house, straining to catch sight of Jesus through the gate, but He was already somewhere inside.

"John! What are you doing?" Peter grabbed John's cloak to pull him back. "They'll see you!"

"That's the idea," John said dryly. "How else do you think we're going to get in?" He pulled away from Peter and walked up to the gate alone. Peter saw him confer briefly with the gatekeeper, who called a priest over. After a few more moments, the gatekeeper stood aside to let John pass, but John turned and motioned forcefully for Peter to come with him.

Peter dragged his feet as he left the shelter of the tall building. He expected to be hauled off in chains at any moment and was pleasantly surprised when no one paid him any particular heed. He had never been inside the high priest's courtyard, and he looked around in awe. Stone buildings ringed the courtyard, with porches all around the lowest story.

The square itself was many times larger than Peter's house and filled with flowering shrubs and fruit trees. The faint scent of almond blossoms floated on the air, and the boughs of a large willow tree hung low over the edge of the central fountain. "I'm going to go sit with the others," Peter told John quietly, trying not to move his lips. "Let's stay separate so maybe no one will recognize us."

"What if they do?" John sighed and found a solitary seat near a doorway with Roman guards stationed outside.

A brazier burned in one corner of the square, and a number of people gathered nearby to ward off the chill of the predawn morning. Peter skulked into the back of the group and stood with his head down, hoping to avoid notice.

A manservant came and added fresh fuel to the fire, and as the flames flared with sudden brightness, the woman next to Peter—one of Caiaphas's housemaids—glanced at him and froze. "Aren't you one of His disciples?" She had seen Jesus on several occasions when He had been in Jerusalem with His disciples. She had wished she could meet Him or at least someone who knew Him.

Peter shrank back in terror. "I don't know what you're talking about," he stammered.

Conversation came to a standstill, and every eye came to rest on Peter and the maid. She looked intently at his face. "But I'm sure I've seen you with Him."

Peter grew angry and afraid. "I don't know Him, I tell you!" he snarled, and from the other side of the courtyard, a rooster's faint crow echoed in the night.

The great oak doors into the makeshift trial chamber flew open with a crash, and Peter looked up with a guilty start. A twitchy, scrawny man flew out, stumbling and bent over as if he had been pushed—or perhaps kicked. Caiaphas followed him out, shaking his fist, his face mottled shades of purple. "Get out!" he shrieked at them. "You pack of idiots, you . . ." Catching sight of someone outside the door, the high priest abruptly fell silent. His eyes narrowed to slits, and his beard seemed to stand nearly straight out. "This is your doing," he said to the man, his voice low and menacing, "and I'll deal with you later." Then the doors slammed shut again.

The man who had incurred Caiaphas's wrath turned, and Peter saw with shock that it was Malchus. Immediately Peter turned away lest he should be recognized and betrayed. One of the men by the fire spoke up, and Peter listened intently. "Who was that man who just came flying out of there?" the man asked.

The maid at his elbow piped up. "That was one of the witnesses. Obviously he didn't tell his 'true' story the way he was paid to tell it."

They all laughed, Peter the loudest of all. Trying to make sure he blended in, Peter only succeeded in drawing unwanted attention to himself. His forced guffaws caused everyone to look his way, and he flushed scarlet. Another of the maids laughed, "Looks like that high and mighty Malchus finally found out he's just a servant like the rest of us."

"Not so," quipped another. "Caiaphas is just treating Malchus like he does his own son." The cruelty of the high priest toward his fragile, mincing son, as well as the marked favoritism he showed to the more rugged Malchus, was a frequent topic of gossip among the servants.

Several men who clustered nearest the fire began a stream of crude jokes about the Teacher of Nazareth. Still trying desperately to blend in, Peter contributed a choice comment he had heard once questioning the virtue of Jesus' mother. But his forced gaiety only deepened their suspicions, and one of the men turned to him. "You talk just like a Galilean," he accused. "You *are* a follower of that Man. I'm sure of it."

Peter let out a blistering oath. "I told you, I don't know Him!" They left him alone after that, sure he was lying but unwilling to provoke him into proving himself with his fists.

An hour before sunrise, the great oak doors opened, and the guards brought Jesus out under the balcony. One cheek showed a bright red mark where one of His accusers had slapped Him, hard. Ignoring the soldiers, twenty or thirty of the men who had been hanging around the courtyard advanced toward Him, pushed Him to the ground, and began beating Him severely. Jesus didn't raise a hand in His own defense as they spat on Him and ripped out handfuls of His hair and beard. Peter tried not to look, knowing his face would betray him if he did.

He felt a touch on his arm. "Peter? Is that you?"

The man tried to speak quietly, unlike Peter. "Leave me alone!" he shouted. "My name is Simon, and I don't know what you're talking about!" Desperately afraid in spite of his bold denials, Peter's only thought was that this man, a known servant of Caiaphas, would quickly denounce him to his master.

Othniel, his face drawn, lowered his voice still further. "I was supposed to kill Lazarus." By now he was whispering. "I couldn't—the angel wouldn't let me. You have to help me tell them that Jesus is the Son of God."

"Jesus? Jesus who?" Peter, furious now, wouldn't listen. "I've never even met the Man!" He tore away from Othniel, frantically trying to escape the persistent servant.

Othniel reached out, trying with growing desperation to stop Peter from getting away. "But I saw you in the Garden. I know you were with Him!"

Peter shook his hand off angrily. "I told you before, and I'm telling you again—I don't know Him!" And from his mouth flowed such foul oaths that even his hardened listeners were shocked. His diatribe broke off in mid sentence when a rooster, that had awakened and was confused by the light and noise, began to crow loudly. Peter stopped shouting, and a terrible change came over his face. He remembered what Jesus had said just hours before—"You will deny Me three times before the rooster crows twice." At that moment, the crowd surrounding Jesus parted for a moment, and His eyes met Peter's across the courtyard. A knife thrust could have hurt Peter no more than the look on Jesus' face just then. The agony of His beating, the stinging raw patches on His cheeks, the sense of abandonment as His Father withdrew from Him, all were magnified by this final betrayal by one of His most trusted followers. Peter saw not a trace of reproach or reproof in Jesus' face, however—only an overwhelming, almost inhuman grief.

An eerie wail bubbled up in his throat, and he dashed for the gate. The gatekeeper let him go, thinking with satisfaction how right his master had been to order him to allow the followers of Jesus to witness every possible humiliation of their Master. The man fleeing out into the brick-lined streets of Jerusalem had certainly looked disheartened enough.

Peter ran until the pain in his side forced him to slow his mad pace. He had run with no conscious thought of where he was going; he just ran blindly down one street after another until the city was behind him. Yet his feet led him unerringly to the gate of Gethsemane. His senses returning at last, Peter walked slowly in, drawn somehow to the very heart of the Garden. He knelt in the same place he had seen the angel only a few short hours before and dug his fingers into the dewy grass in a spasm of anguish. Convulsive sobs shook his frame as he lay on the cold earth and wished fervently that he had never been born.

"That's it. Very good, very good." Set smiled. "It's such a small step from wishing you had never been born to wishing you were dead. Come on, it's not so hard. Say it after me. 'I wish I were dead. I wish I were dead.'"

Consumed by blackness and despair, Peter obediently repeated, "I wish I were dead."

"You should be dead," Set screamed at him. "You broke your oath, the vow you made before them all. Do you remember what you said? 'I swear in the sight of Adonai that I will forfeit my life before I ever desert Jesus again. And if I ever break this oath, I vow to end my own life rather than face another day with such treachery on my head.' Those were your exact words.

"But then you deserted Jesus. When He needed you most, you ran. Instead of leaping to His defense when those terrible men almost killed Him, you cursed and swore and took His name in vain. You aren't good enough to be one of His followers. You know you can't go back to the others after this. How will you face your wife? Your two sweet, innocent little boys will never see you in the same way again. They'll look at you and know what you've done. They'll hate you for it too. There's no other way. You must die!"

Set picked up a length of rope dropped by a member of the mob. "One more time, just say it with me. 'I broke my oath. I'd be better off dead. I'll just end my own life here so I can retain at least the last dregs of my honor.'" And he laid the rope in front of Peter's outstretched hands.

Peter writhed in an agony of self-loathing. He could see as plainly as if he were still there the day he had made his solemn vow, and though he might have fractured it a few times, never before had he entirely shattered it. He felt so helpless, with no idea what he should do next. Unbidden, the answer came to him, and he sobbed, "I broke my oath. I'd be better off dead! I'll just end my own life here so I can retain at least the last dregs of my honor."

As he fell again to the ground in a fresh storm of tears, his hand closed on something fibrous and rough. Lifting his head, he saw a rope in the grass right there in front of him, clutched firmly in his fingers. *It's a sign! Adonai wants me to fulfill my oath to Him.* He wiped his nose on his sleeve, blinked his aching eyes, and looked contemplatively at the trees around him.

Chapter 34

*Y*ou can't be here." Set drew his waving crooked sword, ready to contest the issue if necessary. "He belongs to us now, and there's nothing you can do about it."

Tarik merely echoed the words of his Commander, "The Father rebukes you," adding, "and besides, Jesus' prayer gives me all the right I need."

Set shuddered at the sound of that name on the lips of a messenger of heaven. "All right, all right! It won't matter anyway. Nothing you can do will stop him."

Firing a swift prayer for help to the Father, Tarik stepped in close to his charge. "Peter, you don't have to do this. There is another way."

But I promised, Peter thought, believing he was arguing with himself. I have to keep this promise, at least.

"It was a wicked, foolish promise, and Adonai will count it as a great sin if you do not break it. Just ask Him for forgiveness, and it will be blotted from the books. That's all you have to do to clear this stain forever."

"But you betrayed Jesus," Set reminded. "Death at your own hand is far better than you deserve. Quick! Get it done before anyone finds out you're here. Just get it over with!"

Tarik floated in front of the despondent man, looking right into his eyes. The words Jesus had said such a short time earlier came to his mind, and he felt moved to speak them to the mind of his charge.

"Let not your heart be troubled. Believe in God, believe also in Me."

Peter began to tremble. "In My Father's house are many mansions. If it were not so, I would have told you." Tears sprang up anew, and Peter thought he could almost hear the voice of Jesus speaking to him once more. "I go to prepare a place for you, and if I go to prepare a place for you, I will come again and receive you unto Myself, that where I am, there you may be, also."

A longing for that place of beauty and peace welled up in Peter's heart, and he realized that what he was considering would prevent him from ever reaching it. He cast the rope from himself in disgust. A completely broken man, he knelt in the sight of God and poured out his sorrow and woe. This time as he cried, the tears spoke of repentance and healing.

Nearby, two little demons laughed and cheered as they watched Set go down in flaming defeat. "I told you it would work," Oreb crowed. "Now we'll get our jobs back."

"I hate to admit it, but you were right. I can't wait to see what his penalty is." Zeeb smiled, thinking of any number of torments that seemed suitable.

Just then a rebel scout flew by. "Did you hear? We got Judas. The dogs are eating his body right now."

"We'll be right behind you," Oreb called. "I wouldn't want to miss that for anything!"

There in the Garden, Peter lost all sense of time. The sun was high when he wiped his face on the front of his robe, the same robe he had worn the day Jesus rode into Jerusalem. That thought almost overcame the tenuous hold he kept on his emotions, but he pressed on, tottering to the entrance of the orchard and making his uncertain way back toward Jerusalem.

The bright sunlight made him squint, his eyes watery and sore from hours of weeping. He didn't notice at first that the usually crowded streets were nearly empty. Impulsively, he stopped a woman who was hurrying to fetch water. "Do you have any word of Jesus?"

Eyes wide, she looked fearfully at him and would have passed on, but he detained her. "Please—I'm a friend of His, and I must find out what happened to Him."

She backed up a step, but answered willingly enough. "After the Sanhedrin condemned Him, I heard they sent Him to Pilate, and then to Herod. I haven't heard anything else since."

"Condemned?" It hadn't occurred to Peter that the Sanhedrin would gain a conviction, and so speedily too. Although he knew very little about legal matters, he was sure a death trial ought to have taken longer than that. Pilate's involvement was a very feeble foundation on which to pin any hope, either. The Roman procurator was cruel and unpredictable; more than once he had willingly condemned an innocent man to keep the priests in his debt.

Herod was worse still. In the time since he had ordered the death of the Baptist, he had grown increasingly brutal, trying, with a river of blood, to wash John from his mind. Belatedly, Peter realized the woman was still staring at him, her terra cotta jar balanced on her head. "Sorry. I mean . . . thank you. Did I mention that I'm a friend of Jesus?"

Herod's palace was deserted, save for the guards at the gate. Peter felt his stomach drop as he took in their polished armor and keen weapons, but nothing could stay him from his course. He walked up to them on quaking legs, taking no notice as they laughed at his disheveled appearance. "Excuse me, I'm a friend of Jesus. Is He still here?"

"His Majesty the King has already left." Carried away with his own cleverness, the guard struggled to suppress his amusement. "I can see, good sir, that you must be an important man in His kingdom. One of His chief princes, perhaps." The other guard snickered at his companion's wit.

"Where is He?" Peter ignored the reminder of all his ruined hopes and dreams. "I have to find Him!"

The first guard rolled his eyes. "He went back to Pilate. You can probably still find Him there."

"And wearing His royal robes too." The second guard laughed outright then.

"Thank you," Peter called back as he sped away.

To prevent any uprising during the Jewish festivals, extra companies of Roman soldiers were stationed in Jerusalem. Pilate, himself, stayed in the Tower of Antonia, along the northern perimeter of the temple. By the time Peter reached it, having run across the city from Herod's palace, abutting the western wall of Jerusalem, he was panting and out of breath. From far off, a rhythmic rumbling sound filled the air. As Peter drew nearer, words began to emerge from the dense cloud of noise. *"Barabbas! Barabbas! Barabbas! Barabbas!"* He ran faster, holding his side. Again and again the pitiless mob shouted the name of their rebel messiah.

All heaven watched in mute horror as Satan cloaked himself once more in the form of Zarad, preparing for the last act in this battle to the death. The insurgent general well knew that if Jesus died with no sin to blot His record, his own doom would be assured. For more than four millennia, Satan had stored up anger, hatred, and malicious plotting against this day when the Son of God would be delivered fully into his power. Now, he girded himself for the struggle, finding a delicious irony in fighting the God-Man, with both of them in human form. Despite its limitations, a body would allow him to stand defiantly before the Son and scream out his hatred and defiance. He could hardly wait.

Gathering sixty-six of his top commanders about him, Satan pushed his way into the crowd at the fortress. His demons spread throughout the assembled mob. They were ready when Pilate appeared again at the balcony, leaning heavily on the railing. "What do you want me to do?" he asked the priests in exasperation. "You haven't proved a single charge against this Man, and I already told you I can find nothing wrong with Him. Even Herod, a fellow Galilean, did not condemn Him!"

Pilate teetered on the verge of a crucial decision. On the one hand, Caesar had already promised dire consequences if the governor wreaked any more havoc among the Jews and caused more unrest in the Roman Empire. Under usual circumstances, the decision would have been made before he ever heard a word of the case, a death warrant at the ready, awaiting only his seal. But on the other hand, Pilate had never met anyone like Jesus of Nazareth.

"My kingdom is not of this world." The words rang in the ears of the Roman governor. Whatever Jesus might be, He was clearly no threat to the power of Caesar. Something in the way the prisoner carried Himself unnerved Pilate. The quiet dignity and regal carriage bespoke a rank Pilate could not begin to understand. And when he looked into Jesus' eyes—those terrible, wonderful eyes—he fought the inexplicable urge to bow in worship.

Caiaphas waited impatiently for Pilate to speak. The governor was silent a long while, finally snapping, "Very well, I will have Him scourged and then release Him."

The high priest smiled in satisfaction. He had found a weakness in his frequent adversary and fully intended to exploit it. The moment Pilate ordered the scourging, he might as well have signed the death warrant on the spot. At last confident of his ultimate victory, Caiaphas turned his captive over to the Roman soldiers willingly enough.

Satan, or rather, Zarad, started when a messenger ran to the front of the crowd, waving a sealed scroll. This was not a part of his carefully scripted choreography. Pilate turned to go inside, waving the messenger away. "This is not a good time, Valerius."

"It's from Claudia," the boy shouted up to him. "She says it's urgent."

Pilate threw up his hands. "Very well, bring it up."

Zarad sent a mental demand to know the contents of the missive immediately. In a moment, a reproduction appeared in his mind. "My very dear husband," it read, "have nothing to do with this good Man. I have been greatly troubled in a dream because of Him. I fear nothing but danger will be the result if you bring any harm upon His head."

A demon stood on Pilate's left, and a holy angel on his right, as he wrestled with the divine warning, this one last opportunity to turn away from destruction. For a moment it seemed as if the message from God might prevail, but then the tempter suggested, "Why not call for Barabbas and let the people choose? Caiaphas will never let him go free, not after how hard he worked to help you capture him. And no matter what happens, the responsibility, then, will belong to someone else." Pilate clung to that idea like a drowning man, and calling a guard to him, he gave the fateful order.

Only minutes passed before Pilate stood under the archway with a prisoner on either side. The contrast could not have been more pointed. On one hand stood Jesus, with a stateliness that a tattered and bloody robe could not hide. A thorny crown, meant to humiliate Him, served only to emphasize His nobility, authority, and barely restrained power. Barabbas, too, was restrained, but only by his chains and a dirty leather gag tied tightly around his mouth. Pilate was quite pleased with the disparity in their appearance, feeling sure that the people would take pity on the gentle Teacher.

"Since it is the day of your feast," Pilate announced expansively, *"I will release one prisoner. I will even allow you to choose which one. Today, you may choose between Jesus,"* he held out his right hand, *"and Barabbas."* He indicated the man on his left.

Instantly the sound swelled to deafening proportions. *"Barabbas! Barabbas! Barabbas! Barabbas!"* The frenzied mob chanted the name, led by Zarad and his cohorts. *A few shouted the name of Jesus, but they were drowned out by the roar of the crowd.*

Pilate desperately attempted to bring the people back to order. This was not what he had expected. "Then what shall I do with Jesus?" he shouted, panicking.

"Crucify Him!" shouted one of the demon-men near the front of the crowd. *Instantly, the mob repeated it. "Crucify Him! Crucify Him! Crucify Him!"*

Pilate called for a bowl of water and thrust his hands in, careless of the water that spilled over the side and onto the ground. "I am innocent of this just Man's blood," he told the priests, *sounding as if he were trying to convince himself. "He is your responsibility."*

Caiaphas rubbed his hands together, gleefully accepting the curse that would linger through the ages. "His blood be on us and on our children," he agreed. *Then, like the puppet of the dark army that he had become, he ordered the guards, "Scourge him again!"*

Peter fell to his knees as the water dripped from Pilate's outstretched fingers. The grim-faced procurator took the towel offered by his servant, no emotion visible as he painstakingly dried his hands. *Crucify Him!* Peter did not know how he could go on breathing while such a tragedy took place. He buried his face in his hands, praying that he might suddenly wake up and find it had all been a dream.

Barabbas, freed of his bonds, walked disbelievingly down the steps and quickly disappeared into the crowd. Jesus meekly submitted to another beating, this one far worse than the first. Pieces of corroded iron, fastened to the strands of the whip, ripped into His back and tore His bruised flesh each time the soldier pulled back the whip for another stroke. Many men would have died from the first scourging alone. Not only did Jesus survive, but through it all He never once cried out.

Chapter 34

At the Tower Gate, Jesus was joined by two condemned robbers, Arnon and Elan, who had been scheduled to die with their leader, Barabbas. Peter was unhappy that it took him nearly a minute to recognize the distinctively red-haired brothers from Jericho, but had to excuse himself on the grounds of unusual distress. Commander Marcus, who had assisted in the capture of all three robbers, organized his one hundred elite soldiers into a barrier to make room for the prisoners to walk safely through the screaming mob. Arnon and Elan carried their own crosses, but the rough beam Jesus bore had been made for Barabbas.

Thousands joined the procession as it wound its way through the streets of Jerusalem. Peter tried to push his way to a better vantage point, but it looked as if it would be impossible to get through. He could tell at a glance that other followers of Jesus were with him in the crowd, for their sorrow mirrored his own, and they did not join in the mocking.

Knowing that there would likely be followers of Jesus among the people, Caiaphas had spread the word that all such would be spared His fate, now that their Leader was to die in such disgrace. By this, just as he had by welcoming any of Jesus' disciples to his courtyard during the trial before the Sanhedrin, the high priest hoped to head off any future unrest by letting Jesus' followers see for themselves the full cost of going against the established system.

Cursing all the way, Arnon and Elan carried their crosses with relative ease, though the two were pale and faint from their time in an underground cell on an inadequate diet. Jesus, however, dizzy and weak from loss of blood, stumbled and fell repeatedly under His weighty burden. Each time, a Roman spear pricked Him in the back until He struggled once more to His feet.

At last, Jesus fell once more, and the experienced Roman general could see that He simply was unable to reach Golgotha without assistance. Scanning the crowd, General Marcus saw a brawny man gazing with pity on the fallen prisoner. *Perfect,* he thought to himself. "You there! Carry this man's cross," he ordered, motioning to the young man.

Simon, a Cyrenian in town to observe the Passover, obeyed instantly, not stopping to question even for a moment. Revealing a dark muscular torso, he stripped off his outer garment, handing it to his sons, Alexander and Rufus. Willingly, he bent and lifted the cross onto his own back, stepping away so Jesus would have room to stand. It would have been useless to complain that this defilement would prevent him from joining in the Passover celebration he had traveled so far to enjoy. With his eyes, he reassured his sons that he would be all right.

Try though he might, Jesus could not rise to His feet even without the weight of the cross. The general finally gave in and extended his hand, moved with a human sympathy he thought he no longer possessed. At the next step, Jesus stumbled again and nearly fell.

"Come over here," Simon said softly. "Lean on me."

Slowly the procession moved forward once more. Jesus depended almost entirely on the strength of the Cyrenian to support Him. From far back in the crowd, Peter jumped as high as he could, trying to see ahead. A stout woman turned indignantly to him as his elbow hit her well-padded shoulder on the way down. "Sorry," Peter apologized distractedly. "It's just that I'm a friend of His, and I can't see what's happening." Hardly mollified, the woman turned away with a sniff of disdain.

A short distance outside the Damascus Gate, a cliff rose above a vacant field. On it, a dead tree stood silhouetted against the sky. Dangling from one outflung branch hung a broken rope, a ravaged carcass below providing a feast for the pack of wild dogs that frequented the area, combing through the refuse for food. By the time Peter was close enough to see what lay there, little was left of the man who had betrayed his Master into the hands of the priests. Several ashen-faced men with iron stomachs carried away the wrapped remains of Judas.

The crowd hushed its mocking as those close enough saw the dreadful scene. Many looked anxiously up into the gathering clouds, fearful that the swift wrath of Jehovah might fall on them as well.

As Peter looked up at the rope, a chill shook him. But for the mercy of Adonai, he might have shared the gruesome fate of his much-admired companion. "Thank You, Father," he whispered, heart aching. "I don't understand why this is happening, but help me to trust You."

Farther on, off to the west side of the Damascus Road, the crowd made its way to the site of the scheduled execution. The hill had been christened Golgotha, or "Place of the Skull." Its resemblance to an actual skull and its proximity to the road made it a preferred spot for important executions. As the procession drew near, the soldiers carelessly removed the garments of their prisoners, leaving their naked bodies fully exposed for all to see.

They stopped at the base of Golgotha, and Peter watched with mounting horror as three of the Roman guard lifted three square stones, revealing holes already carved deeply enough into the bedrock to support the base of each cross.

Deftly following Pilate's orders with the ease that comes from long practice, they nailed hand-lettered signs above each cross, with the crimes of each criminal emblazoned in three languages. Peter's legs gave out at last, and he sat, weeping quietly and praying for a miracle. Even now, he knew, God could still work a miracle and deliver Jesus. The more he thought about it, the more he believed that was what would probably happen.

Jesus stooped over, swaying a little, His hands covering all they could so as to preserve His last bit of modesty for as long as possible. Watching the difference between his Master and the other men, Peter was not surprised when the two brothers fought savagely as the soldiers held down their arms and legs, fastening them to the wood with cords. Their screams rent the air as they were nailed in place.

Arnon was loudest and most shrill. "I shouldn't be here! General Marcus, tell them we had a deal. It wasn't supposed to happen this way! I don't deserve to be here." His voice faded, then rose to a shriek as his cross was dropped roughly into its hole. "You moron!" He turned angrily on his brother. "It's all your fault I'm in this mess. If you weren't such a sheep-brained coward, I wouldn't be here at all, dying with nothing but a sissy and a lunatic for company."

"You're the moron," Elan retorted. "You brought that traitor Malchus into our camp in the first place, but could you warn your own brother? No!" Even facing death, they carried on the dispute that had raged all the while they were in the procurator's dungeon.

Holding his breath, Peter prayed with all his might for a miracle. "Please, please, Adonai, hear me! Jesus, Your Son, told us that if we ask anything according to Your will, that You would hear us. I know that the terrible things these men are doing to Jesus are not part of Your will and that You're able to send Your holy angels, or even Moses, to save

Him. Please, hurry! Any second now, it will be too late!" But in spite of his agonized pleas, no angel appeared, and no voice thundered from heaven.

Jesus remained silent as He lay painfully atop the cross, His body reluctantly, forcibly exposed before the hosts of Israel. Like the Passover lamb, He made no outcry when the hammer rang out and the iron spikes traveled agonizingly through His flesh. A sheen of perspiration covered His face as one of the soldiers bent His legs alongside the cross, and the raw wounds on His back came into full contact with the jagged wood.

The hardened soldier placed another spike on the outside of Jesus' heel, hammering it efficiently into place. Though painful, the footing this provided was the only way a prisoner could breathe once stretched and nailed in that awkward position; without it, death by suffocation followed swiftly, in a matter of mere minutes.

Unconsciously, Peter moved forward, finding a spot where he could see more clearly, without being seen by Jesus. He was still far too ashamed to face his Master directly. Clinging to a rock, he cried out when the soldiers thrust the cross violently into the deep hole, causing excruciating pain to the hands and feet of the patient Sufferer. Peter could barely hear the words as Jesus groaned, "Father, forgive them. They don't know what they're doing."

General Marcus, standing his post at the foot of the cross, looked at the Man in amazement. He had attended many a crucifixion, personally supervising the deaths of hundreds of miscreants, but nothing he had ever seen in his life of soldiering had prepared him for Jesus. Barely living, after hours of unimaginable torment, He used His precious, painfully earned breath to ask forgiveness for the very ones who were killing Him. The general tried hard to set aside his sudden fear as nothing more than meaningless superstition, but couldn't help wondering if maybe the inscription above the dying Man were true: *Jesus of Nazareth, King of the Jews.*

Chapter 35

H
e's my Friend," Peter wept yet again as the centurion saturated a sponge in sour wine, consisting more of vinegar than actual juice, and held it on a stick to reach Jesus' parched lips. Jesus tasted the mixture, but though terribly dehydrated, He would not drink anything that might deaden His senses and give the enemy of souls an advantage over Him.

Below Him, the soldiers wagered for who would get the lovely seamless robe made with such love for the day of the Messiah's coronation. As they had made it, Rimona and Keren never thought that coarse men would someday cast lots for it rather than tear it. Bloodstained it might be, but it was still finer than any garment they possessed, and each soldier wanted it for his own.

The human pawns had reached the limits of what they could do to the battered body of Jesus, and for the first time Zarad stepped to the front of the crowd. He stood defiantly in front of the One who had made him. Jesus had no more tears to shed but felt an infinite sorrow as He looked down at His firstborn, the chief of His creation.

Zarad was unmoved. "If you are truly the Son of God," he sneered, "come down from that cross."

Caiaphas joined his advisor, laughing scornfully. "He saved plenty of others, but he can't save himself, can he? I guess this messiah isn't as strong as he thought he was."

"Where is Your God now?" mocked Zarad. "If You were really His Son, He would save You." He took a step closer. "Look around You. They all hate You. Even the ones You thought were Yours couldn't get away from You fast enough." Then softer, "You must have been mistaken. You only thought you were the Messiah. You're a deluded fool, Jesus!" He spat to rid himself of the taste of that name.

Zarad grew more and more angry when Jesus made no answer. At last he lost his temper entirely and began screaming curses, using the names of God from every language in heaven and earth. The priests and rulers mingled freely with Zarad's men, feeling kinship with them in their mutual hatred, yet amazed by the fervid zeal of the strangers.

To Peter, it seemed as if a strong emanation of evil came from the scoffers, so powerful he could hardly remain upright. The air grew close and thick, making it hard to breathe. Jesus had a hard time, too, pushing Himself up painstakingly for each breath by putting His whole weight on the nails in His heels. Those in the crowd took up their mockery once more, emboldened by the daring insolence of their leaders. Elan joined them, if for no other reason than it helped take his mind off his own suffering.

Arnon's thoughts on the cross turned toward a depressing assessment of the events that had brought him to this miserable end. Though he had shouted his innocence, the presence of the Man beside him convicted him differently. Unbidden, his mind recalled the many crimes he had committed. The offenses ranged from petty thievery to out-and-out murder. He included all the camel trains plundered, plus the robbery and beating of Tobias, the man who had been saved by the Samaritan. Should he count each camel train as a single crime or each person killed? His fevered mind grew bewildered as he tried to think how many separate items he might have stolen, how many innocents he might have murdered. Yes, his first count was definitely too low.

Arnon twisted slightly so he could see Jesus. The suffering on that ruined face could not overshadow the love flowing from the bowed form of the King. As Arnon scanned the crowd, he was surprised to catch the gaze of the disciple who had eyed him with such suspicion on his last visit to Jericho. It had been the day before his capture, the day he almost chose to follow Jesus. Again he heard the words of the priest who had persuaded him that Jesus was an imposter.

"He's illegitimate, you know. Everyone knows what kind of woman his mother is. He never went to our schools, either, and yet he sets aside the laws of our fathers. Look at the way he hypnotizes the people! He must have a demon in him to work those magical healings. Turn back while you still can, before he bewitches you too."

Now it was too late to go back and make his choice over again, but Arnon couldn't help wishing that he could be allowed to go free just for a moment even, just long enough to bow down before Jesus and ask for His mercy. His sins rose up before him in vivid detail.

He finally rebuked Elan at noon, as thick clouds blotted out the sun. "My brother, don't you have any respect for God? You know we both are getting what we deserve, but Jesus is innocent." Elan swore at his brother and steadfastly continued his mockery.

Arnon strained for a last glimpse of Jesus before the strange darkness made it impossible to see anything. "Lord," he begged, his voice trembling with pent-up emotion, "please remember me when You come into Your kingdom."

For just a moment the gaunt face of the Lamb lit up with joy, and He smiled faintly at the penitent thief. "Today, I give you My promise. You will be with Me in Paradise." With a sob, Arnon breathed a sigh of relief as the weight of his sins mysteriously slipped from his shoulders. A single ray of light shone upon the Son of God for a moment, illuminating the swelling darkness, just before everything for miles around went black.

The spiritual darkness was complete, as well. Tarik stood next to Peter, his borrowed glory from the Father completely extinguished in every dimension. Every indication of the Father's presence had been withdrawn from His agonizing Son as Jesus took the sins of the world fully upon Himself.

Lightning flashed all around, the only light that could be seen for miles. While this supernatural display hid the dying throes of the Savior from prying human eyes, it would have been far easier for Tarik and his companions if it had hidden the scene from the angels, as well. It was all they could do to watch their closest Friend suffer such unspeakable torment.

In the midst of his grief, Tarik couldn't help but admire General Marcus, who remained bravely at his post while the world fell apart around him. He wished Peter could see him and take comfort from his steadfast strength.

Satan and his "men" became increasingly shrill as the afternoon wore on. But many of his human supporters, frightened by the unnatural darkness, fumbled their way back into Jerusalem. That hadn't been part of his hellish script, either.

It was midafternoon before the blackness diminished somewhat. In the eerie glow, Peter could now see everything and everyone except his dear Master. A mysterious cloud continued to hide Him from view, while writhing lightning encircled the place where He suffered. "See?" Caiaphas wagged his gray beard, assuming a pose of great wisdom. "He took the place of God, and now God is punishing him. He is doomed!"

A thick cloud still hung low over Jerusalem, spilling over the countryside to fill the plains and valleys below, when from the middle cross came a heartbreaking cry. "My God, My God, why have You forsaken Me?" The Son of God wept while the earth itself trembled in pangs of sympathy.

Satan almost jumped with excitement, shaking his fists as he tasted the hope of victory. "Come on, my followers! We're almost there!" Together they sent up a renewed chorus of insults, taking full advantage of this first display of seeming weakness.

In a soft, rasping voice, Jesus said, "I thirst."

When General Marcus looked up to see the swollen face of Jesus for the first time in many hours, he could hardly contain his shock. No other prisoner had ever been so terribly wounded as this. Jesus was bruised and bloody, His lips cracked and dry. With each breath, His rib cage heaved convulsively.

His legs trembled with the effort of pushing upward to make possible each agonizing gasp. His torn back grated up and down the beam. Every citizen of heaven sobbed brokenly as General Marcus dipped the sponge once more in the wine and myrrh.

Jesus drank this time, knowing the pain-deadening mixture could not numb His mind in the moments He had left. So parched was He that the success of His victory cry depended entirely on the kindness of a pagan Roman soldier.

By this time Peter had all but given up hope, and Tarik sheltered his pain-wracked charge in his arms as Jesus gathered the last remnants of His strength and shouted, "It is finished!" Exhausted, His work completed, He gave His life into the faithful keeping of His Father. As if in reply, the glory of the Father ignited the sky, descending to cover the limp body of His Son with a robe of pure light. From the voices of countless sinless beings came a massive shout of victory.

"No!" Zarad screamed, the word barely discernible in his garbled outburst. In a stupor, Peter transferred his stricken gaze from the form of his Master to the tall man dressed in black. Zarad shook both fists at the sky. "No!" he shrieked again, disappearing instantly into a deeper facet of the universe. Thunder rumbled as the air crashed in behind him at his abrupt departure, and those humans who saw him go blinked in disbelief. Peter rubbed his eyes, and when he looked again, Zarad's men had also disappeared, the gaping spaces in the crowd the only sign they had been there at all.

Tarik watched as the Satan flew farther and faster, away from earth and toward the farthest planet to orbit the sun. If he had hoped to go farther, he was doomed to disappointment. An unseen, impenetrable obstruction barred his way, limiting him to the area right around the poor little diseased solar system where humankind was born. Until that day, Satan had claimed his rights as prince of the world, forcing his way even into the councils of heaven as the true delegate of "his" planet. Now the earth had a new Prince—a new Representative to stand in the heavenly places.

Peter clung to the ground as a great earthquake shook the earth. Immense rocks broke away from their cradle in the mountains, crushing everything in their wake. Even graves were opened, hurling forth their dead. As all creation quivered in its sorrow and rejoicing, Tarik shielded Peter from many a painful blow, singing a soothing melody of salvation in his ear.

In the temple, the thick purple curtain, woven with cherubim of gold and covering the Most Holy Place from unsanctified eyes, ripped suddenly from top to bottom, torn by Gabriel in heaven's moment of thrilling triumph. The ark of the covenant, which Ezekiel and a handful of loyal priests had hidden just before Jerusalem fell into the hands of Nebuchadnezzar, no longer rested there. In its place there was only the simple table that had been substituted for the missing ark when the temple was rebuilt. Exposed to the view of even the lowliest priest who might wander by, that most sacred place in all Israel was now polluted. The priest who had taken Caiaphas's place for the evening sacrifice stared blankly into the open chamber, his eyes bulging with shock. As both hands dropped limply to his sides and the knife clattered to the floor, the Passover lamb fled with a startled bleat.

Brought to his knees at the foot of the cross, General Marcus Aburius Geminus, the proud centurion of Rome, cried out with new humility, "Truly this Man was the Son of God!"

The earthquake ended suddenly, and Peter shakily stood to his feet. The sun shone once more, and the sounds of nature filled the air. Everything seemed unchanged, until he looked again at the disfigured body of his Lord. Dropping to his hands and knees, he retched until his stomach was dry then crept as close as he could to the red and silver line of Roman guards.

Ill at ease, though unrepentant, Caiaphas and his father-in-law, Annas, went back before Pilate. Dripping with false piety, they pleaded with the governor to remove Jesus from the cross for burial and to break the legs of the other two men, so that the Sabbath would not be desecrated by having such an unseemly display of bodies still on their crosses during those hallowed hours.

The irony of their request was not entirely lost on Pilate, but he agreed, glancing frequently over his shoulder, a worried expression marring his official dignity. Before retiring, he gave additional orders for a renewal of the guard.

The more aged Annas at last returned to his home, satisfied with his long day's labor, but Caiaphas was soon back at Golgotha to personally verify that Pilate's orders were obeyed. Smiling benignly, he nodded approvingly as one of the soldiers picked up a club near the base of one cross, and walked over to the three men who hung there.

Arnon was first. The crushing blow to his lower legs nearly made him pass out, but though he groaned, he did not speak aloud. General Marcus nodded to the soldier to finish the gruesome task. Moments later, the world seemed to spin as Arnon died, with faint whisper on his lips, "Forgive him. Please forgive Joseph Caiaphas."

Elan stood as high as he could, screaming curses at the approaching soldier. Peter heard the terrible crunch of shattering bone, and the robber drooped on the cross. As Elan's heart slowed and his vision faded, still with his last scrap of awareness, he mouthed his final invectives.

When the soldier came to Jesus, it was obvious that He was already dead. Following procedure, the soldier thrust his spear in between two of the ribs. A fountain gushed out, golden liquid and thickened blood, running into the deep crack that opened at the base of the cross. Peter vomited again as the Roman turned to the centurion and reported, "He's dead."

General Marcus sighed. "I'd better go and tell Pilate myself. Leave Him there until I get back."

Near the cross, a small group of Jesus' followers, lost and alone, waited to receive His body. John held the grief-stricken mother of Jesus, supporting her in his arms. Peter sat a short distance away, feeling he was no longer worthy to be included with the others. Exhausted and deep in thought, he didn't hear the footsteps behind him. Apparently the approaching man didn't notice him, either, because he stumbled as he bumped into the penitent disciple. Fearful, Peter jumped, turning to see Malchus standing behind him.

"I'm sorry," Malchus said, reaching out his hand in friendship.

Peter looked away, hesitating a moment before reaching out. "I'm sorry too." He began to sob. "I'm one of His followers, you know."

The beautiful woman at Malchus's side looked tenderly down at Peter, rightly suspecting he had repeated those words to a good many people since his flamboyant denial. "I know," she said softly. "We both know."

Peter covered his face. In a muffled voice he answered, "It's too late to tell Him. I wish I could, but it's too late."

General Marcus returned just then, leading two wealthy men wearing robes that marked them as members of the Sanhedrin. Joseph of Arimathea walked by the general's side, and Nicodemus, burdened with a huge bag, followed behind. "John," Joseph called out to the son of Zebedee, "don't worry about the burial. Pilate said we can use my tomb, and Nicodemus has the spices." Unwilling to delegate the task to a servant, Nicodemus himself carried the myrrh and aloes; together they totaled about the weight of a grown woman. Though afraid to support Jesus openly during His life, they were heedless now of all worldly concerns in their great desire to be with Jesus.

Two of the most brilliant judges Israel ever had arduously pulled out the nails and lowered the stiffening body of Jesus from the cross. Every inch of Him was covered in gore, and little intact skin remained anywhere on His body, but these two honored members of Israel's ruling assembly unhesitatingly clasped His body to their breasts, caring only that they were at last by the side of Jesus.

Martha, always at her best in a crisis, had brought the lengthy cloth strips needed for the burial and hurried to restore the modesty of the Master.

"The others are both dead now too," a soldier called to General Marcus. "What do I do with them?"

The general meticulously inspected the bodies of the thieves. "It looks like you're right, but make sure they're dead, and then throw them on that rubbish heap over there." He pointed to a garbage heap across the way. The soldier quickly complied, pulling the executed criminals down, ripping the mottled hands and feet in the process, and dragging them off to discard with the rest of the city's trash.

By the time they finished, the other soldiers had already restored the scene of the crucifixion, replaced the stones in the cross holes to keep them clean for the next time, and picked up all their tools. Whatever else might be said about them, the Romans were quick and efficient.

"All right, men," the general said bracingly, dusting off his hands. "That's all; let's go."

"Wait," protested the high priest, "you can't just give the body to them like that." He pointed to where James and John were just finishing a crude hammock in which to carry their Master's body. "What if they steal it? They'll tell everyone He came back from the dead, and there will be rioting in the streets."

General Marcus sighed, exasperated. "Go and talk to Pilate. My men and I will wait here."

Peter and Malchus stepped forward at the same instant, each wanting to help carry the body of their Lord. Joseph lifted the head, Malchus went to the middle, and Peter gratefully carried the feet. Nicodemus, out of breath and with sweat beading his brow, shifted his large bag of spices to a more comfortable position and followed them.

The tomb Joseph had prepared for his own death was very near, carved out of a stony hillside. It was close enough to Golgotha that they could easily see the exact spot where Jesus had died. Just outside the hewn door, they set the body down carefully to make hasty preparations for the burial. Martha was ready, kneeling next to Jesus holding a cloth and a basin of water.

"I'll do it," Peter volunteered. Martha started to refuse, but something she saw in Peter's face stopped her, and without protest she handed the cloth to him. Starting at the head, Peter washed the blood, dried spittle, and grime from the body of his Lord. As he came to the feet, he wept aloud before them all. "When He was alive, I wouldn't even wash His feet." Peter's voice cracked. "But He washed mine."

Martha's impatience increased as the seconds ticked inexorably away. "We'd better hurry," she finally said. "The sun is almost down, and soon it will be the Sabbath."

"What about the embalming?" Nicodemus asked. "The spices are all here."

"I'll tell you what we'll do," Martha stated so emphatically that no one dared disagree. "Let's wrap the body loosely, and we women will come at dawn on the first day to finish the embalming." Since no one seemed to have a better idea, Martha sent some of the embalming spices home with each of the women who promised to help.

She twined the cloth around Jesus' body simply, folding the arms across the loving heart that beat no more. Again Joseph took the head so he could lead the way into the sepulcher. They laid Jesus on a flat stone slab worked into the floor, reluctantly leaving Him alone in the cold earth.

Caiaphas walked with the relief troops who were to guard the tomb that night. He watched closely as the new centurion readied the seal of the governor. Ten of the soldiers rolled the large round stone in the trench, covering the doorway. By each edge of the stone, another soldier pounded in a metal spike to keep the stone from rolling either way. Stretching the crimson seal across the entrance, the centurion dripped melted wax on it to hold it in place and imprinted it with Pilate's ring.

Then the soldiers spread out through the small garden, guarding against any attempt to steal Jesus' body. Satisfied that everything was as secure as he could make it, Caiaphas returned to the city.

"Any of you who need a place to stay can come with me," Joseph invited.

"I have plenty of room too," Nicodemus joined in.

"Thank you." James and John accepted the hospitality offered to them, as did most of the others. Andrew, too tired and sick at heart to speak to anyone, wandered away in search of his wife. Wrapped up in his own world of sorrow, he didn't even think of his brother.

They were all leaving when Mary of Bethany, of all people, came to where Peter had slumped dejectedly on a rock, and laid an understanding hand on his arm. "Your family is in the Pilgrims' Camp. I know you'll want to see them, and if you come with me I'll take you where they are." Her eyes and nose were red, but the deep, sustaining peace never once left her face.

"I might as well." He rested his head on his knees. "There's nowhere else for me to be."

Chapter 36

Rimona waited for him outside her tent, arms open to receive him. Peter walked into them, needing the comfort that warmly encircled him. "Thank you, Mary." Rimona's voice was muffled against her husband's robe.

"You're welcome." Mary did her best to be brave. "He told us this would happen. We should have been better prepared. *I* should have been better prepared."

"Mama, what's wrong with Abba?" Seth tugged on Rimona's sleeve. Batia chased after the small boy and hustled him back to her tent.

"We'll talk about it later," Rimona called after him, turning back to Mary. "You *were* ready, far more than any of us," she reassured her friend. "Remember what He said? That you prepared His body for burial with the perfume? I only wish now that I had helped."

Peter wordlessly resisted all Rimona's efforts to care for him, steadfastly refusing to eat or sleep. From the doorway of the tent, pitched at the northern corner of the camp, he could almost see the garden that held the tomb. There he sat far into the night, absently stroking the bloodstains on his chest.

He might have slept a little during the night, but the rising sun found him in the same spot, staring, unblinking, at the place where all his hopes and dreams had perished. Through the hours of the Sabbath, he never moved, though Rimona at last persuaded him to drink a bit of water.

As it began to get dark, Peter called his wife to him. "You're not safe here," he said, his voice hoarse and rasping. "You're not safe around me, either. It's only a matter of time until the priests change their minds and come after us too. You need to be far away when that happens. Zebedee will be taking Salome back to Capernaum, and I'm sure you can travel with them."

"Aren't you coming?" Rimona was alarmed.

"At some point, but," he broke down crying again, "I just can't bear to leave Him yet."

"Very well," Rimona said decisively, "we'll leave first thing in the morning. I need to start getting ready now—are you coming to bed?"

Peter rubbed his irritated, bloodshot eyes. "Not yet. Later, maybe. But not yet." Resuming his vigil, he gazed faithfully at the burial place of his Master as the darkness deepened around him. At last, during the third watch of the night, when the rounded moon had nearly completed its journey across the sky, the weary disciple slumped to the ground and slept.

It was pretty typical, really. Peter had slept through all the other major events during Jesus' time on earth. Why should this one be an exception? At the appointed hour, Gabriel left his place beside the throne, throwing out a path of light through the far reaches of space.

Plunging through the clouded atmosphere of the first heaven, he did nothing to shield his radiance from the eyes of men, alighting unerringly inside the ring of soldiers and directly in front of the door of the tomb. Demon and man alike fell to the earth, unable to withstand the glory of the Father and His messenger. The pure white light lit the countryside for miles around, bathing the slumbering form of Peter in its brilliance.

The guards twitched feebly then lay still, luminous particles absorbing slowly into every inch of exposed flesh. Trillions of wicked angels, their number in full assembly for the first time since the early days of man, hid their faces from the blinding sight. Satan raised up on one hand, covering his eyes with the other, but even his insolence dimmed somewhat as he shouted a pained challenge at the angel who had taken his place in the celestial courts.

Chapter 36

"*Why are you here? This is my territory, and this grave belongs to me!*" *Tarik found these words oddly reminiscent of Moses' resurrection.*

Gabriel looked out across the vast sea of cowering demons, each one once a cherished friend. Closest of all had been Lucifer, and for thousands of years Gabriel had yearned in sympathy for his fallen comrade, wishing he might repent and be restored. Now, after seeing the depths to which Satan was willing to go as he tried to overthrow the government of righteousness, relishing every drop of blood spilled from the broken body of Jesus, no last bit of that sympathy for his rebel friend remained in Gabriel's heart. Not a particle of hatred marred the pure heart of Gabriel, but he was filled with an unwavering resolve to see justice come at last.

The mighty angel of the Highest raised his sword aloft. "Son of God!" His voice echoed through the land like thunder. "Your Father calls You. Arise!"

Gabriel threw his arms open wide, and in obedience to his visual command, the broad stone at the entrance to the grave rolled effortlessly away from the opening to the tomb, although it had taken ten Roman soldiers to put it in place. The broken seal fluttered to and fro across the round black opening. One spike still protruded from the rock face by the door. The other was gone, sheared off flush with the embankment.

A stupendous flash burst from the tomb, so bright that Gabriel, for all his radiance, cast a shadow over several of the stricken guards. A colossal earthquake shuddered through the land of Israel, toppling stones and ripping at the ground. Another angel entered the tomb, unrolling the bindings Martha had wrapped around Jesus. Raised at His Father's call by the life within Himself, Jesus stood, then bent to pick up the linen strips. He brushed back a fall of white hair as He straightened. Folding the grave clothes with precision, He set them at the foot of the stone where He had lain. Then, overflowing with joy, He left the tomb behind and embraced His treasured general.

Jesus turned to face the plains of Judea, holding up His scarred hands. At the sound of His voice, the multitude whose graves had opened in the great earthquake now stirred to life once more, coming forth immortal, new. From all directions they came to Him, flying on swift wings. Some, raised from an era near the dawn of time, were extraordinarily tall, while others were more typical of that time. But each had a glorified body, just as Jesus did, and soon they would all grow to an even greater height, as Moses, Enoch, and Elijah had done in their turn.

One last task was left for Jesus to do. Facing the refuse heap across the road, He located the remaining vestiges of the two thieves. "Arnon," He called insistently. "Arnon, get up!"

Peter woke, feeling the ground heave beneath his prone body. He blinked sleepily, trying to remember where he was. As his hands touched the stiff robe he still wore, revulsion shook him, and he remembered the tragedy anew.

His eyes blurred, and his head ached. How he needed a bath! His stomach growled, reminding him he hadn't eaten for several days. As he looked about, trying to judge the length of time before sunup, he saw a set of strange lights moving through the air and converging near the area of the tomb.

"What is it?" The soft whisper beside him startled Peter.

"I don't know." He started to reach for Rimona, but thought better of it as a wave of odor rose, stirred by his gesture. "It doesn't matter anyway."

"We're about to leave. Did you want to keep the tent?"

"No." Peter shook his head. "I'm used to sleeping outside."

As Rimona efficiently dismantled their temporary quarters, John made his way through the dimness to see them. He sat down next to Peter on the ground, patting his friend on the arm. A moment later he pulled back, nose wrinkling at the smell. "Peter, you look awful! Why don't you come with me to Joseph's house and get cleaned up? It looks like you could use a good meal too."

Peter half turned away from John. "I don't deserve it, not after what I did."

"None of us deserve it." John's face was pale and earnest. "We all ran away. We all deserted Jesus when He needed us the most. Believe me, my friend, none of us are in any position to look down on you."

The tight band across Peter's chest eased a bit, though he continued to protest. "But I denied Him in front of a whole crowd. I cursed. I swore." Tears came to his eyes. "He was watching me when I mocked Him before His enemies. None of you did that."

"It doesn't matter what you did," Rimona interrupted. "The important thing is, did you ask Adonai for forgiveness? Surely if He forgave our friend Mary seven times, and told you to forgive each other seventy times seven, He'll forgive you too."

"I did ask for forgiveness," Peter said.

"Then you are already forgiven," John replied emphatically. "Now, are you coming with me, or not?"

"Go," Rimona ordered. "We'll be fine." She kissed Peter on his grubby cheek. "I love you. I'll meet you at home."

Peter followed John toward the city gate, the same one through which Jesus had walked on that unforgettable preparation day. As they neared the entrance, a woman ran toward them, her unbound hair streaming out behind her. After his years with Jesus, Peter would have recognized those tresses anywhere.

"Mary, what's wrong?"

"Come quickly! Something awful has happened! Someone has tampered with the tomb, and I don't know what to do." Tears ran down her face as she took both men by the hands, dragging them along.

"Mary, please! You've got to slow down—I can't go this fast." Peter tried to pull away from her insistent tugging, holding one hand to his throbbing head.

"Faster! It might already be too late!" Mary pulled harder, until both exhausted men had to run to keep up with her.

The lovely little garden showed signs of many visitors. The soldiers had carelessly trampled some of the smaller bushes, and the paths were filled with footprints. Just as Mary had said, the stone was gone from the grave. Pushing John aside so he could enter the tomb, Peter needed only a single glance to know that Jesus' body was no longer there.

He reeled in shock as Mary turned to them, gesturing excitedly. "See? I told you—someone must have taken Him! But where?" Her face crumpled, and she moved to lean on Peter for support, but as she got close enough to smell him, she changed her mind at the last instant and went to John instead, wailing, "What are we going to do?"

In disbelief, Peter looked again into the tomb. It was still empty. He tried to straighten up, but all around him, the garden slowly faded to black. "Peter!" He dimly heard John cry out, only vaguely aware of being lifted and held.

"Leave me alone," he said querulously.

"I have to get him back to the city," John apologized to Mary. "He hasn't eaten since, well, probably Thursday night." He looked down in revulsion. "And he definitely hasn't washed. Now I'll have to take a bath too."

"You go ahead. That's all right." Mary wiped her eyes and sniffed hard. "I just want to stay here a little longer. Maybe someone will come along who knows something. I'll let you know if I find out anything new."

With much exertion, John succeeded in getting Peter cleaned and fed, and then the two walked across the city to meet with the others. Peter felt fresh pain as he climbed the stairs to the upper room where he had last fellowshiped with Jesus. All that day, the room was to become a sanctuary to the disciples as they hid from fevered allegations that they had stolen the body of their Lord. The wrath of the rulers threatened to break over them, and they feared to leave their concealment lest they, too, suffer a gruesome death.

By noon, the eleven disciples received the first of three strange reports. A number of different women, Mary among them, claimed to have seen Jesus—alive—and talked with Him. The sister of Martha spoke to them with all her customary vitality and enthusiasm. "He is risen! Really, He is, and He said for all of you to meet Him in Galilee. Peter, He mentioned you especially—He wants to see you!"

Not daring to believe, Peter said mournfully, "We trusted that He was the One who would save Israel." And so instead of rejoicing in heaven's victory, the closest earthly companions of the Savior continued in their useless, hopeless anguish.

As He had explained to Mary, Jesus made a rapid journey to heaven, eager for the assurance that the Father had accepted His sacrifice. Then He returned just as swiftly to earth, appearing to numerous sorrowing followers. Even when He came to the eleven where they still waited in the upper room, they didn't believe at first that it was He.

Jesus ate and drank in their presence, showing them the scars in His hands and feet. At last they believed, but when He disappeared without a definite appointment to see them again, discouragement set in once more among them. Not knowing what else to do, seven of them at last started out for Galilee and home, hoping and praying that they would see Jesus there.

Peter sat between Andrew and John, staring out across the waters of the lake. "He's not here yet." James stated the obvious.

Matthew leaned his back against the wall of Andrew's house. "We've been here all day. I wonder how long we're going to have to wait?"

"I don't know about any of you," Andrew put in, "but I'm going to have to get some new clothes tomorrow. Mine are pretty much just rags."

"Mine are worse than yours." Peter held up the tattered edge of his robe for Andrew to see. "We'd better do something quickly, or they might have to start a poor fund for us."

"I don't have any money." Andrew raised his eyebrows as the realization sank in. "Judas had all the money in his purse."

"Why don't we just go fishing?" Peter brightened at the thought. "It'll give us something to do while we wait, and maybe we can catch enough to get some decent clothes. Our families would probably appreciate the food too."

"What are we waiting for?" Suddenly energized, James ran to the shore, where Peter and Andrew's boat leaned on its side.

In a few minutes they were ready to go, eagerly shoving the boat out into the water. Peter stretched and yawned, enjoying the feel of the sun on his back, the wind in his hair, and the boat rocking under his feet. "It's sure good to be back!"

"Remember when Jesus calmed the storm?" Philip gazed off into the water as the sun set.

"Which time?" Andrew clapped his brother on the shoulder. "The first time, or the time my clever brother sank like a stone?"

"And over there," James added, pointing to the opposite shore, "He fed all those thousands of people with one boy's lunch, remember?"

"Remember how He would sing to us? Nothing else has ever sounded so beautiful." Nathanael fingered his flute wistfully.

"Why don't you play for us?" Peter surprised himself by asking.

Nathanael needed no second invitation, drawing out the carved wooden instrument. First, he played the Passover hallel, the last song Jesus had ever sung to them. The uplifting tunes which followed called to mind the many happy times they had shared over the past three years.

Peter found his melancholy deepening. About two years before, he had brashly wished that everyone in the crowd would know his name. He had gotten what he wanted, but unfortunately not in just the way he had hoped. Now he feared he would always be first recognized as the disciple who had denied his Lord.

As the night wore on with not a fish to be found, Peter began to question his future. Once he had believed his destiny would lead him to a palace, but all he had left of his aspirations was an empty fishing net. Instead of being a wealthy, powerful man, he was little better than a beggar dressed in rags. *Adonai, help me,* he pleaded. *What should I do? Nothing has turned out like I planned, and I feel so lost. Please, just show me what You want me to do.*

There was no vision, no special revelation, and Peter was just as confused as before when the men called off their fruitless quest and turned back toward the shore. They were quite close to land when he first saw the stranger walking slowly along the water's edge. The man waved to them, asking cheerily, "Did you catch any fish, boys?"

"Not even one," John called back. "We just gave up."

The stranger cupped his hands around his mouth to carry the sound farther. "Throw your net on the right side, and you will find your fish."

With peculiar expressions on their faces, they did as they were told. As soon as they tried to draw the net in, they saw it was so full of fish that the net was about to break. Even working together, they could not pull it into the boat.

"It's Jesus!" Peter let go of his portion of the net and dived into the water, cutting smoothly through the lapping waves in his eagerness to see the Master.

A light came over the faces of the other weary men as they struggled to shore, Matthew and Nathanael doing their best to row while the experienced fishermen held the squirming catch. Belatedly realizing the predicament the others were in, Peter waded back out into the water to help them bring in the net.

A noisy, joyous bunch secured the catch and sat down to eat the meal Jesus had prepared for them with His own hands. As Peter took his first crispy bite of fried fish, Jesus asked him, "Simon, son of Jonas, do you love Me more than any of the others?"

Chapter 36

No pompous, overconfident reply came from Peter this time. He knew all too well the weakness of his own soul. He dropped his gaze to the ground. "Yes, Lord, You know I love You," he replied humbly.

"Then feed My lambs."

Jesus went on talking to the others, but a few minutes later turned to Peter again. "Simon, son of Jonas, do you love Me?"

Peter hid his eyes with his hand, cut deeply but knowing the question was justified. Again, he gave the same reply. "Yes, Lord, You know that I love You." His companions all noticed the contrast between his previous arrogance and his present meekness.

"Feed My sheep," Jesus told him.

Peter picked up another slice of fish and chewed it slowly. He didn't blame Jesus for doubting him, but wished he knew what it would take to restore the Master's trust in him. He was still deep in thought when Jesus turned to him the third time. "Simon, son of Jonas, do you love Me?"

The other disciples looked away, trying to protect Peter from further embarrassment. Tears came to Peter's eyes, and in a choked voice he said sadly, "Lord, You know everything. You know that I love You."

Jesus looked at the heartsick man with kindness and love. "Feed My sheep," He repeated softly.

At last, Peter understood what Jesus was trying to do. Three times he had publicly betrayed his Lord, and three times he was being given the chance to publicly express his faith. For the first time since Jesus died, Peter felt as if he could be truly restored.

As they finished eating, Peter followed Jesus down the beach, not wanting to let Him out of sight. Jesus turned soberly to His faithful disciple. "When you were young, you went wherever you wanted and took care of yourself, but when you are old, you will stretch out your hands and be carried to a place you do not want to go."

It took Peter a moment to cut through the poetic language and reach the meaning, but when he did, his eyes lit up. "Do You mean that I will be crucified, like You?" The hands he held out to Jesus trembled a bit as he knelt there in the sand. "Thank You for giving me another chance. I won't let You down this time!"

Jesus lifted him to his feet, placing both hands on his shoulders. Looking deeply into Peter's eyes, He said as He had at the beginning, "Follow Me."

Chapter 37

*I*t was a truly glum assembly as every rebel answered the summons to a vast session devoted to regrouping their strategy. A temporary and unexpected peace spread over the world as they gathered amid the crumbled ruins and blowing sand of old Babylon. The insurgent commander stood, motioning to silence the ugly murmuring of his malcontented troops. Behind him, his top generals regarded their underlings balefully.

"Believe me, I know what you're thinking. You feel as if we have lost, and some of you may even be tempted to surrender to our enemy and get it over with. Yes, it's very true that the last few years haven't turned out exactly the way we'd planned." Muffled snorts of derision greeted this colossal under-statement. "But we still have many options left open to us." Openly scornful laughter broke out this time, but Satan ignored it and continued.

"A victory before the cross," he gagged at the hateful word, "would have ensured our survival, but there is another way. It can work the same way it almost did in Noah's day, curse him, because if ever a time comes when every single human on earth has chosen our side, ultimate victory will still be ours."

"That's a pretty big load of perjury, even for the father of lies," Oreb muttered to Zeeb. "We lost, plain and simple. All we've got left now is to try and take as many of the humans with us as we can."

"It sounds so good, that it's too bad it won't work." Zeeb shook his head sorrowfully. "Of course, the enemy will never let it come to that, but it sounds *so inspiring, and so . . . possible. I wish it were true." Belatedly aware that a hush had descended over the entire assembly and that every eye was fixed on him, Zeeb looked around blankly as his words trailed away into silence.*

"Well, what are you waiting for? Oreb and Zeeb, both of you come up here—now!" Impatience tinged their commander's voice, and he enunciated very clearly as if speaking to children. "I am giving you your old jobs back. With the increase in status for each of your sinners, it practically amounts to a promotion. No," he held up his hand, "don't bother to get excited. Believe me, I'd put someone else in your place if I could. Dagon is the only one of the miserable lot of you that really deserves a promotion, since he added Judas to the tens of thousands of Israelites and Philistines that have already been his personal conquests.

"Set and Ares, you incompetent cretins, don't think I don't notice you try-ing to sneak off. Set, I hear that an opening as Father Damballah has just opened up on a mountainous little island called Ayiti, off the coast of the great Undiscovered Land to the west. As you find the worship of the humans so enjoyable, this should be an ideal assignment for you."

Set's mouth dropped open. He had been prepared for a certain amount of recrimination, but this was terrible! To have to leave behind the glitter-ing gold and stately palaces of the sophisticated Egyptians and head for a squalid, insignificant outpost among already superstitious people, an assign-ment that could be handled easily by the greenest tempter, was more than he could accept without protest. "Your highness," his tone was aggrieved, "of course we can agree that the outcome was not what we would have most desired, but I don't believe that any of the blame rests on me. I performed my job as well as anyone—even you—could have done, and I don't deserve this demotion."

"Then don't think of it as a demotion." The commander bared his teeth in a mocking sneer. "Think of it as a lateral transfer." He turned to Ares. "As for you—"

"We're being a bit hypocritical, aren't we?" asked Ares snidely. "After all, it's not like you made such a stunning success out of your part, either, and I don't see you taking any demotions. In fact, through your incompetence, the death warrant for each of us has now been signed!"

Rage flashed in Satan's eyes, but he replied evenly, "Ares, I would kill you on the spot for your gross insubordination, but rebellion is a trait I value.

Still, it must be curbed and channeled properly. Therefore, I sentence you to a year of torture at the hands of your peers, at the end of which you will join the ranks of our record-keepers for a thousand years or until the final battle, whichever comes first.

"The rest of you, continue to carry out our plans. Remember the three D's: Discourage, Distract, and Divert. Billions will enter our path through one of these three doors. Do as much damage as you can; every blow you strike to the heart of our enemy is one stroke closer to our freedom! Dismissed!"

At that, they scattered to their posts around the world, freshly determined to spread their evil and drag the race of men to new depths of depravity. Each heart nursed the burning determination that, if the Almighty was truly going to destroy them as He had said, they would take as many of His beloved children with them as they could.

Just before He returned to heaven, Jesus gathered His disciples together for one last meal. As they broke bread together, He continued to share the instructions He wanted them to follow after His departure.

"I want to give you a special promise from My Father. You must stay in the city of Jerusalem until I send My power to you. The Holy Spirit will come over you, and you will be My witnesses, not only in Jerusalem and Judea, but in Samaria, and the farthest parts of the earth."

Peter followed Jesus to the top of the Mount of Olives, pressing close as he sensed their time together was short. A crowd followed at a distance, and near the crest of the hill a man broke away and ran to catch up with Jesus.

Peter heard the footsteps behind him, and turned to see that it was Malchus. The man who had been one of the Teacher's most cynical and determined opponents bowed in the dust to worship his Lord. "I'm so sorry, Jesus," he said humbly. "Please forgive me for all the things I did to hurt You. And thank You."

"You're welcome." Jesus pulled Malchus to his feet, embracing him. "I forgave you a long time ago, Malchus." With a spark of humor, He touched the side of Malchus's head. "He that hath an ear, let him hear."

Malchus grinned. "I'm listening now, Master."

Jesus continued on to the top of the hill, where a group of magnificent humans awaited His arrival. Peter recognized Arnon there, and John the Baptist. It appeared Jesus hadn't forgotten his cousin after all. After the weeks the glorified ones had just spent preaching on the street corners of Jerusalem, Caiaphas, Herod, and Pilate had dissolved into nervous wrecks, fearing that at any moment they might be brought face to face with the One they had crucified. Others of the grand company had spread through the countryside, glowing as they told the good news of salvation.

The cloud of witnesses went up first. Jesus stayed as long as He could, but a powerful force pulled Him away from the gravity of earth. Finally, all Peter could see was a tiny speck against the cerulean sky, until a drifting cloud blew by and hid Him from sight.

While angels swirled about the figure of Jesus in the heavens, controversy about Him swirled on earth. Caiaphas conspired with Pilate and the Roman guards to put about the story that the guards had fallen asleep and that the disciples had come and stolen Jesus' body while the soldiers slept. Due to the fact that the penalty for sleeping on duty was death, it took a heavy purse and many assurances of safety before the still glowing, strangely luminous guards consented.

While shouting matches broke out in the city streets as to whether the priests were being truthful about the Resurrection, shouts of praise rose high from throngs of angels as they walked on streets of gold. When the escort drew near, Moses waited at the gate.

The angels surrounding the Savior sang out, "Lift up your heads, oh ye gates, and be ye lifted up, ye everlasting doors, and the King of glory shall come in!"

Knowing the answer and smiling as they sang the challenge, the angels there at the gate asked, "Who is this King of glory?"

Louder and more majestic came the response, "The Lord, strong and mighty, the Lord mighty in battle."

The Conqueror stepped onto the foundations of the City and walked toward the entrance. Moses threw open the gates to receive Him, took off his crown, and laid it at Jesus' nail-pierced feet. It was a long time before he stood, Enoch and Elijah by his side, and held out his arms. "My Master, My Lord. Welcome home!"

In the days leading up to Pentecost, many of Jesus' followers obeyed His command, lingering in the city of Jerusalem and preparing to receive the gift of the Holy Spirit. By day, they taught in the temple, opening the prophecies that pointed to the suffering and death of the Messiah. Many, even among the priests, embraced the controversial teachings and joined the ranks of the believers.

Having left the boys with her mother, Rimona returned to her husband, never leaving his side. More than ever before, she wanted to find the unity that Jesus had promised.

In the evening, and far into the night, the faithful assembled to pray together, searching their hearts and making a full confession of sin. As they prepared to take the gospel to the world, they realized with dismay the many chances they had wasted during the past three years, missed opportunities to show their love for Jesus, and lost time they could have spent in service to others. Memories of their unbelief caused them much pain and helped them renew their efforts to share their strengthened faith with the world.

The Day of Pentecost found the disciples, as well as many others, assembled yet again, at last completely in harmony. Their prayers were for each other, and that the world might know the living Word that they would speak. While these petitions were still on their lips, a great wind rushed into the room, extinguishing every candle. With a strange glow, it spread over them, appearing as a flame over each bowed head.

Peter felt the warmth of that divine fire spread through his veins, and a holy excitement filled him. All doubts about what he should do melted away. The zeal burning in his breast demanded immediate expression and in only one possible way. He would go out and preach!

Hand in hand with Rimona, he joined the others as they spread through the crowd that attended the feast, laughing and shouting his joy. Two priests passed by, looking with horror at the exuberant spectacle of Peter preaching fervently to a small group of foreigners, also come to enjoy the harvest celebration.

"He must be drunk," exclaimed one of the priests.

The other listened intently for a moment. "I'm not so sure. How can he be drunk in Greek? And I'm not positive, but I think that the woman next to him is speaking Parthian!"

Peter was delighted with the new ability bestowed on him to speak fluently in several languages. Boldly and eloquently, he rebuked the murderous priests for their efforts to hinder the work of God, and about three thousand were converted on the Day of Pentecost alone.

The Pharisees and Sadducees were beside themselves at this and tried to silence Peter by any means possible. After they had captured him and thrown him into prison, along with John, they were appalled to find the two disciples busily preaching and working miracles in the synagogue the very next morning. A peculiar story circulated that an angel had released them from their cell. When nothing else worked, the desperate rulers at last dragged Peter and John before the Sanhedrin.

Less than two months before, fear of these men had caused Peter to deny his Lord with cursing, but now, standing in the Hall of Hewn Stone among the very men who had brought about the death of Jesus, he did not hesitate.

Caiaphas fixed a baleful glare on the radiant apostle and drummed his fingers on one knee. "By what power, or by whose name do you do these things?"

Peter took a deep breath, thrilling as the power of the Holy Spirit filled him. "You rulers of the people, the elders of Israel," he thundered, "if we are going to be questioned today for helping that poor crippled man and have to give an account for what method we used to make him whole, then we want you all to know something. It was by the name of Jesus Christ of Nazareth, whom all of *you*," he pointed his finger around the circle, "crucified, and whom God raised from the dead. It was by His power that the crippled man was made whole and stands here before you."

The entire Sanhedrin sat dumbfounded as this uneducated fisherman rebuked them. Shaking one finger at Caiaphas, Peter went on. "Jesus is the Stone that you builders rejected, and now He has become the Chief Cornerstone. Salvation comes only through Jesus, and His name is the only one given under heaven, by which we must be saved!" Shocked into silence at the boldness of one they had thought to intimidate, the Sanhedrin marveled at his words.

Sitting in the front row of the novices, a brilliant young lawyer and student of Gamaliel, Saul by name, listened intently to each word. The novice on his right gawked, amazed, at the inspired and logical summation. He grabbed hold of Saul's arm, never taking his eyes off the prisoners who were even then being released to preach again. "Can you believe that?" he marveled. "Those two men are ignorant and uneducated, but even the finest legal minds in the nation cannot best them."

Saul nodded slowly, removing his arm from the offending grasp. "It's easy to tell they've been with Jesus."

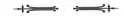

And there are also many other things which Jesus did,
The which, if they should be written every one,
I suppose that even the world itself could not contain
The books that should be written
(John 21:25).

Epilogue

The old man sat on the cold stone floor, fingering the shackles that bound his wrists and ankles. His back ached, and he was hungry. Probably by now he would have starved if not for the valiant efforts of his younger son and nieces. Such good children they had always been, he reflected with pleasure. Jered, his elder son, was preaching in Asia, winning countless thousands to Christ. And how he missed his dear Rimona in the years since she had died.

Seth, his younger son, had brought his twin cousins with him to Rome, much against the old man's wishes, and they all cared for him in his imprisonment—as often as the guards allowed. Risking the displeasure of the emperor, Peter's nieces, Abitalia and Adelia, sent nourishing food, along with the woolen blanket that provided his only warmth. He wished he could see their beautiful faces once more before he died, those sweet, wonderful girls.

On the morrow he was to be executed by crucifixion, and already he had decided to request that he be nailed upside down, feeling unworthy to die in the same manner as had his Master. In his prayers, he did not plead for deliverance. "Lord, make me able to bear the pain for Your sake," was all he asked. All the same, he kept a watchful eye on the door of his cell, hoping to see a familiar angelic face.

The night wore on, and his heavy eyelids closed at last. A glowing figure slipped into the cell with him and knelt at his side. "Peter, wake up."

He opened his eyes. "Moses? Is that really you? You look just the same as you did on the mountain so many years ago. But I guess I should have expected that." He shook the chains on his arms, but they remained fast.

Moses nodded, sitting down comfortably next to him on the hard floor. "Jesus sent me with a message for you."

"For me?" Peter's hazy brown eyes filled with tears that spilled down onto his snowy beard. "He sent you for me?"

"Yes, Peter. He wanted you to know that He will be with you in the morning, though you will not see Him. He has prepared a mansion for you and is saving a jeweled crown just for you."

Peter laughed shakily. "I always did want a mansion, but I didn't exactly get it down here, did I?"

"Trust me, you won't be disappointed."

"Is my angel here?"

"Yes. He's right there next to you, in the same place he's been since the day you were born."

"He isn't coming to rescue me this time, is he?"

Moses could see by his face that Peter already knew the answer. "No, Peter, not this time. You've come to the end of your race here on earth, but your place in heaven is assured."

He shook his head. "I still don't deserve it—I feel so sinful."

"I don't deserve it, either, but the blood of the Lamb washed away all our sins. I've seen your book, Peter. Across every page it is marked with red letters that say, 'Forgiven.' Your sins have been blotted out."

"Thank you for telling me all this. I can bear anything, as long as I know Jesus is with me."

The tall man stood, the time for his visit at an end. "Goodbye, Peter. You don't know how much I look forward to meeting with you in the kingdom. After your suffering comes to an end, it will seem like only a moment before Jesus comes to call you out of the grave, just as He did me. Until then, I'll be waiting at the gate for you—waiting to welcome you home."

Slowly, the messenger faded out of his sight. The man of God sat there in the solitary blackness, cut off from among men, but never abandoned—and never alone.

Bible quote credits

Chapter 3
Isaiah 35:1–8, NIV.

Chapter 4
Malachi 3:1–3, KJV.
Psalm 69:9, NIV.

Chapter 7
Psalm 91:1–4, NKJV.
Psalm 91:5–12, NKJV.

Chapter 8
Deuteronomy 8:2, 3, NIV.
Deuteronomy 6:16–19, NIV.

Chapter 12
Isaiah 9:1, 2, NIV.
Isaiah 41:17–20, NIV.
Isaiah 61:1, 2, NIV.

Chapter 18
Psalm 103:1–4, NKJV.

Chapter 30
Zechariah 9:9, version undetermined.

If you enjoyed this book, you may also enjoy these missionary stories.

Lotus Blossom Returns
Sandy Zaugg

The remarkable life of Florence Nagel Longway Howlett.

Born two months early to missionary parents Sherman and Mary Nagel, Florence Ione Nagel seemed eager to see China. Called "Fa Lien" (Lotus Blossom) by the Chinese, Florence's love for the people and the culture of this far eastern country was indomitable.

College would call her away, but this young missionary was determined to return to her beloved China someday. The long road back was paved with war, bedbugs, emergency plane landings, heartbreak, floods, and seemingly "impossible" challenges. But what Lotus Blossom knew, and what, you, too, will discover as you read, is that nothing is impossible with God. *Lotus Blossom Returns* gives a fascinating history of the Adventist work in China through the eyes of one of its still-living pioneers.
Paperback, 192 pages.   0-8163-2044-6   US$14.99

Mission Miracles
Eileen Lantry and *David Gates*

Mission Miracles chronicles more miracle stories of David and Becky Gates, "God-supported" missionaries to the Amerindians of Guyana and Venezuela. As you read what God has done for their ministry, think again about what God can do through your service to Him.
Paperback, 208 pages.   0-8163-2186-8.   US$14.99

Order from your ABC by calling **1-800-765-6955**, or get online and shop our virtual store at **http://www.AdventistBookCenter.com**.

- Read a chapter from your favorite book
- Order online
- Sign up for e-mail notices on new products

Prices subject to change without notice.